To:	To:
From: HARVEY	From: HARVEY
Due Back:	Due Back:
ILL No.: No Renew	ILL No.: No Renew
To:	To:
From: HARVEY	From: HARVEY
Due Back:	Due Back:
ILL No.: No Renew	ILL No.: No Renew
To:	To:
From: HARVEY	From: HARVEY
Due Back:	Due Back:
ILL No.: No Renew	ILL No.: No Renew
To:	To:
From: HARVEY	From: HARVEY
Due Back:	Due Back:
ILL No.: No Renew	ILL No.: No Renew

Please initial below if you would like to record that you have read this book.

TRUTH, BY
OMISSION

TRUTH, BY OMISSION

DANIEL BEAMISH

BLACK STONE
PUBLISHING

Copyright © 2019 by Daniel Beamish
Published in 2019 by Blackstone Publishing
Cover and book design by Sean M. Thomas

The characters and events in this book are fictitious.
Any similarity to real persons, living or dead,
is coincidental and not intended by the author.

Printed in the United States of America

First edition: 2019
ISBN 978-1-9825-4477-5
Fiction / Literary

1 3 5 7 9 10 8 6 4 2

CIP data for this book is available
from the Library of Congress

Blackstone Publishing
31 Mistletoe Rd.
Ashland, OR 97520

www.BlackstonePublishing.com

The End of the Beginning

I was one month shy of my eighth birthday when I first saw one person kill another; nine when I first committed the same atrocity—my misconceived and futile attempt at justice. I have since learned that one depravity can never excuse another. I've also come to know that the hand we are dealt in life can still be played many ways: that the ledger of eternal fate is not preordained, and that each act of human kindness can indeed make a difference.

Me

It was a daily ritual for Auntie Nyaka and me to walk the path from our home through the lush jungle, making noise and song as much for our own play and amusement as to let the creatures of the river know that we were approaching. We villagers lived in a symbiotic relationship of respect with the hippos and crocodiles that also used the waterway and none of us wanted to tip the precious balance, fine-tuned over many generations. We each kept our distance and tried not to surprise the other, us out of fear of being devoured, the beasts trying to avoid slaughter.

The length of the path itself was part of the détente. Our homes were built far enough from the water that the creatures would not venture the distance and take us unawares. The daily treks to the river involved the older boys swinging their machetes to keep the path clear. If this was not done regularly the way would be lost to the jungle in a matter of weeks. Uncle Dzigbote would jest and tell me often that the only thing growing

faster than the jungle was me. At seven I was as big as some of the older
boys, and Auntie Nyaka even referred to me as her "little man." And as
predictably as the day would dawn, on every river trek I bemoaned not
yet being given my own machete. But Uncle Dzigbote knew too well the
dangers of the weighty blades.

The machetes served a second purpose: to lop off the heads of the
mambas, vipers, and adders that camouflaged themselves so well in the
trees and on the ground, and even in the water. There was no truce possible
with the snakes. We feared and hated them, and I suspect they felt the
same for us. When we could avoid each other we would, but if either of
us got the chance we would kill the other, us with our machetes and them
with their needle teeth.

So, when Auntie Nyaka and I—neither of us wielders of a machete—
walked the path alone we had to be especially loud and vigilant. We usually
sang the songs that Auntie's mother had taught her. Those were the ones
that I liked, the ones that made me laugh and her smile. Sometimes she
would sing the songs that the white Christ-men had taught her, but those
didn't make me happy. They were not the joyous songs of our people. They
were sad songs, songs of subservience.

The last time Auntie Nyaka and I walked the path to where it met
the bank of the river, I charged down the dirt and log steps while Auntie
descended them gracefully. These were the steps which the men of the
village had to repound into the mud walls after each wet season finished
and the level of the river dropped a good eight feet. I stripped off my
blue shorts with the three white stripes down the side, the full extent of
my wardrobe, and threw them ahead to the foot of the bank. They had
arrived in a bundle, brought by the Christ-men and picked through by
the children of the village. From the debris at the river's edge I plucked
as large a piece of driftwood as I could swing and beat the surface of the
water until Auntie made it down the steps. Once reasonably sure that
there were no hippos or crocs lurking in the silty brown water, I slid down
the submersed edge of the bank until I floated free of the bottom.

Auntie Nyaka unwound the single bolt of multicolored cloth that
packaged her so elegantly and tossed it over the branches the village women

had erected for drying laundry. I paid no attention to her nakedness as she plunged into the water with me. As always, she tired of water play before I did and went to the bank to fetch my small shorts and her long cloth. Squatting at the water's edge she immersed and scrubbed them both, then draped them on the branches to dry in the sun. A few steps upstream the waterway curved around a shoal of pebbles that reached out into it. Auntie loved to stretch out there, basking under the blazing African sun. She laid down, patient as always, waiting for me to play myself tired.

I had swum near the far bank when I heard a somewhat familiar *pud, pud, pud* creeping slowly closer, slowly louder, from downstream. Before I could even see the boat, Auntie Nyaka was shouting and waving frantically. I looked to her as she stood totally naked on the shoal gesturing for me to get away, but her hysterics were confusing. With my head peeking above the water's surface, I turned back to the *pud, pud, pud,* which was becoming louder, slowly exposing the source as it inched around the curve of the river. Auntie's alarm gradually began to register, and I paddled myself close to the far shore until my feet took purchase on the muddy bottom. Crouching in the water among the overhanging branches I watched both the opposite shore—where a panicked Auntie Nyaka wrapped herself in her bolt—and the boat, now fully in view as it *pudded* upstream toward us.

The craft's large flat deck carried four men, one of whom controlled the motor at the back. The other three stood at the front, signaling the man in the back toward Auntie Nyaka's shoal. The *pud, pud, pud* quickened, becoming louder, the gap between Auntie and the boat closing faster and faster. She glanced my way, making sure that I was well concealed. The motor cut, leaving the sounds of four men shouting over one another in a language I was unfamiliar with as the front of the flat deck slid onto the pebbled shoal.

Auntie Nyaka defiantly maintained her position on the bank and spoke to them in the dialect of our village. When they didn't answer she repeated in Kinyarwanda, and when they seemed not to understand that she switched to Swahili.

"We have nothing here for you. Please continue your voyage in peace, health, and happiness."

"We've been looking for the fruit of the jungle," one of them responded in Swahili. "I think we have found it."

"Please, please continue your journey," Auntie Nyaka said, slowly backing away.

Ignoring her plea, they leapt from the boat, one of them grabbing her around the waist from behind. But before he could cover her mouth with his other hand she let out a piercing scream. A second man, a fat one, pointed a pistol into the air and fired it. The suddenness of the sound stunned me. I watched the first man hold Auntie tightly as another roughly slashed open her bolt. Suddenly her nakedness, which had never before seemed anything but calm beauty, became a shameful exposure. She struggled futilely against the grip of the slick black muscles wrapped around her, managing only a few loud shrieks before one of the men, using a section of her own clothing, stuffed her mouth. Auntie was no match for the four men as she was thrown down and pounced upon. One held her arms, pinning her shoulders to the ground. The fat one, the one with the gun, laid it aside and knelt over her. He opened his pants and prodded, forcing himself on her. I had seen Auntie Nyaka take Uncle Dzigbote inside her many times before. In the single room of our mud hut there was scant opportunity for privacy, not that privacy was called for in the loving environment of our little home. When Uncle Dzigbote came to Auntie strong and hard the two of them were gentle and quiet together. Hardly ever speaking, they caressed each other, covered each other with kisses, and when finished, held each other tightly. Then they would welcome me between them, and the three of us often fell asleep like this.

But now Auntie Nyaka struggled to keep this stranger away from her. She fought hard as the others beat her about her head until she gave in and collapsed limp, allowing the brute to thrust into her. I could not remain quiet witness to the violence, and I shouted at the men, swimming toward them as quickly as I could. The surprise of a child appearing in the water and yelling at them was acknowledged with mere glances and laughs. The one on top of Auntie paid me no heed whatsoever as he grunted and panted his brutal business.

I planned to jump on his back and make him stop. I just needed to get there. I felt my toes in the mud. My feet grabbed. I shouted and cried, hauling my small body out of the water to save Auntie. But before I could rescue her, Uncle Dzigbote was running down the bank, slipping in the mud, not bothering with the pounded steps. His appearance startled the four men as much as it surprised me. Their hesitation allowed him the moment he needed to grab the collar of the one facedown on Auntie. Ripping him backward with one massive pull, the man landed sprawling on the shoal. Uncle Dzigbote was bigger and stronger than any of the strangers. I kept coming forward to help him. I wanted to be able to hurt these men that had hurt Auntie. But without even seeing it coming, I was scooped up in the arm of the fat one who had fired the pistol. The pistol was now in his right hand, with me wrapped into his left arm. For a long moment no one moved. The other three men stood still. Auntie Nyaka, still restrained, sobbed. Uncle Dzigbote did not move. He looked into my eyes and I stared back, imploring his might and his help. He was so close to me we could almost have touched if we would have both stretched out our arms. I did reach out to him, willing him to stretch toward me, but at that very moment the pistol was raised by an extended arm. It reached level with Uncle Dzigbote's face, a foot or two away. His eyes were still tethered to mine, so neither of us saw the trigger being pulled.

The sound was so loud that my eyes squeezed shut, losing my bond with Uncle Dzigbote. A warm sticky wetness covered my face and seeped into my eyes as they reopened, stinging them. The hulk of Uncle Dzigbote staggered backward and toppled over on his heels. I looked to Auntie Nyaka, still held by one of the men. I think she was screaming from within the muffle of her gag. The men shouted to each other, but I heard nothing, save the loud ringing in my head.

I kicked and pounded the brute who held me until another of the men stuffed my mouth with cloth and tied me to the deck of the boat with a length of rope. From there I watched the men roll the lifeless body of Uncle Dzigbote into the river where it casually disappeared into the silty brown water. I searched the path and the jungle for help and it was there—I saw them, the men of our village, concealed along the upper bank, too frightened to act. I looked away as each of the strangers took a turn with Auntie Nyaka.

I saw my second killing when they were finished with Auntie Nyaka.

Stephanie

Now, after so many years and so many deaths, I ought to be immunized against them, hardened to them, but this one is unlike any I have faced before. Nothing, nothing, can prepare one for the death of one's only child. We saw the counselors, the same counselors I have sent so many of my own patients' families to see. We listened to their advice, tried to do everything they recommended. I have to believe it made a difference for our little Steph. Surely it helped her. *Please let it have helped her.* But everything that we did, and tried to do, seems insubstantial when measured against her challenge. There was so little we could really do, so very little.

This shouldn't have surprised me. I've had young patients die. Not a lot, but a few. I know everything the counselors say to parents; I've said it all myself. Now, when I really think about it, it's a lot of clinical gibberish. There's nothing in this advice that truly helps a parent convey their love to a dying daughter or makes the loss any less painful. There's a lot of advice about how to "manage" the child, how to make things easier, maybe less confusing, perhaps make them a little less afraid of their own death. I hope this helped Steph … somehow.

"I'm exhausted, Freddie. I feel emptied out, empty of everything." Anna is lying beside me on the twin bed in Stephanie's room. We're not cuddled together or holding each other. We're both just lying there on our backs, each of us too exhausted to clasp the other. I know exactly how she is feeling. There is nothing left inside me, either. I think even my soul has left me, I feel so empty. I want to be strong for Anna, but I just don't have the energy. A knight of a husband would muster a rally and say the right thing. But I am no knight.

The best I can manage is a lame, "I know, Anna, I know." I feel tears running down both sides of my face and I'm not sure whether they are for Anna, for Stephanie, or for my own pathetic self.

It's our first day home after driving back from Anna's parents' place in the Springs. We lingered there for two days after Stephanie's burial in the cemetery on the family farm. Her mom was busy cooking and sent back enough food to stock the refrigerator for several days. Her dad said he'd drive us home to Boulder, but we needed some time alone and refused the kind offer. They're both amazing. They've been real troupers, because this was their loss, too. Stephanie was special to them. It was evident whenever they were with her. They were ten years younger around her; she energized them. They've done so much to help us over the last few days and weeks. But they have to get back to their own lives, do their grieving alone, as do Anna and I.

It's now exactly one week since Stephanie let out a tiny hollow breath and just never took in another one—not even eight months since we first thought something might be wrong, seven since the confirmed diagnosis.

Steph had carried a note home from her fourth-grade gym teacher but forgot to give it to us for two days, until Anna found it while packing her lunch. Nothing alarming, she seemed to have been wheezing. Perhaps we should have her checked for asthma. I knew she didn't have asthma. That evening I called Steph into my study. Even as my young lady of nine, I didn't need to invite her up onto my lap. It was her first choice of a seat whenever we were together.

"I'm sorry, Daddy."

"What are you sorry for, sweets?"

"I didn't give Mom the note from Miss Newlin. Am I in trouble?"

"No, you're not in trouble, but you know you have to try harder to remember these things."

"But am I in trouble from Miss Newlin?"

"Not at all … she wants me to take a listen to you." She had her pajamas on, and I stretched the front collar down with my stethoscope and placed it on her upper chest, one side and then the other. Not the perfect smooth sound of air exchanging that I'd have liked, but not bad. "Turn a bit, honey, and let Daddy listen to your back." I reached up under her pajamas and listened again from the back of her ribs, on both sides. Certainly not a wheezing. Perhaps she had a touch of a cold a few days ago.

"Am I okay?"

I bounced her and tickled her ribs as I'd been doing all her life. "You're perfect … you're my perfect little princess."

And she was perfect to me, to both of us. Her soft, caramel skin, a blend of Anna's pale white and my own deep African black, was totally unblemished. She wasn't old enough to have been scarred by even a pimple yet. Her rounded little nose was very like her mother's, not brutishly flat like mine. Her eyes were bright and wide, like her mother's, but obsidian black, like mine rather than the blue of Anna's. She often fretted over the trouble her rag-doll hair gave her, but to both Anna and I it was worth all the time it took. Never an Afro, difficult to straighten, it was her most distinguishing feature.

Could any other child have been so easy to love? If she ever gave us grief it was so minuscule that I can't remember it. I stood up, lifting her from my lap to my arms, and then up over my shoulder, tapping her bum and tickling the back of her leg behind the knee until her laughter took her breath away. That was when I noticed the huffing. I didn't need a stethoscope to know that something wasn't quite right.

A routine X-ray is no longer routine when it is done on your own child. You're no longer a physician ordering it, you're a parent dreading it. And all the clinical composure from years of reading and interpreting CT reports doesn't do a damn bit of good when you have to explain them to your own wife. I know too much about this stuff. I can't *not* panic. Like every parent, I'm sure there is a mistake, a mix-up with reports, something wrong at the lab. Even my clinical side says there might be a mistake. Type III pleuropulmonary blastoma is rare in children over the age of five. Rare, but not unheard of.

As much as we'd like it to be, I know the biopsy isn't wrong. When things move on to MRIs and then the tissue biopsies, I'm out of my league. Colleagues, experts in the field, completely relegate me to being another frightened parent. Metastasized malignancies show up in the brain. They are extremely invasive and inoperable. I must have learned this in med school.

I learned it all over again.

By this point Anna and I had both slowed down our practices. We wanted to spend as much time as possible by our little angel's side while she bravely faced the regimen of treatments for the cancer that had taken hold. I saw no patients after lunch, and Anna reduced her workload so that she could manage it during the afternoons. She could do most of her work from home. Anna is a partner in a small local law firm, Tierney, Thomas, and May, which specializes in immigration law. They were as understanding and supportive of us during this period as the partners at my own downtown clinic. We adapted into the routine of getting up around five. I scheduled patients early, went to my clinic first thing, and arrived at the hospital during the lunch hour. Anna arrived there before breakfast, sometimes before Steph was even awake, and left for a few hours when I took over. She'd come back around dinnertime, and neither of us would leave until Steph had fallen asleep; most of the time we sat there quietly for several hours afterward, just watching the gentle heft of the blankets as she slept. For months we never ate a meal at home; it was takeout at Steph's bedside for us and a hospital tray for her.

A month ago we started taking turns staying all night, one of us climbing into the hospital bed and gently cuddling our little princess. But there was no sleep on those nights for either of us. When I was at home alone in bed I worried, I doubted, I prayed to gods I didn't believe in, just in case. I wallowed in pity. And the nights I was at the hospital I lay awake, trying not to move lest I jerk one of the drip lines feeding into her delicate little veins, willing a miracle with all my might.

Several times we were lulled into false hopes. Stephanie would tell us the pain was gone. She wanted to go home. Could we play a game with her? She wanted to walk to the playroom down the hall where she could hear the other kids. For these brief moments she had more energy than either of us, than both of us.

When Anna and I met up at the hospital these mornings I didn't need her to tell me that she'd had as little sleep as I'd had. Her movements were slow, her eyes dull, her hair had no sheen, and her fingernails began to crack. The life was draining from all three of us. The nurses at the hospital began to treat us like copatients. They brought us water and snacks when we stopped bothering to even pick up takeout.

Eventually, we both insisted on staying, refusing to leave. On the fifth night of this, Anna's parents stayed late at the hospital as well, waiting outside in the hall. Her brother and his wife and two boys were staying at our house. We wanted to be alone in the room with her. She hadn't opened her eyes for hours. I knew she wasn't sleeping. She was in a fitful coma, but we pretended between us, without saying it, that she had slipped into peaceful dreams. That's what we wanted for her. But I had seen many deaths and I knew they seldom came peacefully.

Steph no longer breathed, she gulped in bits of air at irregular intervals and expelled them in long slow bellows. I could hear it all in my dozing state midway between half sleep and total exhaustion. My eyes popped open when the next gulp of air didn't happen. I squeezed Anna's hand, and she woke in the chair beside me. She bent over the bedside and cuddled the frail skeleton of our daughter, her previously effulgent caramel skin now a pallid beige, her springy curls long ago fallen out, leaving a tiny bald orb easily cradled in one palm.

We cried without making a sound, my tears running off my cheeks, sponging into Anna's already matted blond hair, now tucked beneath my chin. Her tears rolled even more copiously, drenching the single sheet that covered Steph. We sat like this for a long time, neither of us with any will to do anything save hold our baby, hold each other.

Dutifully taking the advice of the counselors, we had already made all the funeral arrangements but there was still a lot to do. Anna's family helped out immensely. They've been a rock to us since her parents embraced me as a second son. Anna and I muddled through four days of condolences from extended family, friends, colleagues, and remote acquaintances.

Two things stand out as especially touching to me—Stephanie's school friends and my own patients. Every single child in Steph's class, all twenty-six of them, and their parents made it out to the wake and the funeral, and a few of her closest friends and their parents even made the two-hour drive to the interment at the small plot on Anna's old family farmstead in Colorado Springs. For most of them it was their first experience with death. I wondered what they thought. How will death affect them throughout the rest of their lives? They'll all soon enough lose relatives, a parent, a grandparent, a sibling. Some of them will witness violence and accidents. Some may become policemen or firefighters or soldiers and have to see more than their share of death. I only hope that none will have to experience all the deaths I've known.

My patients, many of whom I really didn't even know all that well, came out in numbers that I would have never expected. I was touched by how they wanted to give back some healing now that I was in need. They turned the tables on me, asking about *my* family and *my* well-being. And I was grateful to them all. It helped reaffirm what I believe to be one of the basic truisms of medicine—that compassion and empathy go a long way in the healing process.

But now we're alone here, Anna and I. Alone for the first time in nearly ten years, and we are empty and exhausted. Side by side on Stephanie's bed, tears puddling and spilling over, we take in all of what used to be Stephanie's—a constellation of glow-in-the-dark moons and stars stuck to the ceiling; *National Geographic* animal posters; photos of her school friends; a collection of stuffed animals, from the ratty little dinosaur that she used to suck on in her crib to a giant panda that her grandpa won for her just this last summer at the fair; an I AM AFRICA poster. We are surrounded by a mix of things that tell us our little baby girl was turning into a young lady. But now we will never see her giddy with her first love, or graduate, or learn to drive, or go to the prom, or get engaged, or have her own children.

I know we've been lying here for a while because through the window I've watched the sky go from cloudy gray to indigo purple. Anna has finally fallen asleep, but she holds my hand with her fingers twined into mine. She's always been a good sleeper. She can sleep anywhere, any time of day. We've had a lot of jokes between us about that over the years.

I, on the other hand, want desperately for more sleep. For years my sleep was sparse and haunted by the atrocities I'd seen. There was a brief time, during my years in France, when Anna and I first met, where I enjoyed long, blissful sleeps. I was lost in Anna's newly cast spell and we spent time in bed together, totally oblivious to the rest of the world, to any past demons. We gaily lounged through whole weekends without ever getting dressed and hardly leaving the bed. But life overtook us, as it does all new lovers, and those carefree days are now relegated to memories and yearnings.

All the years of med school and residency helped to banish my recurring nightmares. I didn't have time for such distractions, but I had little time for sleep, either. When I *could* grab a few winks, I was in such a bone-weary state that even my sleep couldn't be distracted. Then my first few years of practicing medicine were as a trauma doctor, usually as junior man on the night shift, in the emergency department at St. Joe's in Denver. It's only been in the last few years again, now that I've joined a group practice, that I've been able to keep more regular hours and get a bit more steady sleep.

But no one can sleep like Anna. And it's not just how much she sleeps, it's the way she sleeps. She's totally peaceful and calm. She hardly breathes, she rarely moves—on the couch, the bed, upright in an airplane or bus, on a chaise by a crowded pool. And she always sleeps with a smile, always that is, until Steph got sick. Since then it's been different. She is sleeping less and fitfully. When I look over at her now her brow is furrowed and her face twitches. Her grip on my hand is alternating from a hard clasp to a flaccid touch, and she makes noises, like she is thinking in her sleep.

I start to selfishly mull over that she is all I have left. I've only ever really, truly loved so few people in my life, and three of these are now gone. Why shouldn't I have been the one to go instead of any of them? How sad for me to be left to grieve, to be burdened with the weight of their deaths. But how can I even think like this? How deplorable, how pathetic am I to think of myself now. Yet it's in me to wallow in this stuff. I've done it all my life. I hate it. I don't want to do it, but it sloshes around inside me. I've felt it before, dark inky purple, swirling, building force into a whirlpool, grabbing, pulling me along, taking me down.

Vincent

I stood atop the battered van while our driver handed bags up to me. We'd be eight in this little van with all the luggage packed up top in the welded-pipe rack. Vincent had wrapped both of his suitcases and my small one each inside its own plastic green garbage bag. This was as much to keep the dust out as to keep the rain off. The rainy season was just letting up, and Vincent had judged that the roads should be passable without too much trouble. We were leaving what had been home to both of us for the past four years, the Nkwenda refugee camp. It was a bittersweet departure. This squalid place had reformed me, proved to me that humanity existed, and inspired some sense of hopefulness out of the despair that was my life. But most of what we were leaving held few pleasant memories for me.

The camp had been built four years earlier by the United Nations Assistance Mission for Rwanda to house the masses fleeing the civil war. It was a noble project on behalf of the world, an attempt to stave off starvation and death and provide housing for up to five thousand refugees. But within two years the population of the camp had swelled to more than fifty thousand. I was among that number, and Dr. Vincent Bergeron was one of two doctors who futilely, desperately treated us. By the time I left, most of the other fifty thousand had already moved out, and many others were buried or cremated downwind of the camp. The original service tents, emblazoned on the roofs with the large UN logo in hopes of preventing "friendly fire" from one of the several militaries operating in the area, were now threadbare and blackened by the mold that crept over them continuously during the nine-month rainy seasons. A few thousand other tents, or more accurately, tarps pulled over sticks, remained and housed those still too fearful to return to their homes and villages. But they'd have to leave soon; the Tanzanian government was expelling all those who were left, and the UN was wrapping up its mission.

From my vantage on the roof of the van I could see the whole of the camp—what was once the camp. The single main road that remained ran straight down the center and was rutted deep. It was almost impassable, with potholes like artillery craters. On either side lay acres and acres of mud. There was no longer any semblance of paths or roads left in these fields, just garbage strewn everywhere. In a few areas the garbage was piled up in small hills. These were the neighborhoods in the camp where some local leader had the foresight and strength of character to convince the inhabitants to organize themselves into a community of sorts. But most of the camp was just acres of garbage, ankle- and knee-deep, trampled into the mud.

On the outskirts of the camp the forest had been completely cut down for miles to provide families with small amounts of firewood for cooking, warmth, and camaraderie. I had watched the camp swell time and again, each time thinking that surely it had reached its limits, only to see thousands more drift in and expand it further. Each new wave of migrants would dig out the tree roots left by the previous settlers' harvest of wood. These roots became their own first stash of firewood as they settled their families in and covered them with whatever they had carried on their backs or wheeled in their barrows. Every few months the UN convoys arrived with a new truckload of blue tents, all exactly the same, and the camp dwellers would line up, waiting their turn to be handed a new home to pitch in place of the cardboard and rags that they had been using. This was how the camp grew, expanding out concentrically, gobbling the forest ahead of it.

On the day we packed up to leave, the immense African sun burned down on the mud and garbage, cooking it, fermenting it. But I had long since become immune to the stench of human waste mixed with death and refuse. Actually, it was a pleasure to see the sun reaching all the way to the ground since, during most of my past four years at the camp, sunlight was rarely able to filter through the yellow-gray haze that pressed constantly down on us. As a little bit of haze would blow or burn away, it was immediately replenished by the smoke from thousands of small fires that smoldered, many days augmented by the funeral pyres that were required for quicker cleanup of the camp.

Our van held the last of the UN personnel to vacate, and Vincent had arranged for me to ride with them since I would be accompanying him back to France—thanks to my recently granted refugee status. At one time the UN contingent here numbered as high as forty but over the past few months they had gradually been called away. I knew everyone who would be traveling with us, the UN people had been a tight and cohesive group, and they had accepted me as a useful, if not important, part of their workforce. Along with our driver, a Tanzanian national, two of the six traveling with us were logistics coordinators, one was a clerk and accountant, one was the mission lead, another was there as a nurse—also through Médecins Sans Frontières, the same group that Vincent volunteered with. In his late thirties, Vincent had already been through this a few times before, always leaving behind what would never really be a completed job in Africa. Never able to wholly satisfy the demand for the healing and compassion he brought with him.

The land portion of our trip was to take us first to Dodoma, the capital of Tanzania, where the UN had a small permanent office. The office had sent word that my French refugee papers had finally arrived, and they were holding them for us. From Dodoma we would be able to take the highway to Dar es Salaam. And after that we would fly, my first ever time on an airplane, through Zurich and on to Paris.

I lashed the gear tight and slid down from atop the van. Some of the camp dwellers who were still left had come to see us off. Those of us leaving tried to downplay our buoyant feelings, while those left behind forced themselves to offer us pleasant tidings. One of them stepped forward from the small crowd and extended his right arm as if to shake my hand. By the time I noticed there was no hand to shake, rather just a stump at the wrist, Idi Mbuyamba had grabbed my biceps with his left hand and pulled me close. He held me firmly and froze me stiff with his eyes, removing any thoughts of fondness that I was having for the camp.

I was twenty and feeling every bit a man. Idi was fifteen years my senior and certainly no bigger or stronger than I, but locked for these few seconds in his glare I was reverted to a child, mesmerized, intimidated, insecure, beholden. I had known Idi long before we both showed up in the camp and this was how he had made me feel for years. But before I could contemplate what was happening his face broke into a large toothy grin and the spell was broken. "You've done well to find a way out. You won't forget me, will you?" he said and stepped back into the throng.

As we packed ourselves into the van, I despised how once again Idi had found a way to spoil what should have been a moment of achievement for me. The joy of embarking on a new phase in my life was tainted.

Vincent sat in the front seat with the driver, three more on the middle bench, and the last three of us in the back row. As the driver began his navigation of the potholes, I twisted around in the seat, looking through the back window, wanting to say my own goodbye to the camp, but all I could see was Idi waving his handless stump at me.

We headed north and east to Bukoba, on the shore of Lake Victoria. Africa's greatest and the world's third-largest lake, Victoria spills out and becomes the Nile, traveling north for another four thousand miles. We stopped for a few hours to marvel at the vastness of the lake, an ocean to us. Perhaps even more impressive was the freshness of the air that blew off the lake and cleansed our lungs. All eight of us had forgotten the smell of freshness, and we sucked in as much of it as we could. Vincent thought we'd do well if we could make it another three hours due south to Biharamulo, and I was more than happy to put any extra mileage behind us.

The hotel in Biharamulo was a game lodge, out of season at the time and empty. They were glad to have our business, and the porters quickly erected tents for us on wooden platforms. Vincent and I shared a tent, each getting a cot. We sat alone on the porch in front of our tent relishing the quiet. Four years in the camp, there was never quiet. Tents were pitched so close to each other that there was no prospect of privacy. All the sounds of humanity not meant for broadcast were inescapable in the camp, grunts and snorts and farts, spousal squabbles, copulation, childbirth, child death, all day long, every night. Vincent and I sat for a long time in peace, just basking in the silence. Eventually he pulled out his diary and made his entries, just as he'd done every single night we were in the Nkwenda camp. After he'd finished writing down his thoughts he broke the silence.

"Will you miss the camp, Alfred?"

"In some ways … maybe." I tried to sound positive but was unable to escape the stare, then smirk and departing words from Idi.

"What is it you'll miss?" Vincent tried to coax conversation from me.

I thought about this before replying. There were lots of things I surely *wouldn't* miss, but for the sake of conversation, I finally settled on, "Being needed. Since I started helping you I feel like I have a purpose, like I'm needed."

"A basic human requirement, to be needed," he said. "Medicine would make a good profession for you. You'll be needed—more than you'll want sometimes."

"What about you, Vincent? What'll you miss about Nkwenda?"

"I'll miss making a difference. Every day, every hour I spent in that cursed camp I knew I was making a difference. Now, I'm going to go back to fill out forms and requisitions and fight the politics of a big-city hospital, and I'll go home most nights having not made a damn bit of difference."

"Is that why you stayed so long?" I asked. Most doctors did a six-month stint then retreated to the comforts of the first world. Vincent had been there four years, returning home to France only once for about two months to tend to his mother when she was dying.

"Yes that," Vincent replied, and then he added, "and atonement."

"Atonement? For what?"

Vincent was lost in introspection for several moments until the silence was broken by a deep guttural rumble that undulated on the night air. I felt the sound as much as I heard it. He put an extended finger up to his pursed lips and cupped a hand behind his ear.

"Lions," he whispered.

The king of the jungle was more than just that. The way the reverberations rolled through the darkness with firm confidence and certainty, inspiring awe more than instigating fear, made him the supreme presence of an entire continent.

We lolled in the majesty of the resonance for a few minutes after the basal music finished and the echoes floated away. Finally, Vincent restarted the conversation. "If we're lucky we might see some of the game herds in the next couple of days," he said. "Unfortunately, we're too early for the big migrations, but the smaller herds should be gathering."

I was looking forward to the wildlife. I'd seen none since arriving at Nkwenda. Every creature down to the insects had been eaten by the starving hordes. So, the next day when Vincent pointed to the dust storm ahead and identified it as a buffalo herd, I paid careful attention. As we came closer, I could make out the animals, perhaps a hundred or more. I'd never seen them in such numbers, but our driver laughed and told me that during the great migrations they would gather by the thousands, the wildebeests by the hundreds of thousands. Before arriving in the camp I had seen lots of wild game, but only in small bands or as isolated animals. I wondered how so many people could have starved in our camp at Nkwenda when it was just a few days' drive away from so much huntable game. What started as a novelty, seeing the herds of gazelle, zebra, giraffe, topi, and wildebeest, soon became a nuisance as they slowed us down, showing no fear of our approaching vehicle as they grazed by the hundreds on the dirt roadway.

We spent two more nights in small hotels before arriving to three nights of luxury at the Continental in Dodoma. The United Nations provided us with the rooms, truly palatial to me. Vincent smiled as I turned on the tap and ran hot water over my hands. I flushed the toilet four times just to flush it. And then I noticed the cool air pumping from the air conditioner mounted on the wall. I put my hands in the flow and tried to direct it to my face.

"Enjoy that while you can," he said. "You won't find many of those in Paris."

Vincent had told me a lot about Paris, preparing me for what to expect, and this was another bit of information I filed away.

I stayed in the room while Vincent took a cab to the UN offices. The hot water and new bar of soap were a treat to be enjoyed. I filled the tub three times, refilling each time after the water cooled too much. But then when I got out I found the room much too cold. I shut off the air-conditioning and opened the window to allow the heat in.

Three days in Dodoma and I was feeling antsy. I preferred more mileage between us and the camp now that I had my paperwork. I was glad when our driver showed up at the hotel to fetch us. Vincent and I had decided to forgo flying for this leg of our trip, as the others had chosen to do, and instead took the Camry and driver provided by the UN office. I'd never seen the savanna plateau, and Vincent assured me that four more days overland would be a worthwhile experience.

The road from here on was paved and made for smoother travel. We never got as close to the wildlife as we did coming out of the lakes region, but we did see much more of it. In the distance we often spied elephants in large family herds and several times spotted prides of lions. This was the only time in all my life in Africa that I had seen the royal beasts. They were often referred to in my culture, but they had been hunted and driven from our mountain jungles years ago. We stopped by the roadside to sit and watch, and I studied them from a distance, admiring their elegance and gracefulness as they softly padded, a small puff of dust rising with each paw fall. Their dominance required no demonstration as the sounds of their night roars from a few days earlier proved. I saw no parallel at all between these regal creatures and Idi Mbuyamba, who had used his self-proclaimed affinity to the great cats to inspire fear in others. To me, he was much more like the striped hyenas skulking around in the darkness, scavenging off others.

Anna

Four weeks have now dragged by since our Stephanie passed, and we're in the kitchen. Anna has just finished the dinner dishes and sits down across from me on a stool at the island.

"Let's take a trip, Freddie," Anna says. She holds the top of the teapot secure as she pours us each a cup of chamomile.

I look up from the news on my tablet. "Hmmph, where would you like to go, Anna?"

"Anywhere, let's just get out of this house for a while … take some real time off. Let's take the honeymoon we never had." I know what she's doing. She's doing it for me more than her. I've been able to escape sinking into the inky whirlpool for the past month because she's been keeping me above water. She's my brave knight. And I'm embarrassed by it, but also grateful, very grateful.

"Maybe Mexico ... or Hawaii," she says. "Or let's get far away. You could show me Africa. You said we'd go sometime."

We were going to do that with Stephanie. I'd wanted her to see what's out there in the world when she was old enough, to see the beautiful majesty of Africa, even the corruption and bleakness of Africa—her heritage.

"Now wouldn't be a good time for me to show you Africa, Anna. I just can't do Africa now, not yet. And I'm not sure I should take any more time away from the clinic right now. I haven't pulled my share there since Steph got sick. No one's saying anything, but I feel I need to make it up to them a bit."

"Fuck the clinic, Freddie. You've been doing extra time in there the whole last month since Steph died." She's not cautious anymore, I know she's serious by the way she's raised her voice. "That's all in your head ... you don't owe them anything. They're not asking you for anything. You're the one putting all that pressure on yourself." She's right, of course, as she usually is. "Would you expect anything extra from any of them if they lost a child?" she asks. "No. You'd never think of it."

"It's not just the partners, it's my patients," I say.

"No, it's not! They're not getting sick now to make up for the time you were off six months ago." She seldom shouts, so now I'm taking this very seriously. She takes her eyes from mine and looks straight into her cup. "Freddie, we haven't made love for seven months."

I know this, but I've been blocking it out, avoiding thinking about it. "I'm not a nun," she continues. "And I don't want to be. I need you to come back from wherever you've gone. You have to try." I know that she's saying this for me and not for her. She's always put me first, much to my own shame. I know that she would stay celibate if in some way it would be better for me. That's how much she loves me. And I love her just as much. I just have a hard time showing her, unlike the way she so easily shows me.

A thought suddenly comes into my mind, something a counselor from the hospital cautioned us about before Steph died. He said that the statistics for couples separating go way up after the death of a child and they go off the charts when that child was the only one. I love Anna way too much to become one of those statistics.

"Okay, Anna. Let's take a vacation. We'll take our honeymoon, the one we've put off forever. A nice long vacation—maybe Saint Martin, or Jamaica … or anywhere you want, just not Africa right now."

She straightens up on the stool, her face brightening, and it makes me feel like I haven't felt in a long time. Her exuberance is a dappling of light on the surface above my murky depths, and it gives me a fresh breath.

"But let's wait for a month," I say. "We can both tidy up things at work. We'll have Christmas with your family and then we'll go away for the new year. We can take a whole month and get away from winter. It's a good idea, Anna … just the two of us, time just for us."

She comes around the island and sits on my lap, putting both arms around me, hugging tightly. It is the fun happy hug that has been missing for the last nine months. And it cleanses something in me, like an infection being rinsed out of a wound, like the worst is suddenly past and a healing has started.

I immediately decide not to go back into Stephanie's room tonight like I'd planned—like I've been doing for the past month since she passed, going in there and wallowing in thoughts of what we've lost and what we'll never have. Instead, I lift Anna off my lap and direct her down the hall toward our bedroom.

We spend the next four dreamy hours making love like we used to, seventeen years ago, when we first fell in love. We aren't fucking, and we aren't having sex. We're *making love*—laughing, and crying, and holding, and touching, and kissing, and exploring, smelling, tasting, feeling, and crying, and laughing, again and again. We aren't *trying* to make up for the past seven months, but it feels like we might be.

I have to be at the clinic at seven tomorrow morning. I'll need to be up by five to get in a quick workout and then make the commute from Boulder to downtown Denver, yet I don't care that it's now after midnight. Anna has fallen asleep while I lie here awake. Splayed fully naked, on top of the sheets, the low November moon is reflecting a soft light on her. How lucky am I, an orphan out of Africa, lying here in my own home in America, beside this angel of a wife. At thirty-seven she is more beautiful than when we met seventeen years ago. The nubile softness of those times has been sculpted into a sleek sinewy mature body. Her pale skin, dotted with a galaxy of freckles, is complemented by her long blond hair, now cast on the pillow like a veil. Several times she's threatened to crop off that hair simply for practicality, but she never has, knowing how much I adore it. Small breasts, shapely hips, her tummy shows no sign of ever having borne a child. I know she loves me totally and devotedly. How fortunate I am. The slight smile has returned to her face as she lies there, lost in her own dreams, that peaceful smile that has been missing all these past months. I resolve to myself, at this moment, not to let our loss of Stephanie drag either of us down. Content to just enjoy her sleeping presence, I let myself drift back to our first days together.

* * *

I was twenty-one when I first reluctantly met Anna in Paris. It was an arranged meeting, not like a date or anything, but rather a favor to Vincent. Since our meeting in the Nkwenda camp he had become my closest friend. A friend to whom I was deeply indebted, and to whom I would become even further indentured, once this meeting played out.

"Alfred, I know you're extremely busy with your studies, but I was hoping that you could take a few minutes and help me out."

"Of course, Vincent. Anything." We conversed in French, the common language between us.

"There's a reporter, Anna … somebody from the student newspaper at Hautes Études Internationales et Politiques. She's doing a little feature on the experience of African refugees here in Paris. Would you be able to talk to her?"

"Does she want to talk about my experience in Africa or here?" I was reluctant to speak to a stranger about the things that I had seen and done in Africa, but I was happy to talk about my efforts to adapt to European life.

"Hopefully both," he replied. Vincent himself didn't know the worst things from my past, but I would do anything for this man. We'd left Africa a little over a year earlier, and since arriving back in France he'd been tirelessly fundraising for Médecins Sans Frontières and promoting the case for a more open refugee policy here, in addition to his responsibilities at the hospital.

Vincent made arrangements for me to meet the novice reporter at a café near the campus where I was studying. This was a good thing because I couldn't really afford the time away from my studies or the Métro ticket to go anywhere beyond walking distance. As soon as I entered, a rather perky girl with long blond hair and soft, straight bangs stood from a table at the other side of the room and strode my way with one arm reaching out.

"Alfred Olyontombo?"

She took my hand firmly, surprising me with her grip. "Yes, Anna …?"

"Fraser. Anna Fraser. Dr. Bergeron speaks very highly of you. I'm so pleased that you've taken the time to meet with me." Her French was fine, but I noticed an unfamiliar accent to it.

Still slightly off balance from the warmth of her handshake, I stupidly asked her, "How did you know I'm Alfred?"

She half-stepped back, looked at me from head to toe, and then looked around the rest of the café. "You're the only black dude in sight. Doesn't take a Sherlock." I didn't understand this reference at the time, but her spunk impressed me. "Can I get you a coffee?" she asked.

I was too shy to impose on her, but I also didn't want to spend my meager funds on coffee. "No, I'm fine, thank you."

She ordered anyhow. "Two café américain. Do you want cream or sugar?"

"Just black. Thank you." There was a wholesomeness to her and a "take charge" attitude that most Frenchwomen didn't have, at least in my limited experience. I can't explain why, but I suddenly felt a bit inferior in the situation, intimidated.

"Well, I guess we survived," she said as we sat down.

"Survived?"

"Survived. No apocalypse, no second coming, not even a single computer failure reported anywhere in the world. Guess we could have made better use of those billions we got sucked into blowing."

It was only a few days into the new millennium. It took me a moment to clue in to her quip. *Survival* clearly had a much more visceral meaning to me, but I wanted to match her tone. "Doesn't actually feel any more like the future than the last century felt, does it?"

She raised her coffee cup in a toast. "To the next century … peace and harmony."

I touched my cup to hers as I thought about this for a second, reflecting on where I came from and the brighter prospects of a future away from Africa.

She looked me straight in the eyes, obviously noticing my hesitation. "Shall we begin? Please tell me your story."

"My story? What do you want to know?"

"Dr. Bergeron says that he met you in Tanzania and that you then came here as a refugee. Tell me." Her notebook and pen were ready, and she put a small recorder on the table. "Do you mind if I tape? I can't really do shorthand."

"I don't mind at all. Well, I met Vincent … Dr. Bergeron, in a camp … a refugee camp. He was working as a doctor there. He was totally overworked. There was one other doctor, provided by the UN, I think, and two nurses. But they couldn't keep up. We were at least twenty thousand in the camp at that time. There was no water, no food. We were all hungry and most everyone was sick from something. Vincent was a saint there. He—"

"Yes, but what about you?" she interrupted. "I want *your* story. I'd like to make this a personal account, firsthand … from you."

I didn't like talking about myself. It was much easier to talk about others and to talk in generalities. I began to think that perhaps I had gotten myself into something I didn't really want. Completely out of character, I blurted out, "What about you, what's your story?"

She stared at me for a moment, and then I think she sensed my discomfort. "Okay. I'm an American. I've been here for four months studying international politics at HEIP and trying to perfect my French. It's my third year of college, and I volunteer on the student newspaper. It's a way to meet people and force myself to do more writing in French."

"I think your story is better than mine," I said. "Where in America?"

"Colorado Springs."

I shook my head.

"Near Denver. In the middle of the country."

I nodded, but I really knew very little of American geography.

"It's in the mountains."

Mountains I knew about. I'd spent much of my life in them.

"Where are you from? Not the camp—I mean, where were you born?" she asked.

I thought how I might answer this and then decided to be honest. "I'm not sure … a small village, somewhere in the jungle. I know it was a pretty remote village. There were no roads, just a trail to the next village. Most people came by river."

"So, you grew up there, in the jungle?"

"Sort of. In the jungle, anyhow. For the most part."

She noticed the hesitation in my answer and paused to think. "So, um, you went to school there? In the jungle?"

It was at this moment that I made a split-second decision that would follow me to this very day. I liked this girl, and I wanted to be as honest as I could with her. But there were things, many things, that I didn't want to be honest about even with myself. There were things that I had spent the last several years pretending had never happened, pushing them into hiding places in the back of my mind, hoping that if I didn't look at them again, they might eventually disappear. I certainly wasn't going to talk about these things with this person I had only just met. And yet I wanted to be truthful.

So, I decided that I would not lie to her. I might avoid some answers and I might tell her only parts of the story, but I wouldn't tell her any outright lies. And this is what I have done with Anna for the past seventeen years. Everything that has happened over all these years in which we have been together is a wide-open book. We have no secrets between us. We've made it our personal policy. We know each other's deepest fantasies and ambitions. But much of what happened in Africa still remains buried.

The truth I have told Anna about Africa contains no lies, it simply isn't the whole truth. And it began on that very first day I met her with that split-second decision I made. She might have sensed that I wasn't telling her everything, but she was sensitive enough, and kind enough, to not acknowledge it. She never pried any deeper with her questions than I had led her, a sure sign that she was not destined for a career as a reporter. And over the duration of our marriage she has never pushed into those places that she surely knows exist. Perhaps she thinks that eventually I will open up to her, or perhaps she has decided it really doesn't matter anymore. I hope it is the latter. I hope that I have proven to her my goodness, my humanity. I hope that she will never be faced with judging me by any more than the person she has known me to be for seventeen years.

Still, I have been tempted to confess at least the sin of omission—if not the sins themselves—especially recently, during Stephanie's illness. More than once it occurred to me that her sickness might have been some twisted form of karma, a way for the world to get back at me for my horrid transgressions, unscrupulously sweeping Steph and Anna along with me. I even thought about confessing, telling Anna everything, but sober second thoughts prevailed. Would it really cure Steph? Was it likely to do anything other than make Anna hate me?

Our first interview went on that way. I, telling my story with omissions, in return for her telling me hers. I told her how I was orphaned and ended up being schooled by Catholics at a missionary school. She traded me information about the public school system in America.

"What about language?" she asked. "Is French that common in Africa? Do you speak anything else?"

I replied in Kinyarwanda, "I speak several languages." She smiled and asked me to translate. I explained that it was the main language where I was from, but that most of the schooling was done in French.

"So, you speak two languages?"

"And Swahili, and several dialects from the mountains. And English."

She raised her eyebrows, obviously impressed. I learned from her that Americans seldom bother to learn more than English. This seemed odd to me since almost everyone in Africa spoke more than one language and even here, in Europe, most people seemed to speak two or more. She explained that she was an exception in America. "I had a close friend as a child, a Mexican immigrant whose first language was Spanish. I thought it was cool to speak Spanish with her and jumped at the chance to study it in high school. I also took a few French courses and when this opportunity came up, to study for a year here in France, I worked part time at two jobs and convinced my parents to help me out with the rest."

I related to her that it was because of my proficiency in languages that I had met Vincent Bergeron and was ultimately able to come to France.

That first meeting with Anna had been but a trailer for the movie we would make together. It lasted three hours, about two hours longer than I had allotted. But it whetted my interest in Anna the American, and she seemed keen enough to get back together for phase two of the interview.

"There's so much we haven't gotten to yet. Do you think I could impose on you for one more session—at your convenience, of course?" she asked, packing up her things.

"I'd love to," I replied in Kinyarwanda, to which she smiled and raised her eyebrows.

"Maybe you could call me next week and we could try to find a time," I said in English.

I watched her leave the café, and I sat alone for a few minutes. It had been an enjoyable time with her. I thought she was pretty—quite beautiful actually—but had never thought I'd be attracted to a white girl. She certainly wouldn't be attracted to me. I mean, not that she'd demonstrated any prejudice at all, it's just that I never considered myself particularly good-looking. I was as deep a brown as brown could be before it is called black. My lips were just as dark, if not darker, filled with the same brown pigment as my skin, touches of pink hinting at the inside of my mouth. That brown pigment even extended to the whites of my eyes—which I always felt were a pale yellow, not really white. My hair was clipped close, more because my friend François could cut it for free with his clippers than from any sense of fashion. This accentuated the roundness of my head, pure central African. But I was taller than most from this part of Africa—not as tall as those from the north and east, but considerably taller than most others from central Africa. My clothes hid most of the multitude of purple scars that railroaded much of my body, but there was no hiding the one that sloped down from the center of my hairline through my right eyebrow and ended at my jaw. She couldn't *not* have seen that scar. Yet she never stared at it and was kind enough not to ask about it.

I wasn't interested in Anna for anything more than pleasant company and to quench my curiosity of the wider world, at least that's what I told myself. She was a good conversationalist; three hours had gone by very quickly. At that point in my life I honestly had no time for girls as anything more than friends. I was too busy trying to secure a university standing that would get me accepted into medical school somewhere in France.

She called me the next week for the follow-up interview. "Same place?"

"That's fine, but the only time I have this week is Sunday morning," I said.

"That won't interfere with your church?"

"Church?" I was surprised.

"You were schooled by Catholics. Don't you go to church?"

"Hmmph. It definitely won't interfere with church."

I was waiting for her in the café when she arrived. This time she didn't show up in a sweater and jeans. When she removed the heavy winter coat guarding against Paris' damp January she showed off a stylish skirt and trim top. She obviously had another appointment today. I soon learned that it wasn't church though, because when I asked about this she told me that even though her family was Methodist she didn't practice any longer.

We settled into an interview much like the last one. I filled in some details, withheld others, but offered enough to suit her feature story for the school paper. She, in return, traded off any information that I asked about. She learned that my ambition was to become a doctor like my friend Vincent. And I found out that she was planning to take her LSAT when she returned to the United States that summer. She enjoyed her studies in international politics but her real goal was to get into the field of international humanitarian law.

"Fascinating," I said. "What would you do with it?"

"Help people." A simple and blunt answer, but to the point.

"How so? Where?"

"I haven't thought that far ahead yet. It's a big hurdle just to get into law school somewhere. And then there's three years of that before practicing."

The conversation came so easily, and her company was so enjoyable that by midafternoon, nearly four hours after we sat down, I made up my mind that I needed a friend like this. Not a girlfriend like this, just a friend, someone interesting and interested—intellectual, but not in the least haughty, and mostly, a pragmatic humanitarian. I saw this last trait in her and I wanted to be that kind of person as well. I knew my own past and doubted my ability to ever become a humanitarian, but I thought that perhaps if I surrounded myself with others who were, it might polish my tarnish.

While we talked I schemed for an excuse to be able to see her again, just a friendly visit.

"Would you like to see the article before I submit it to my editor?" she asked as she suddenly began packing up.

"Yes. Yes, I would … please," I said, not caring to see the article at all, just jumping at an excuse to see her again.

"Okay, I'll call you when I've got it roughed out. And what about Saturday? Would you like to come to a party, meet some of my friends? You could bring some of yours if you like."

I suspected I wouldn't fit well into this social setting, but there was no way I was turning down the invitation. "I could ask François, he might like to come."

François was my Cameroonian roommate. We were paired purely by chance when I first arrived at the university. After a year together we pooled our resources and rented a small flat close to campus. Neither of us had time for much of a social life, and what little socializing we did was usually done together, each of us acting as a security blanket for the other.

"Sure, bring him along," she said.

"You're off to another appointment?" I asked, probably just unconsciously delaying her departure.

"No, only home to start writing this up."

"Oh, you're all dressed up on a Sunday. I thought that you were, um, either going to church or, maybe, I don't know, going to meet someone."

"I *was* meeting someone." She looked me straight in the eye, and then lit up with a smile before turning to leave. "I'll see you Saturday. I'll call you."

I had to think about this for a moment, and she was out the door before I clued in and blushed, feeling the warm wave start at the top of my head and descend right down through my feet.

François and I attended the party, and to the surprise of both of us found that it wasn't so intimidating. Anna had made an interesting group of friends since arriving in Paris. She was clearly more social than we were, but she gravitated toward people of substance. Her friends were engaging and worldly, many of them supporters of international activist causes. This should have been no surprise because the school where she was studying was well recognized for its international studies program. But when this group got together it wasn't all deep heavy thought. They liked to just hang out and be the kids they were. François and I took to the group immediately, and they accepted us in return.

We were an international bunch with several Europeans and Brits, two other girls from America along with Anna, one from Hong Kong, a Jordanian and an Israeli, and François and I adding the color. Sometimes we played Ping-Pong in one of the dorms or board games at a coffee shop. We went to movies, parties, and other times we'd just lay around "shooting the shit," as the Americans said. I know I spent more one-on-one time in the group with Anna than I did with anyone else. We were simply very comfortable together. This was not a group with boyfriend-girlfriend relationships, just a bunch of platonic equals.

Then one day in March I had a call from Anna. "Freddie," she said, as she had begun calling me that, saying that Alfred was too formal, "do you want to go to Le Mont-Dore next weekend? There's a special on for Friday through Sunday."

Ahmed, the Jordanian, had mentioned to the gang a week or so earlier that we should all go skiing before the season was over. He had never skied and wanted to try it. Some of the rest of us hadn't either, and we all agreed it would be fun.

Embarrassed, I replied, "Anna, I can't afford that."

"It's okay, Freddie … it's all handled. And I've already rented a car. We can go up together. Please," she said. "You said you wanted to learn to ski. It'll be fun. Please?"

Neither François nor I had ever skied. We didn't even like the snow, but skiing sounded like it might be fun. And a weekend away from Paris with the group would be nice.

I acquiesced. "I'm in."

When François arrived home, I told him about the trip. Impossible! He had an organic chem midterm that he was struggling to prepare for. I considered not going if François couldn't, but by now I was more than comfortable enough with the group and I'd already promised Anna I'd ride with her. She arranged to pick me up right after her class on Friday morning, and we left in her small rented car for the five-hour drive.

The back seat was filled with borrowed ski gear. She said we'd have to rent the skis, but that it was all arranged already. I assumed the others would meet us at the resort and were in their own rented or borrowed cars. We fell into lively conversation and the time passed quickly, as it always did when we were together. She spoke mostly in French and I in English, each of us wanting to practice what we needed most. As we left the farm fields south of Paris and rose into the alpine range of southern France, conversation turned to our own home mountains. Anna described the open vistas of the Rocky Mountains surrounding her home in Colorado, and I regaled her with stories of the mountains of my home, the lush jungle that forested the slopes, and the wild creatures I encountered there. She talked fondly of the elk and bears that were abundant in her mountains and then asked if I had ever seen the mountain gorillas. I told her that indeed I had seen the magnificent creatures, but I didn't have the fortitude to own up to my crimes against the innocent beings. Turning my face away from her, I hid the shame that must surely have been painted all over it and added another omission of fact to the tally.

Arrival at the ski village was via a path snaking off the main highway, barely wide enough for us to pass oncoming vehicles. Anna stopped once when we got into the town to ask directions. The passerby pointed us to a group of small cabins at the base of the mountain. It was dark by the time we arrived, but a small neon sign in the window of one, touting VACANCES, indicated an office. Anna went to check in while I waited in the car. There didn't seem to be any sign of the rest of the group yet, but I assumed they were already in one of the cabins.

The cabin, which Anna opened for us with a flourish, turned out to be a cozy little minichalet with three rooms. The main room was a comfortable living space containing a large couch, an oversized chair, a small dining table, and a fully equipped kitchen with the typical French apartment-sized appliances. But most impressively, there was a whole wall dominated by a large stone fireplace and mantel. A small stash of firewood was stacked on the hearth. Faux antiques hung from the walls, adding character to the scene. Opposite the fireplace there were two other doors, one led into a small bathroom and the other into a bedroom with a wardrobe, dresser, and double bed. Anna sunk into the large living room chair while I went to the car to grab our things. I left our personal bags and picked out the groceries and wine.

"I guess we'd better find the others," I said as I set down the armful of goods. "Then we can decide who is where. How many cottages did we get?"

Anna looked at me with an exaggerated innocence, which only served to confuse me.

"Who all is meeting us here?" I asked. "We should be fine with two cabins. One for you and the girls, and one for Ahmed and us guys. Some of us can sleep on the floor and the couch is good for one."

"Freddie, no one else is meeting us here," Anna said. She looked a little confused herself. "I never said anyone else was coming."

This required a moment for me to process. "But I thought the gang was all coming for the weekend. No one else is here?" As I took in a long slow breath I could feel anxiety welling in me. My heart instantly began beating faster, and I had to concentrate hard to think this through clearly. "Just you and me?" Perhaps I didn't say it loudly enough because she didn't even bother to answer my question.

"Do you want help bringing in the other things?"

I was still standing inside the doorway with my outer shoes on. "No need, I can get them."

When I returned with our overnight bags Anna was uncorking one of the bottles. She poured two glasses of wine while I removed my boots and jacket, and then she leaned back against the countertop looking worried as I took a seat in the chair.

"I'm sorry, Freddie. I should have been more clear. I thought you would have known." When I failed to respond, she blurted out, "I'll sleep on the couch."

"Don't be silly, Anna. I'll take the couch."

She grabbed her bag from where I left it and dropped it on the end of the couch, plunking down beside it. "Shotgun," she shouted. I knew what a shotgun was, but I had no idea what she was talking about.

I picked up my own bag and put it on the other end of the couch and sat down as well. Clumsily, awkwardly, we sat there for a moment, side by side. I had a feeling what she might be trying to do, but I wasn't sure. I was afraid to be wrong about it, afraid of my own embarrassment if I was, and afraid of her embarrassment if I was right. And if I *was* right about what I was thinking, I wasn't even sure what I thought about that. This would be a totally different dynamic for us. It could all backfire and totally screw up everything, our good friendship, even our relationship with the rest of our group. I didn't have time for a girlfriend. I was too busy with my studies. I didn't have time for med school *and* women. But surely I was wrong about her intentions. Anna didn't see me that way, in a relationship with her, did she? Maybe I was wrong about that, too. Maybe this was just a casual weekend thing, not a relationship thing. I guess I wouldn't be opposed to something like that, just not with Anna. I thought she was very attractive, but she was much too nice a person. I respected our friendship too much to do something like that. While trying to process all of this I became flustered and my heart was beating faster and faster as my anxiety swelled. I wasn't used to such feelings of uncertainty and lack of control.

Before I could fully process everything, Anna surprised me by lifting a leg over and straddling my lap, facing me. "If we're going to fight over who gets the couch, why don't we just share it? Better still," she said, "I'll share the bed with you. But we can each have our own side if you like."

It was a nice try at lightening up the situation, but it only made my heart beat faster and added a full-out blush. I looked up at her and thought how beautiful she was. Really beautiful. Beautiful in some way that I had not let myself think about before, wholesome and clean and pure and sexy all in one. Clasping her hands around my neck at arm's length she gave me the perfect vantage to study her beauty. I'd seen her this close-up before, but never where I could look right into her eyes and concentrate on them, where I could look in those eyes and not be so shy that I'd immediately look away. They were bright and happy, sparkling blue. She didn't blink at all while I looked into them; she just stared back, and I could see my own miniature reflection in her pupils. I looked down and scanned the rest of her and still she didn't take her eyes off mine. How had I not noticed during the drive all the way up here that she had makeup around her eyes and a blush on her cheeks and lipstick making her lips look even fuller? I knew that she never wore makeup, or hardly ever. Why hadn't I noticed until just then that she had makeup on? While I pondered this and enjoyed her beauty, she leaned toward me and kissed me smack on the lips.

"I have to go pee," she said, jumping up. "Sorry, I should have gone as soon as we got here. I'm bursting." And she left for the bathroom.

Something about the intimacy of that sudden announcement made her even more attractive to me, and I realized that I was in the midst of totally abandoning my defenses. Primal feelings began to mix with my anxiety. But not primal feelings of lust. Primal feelings of wanting to love someone, of just giving in and being totally in the presence of someone. I closed my eyes, enjoying this warm feeling that was swooning over me, and rested back into the couch. I heard Anna come back but I didn't want to open my eyes in case I was wrong about everything and in case this wonderful feeling left me. I wanted to savor it as long as possible.

I felt a glass on my lips, tipping gently for me to sip. Taking it from her I opened my eyes as she sat back down.

"What are you thinking, Freddie?"

Still not sure about giving up my complete guard, I replied with another question. "What are *you* thinking, Anna?"

"I'm thinking … I'm hoping that you aren't mad at me. I hope you're feeling a little bit the way I'm feeling."

"And how are you feeling?"

"I'm feeling like I've fallen in love with you, and you are too stupid, or maybe too busy, to have noticed. Or, maybe you have noticed and you're just not interested."

This was just one example, among many, that endeared Anna to me at that moment and over all our subsequent years together—her forthrightness.

"Stupid *and* busy," I said. "Very stupid … and a little bit busy. Not very good excuses, I guess."

"And what do you think?" she asked.

I had no clue what to answer. I didn't know exactly what she was asking. I wasn't sure if she was asking what I thought about her falling in love with me, or what I thought about me being stupid. So, I lamely sought clarification. "What do *I* think?"

"Should I have told you this? Should I have brought you here this weekend … alone like this?"

"I'd like to learn to ski," I said. At which she closed her eyes and put her hands over her face. Sensing she was about to cry, I instantly wished I could have taken that back. It was clearly the wrong time to have tried to be humorous. I set my glass on the side table, swung a leg over, straddling her lap, pried her hands from her face and kissed her on the lips. More than on the lips, we kissed passionately, neither of us letting it come to an end for the longest time. Even then, it was only to push her back fully on the couch and lay on top of her where I could feel the full length of her body against mine.

I never did learn to ski until several years later when we moved to Colorado. We didn't even get to the hill that weekend. In fact, we only made two trips outside the cabin, both for more wine. We used every piece of firewood that they had left us, weren't out of the bed long enough to ever bother making it, and brought home most of the food that we had taken up with us.

This was far from the first time I had been with a woman, but this was the first time I understood what was meant by *making love* with someone. No one had to tell us we were making love, we knew it. We knew it was different than what either of us had ever experienced before. The fullness of me enraptured with every inch of her creamy white body and her fascination with the entirety of my muscular ebony frame simply fueled more admiration for each other. We made no verbal pledges at all, but we both somehow knew we were now committed to each other—it was a given, an unspoken dedication.

That was the beginning of us—us together. Many times over the years we've laughed and joked about that first weekend together. I tease her about deceiving and trapping me, and she claims I was just so blind that I missed all the hints she had been dropping for weeks. It's one of our go-to stories when we are at parties. And it's one of my go-to memories whenever I am away from her for any length of time. We celebrate this weekend in March as our anniversary, since it has more meaning for both of us than our formal wedding date, which wasn't actually all that formal.

* * *

With Anna lying here beside me, now, seventeen years after that first blissful weekend together in Le Mont-Dore, her peaceful, slight smile is finally showing signs of returning. Her face is softening as she sleeps. I haven't seen this from her in months. Perhaps tonight is a turning point—for both of us. I certainly hope it is. I know things will never be the same, that our lives are now headed in a much different direction than they were a month ago, before we buried our sweet baby. Watching Anna sleep, I resolve to do my part in helping us move through this horrible chapter in our life.

Later this morning, when I go into work, I'll start to clear my schedule for January. I'll talk to Mark, Brie, and Luis, my partners in the clinical practice that we share. They'll understand. They've been urging me to take some time off. I suppose they've noticed the changes in me since Steph passed, all the little things that I hadn't noticed in myself, all the things that others had probably also noticed. Anna has certainly had to put up with changes in me. Maybe I'm past that now. Tonight was a good start. I feel refreshed, rejuvenated, ready to move on. I'll let Anna make the plans and reservations for our vacation. She'll enjoy searching all the options and then surprising me with a booking. It doesn't matter to me where we go. Anna needs a good break as much as I do, and we both need the time together to reconnect and recharge.

But as the hours pass and sleep eludes me, the feeling of rejuvenation slips away. Glancing at the clock again, it's 3:00, and I'm now wishing desperately for some sleep. I need at least a few hours before going to the clinic, knowing that without it I won't be able to function well. I'm having one of those nights where the harder I try to fall asleep the more awake I feel; the more I try to relax and empty my mind, the more it fills up and flits from one thought to another. I roll my head to the side and see Anna still soundly asleep, the peaceful smile of old still resting on her serene countenance. Cautious not to wake her, I roll on my side and prop myself up on my elbow, affording a better view. The moon, slightly lower now, lays a pale-yellow glow across her nakedness. I am tempted to lean over and touch my lips to her body, stroke her back to arousal and make love again. But I know how much she needs this rest, depleted after months of care and worry for Stephanie, so I content myself with just looking.

I watch her for a few minutes longer and then lay back down, looking up at the ceiling, staring at nothing in particular, wishing for sleep. Bored with this I glance around the room. Elongated shadows cast by the moonlight accentuate every article in the room, the bed plush with a deep mattress, the recliner chair I use for quiet reading, Anna's vanity, her jewelry box, the television affixed into a custom wall unit, the overpriced print hanging above the bed. All of these *things,* and this is just our bedroom. Beyond the door there are three full bathrooms, Steph's room, a spare bedroom, the living room lavish with furniture we never even sit in, the den with the large screen television and custom sound system, my office lined with shelves filled with books, Anna's office furnished the same, a playroom, and a gym in the basement, two vehicles in the garage. All of this *stuff,* accumulated over the years. And to what end?

When Anna and I left Paris sixteen years ago we had two suitcases each, having given away all of our limited possessions that wouldn't fit in the airline baggage allotment. And for the year and a half before that we'd lived like so many other students, never missing what we didn't have, optimistic that life would provide whatever we needed, and sustained by the exuberance of youthful love.

Us, France

The drive back from Le Mont-Dore after our first weekend together in the ski chalet was bittersweet, neither of us wanting the fairy tale to end but both of us excited to see where this uncertain new relationship might take us. We were careful as we tested the tentative limits of what we had started, both tiptoeing, trying not to overstep our boundaries. I was concerned about what the others would think if we were to let them know that we had spent the weekend together, but Anna couldn't care less about it. I also fretted about what they all might think of Anna and me being in some sort of relationship. Typically, I overthought everything, and Anna was her carefree self, not worrying ahead of time about things that didn't need excess energy wasted on them. This has remained one of my faults that I can't seem to correct, while Anna's carefree spirit continues to be one of those qualities that just endears her to me all the more.

On the drive home I raised one of my worries. "What do you think I should tell François?"

"About what?"

"About us, the weekend alone." It was obvious to me.

"We'll tell him we had a great time alone together." That seemed pretty obvious to her.

"What about the rest of the gang?"

"Same thing. We had a great time alone together," she said, looking straight ahead at the road.

She didn't seem to understand how much more complicated everything really was. The dynamics of my relationship with François would surely change, and the whole dynamic of the group could also change. I was worried about whether they would even accept us as a couple and whether we could still count on their friendships.

"It's not that simple, Anna."

She slowed down the car a bit so that she could glance at me while she drove and talked. "Alfred, they all knew we were going away for the weekend. And they all know how I feel about you. You're the only one who seemed not to understand."

This was definitely news to me. "What do you mean they all know? François doesn't know. He'd have told me something."

"François knows. He's the one who came up with the idea of us going away for the weekend," she said.

"No! I guess I'm pretty thick."

"Yes, you are." She smiled. "Everyone knows. So, we might as well just get it all out in the open as soon as we can. As soon as we see them we'll tell them we had a fantastic time, we got along great and fucked our brains out all weekend."

Not exactly the way I would have put it, but just a bit more of Anna's charming American forthrightness.

A little while later, after several miles of silence between us, Anna raised another topic. "Freddie, I'd like to tell my parents about you. But I'm not sure what to say."

"Why not just tell them that we're getting along great, having a fantastic time, and fucking our brains out?"

We both laughed at this as she eased on the brake again. And then we just contagiously laughed at each other, laughing until tears streamed from us both.

Once we got over our hysterics I ventured to ask, "Will they have a problem with me being black?"

"God, no," she replied quickly. "That won't be an issue."

And it wasn't. Just like the whole thing of Anna and me hooking up wasn't an issue to François or any of our friends. There were a few practical things that might have been concerns but no one ever made a big deal of them, like François having to put up with Anna's and my lovemaking every time she stayed over at our place, especially when it quickly morphed from pure lovemaking into sexual antics. And then there were times when we just wanted to be alone and some of the others couldn't get their heads around that. But it all worked out fine, once again confirming Anna to be right in not wasting time worrying about needless things.

Anna proved to be unbelievably patient and considerate in not prying into those areas of my past in Africa that I had shied away from. Then one night not too long after our trip to Le Mont-Dore, we were lying in her bed facing each other, existing in that zone of pleasure right after having made love, when she reached up and traced the scar on my face, from my hairline right down through my eyebrow to the side of my jaw.

"Is there a story with this?"

I was embarrassed by this permanent record of my past, ashamed of it. I tried to ignore it, but it faced me every time I looked in a mirror. I had pretended that Anna somehow hadn't noticed. But of course, she had seen it. It glared out at everyone who looked at me. She just had been considerate enough to have never brought it up until today. But why shouldn't she ask now? We had shared so many things already—personal things, family things, aspirations.

"A machete," I said. "We all used them in my village from the time we were very young." This was true, just not quite the whole truth. I hoped it would suffice. And it did, sort of, until she gently rolled me onto my stomach and began to trace the patchwork of scars on my back.

"What about these? These aren't from a machete."

"No, no, they're not. Those are proof that there is still a lot of work to be done in Africa."

She continued in silence, softly tracing the scars with her finger. Again, I had not lied to her, just avoided part of the truth. I hoped that this answer would suffice because I had begun to weep into my pillow. I attempted to stifle my tears as the shame made me tense and the weeping turned to sobs. I was ashamed at what those scars really said about me, ashamed at the person I really was, ashamed that I couldn't tell Anna the whole truth, ashamed that I was lying there crying in front of her.

Anna pulled on me to turn me onto my back. I rolled over but brought the pillow around with me to keep it over my face, shielding my shame from her. She took the pillow and pulled it away, and I cried, cried like a baby, uncontrollably. She wrapped me in her arms, and I knew she was crying too. I just let her cradle me like an infant, let her mother me to sleep.

Anna never asked me again about my scars. She often traces them softly when we lay together but she never asks about them.

Stephanie, however, asked a few times. "Daddy, what are those marks on you?"

And Anna discreetly interjected for me. "Childhood can be hard in Africa, Steph. Someday Daddy might tell you, not today though, honey."

There was another elephant in the room during those early days and weeks of our relationship, and it had nothing to do with my past. It was mid-April and the school term was ending in about six weeks. I had lined up a job through Vincent as a hospital orderly for the summer months. I'd also tried to study ahead as much as I could and to prepare my applications for med school. But Anna was due to go home. She had been accepted at HEIP for only one school year and that was almost up. She was planning to take her LSAT during the summer and complete her degree at the University of Colorado, where she had started it. I dared not mention the topic, not wanting to jinx or dampen the charm that we had going, but I thought of it daily. I was pretty sure that Anna was thinking of it too, and not knowing what to do about it, either. Then it came up finally.

"I bought my ticket home today," she said as she sat down at our usual table in the café. "I leave on June sixth."

This was the deflating news that I had known would come eventually. I looked down and nodded my head, a little bit afraid I might start crying if I looked directly at her. I didn't want to speak for the same reason.

"And I've registered to take the LSAT on August first," she said. "Then I'll be back here August fourteenth."

"You're coming back for a few weeks before you start school? That's great!" I was ecstatic. I hadn't expected this. I thought maybe we could somehow get a visit in over Christmas or something. This was way better than I had hoped for.

"Yeah. I'll have a few weeks of vacation and then I'll continue on here at HEIP. They've accepted me for my final year of undergrad!"

I was ecstatic. And she was beaming at being able to deliver me such a surprise, leaving no doubt that she was every bit as happy. I spilled both coffees as I sprawled across the table to hug her.

"What about your family? What did your parents say?"

"They're a little disappointed that I won't be staying home but I convinced them that the international undergrad would come in handy, maybe even get me into a better law school. Daddy figured out right away that there must be a man involved, and Mom swears that she didn't tell him. They said they'd help me out again, but I had to promise them both that I would return to the States after graduating."

Even with this great news I immediately set to worrying about the new doomsday to come, now simply postponed to fifteen months away. Anna wouldn't even talk about that situation. She was so much better at living and enjoying the moment than I. But we had our reprieve. She'd only be gone for a few months over the summer.

We spent the last couple of months we had together before Anna returned to America just being young lovers. We had very limited funds, but that didn't matter, we had each other. We found a small apartment, even by Parisian standards, and I moved in the week after Anna left for home. I tried to fix it up the way I thought she would like it, and I worked hard to keep it scrupulously clean, even though I knew she wouldn't be back for two months. I just didn't want to disappoint Anna in any way, even if she wasn't there to see it. Silly.

In some ways the two months seemed to go by slowly, but in other ways they just flew by. My job as an orderly at the hospital kept me busy much of the time. Vincent had assured me that a job like that would not hurt on my résumé when I applied for med school. I was able to pick up a full seven-hour shift each day because many of the regular staff were on holiday. This allowed me about eight hours per day of good solid study time. I was very diligent about my studies and hardly took a day off from them while I waited for Anna's return. So that's what made time pass—work and study.

I usually studied in the library because there was a free internet connection there for students. In those days no students could afford internet at home, and it wasn't all that common even for those with money. But with the connection at the library I was able to send Anna an email every day and retrieve the ones that she sent to me. Neither of us really seemed to have a lot of news to share, those emails were just the babble of lovers in love. Everything about Anna seemed exciting to me. She could tell me that she went to the dry cleaners for her mother that day and I thought it was just the nicest thing and wished I could have gone to the dry cleaners with her. I'm sure my news was even less exciting than hers because my routine was more mundane and predictable.

Toward the end of July I began worrying again. I started to doubt myself and our relationship. What did Anna see in me? What did I have to offer her? I had no money, no family. Most of all, I had no past that I could share with Anna. I literally had nothing to offer her in return for all that she had to give me. I was alone in Paris. It was stinking hot and humid during late July in our apartment with only one window. Many nights I couldn't sleep because of the stifling lack of fresh air, and while I lay there awake these doubts came alive within me. These demons got me to thinking that maybe I was experiencing some kind of cruel joke and that Anna had no intention of coming back.

Even as I waited outside the customs arrival area in De Gaulle on the morning of August 14, some of these thoughts passed through my mind. It wasn't until I saw her emerge from the tinted automated doors, drop her bags right there in the midst of all the human traffic, and come running toward me, that I fully believed she would be back. Five feet seven inches of glowing joy hugged me tightly, and I hugged it all back, squeezing hard, not wanting to let go.

We settled into our own cozy little domestic situation. This was something totally new to me since I had never lived with a girl before. The adjustments were a pleasant adventure. I learned about smells in a home—keeping down the bad ones, burning a little incense, scented candles now and then. Apparently, what I thought was clean really wasn't. I had my first experiences with monthly hormone invasions and adding tampons to the grocery list. But all these minor inconveniences were insignificant compared to the happiness that being with Anna brought me.

Six weeks after Anna landed back in Paris, a piece of mail arrived at our apartment from Newtown, Pennsylvania. Anna spotted the letter and the LSAT logo on it.

"Oh my god, Freddie. I'm afraid to open it."

I sank back onto the sofa, and she plunked down beside me with the envelope in hand.

"You open it," she said and handed it to me.

I tore open the envelope and pulled out the folded insert. I was just about to unfold it when she snatched it from me. "Okay, I'll do it."

"Woo-hoo," she screamed. "I made it!" She paused for a minute and then made a funny little face by scrunching her upper lip. "I was hoping to do a little better. But this should get me in ... somewhere."

Her 150 LSAT score wasn't stellar, and it wouldn't get her into the top schools, but it would get her into a decent school, and she was plenty happy with that. Anna was always content with *good enough* and never pressured herself for perfection the way I always burdened myself.

"Let's celebrate tonight," I said.

Later that evening, over a bottle of wine and packages of takeout, Anna mused about where she might apply to get into a law program.

"Why not just hit them all up and see where you get accepted? Make a decision after that," I said. I was trying not to think about the reality that she would be going away again in less than a year, and this time she wouldn't be coming back.

That was when she caught me off guard by saying, "I don't want to go to any of them."

"That's crazy. This is your dream. This is what you have worked so hard for. What are you talking about?"

"No, Freddie. I don't want to go to any of them. I don't want to leave you. I wasn't happy the last two months away from you. I don't want to go again."

"Nonsense. You have to go, Anna."

"I don't want to leave you. I won't go."

I was honored that she would consider foregoing law school to be with me and realized right then that she was as much in love with me as I was with her. But to make a sacrifice like that just didn't make sense. I called the hospital the next day and left a message for Vincent, asking him to call me when he had a moment. After trading phone messages for two days we finally arranged to meet in the hospital cafeteria the following day. Neither of us had had much time to get together recently and he greeted me warmly with a tight hug.

"Alfred, you're looking great. Between that lovely American girl and fattening French food you look … healthy."

No one comes to France from a refugee camp in Africa and doesn't put on some weight. But not many would get to meet someone like Anna. Between the two, Vincent had hit it on the nose: I was very healthy and incredibly happy.

"I need some advice, Vincent. About Anna. She got her LSAT results back, and they're not too bad."

"That's great."

"Yes, but now she's threatening to not even go to law school. She wants to stay here … because of me. I can't let her do that."

He thought about this for barely a moment and then said, "Have you thought of going with her?"

"Go with her? To America? I can't. I could never get into the US. You know how much work it was for you to get me in here. I wouldn't want to leave you. I've just about got my applications all set to send out for school next fall."

"There are medical schools in America … a lot of them. Good ones. It's a bit of a different process but your marks are good." Vincent looked at me.

I had thought of this before, but I'd always quickly dismissed the idea. It seemed futile to even dream it.

"Let's think about this for a while," Vincent said. "Nothing's impossible. And don't ever think about staying around here for me. I'll be leaving again soon to go back to Africa, anyhow. I'll be gone for at least two years this time."

Later that night I mentioned to Anna that I had seen Vincent.

"Oh, how is he?"

"He's getting ready to go back to Africa with Médecins Sans Frontières."

"Back to Tanzania?" she asked.

"No, eastern Nigeria this time."

"Oh, Freddie, why would he go there of all places? It's the most dangerous spot on the continent. The terrorists are running rampant there and a Western doctor will be a prime target." She was quite concerned.

"He says that's where he's needed the most." Anna looked worried. She was well versed in the geopolitical situation of this part of the world. It was the focus of her schooling. To distract her I said, "I went to see him about us. About your wanting to stay here rather than do law in America."

Anna didn't respond. She just looked at me, waiting for me to continue.

"He thinks you can't miss an opportunity like this—that you should go back."

"Of course he'd take your side, Freddie."

"He didn't take my side. It's not about taking sides. I just asked him for his advice. He said you *have* to go to law school." I waited for her to react but again she wouldn't respond. She looked down in thought. I ventured a little further. "He did have a suggestion, though. He said that I should go with you. To America."

Her gaze shot back up quickly, and I could see the wheels turning in her eyes.

I spent the next several days researching the logistics of me doing med school in the United States, but Anna was working on her own plan which she popped on me quite unexpectedly.

"I can get you into the US, Freddie."

"How's that?" I asked.

"Well, we'd have to be married for at least twelve months, but then you can come."

"You would marry me, just to do that? To get me into the US?" She never ceased to amaze me.

But then with deadpan seriousness she said, "No, I wouldn't. I wouldn't marry you to get you into the US."

This popped my bubble. And she could see the disappointment on my face.

"I'd marry you because I love you, stupid."

We both stood up at the same time, grabbing for the other. I squeezed her tight and kissed the top of her head. She seemed content just to be held for a long while, but then stepped back.

"Would you marry *me*, Freddie?"

"Now who's being stupid, Anna?"

By the end of the second bottle of wine we had our futures totally mapped out. We knew where we'd be going to school, working, living, and how many gorgeous little American children we'd have. The next morning at breakfast, in the light of sobriety, we got down to the more realistic details. We carefully went over the paperwork that Anna had collected from the American embassy. As the spouse of an American citizen it would be much easier for me to get a student visa, and once we were married for twelve months I would qualify for a green card. That would allow me to get a job.

Vincent was thrilled to hear that we had a plan for both school and marriage, and he gladly helped us make both a reality. As my sponsor, he filled out the necessary forms, and once we had them notarized, he even went with us back to city hall. He also found the Paris MCAT schedule for me. I could either take it in October or January. But it had to be October, only four weeks away, because January wouldn't allow me enough time to get med school applications in for the next school year. In a huge gift of generosity, Vincent rearranged his shifts so that he could help me cram for my MCAT. We met each afternoon in his office at the hospital and studied until midnight. A few days after starting this routine Anna began to bring dinner in to us, after she finished her own studies.

This went on every single day for four weeks until Thursday, October 26, when I took the exam. I was completely exhausted after the test and there was no celebration. We saved that for the next day.

On Friday, October 27, 2000, Anna and I were married, less than ten months after we first met. Yet it all felt so perfect, seemed so natural. The only person we told about it was Vincent, and he insisted on going back with us to city hall once more. No new clothes, no flowers, no party. No money for any of that. We saved everything we could in the hopes that we would soon be going to America. I did buy Anna a ring, a plain gold band, and promised her that, when we could afford it, I would buy her a diamond. I bought my own wedding ring, a stainless steel key ring that fit my finger perfectly. It cost me forty-nine cents, and I've never taken it off in all these years. Vincent, generous as always, took us out for lunch and then handed us the keys to his car.

"Use it for the weekend. And here's your reservation." He gave us a piece of paper with the name of a hotel in Auxerre. "It's beautiful there this time of year. They're bringing in the grapes."

We went, and we loved it. The rolling hills, miles on miles of vineyards, the musty sweet smell of harvest, an enchanted weekend for two kids. And we loved each other. We were high on each other, high on our dreams of going to America together, starting careers, starting a family. It was the beginning of an enthralling adventure together.

Opportunities for foreign scholarships were limited, and as it turned out, the University of Pittsburgh was the one place that did offer them where Anna and I could both do our studies, hers in law and mine in medicine. I traveled there for my interview and two days after returning got an invite from Vincent for a small get-together at his apartment.

He was leaving the next week for his commitment with Médecins Sans Frontières and had invited a few doctors and friends over. Some of his colleagues were also involved in the MSF program, all good people. They'd have to be to give up substantial portions of their comfortable lives in France to go and work for free in some of the most impoverished and dangerous places in the world. Some of them left families behind, usually for shorter commitments than Vincent made, but he wasn't married and had no children. He planned to be gone for two years this time, and I'd spent much of my overnight return flight from America thinking about what it would be like not to have Vincent around. If I were successful in getting into Pitt med school it might be a lot longer than two years before I would see him again.

True, I now had Anna, but Vincent was a stalwart surrogate father to me. Like Anna he saw things in me that I wasn't able to see in myself. For some reason, right from our first meeting in the camp in Tanzania, he took me in as a part-apprentice, part-friend, part-son, and part-project. And, also like Anna, he did this totally devoid of judgment, never prying into my past, never poking my wounds.

Vincent was the one who insisted that I continue my education during my years living in the squalor of the Nkwenda camp. And then he sponsored me through the French government's refugee program, acting as my surety. Without him I wouldn't have had this chance at a better life in Europe. He encouraged my interest in studying and made me want to go further into medicine. It was his model of generosity and basic human kindness and compassion to which I aspired. And, if it wasn't for him, I'd have never met Anna. I wanted to tell him how much he meant to me, but this little party wasn't the right forum; there were too many others saying their goodbyes.

A few days later I rode the train to the airport, sitting beside Vincent. I lugged one of his two suitcases for him. He had done these trips before and knew that not only was there no room for a lot of personal items, there was no need for them. Where he was going the accommodations wouldn't permit excess, and he was the type of person who thought he could mesh with the locals better if he lived like them. Most of the MSF doctors understood this concept, not many of the United Nations doctors did. They still made good salaries even amid the destitution of the third world.

I suppose both of us had the same thoughts about parting because neither of us seemed ready to address it in conversation. Instead, Vincent said, "You can try to send me an email as soon as you hear back from Pittsburgh, but you'll have to send me a letter right away too, since I have no idea when I'll get close to internet access."

"Of course," I replied. "I don't know what I'll do if I don't get accepted."

"Sure you do. You'll fall back on UPMC here in France. If Pittsburgh doesn't work out, you commit right away to Curie. Most people would die to be in your position with an acceptance there." He sounded firm and fatherly.

UPMC was one of the top med schools in France, but my attendance there meant that either Anna didn't go to law school, or she would have to go in the US while I studied in France. I refused to face this possibility until I heard back from Pitt. "At least if I stay here in France I'll see you when you get back," I said. "If I go to the US, I don't know when I'll get to see you next."

I had finally broached the subject. I was starting to feel despondent as the train approached the airport, and I wanted him to say something firm and fatherly about this. I was hopeful that his practical wisdom would buttress me against my clear weakness. Instead he put an arm over my shoulders and looked right at me, not saying anything for a moment. His eyes pooled with water that spilled over his cheeks. Pulling me close, he wrapped his other hand around the back of my neck in an intimate cradle and pressed the side of his face tight to mine. "Alfred, I love you. I love you. I'm going to miss you," he whispered in my ear.

It dawned on me that this was the first time since my early childhood that anyone other than Anna had said that they loved me. Through the lump in my throat, all I could muster was, "Thank you. Thank you, Vincent … for everything. Thank you. You know I'll always love you."

We clung to each other, two grown men sobbing together in public, neither of us caring what anyone around us thought. And neither of us said another word until the train pulled into the platform. I waited at the check-in and then accompanied Vincent to the security line. We made promises to write and stay in touch and then, as the line reached the security point, we hugged one last time and kissed each other on both cheeks with meaning.

* * *

A few months after Vincent's departure everything was going our way. Anna and I were both accepted into our programs at the University of Pittsburgh, I with a scholarship. Anna was soon going home to America; I was soon going to America. We had each other and we had everything to look forward to—our whole lives ahead of us.

Floating in confidence, we dreamed great plans. Once we finished our studies at Pittsburgh we would go overseas together and work someplace in the developing world. We both spoke French and English. Anna was good in Spanish, and I in Swahili and other less important languages. There would be lots of places we could work to help people. We could start our own practices anywhere in the US. Anna would do legal aid work, and I'd treat the poor there, although I couldn't imagine poor people in the US. No one coming from Africa, as I did, can fathom that there might be poverty in the richest place on earth.

For weeks, we sailed along in our reverie. And there was no reason for it to be interrupted. No one could be more grateful than I for my circumstances. An orphan from darkest Africa, not even a road to our village upriver in the jungle, was graduating from a university with a degree in biochemistry, about to fly to America to become a doctor, in love with the most beautiful, caring person in the world. I fully knew how fortunate I was.

Why then did I suddenly begin to throw a blanket over it all, drape it in darkness, drag Anna down with me? In a matter of days I went from peak to pit.

"What's going on, Freddie?" Anna sat back down on the bed beside me. She was dressed and ready for classes. I was still lying in the dimness of our windowless bedroom.

"Go ahead, Anna. I'm just staying around here for a while. I'll get going soon."

"That's what you said yesterday, and you didn't leave the flat. What's wrong? Everything was going so well a few days ago."

I didn't know how to answer, everything *was* going so well just a few days ago. I was basking in all the great things that were happening to us, enjoying planning our new start in America together, and then I had a few thoughts cross my mind that maybe I didn't deserve it.

"Why should I be the one who gets to go to med school in America? What about the millions of more deserving kids in Africa who aren't getting this chance that I am stealing from them?"

"What are you talking about? You're not stealing anything from anyone." She sounded incredulous.

"What makes me deserving, Anna?"

"You've worked damned hard, that's what."

"What makes me even deserve *you*, Anna?"

I searched for some excuse for my glum mood. These thoughts had been short-circuiting in my brain for a few days now. This was the first I had verbalized them, and they sounded totally pathetic. In some perverted way, I was juxtaposing my current good fortune with the wretchedness of my childhood in Africa, and not just the poverty and tragedy of so many millions of Africans, but my particularly wretched upbringing. I simply wasn't worthy of any of the good things that were now happening to me.

"What's wrong, Freddie? Why are you saying these things?" She stroked my head tenderly while I looked away from her, shamed. "You're sad. What are you sad about?"

"I don't know." I slowly rolled my head side to side. "I know logically, intellectually, there is nothing going wrong in my life. I should be happy. I can't explain it. I've tried to think myself out of it, but it's some kind of weird feeling that's drawing me in. I'm not sad, I'm not mad, I'm not angry. I just don't know. It's like some deep, sullen, inexplicable despair. I can't figure it out." I wanted to be able to explain it, to Anna, to myself. But I couldn't put it into words.

Later that afternoon, when Anna arrived home and saw me still in bed, she came in and sat down again.

"Have you been in here all day?"

"No." I said it with no conviction, not really wanting her to believe me.

"Well then, how were your classes?"

"Fine."

She frowned, knowing it wasn't true but rather a plea for understanding. "You've got to pull yourself out of this funk. You've got exams starting in two weeks. I'm pretty sure that scholarship of yours has a void clause if you fail your final term."

I knew she was right, but I couldn't seem to conquer the inertia and begin to pull out of my "funk." The next two weeks were rotten, and so were the three weeks of exams following that. Just plain rotten. I existed, that's all I did. I got by, just existing. And if it was bad for me, it was worse for Anna. Because she couldn't understand, any more than I could, what was wrong, what was happening. This was my first experience with the inky purple whirlpool that would catch me several more times over the course of my life, especially when things were going well for me, but, oddly, almost never when they were going badly. The bad times and the tough times I could always deal with—just look at the atrocities I had already dealt with in Africa. It was the good times that caught me unaware, always the good times dragging me back to the whirlpools of Africa.

I've since learned the clinical diagnosis and can recognize it quickly in my patients. My mild depressions could be called funks, as Anna stated. They've never been bad enough for me to think that I need medication, but it's probably borderline. That first funk nearly cost me my final term grades, and it took all my strength to drag myself through exams. And then two weeks after exams, a few days before we left France for America, the ink dissipated, the current slowed down, and I stuck my head out of the water and gulped fresh air. As quickly as it had settled upon me, it left me.

"I think it was stress," said Anna. "The stress of the exams, and once they were over it was gone."

I smiled. If only it were that simple. "But I wasn't stressed about school. I was in total command. I didn't get stressed until I lost control. And I don't know what made me lose control."

"I'm just glad you're back, Freddie."

"I'm glad too, Anna. I wouldn't have wanted your parents to see me like that. Thank you for being so good with me the last little while."

"François and the others want to come over on Friday to say goodbye," Anna said, changing the subject.

A week earlier I would have dreaded the prospect, but at that moment I welcomed it. "Super. We have to convince them to come and visit us in America." We really were going to miss them. We'd all been a very tight group of friends over the past couple of years. Somehow though, it wasn't a sad parting with them. It was joyful and positive. We were all young and knew we'd get together again. They all wanted to see America and now they'd have a good excuse, and a couch to sleep on when they got there.

Anna and I took the same train that Vincent and I had taken barely two months ago. This time it wasn't heading toward a sad separation, but rather a joyful beginning to the adventure of the rest of our lives together. As the train pulled into the De Gaulle station we were jittery with excitement, anxious to get to America. We each had our own backpack slung over a shoulder holding our travel documents and extra water bottles and sandwiches—enough to get us through twelve hours of flight and two hours of a layover in Newark before arriving in Denver. Airports were still confusing to me. A one-way to Paris from Tanzania and a round-trip to Pittsburgh were my complete résumé of previous air travel.

At the ticket counter the attendant quickly scanned passes and IDs, processing the line of passengers. Anna handed over her USA passport.

"Anna Fraser?" The attendant glanced up perfunctorily as she processed entries into her terminal, printed a card, and tagged luggage. "Your boarding pass, Mademoiselle Fraser. Have a nice flight."

Anna stepped aside while I handed the attendant my Rwandan passport.

"Mr. Alfred Oly-Oly-on-tom-bo?" She stumbled over my last name and then looked from the passport picture to my face and back again—and then again, once more. This wasn't unusual for me. I knew that the scar on my forehead and the scar in my picture were as good as fingerprints for my identity. When people were first forced to look at me, it often took a second or third glance to register properly. That no longer bothered me, and I knew that most people were uncomfortable themselves because they'd focused on it. I could see Anna was disconcerted while the attendant processed me. She was still embarrassed for me when others made an issue of my facial deformity.

"Thank you, monsieur, have a nice flight." She handed me my documents.

Each now carrying only our own backpack, we started toward the security checkpoint and Anna tugged at my sweater. "Alfred, can I see your passport?"

I handed it to her as we kept walking.

"This is from Rwanda," she stated and asked at the same time.

"Yes."

"I thought you were Tanzanian. You said you came from Tanzania."

This was another of my omissions, and I was caught out in it, as I knew I would be eventually. But there was nothing here to hide, except perhaps some of my own uncertainty, and the fact that I'd rather forget most of Rwanda.

"I did come from Tanzania. I came here from Tanzania, and Rwanda before that."

"You never told me." Another statement and question at the same time.

"It never came up, and you never asked." I could tell she was disappointed, everything drooped, her shoulders, her entire face. I felt terrible for letting her down. I probably should have told her before. "I'm sorry, Anna, it just didn't seem important."

The line had moved us close to the first security check. "What else doesn't seem important? Is there more you should tell me?"

"Honestly, Anna, there's lots more I'd like to tell you. And I will, sometime. Please, just not now. If we make a scene here, they won't even let us on the plane."

As soon as we'd made it through to the other side of the security check, she started with her questions again while we walked toward our gate.

"So, you're Rwandan?"

"I'm not positive, but I think I'm Rwandan. I lived most of my life in Rwanda, and was given a Rwandan passport. I suppose that makes me Rwandan." I paused for a moment. "Does it make a difference?"

She ignored my question and asked another of her own. "Why couldn't you tell me?"

I stopped, turned to face her, and held her by each shoulder at arm's length. "Anna, there are six million people trying to forget Rwanda. I've never lied to you, but there's a lot you don't want to know."

"Alfred, we're married. I want to know everything about you."

She wasn't angry. She was disappointed. Her eyes, her entire face was begging for more of an explanation. How could I blame her for wanting to know the full truth?

I hung my head and nodded. "Let's find our gate. I'll tell you."

We had more than an hour to wait in the departure area, plenty of time for me to give Anna a history lesson on Rwanda in the early nineties. As a student of international studies she'd heard some of the story, but not told in the way that someone who lived through it tells it. I related what happened in a fashion typical of most war survivors: I painted a panorama of the broader landscape and avoided the pain of the finer personal details. She didn't need to know these, and I'd worked hard to forget them myself.

The hour passed quickly, and our flight was called. After bumping our way down the aisle and settling into our seats, Anna took my hand and squeezed it, turned sideways in the seat and kissed me on my upper cheek, purposely or accidentally, I'm not sure, but landing it right on my scar.

In all the years since, Anna has never pushed, never pried into these personal horrors. Instead, she's kindly and gently helped me nurse the wounds that I hope will never need to be reopened, and she's patiently let me offer her morsels of Rwanda on my own time. She continued to hold my hand for much of the flight while I sank back and closed my eyes, unable now to stop thinking about Rwanda, Tanzania, Africa … and all that I'd omitted.

Rwanda

After filling a small rucksack with as much food as I could stuff into it and hastily departing the convent, I headed east. The roads were surprisingly busy with vehicles, even at this early hour of the morning, almost all of them heading in one direction—out. Everyone and everything was leaving Kigali, Rwanda's capital city. Hardly anyone was going the other way. I thought that perhaps I would hitch a ride on a passing truck. Each time a vehicle approached I turned around and put my arm out hoping it would stop, but none even bothered to slow down. I understood their reluctance; no one in Kigali trusted anyone else, especially at this time of day. I considered just walking but reasoned that a quicker departure would be better. If I was going to put any speedy distance between the convent and myself I'd have to find a ride.

I watched a one-ton flatbed pass me and then followed its taillights as it slowed down about a hundred yards ahead and turned off into the gravel parking lot of a small roadside shop. By the time I had walked the distance to where it was stopped, the driver was just returning to his truck. I approached him with a friendly greeting.

"Can I hitch a ride in the back of your truck?"

"There's room, if you want. I'm only going as far as Kayonza, and it'll cost you one thousand Rwandan francs. But I'll take five dollars US if you have it."

I only had the two thousand francs I'd taken from the convent and I certainly wasn't about to turn over half of it just to get me the sixty miles to Kayonza. I planned to go a lot farther than that.

"I'll give you one hundred francs."

As if he had never even encountered me he climbed into his truck, slammed the door, started it up, and backed around, almost right into me. To avoid being hit I leapt up onto the flatbed. He pulled the truck ahead and turned back east onto the road. In the darkness I could make out five other bodies, backs propped up against the racks on the side of the truck. In the front of the truck bed burlap sacks of root crops were piled and covered with a mildewed canvas tarp. None of the five bothered to acknowledge me, so I shifted around and joined them, leaning my back against one of the side rails. The truck had little suspension, and we bounced jarringly along. This was a paved road but was in such disrepair that a gravel road would have been better. It, like most of the other roads in the area, had been built and paved thirty years earlier in the midsixties. Right after the Rwandan independence in 1962 the new governments wanted to demonstrate their largesse and paved a series of roads linking disparate parts of the country, but none of the succeeding governments had the money necessary to repair them or do upkeep. As these paved roads became potholed and washouts from seasonal flooding swept parts of them away the remaining pavement sometimes became more of an impediment than a help.

Dawn was just starting to break, and I watched the landscape slowly move past us. The sides of the road were filthy with trash carelessly discarded by others who didn't want to be troubled carrying anything extra with them. Makeshift tents and plastic tarp lean-tos were pitched irregularly along the roadside where families had stopped for the night. Someone sat awake at each of these campsites, keeping guard against looters and bandits who might find them easy prey. Other early risers were out walking on the sides of the road trying to hitch rides, but our driver ignored them.

As the morning sky gradually lightened, the large body across from me began to stir and straightened himself up. He measured me and then said, "He's going to be stopping in Nyagasambu. He might kill you if he finds you on his truck."

With as much bravado as a youth of nearly sixteen could feign I replied, "Perhaps I'll kill him first." To which the man laughed uproariously. The guffaws woke up everyone else. He had no idea how many people I had already killed. And he had no idea how old I was. I was big for my age and had already been passing for older. I was insulted and embarrassed by his mockery.

"If he doesn't kill you he'll probably beat you." The man continued to laugh. When he was finished making fun of me he said, "Give me two hundred francs, and we'll hide you at Nyagasambu. We can put you under the tarp."

"I haven't got any money."

"I know you have at least one hundred. Give it to me and we'll hide you."

I had divided up my two thousand francs that I had taken from the sisters at the convent, putting five hundred in the soles of my shoes, five hundred each in two different places in my rucksack, and five hundred in my shorts. I pulled out this wad and gave the man one hundred francs.

"I'll tell you when we get close and show you how to hide," he said.

The other four were all awake now and I could tell that it was a family: the father and mother; two sons, both younger than me; and a girl around nine. After a while the mother reached into a sack beside her and pulled out a flat round loaf of honey bread, which she partitioned and passed around. She set a small bowl of bean paste in the center for them to scoop out. No one offered me any, so I opened my rucksack and took out a plantain.

One of the boys ventured to make conversation with me. "Where are you going?" he asked.

"North. And then probably Tanzania," I replied.

"Where is your family?" the little girl asked.

"I'll meet them in the north," I said.

By now I'd become a very good liar and they all accepted this story. I still wasn't sure whether I'd go to Tanzania, but I had decided to go north, initially. Maybe I could hide out there, or maybe I'd try to blend in with the masses and make it to one of the camps. Most everyone else in Kigali and west of there was headed toward Zaire. It was the obvious route out of the country since there were more roads and they were better. Also, word had passed back that camps were indeed there. Camps in Tanzania were still just an unconfirmed rumor.

An hour later, as we lumbered into Nyagasambu, the father crawled to the front and drew back the tarp. He rearranged the sacks of cassava and turnips, creating a small space for me at the bottom and then pulled the tarp back in place. A few minutes later the truck came to a stop and the door slammed.

"How many bags do you want?" the father asked the driver.

"Ten here. The rest will come out at Kayonza."

The man and his two sons lifted the tarp partially away and took ten sacks from the pile. They stacked them on the edge of the truck, returned the tarp into place, and jumped down to help carry the sacks to the front door of the shop. Afterward, they loaded themselves back on the truck and the driver put it in gear. Once we were rolling eastward again the father lifted the tarp.

"It's safe to come out now."

I climbed up and over the remaining sacks. "Thank you," I said.

He put his palm out to me. "Two hundred more."

"I paid you one hundred already."

"That was to Nyagasambu. It's another two hundred to Kayonza."

I thought about arguing with him but realizing it was probably futile, I slapped another two hundred francs into his open palm.

"Plus fruit." He had seen inside my rucksack. "For everyone." He gestured to the rest of his family.

I opened my bag and passed out a plantain to each of them.

Another two hours passed with the family conversing among

themselves. I kept one eye on them and the other on the countryside as we drove along. It was nearly nine in the morning and the sun had risen enough to make things steamy. The makeshift campsites along the side of the road had been packed up, and they were being trundled by all manner of carts and wagons as people moved east toward the Tanzanian border.

As we entered the outskirts of Kayonza the father finally addressed me with a jerk of his neck. "Help us move these." He pulled the blackened tarp back and we shuffled the two dozen remaining food sacks toward the back of the truck bed. "Lay down here, tight to the front. We'll cover you with the tarp."

"Thank you, but I'll just jump off here before he stops and sees me."

"After he unloads these at the market he goes north on Route 5 with an empty load for another one hundred miles. You might as well stay and ride. He'll never know."

The truck turned off the main road and was slowing as we approached the market ahead. I thought about jumping off but chose to stay put for the free ride farther north. I laid down with my rucksack and let them cover me with the old tarp. The father then kneeled down on top of me, trapping me under the tarp. Peeling it partially back he stuck his open palm in my face. "The other two hundred."

"You fucker," I said, regretting having let my guard down to trust anyone.

"Hey, it's a cheap ride if you make it all the way to Nyagatare. You saw what he wanted to charge you just to come this far."

The truck was slowing to a stop. I reluctantly reached into my pocket and pulled out my last two hundred francs from there. He covered me back over as the truck door slammed. I could hear the boys and the father as they helped the driver unload. The bed of the truck bounced and swayed as they jumped up and down and moved the sacks around. After they had finished and the family had departed, the truck bed bumped once more. I heard the sound of footsteps approaching, and then I felt the heavy weight of a knee come down on my ribs through the tarp. The tarp pulled back and the barrel of a small revolver was pressed against my temple.

"I told you it was one thousand francs to ride here."

"I haven't got any money. Those people took everything."

"Give me the bag." He reached under the tarp, yanked out my rucksack, and turned it upside down dumping out the contents on the floorboards. He easily found the five hundred francs in the bottom of the bag and the other five hundred in the side pouch.

"Now get off my truck."

Crawling from under the tarp, I attempted to pick up my food, but was discouraged with a hard kick to the side of my head from his boot. Clutching the empty rucksack, I scampered down and walked backward from the truck. I kept my eyes fixed on his, having learned long ago that a dog is less likely to bite if you're staring it down rather than turning from it. I didn't stop watching him until he had stowed my food in the cab of his truck and parked his own ass in the seat.

I scooped a drink from the well in the market square, then spent two hundred of my last francs, which I had hidden in my shoes, on bananas and plantains. After asking directions to Route 5, I set out on foot. There was almost no traffic on this road. It seemed that anyone who was heading to the UN camps in Tanzania was continuing straight east from Kayonza. The border was only twenty-five miles from there. But I took the road heading north, seeking territory that I was more familiar with.

I walked the remainder of that day and then all of the next before I started to see small groups of people also walking the road north. Here and there, from out of the bush along the road, families and small bands emerged, pushed their carts through the ditch, and plodded along with the rest of us. I was healthier and better fed than most of those who came from the small villages that were tucked back into the jungle. My relatively prosperous time at the convent school was evidenced by the contrast with the swollen bellies of the children and the protruding rib cages of adults. There was a cautious camaraderie among the common travelers and a good handful of languages bantered about. Most of them I could understand well—Kinyarwanda, Swahili, a couple of the northeast dialects. A few spoke some French and a few others, Arabic. I'd had no chance to learn any Arabic in the past, and I passed time on the road learning a few words from anyone who would converse with me.

As careful as I was about conserving my food it only lasted three days. I wasn't sure what to do. Water was never a problem, as creeks and streams ran steadily this time of year, but food was scarce. I had seen several of the walkers selling and bartering from among their supplies and I thought of buying something from them, but after my experience in Kayonza I didn't want anyone to know that I had any money. I certainly didn't have anything with which to barter: shorts and a T-shirt, shoes with no socks, and an empty rucksack were all that I had.

I walked the fourth day with no food, and on the fifth I encountered a family of eight. A father and grandfather carried dried firewood and tools on their backs, the mother and grandmother had their heads piled high, each with three large baskets stacked one on top of the other. One of the daughters, about twelve, carried a crippled young boy on her back, and a younger daughter of about seven cradled a crying infant in her arms. The children were emaciated. It took three tries at a language before they understood me.

"Here. Put the baby in here." I opened my rucksack and we sat the little fellow down inside it with his head sticking out the top. Then I traded the older daughter the rucksack for the crippled boy, taking him in my arms. She strapped the rucksack on her back, and we continued on our way. The father came up beside me on the road.

"Thank you. We had no food to leave with. I don't think my kids will make it much farther."

"Do you know how far to the next village?" I asked, contemplating buying something for us all.

"There are no more villages until we get to the Bganga road, maybe two or three days' walk yet. Soon we'll see the vultures, though."

I didn't understand his reference. "Vultures?"

"The scavengers among men. Soon those with food will bleed the rest of us of everything we have. And when we start to fall behind, others will pick anything that is left from our carcasses."

He was right. Small vendors started to appear along the roadside. They hawked corn and beans and cassava and plantains. One man had three small skinned monkey carcasses, putrid and crawling with flies, which he dangled from a pole. "Fresh meat, one thousand francs apiece," he shouted. These, like everything else, were being peddled at prices four and five times what they sold for forty miles south in Kayonza. I still didn't want to admit I had any money, not able to trust even this starving man with his aging parents and children.

Up ahead, a crowd was gathered on the road. Reaching the mob, I stretched to look over the tops of their heads. From there I could see that they were congregated around the same truck that I had ridden in five days earlier, and the same family that had taken my money was staging a market from the back of the truck. The truck driver lay sleeping on the grass around the front, in the shade of the cab, while the family of sellers teased the starving crowd by asking exorbitant prices for fresh fruit, cheese, and bread.

"Look after your son." I set down the crippled child. "I'm going to get us some food."

I walked to the front of the truck and then crept quietly to where the driver lay dozing. Swinging my leg back, and with all my heft, I kicked him in the side of the head as hard as I could, twice. Before he could recover I reached to his belt, took the handgun, and pressed it to his temple. I was fully prepared to kill him, my eternal fate having been already sealed; one more murder was not going to alter the ledger of my accounting even if there might be a god.

"You owe me some food," I said, close into his ear.

When his head had cleared, and without moving it, he turned his eyes to the side to see me.

"Yes … yes … I have some food for you."

"And fifteen hundred francs." I pressed the gun tighter to his head.

"Certainly."

"Turn onto your stomach," I ordered him. He rolled over, and I pressed the gun to the back of his skull. "Who is the other guy selling that food?"

"He's my brother."

"What's his name?"

"Bagwa," he answered.

"You call for Bagwa to come around here."

"Bagwa," he shouted. "Come here. Bagwa!"

Bagwa was caught by surprise at the sight of me holding a gun to his prone brother's head, my knee firmly planted in his back. The truck driver's face was swollen and he was sweating profusely.

"Bagwa," I asked, "you love your brother?"

"Yes."

"Then go around to the back of the crowd. You'll find a family there with a crippled boy. You know my rucksack; it has a baby in it. You take a hamper of the best of the food you have on this truck and take it to them—enough for four or five days. Don't even think about cheating them. Then bring me something to eat."

While Bagwa went to get the food I reached into the truck driver's pockets and found twenty-two hundred francs. I counted out the fifteen hundred francs he and his brother had taken from me and stuffed it in my pocket.

When Bagwa returned and dropped some cheese and fruit on the ground he said, "You can let him go. I have given them their food and here is yours."

"Bagwa, I should thank you for the lesson you taught me on the truck, to bargain in parcels. Now go get up on the truck and pass out every bit of food you have left to the rest of those people. Divide it fairly. Then come back here and I'll let him go."

When Bagwa left the second time, I swiftly swung the butt of the gun in a full arching backhand that caught the driver unaware in the temple. His head dropped forward, and his body slumped beneath me. By the time Bagwa had doled out all the food on the truck, I'd gathered up my share from the ground and made my way back into the crowd, taking the loaded gun with me. Sidling into the girl with my rucksack, I squeezed her hand around the seven hundred francs I still clutched and then slipped away.

Two days' walk later, the long file of migrants turned off onto the Bganga road, heading east toward Tanzania. The Bganga road was little more than a gravel cart track. It looked like a well-populated area, judging by all the huts and stone-block homes along the road, but they were mostly empty now—not even enough left in them for the scavengers to pick.

At two hundred francs per plantain, my food and money had run out after two days, near where the Bganga road ended. Carts and trailers and wheelbarrows were left abandoned there. A column of people led single file into the jungle following a walking trail, and I followed them, too hungry to venture out on my own. I stepped up beside another traveler.

"Have you any idea where this will take us?" I asked him.

"They say the United Nations has built a camp across the border."

"They say. But does anyone know for sure?"

"No one is coming back this way, so there must be something ahead," he said.

And that made some sense. So, I walked on with the wretched crowd of humanity, blindly hoping that the world had heard our call and sent something to help us.

The only way we knew that we had arrived in Tanzania was that the path through the jungle suddenly broke out to a gravel road. Locals living in the homes along this road pointed us another ten miles farther and promised we would find the newly built camp, which the UN was still installing at Nkwenda. They offered us water but had little food of their own to share. Those who sold food asked a fair price and didn't try to gouge us like our own people had done.

I was young and strong enough to make it another ten miles, but there were many who died on this last stretch of road. How sad to make it all this way and not be able to go the final few steps. When the road crested a hilltop I could see below in the valley, less than a mile away, a village of blue tents. In sight of our goal, an old lady beside me, struggling along with a walking stick, suddenly dropped to her knees and fell face forward on the road. I loaded the lady's bags on my empty back and picked her up, putting her over my shoulder, carrying her the last distance to the tent village. As gently as I could, I set her down in front of a large white tent with bold letters stamped on the roof, UN. But by then she had stopped breathing.

America

The pale-yellow moonlight has been replaced by a blue-gray that signals impending dawn in the beautiful Colorado sky, finally. I've slept very little after the hours of making love with Anna, the first time in seven months, and then still more sleepless hours spent reliving that first year with Anna in Paris. Yet I feel reasonably refreshed, rekindled by the intimacy shared with Anna and the hope that we can somehow start our lives all over again. We still have each other, and we still have the cherished memories of our stricken angel. The funk that has been dragging me down for the past month since Steph's death is waning. I recognize this feeling. I've been waiting for it and I want to hasten it, but past experience tells me, *It's coming, be patient a little longer.*

Kissing Anna and leaving her to sleep, I climb from the bed and make my way to the kitchen. The coffee is brewed and the smell alone stimulates me. I flip on the light and another level of consciousness takes hold.

A quick coffee and my mind is working, almost normal, certainly a lot more positively than it has over the past month. Twenty minutes on a spin bike in the basement, rehashing Anna's suggestion. Yes, this will be good for us both, a vacation, the honeymoon we never really had, somewhere warm, Jamaica, the Caribbean. First thing in the new year is ideal, we'll do Christmas here with Anna's family—it'll be good to have them around— and then we'll get away from Colorado during the coldest time. Twenty minutes at the weights feels good after missing a few days. Twenty more minutes with a shower and another cup of coffee. Throw the curtains open. "It's time, baby." A kiss on her cheek, like I make sure I do every single morning when I wake her. "Thank you for last night. You'll start looking into flights and places today? Maybe confirm what's happening with your parents and brother at Christmas?" Anna gave a sleepy nod. "You here when I get back tonight? See you around six. Love you, hon." An easy forty minutes this time of the morning on the 36 downtown to Sun Valley.

I've been making this drive in from Boulder to downtown Denver for the past five years. That was when I was invited by the three founding partners, Dr. Mark Su, Dr. Brie Ferguson, and Dr. Luis Davila, to join them at their clinic. The three of them had established the Sun Valley Family Health Center four years earlier to provide family care to the poorest of Denver's old inner city. They were all passionately dedicated to their Hippocratic oath, and it only took Anna and me one night to accept their invitation to join them. I'd been doing emergency trauma at St. Joe's hospital for three years after finishing my residency, but I was low on the totem pole and I was still drawing mostly night shifts and almost every weekend and holiday. Stephanie was four at that time, and I wanted something more regular, stable. I negotiated a buy-in to the practice with Mark, Brie, and Luis, and Anna and I bought our house in Boulder soon after. It was a little farther to Anna's parents in Colorado Springs, but the schools would be better for Stephanie, who would start pre-K in the fall. The commute wasn't too bad for me since I went in before morning rush hour and came home after the afternoon rush.

This morning there is no traffic at all at 6:40 when I pull off the street into the clinic parking lot. There's parking only for the staff since most of our patients don't own cars. We try to make it our policy not to turn anyone away, coverage or not. Staff is lean, just three others in the office full time. Rosa has been there since it started; she does office admin, fills in on reception, helps with translation, and will even do cleanup when the janitorial company can't make it out. Abi and Jamie split the reception, scheduling, and filing duties.

The clinic space itself is a bit tight, but we make do. It used to be the office portion of the McGill Bros. Bindery Company, then sat empty for several years before Mark, Brie, and Luis got together and bought up the entire old factory building. They took the offices for their clinic and rented the factory floor back to the city at cost for use as a drop-in space for kids' after-school programs. There's always a lot of activity around the property, and because of the work that we do, and the kids' space in the building, we're pretty much spared a lot of the criminal activity that the neighborhood is generally known for.

Entering my office, I see that Abi and Jamie placed a small stack of charts, scans, and lab results in my in-basket before they left last night. These will be the things that need attention right away, along with the files of my patients scheduled for today. The office is small, but it's adequate. The other partners endure equally tiny quarters so that we can have more exam-room space. We never have enough space in the waiting room, largely because in addition to our scheduled patients we also operate as a sort of drop-in clinic. We try not to encourage it, but everyone in the neighborhood knows that we won't turn anyone away, and it's a lot easier for a single mom with three or four small kids to come by our place rather than take the bus to the community health-care centers on the edges of town.

I've just started to peruse my inbox when Mark Su knocks on the open door and steps in. The partners arrive early, all of us wanting to pull our share of the endless load.

Mark has a file in one hand. "Morning, Doctor," he says.

"Morning, Mark."

"Mind if I sit down?" he asks as he drops into the seat across from my desk. "I've got the Nunez boy's file here. Ricky."

"Oh yes, he's my patient. Did the girls put it on the wrong desk?" I ask.

"No. Rosa brought his CT scan results to me last night. She thought that maybe I should deliver them to you."

Ricky Nunez is the oldest of five brothers; he's fourteen. His single mother works two jobs to support them and Ricky quit the varsity basketball team to take a job after school to help her out. He'd noticed a small lump in his testicles about four months ago and said that he didn't come to see me because he didn't want to lose a paycheck. This may have been partially true, but more likely he was too embarrassed. A week ago his testicles were so swollen that he finally made the trip in.

"I didn't expect them to come back good," I say.

"They're not good at all," said Mark. "He's got spots all over his lungs. He'll need biopsies right away, but that's just a formality."

I reach across to take the report from him. "I'll call his mom this morning."

"Alfred, we all thought that maybe you'd want one of us to handle it. We don't mind helping out."

I know what he means, they are trying to spare me the pain of reliving my experience with Stephanie so soon after her illness and passing. They are great colleagues; they really care about the patients—and me.

"That's all right, Mark. I can do it. I'm feeling a lot better than I was a few days ago. Besides, who better to help a parent facing this than one who's been through it?"

"Are you sure?" he asks. His concern is sincere. "We don't mind at all."

"I really appreciate that, Mark. I might have Rosa come in, though; my Spanish isn't good enough to trust with something like this."

"Sure, no problem."

"Oh, Mark, one other thing, while you're here. I'm going to take your suggestion and take some time off. Anna and I are going south for a few weeks. We thought right after Christmas, if that's okay with you and Brie and Luis. If no one else was planning on being away."

"Excellent," Mark says. "I'm glad. You both need it. Take a whole month off. Go crazy."

"Anna's organizing it. I doubt it'll be a month. I might really go crazy if I were off that long."

"Alfred, why don't you slow down on the hours a bit for the next month? At least until you get away for that vacation. We've all been worried you're going to burn out and then we'll lose you permanently."

I smile at him. "Anna's been saying the same thing. And I've already promised her I'll do that. Thanks, Mark." I reach across to shake his hand. "I appreciate the support."

After taking a look at Ricky's file, I decide that if I call right now I might get them both at home, before Ricky leaves for school and his mother for her job. As soon as Rosa gets in I'll ask her to make space on my schedule later this afternoon for the Nunezes, and I'll see if she can sit in with me just to make sure everything is translated properly.

Languages have always come easy to me. We spoke three in my village before I was taken. Bufumbwa was the first language of the village, a dialect really, and spoken by some neighboring villages as well. Kinyarwanda is the national language of Rwanda, so we all spoke that. It was the language of our early schooling, and Swahili was the common language of the greater area of central Africa. People from our village typically conversed in Bufumbwa. School and any official dealings or interactions with the government were in Kinyarwanda. And general trade and commerce were conducted in Swahili. I learned all three by the time I was five. I picked up several more dialects before leaving Africa. These were mostly variations on the languages I already spoke, and a keen ear made it easy for me to learn them. For a period during my older schooling in Kigali, and then again for four years in the refugee camp, I honed my French and got a good start in English. French was the colonial language of Rwanda under its Belgian rule, and many people still considered it a necessity for advancement. And in the UN camp English was the common language of choice for the staff and volunteers. Once I got to Denver to do my residency, I understood why Anna had learned Spanish during her youth; it was the second language of Colorado. I practiced it a bit during residency but got serious about it when I joined the clinic. For most of our patients Spanish is their first language, and for many it's all they speak.

Late in the afternoon Rosa pops into my exam room right after my last patient has left. "Pina Nunez is here," she says. "Do you want to see her right now?"

"Sure. Send her in please, Rosa. And you'll sit in, too?"

Pina Nunez hardly seems old enough to have a son of fourteen; she's not yet thirty herself. And she has four other boys, the youngest five. The sunken eye sockets and pockmarks on her face give away the tough battle she has waged with drugs over the years. As far as I know she's clean now, but that could change at any time. I'm worried that the news I'm about to give her could push her in a bad direction again.

"*Buenas tardes, Pina. Gracias por venir*," I greet her.

"Hello, Dr. Olyontombo. I'm fine in English if that's better for you," she says and smiles.

"English is still a little better for me, but I am working on my Spanish," I say.

"You're doing well, Doctor."

"Do you mind if Rosa sits in with us, just in case you have any questions?"

"That would be good. Thank you."

"Where's Ricky?" I ask her. "Is he coming?"

"He has to work at the restaurant. He's afraid he'll lose his job if he asks for time off."

"He should be here for this, Pina. I have the results from the tests we sent him for last week, and they're not good."

She tenses visibly, as if she is about to be hit—and she is, with the news I'm going to deliver. I remember hearing these words myself as a parent not long ago. Anna and I had each other to hang on to; Pina has no one, so I take her hand. Not wanting to make it melodramatic, I just get on with it.

"Pina, Ricky has cancer. The swelling in his testicles is a tumor, and the CAT scan tells us it's in his lungs, too. We won't know exactly how advanced it is until we do an MRI. And we have to biopsy everything to be one hundred percent certain before we can confirm malignancy. But we should expect it. There are things we can do, and we'll get on it right away."

She sits frozen in her seat, staring at me. I'm not certain if she hasn't heard me or perhaps doesn't understand me. "Pina, do you understand? Do you need Rosa to explain?"

"Is this like your little girl had, Doctor?"

"Not quite the same, Pina. But similar."

"Is my Ricky going to die, too?"

"We're going to start on treatments as soon as we can. I know exactly the pediatric oncologist we'll get Ricky in to see. He's the best in Denver."

"Is my Ricky going to die?"

I don't want to lie to her, and Ricky's prognosis is a *little* better than Stephanie's was. I wouldn't have wanted anyone to lie to Anna and me, but we obviously had the advantage of me being a physician. I resort to my well-practiced truths, or perhaps, lies by omission.

"He's young, and he's strong, and he's otherwise healthy; he has a good chance to fight this."

The emotion overwhelms her now, and she breaks down into gasping sobs. Moving closer I put my arm around her, and Rosa takes her other hand. We let her cry for a minute, let her process this news in her own way. I know that Pina has no family in town, her parents are in the US as illegal immigrants and they both work as ranch hands south of here in Alamosa.

"Pina, where are the other boys? You'll need someone at home with you. Do you have a friend you can call?"

"The little ones are next door in the community center, Doctor."

"What about a friend to stay with you at home for tonight, maybe a few days? Could your mother come up?"

"Mama will come. She'll stay with us." Pina is still sobbing but she manages to get it out. "I have to go get my boys, Doctor."

"How are you getting home, Pina?"

"We'll walk. I don't want to go on the bus like this." She wipes away tears with the back of her hand.

"I'm going to drive you, Pina. We'll get the boys and I'll drive you all home. What about Ricky? When is he home?"

"His shift is done at eight. He'll be home after that."

I grab a few things and tidy up while Pina waits with Rosa. She's managed to stop crying but her face and body language shout distress.

"Rosa, would you mind waiting a few minutes longer with Pina? I'll go next door and get the boys."

The door to our clinic is right beside the door to the community center. After exiting one, and before going into the other, I pull out my cell and call Anna, getting her voice mail. "Anna, something's come up, I won't be home until after nine, I'll call you when I'm in the car. Love you, honey."

A sixteen-year-old attendant greets me as I enter the community center. "Hi, Dr. Alfred."

"Hi, Mercedes. Do you know where the Nunez boys are?"

"I think the two older ones are in the gym and the younger two are probably in the art room upstairs. Do you want me to get them?"

"No, I'll go get them. Thanks, Mercedes."

The gym is really just the old main factory floor area from the bindery, but it serves the purpose well. It has a high ceiling and new lighting was installed overhead. Only problem is, it's still got the original concrete floor, not ideal, but workable. It gives the kids a place off the streets, out of the weather, and away from the miscreants who wait to corrupt them. Twice a year the gym is used by the county health department when they send out public health nurses to provide immunizations and general checkups for the young and elderly alike in the neighborhood. On those days Luis, Brie, Mark, and I all pitch in to offer free examinations and advice to anyone who wants to drop by.

A pair of movable basketball hoops are set up at the far end, and some of the older boys have a game running. This end is occupied by boys and girls playing a game of dodgeball. I spot the two Nunez boys, laughing and having a good time. I wave to them just as the ball flies into my vision. Ducking quickly, I look around to see who threw it. Two girls about Stephanie's age laugh and shout, "Come play with us, Dr. Alfred."

I know several of the kids in the gym, a few of them are my patients and others I met just dropping in to play with them.

"Yes, Doctor, play on our team," someone else shouts.

"Another time, girls." I wave again for Marcus and Adrian Nunez, and they come running over.

"Is Mom waiting for us, Dr. Alfred?" Marcus asks.

"She is, Marcus. I'm going to give you a lift home tonight. Would you mind running upstairs and getting your brothers?"

Marcus runs off leaving Adrian to ask, "How come you're going to drive us home, Doctor?"

"Your mom just needs a hand for a bit. And I want to see Ricky when he gets home," I answer.

The two younger boys come down the stairs dragging their jackets. When Ronny, the youngest, sees me, he drops his coat and runs right to me, jumping into my arms. "Dr. Alfred, you're driving us home?"

None of the boys know their fathers, and they crave male attention. Ronny is the most affectionate of the brood and still wants to be cuddled. I carry him next door with the others in tow; we collect Pina and all load into my SUV.

They live in one of the older tenements, two bedrooms for the whole family, the three eldest boys in one and the two younger in the other with Pina. The living room and kitchen are both cramped, but the boys are happy to show me their home and have me as a guest. Pina and Adrian set to making supper while the other boys entertain me. Ronny sits on my lap and at one point, with the brashness of youth, leans back and asks, "Dr. Alfred, what happened to your face?"

"Stop it, Ronny," Marcus says. "You're not supposed to ask him that. Mom's told you before."

"But I want to know," his little brother responds.

"An accident with a machete, Ronny," I say.

"What's a machete?"

"It's like a sword, stupid. Don't ask him these questions," Marcus says.

"Were you in a sword fight?" Joe asks. "Like a pirate?"

"Can I touch it?" Ronny asks.

"Ronny!" Marcus shouts.

I smile at them. "Sure, go ahead and touch it."

Ronny reaches out to trace the line of the scar, starting at my forehead, following it across my eyebrow and down the side of my face to my jaw. Joe reaches up for a turn. "Does it hurt, Dr. Alfred?"

Hmm. No one has ever asked me that before. It does hurt, actually. It hurts to wear it every day, as a reminder of a previous life, a life I've now spent nearly two decades trying to erase—or at least make up for. But instead of admitting to the pain I reply, "No, Joe, it doesn't hurt."

After dinner Pina can't thank me enough for staying around until Ricky gets home. I am still not sure how to handle this, how to give the news to Ricky. When he finally arrives a little after eight o'clock he sees me as soon as he comes in the door. "Dr. Olyontombo? What are you doing here?"

"Hi, Ricky." I want to force a smile but none will come out. It's just as well, he takes my cue.

"Something's wrong?" he asks, cocking his head slightly and looking from me to his mother. He sees her trying to look composed, but she's snuffling and her eyes are wet. She looks older than she did when she came into my office just four hours ago. I know how this ages a parent. I also know it's only just starting for her.

I inhale deeply. "Yes, Ricky. I have your CAT scan results. A few things have come back as problems." Ricky is silent. He looks again to his mother, who steps in to hug him, and I continue. "Ricky, it looks like there are some tumors on your lungs. We need to do some more tests."

The news sinks in. He looks confused, and yet comprehending at the same time. He bites the side of his lower lip and nods ever so slightly as his eyes begin to water up. He's tall at fourteen, taller than his mother, and he stands proud, hugging her to his side.

"What do we do now, Doctor?" he asks me over the top of her head.

"I'm going to make all the arrangements for your next tests. I'll call you in a few days. I'll let you and your mom know everything you need to do."

"What about my job? We need my job." He gives his mom a squeeze.

Only fourteen years old, yet Ricky is taking this like a man. He's concerned about his family; he's comforting his mother. He's certainly making this easier on me. After giving him the details and making sure that Pina and the other kids are okay I get up to leave, and Ricky sees me to the door.

"Thank you, Doctor," Ricky says. "Thank you for coming over here and helping Mom. And me. I know you didn't have to."

I sit in the SUV for a minute before starting the ignition. I feel like shit. I want to do more for this kid, more for his mom and brothers. I'd trade places with him if I could. Ricky's done nothing to deserve this sentence. I have. I wish I were half the man that Ricky is.

What started out as a pretty good day, making love with Anna into the early hours, plans to take our honeymoon vacation, and my resolve to move forward after a month of sulky mourning for my baby girl, is ending on a bit of a downer. Just last night I promised Anna that I'd put in a little less time at work and get home earlier in the evenings, and here it is now almost nine o'clock. I have to call her.

"Anna, hon, I'm really sorry—"

"Freddie, I tried calling you. There was no answer on your cell or at the office. I was worried. Are you okay?"

"I wasn't at the office, and I turned off the ringer for a while. I was with one of my patients and his family. He's just a kid, Anna. A little older than Steph ... almost the same thing."

"As bad?"

"Not quite ... yet. I'll be home in thirty. I'll tell you about it then."

"Are you okay, Freddie?" she asks.

"Sort of. Anna, I'm sorry I'm late. I'm sorry."

"Freddie, I love you."

"I know. I know you do. Thank you, Anna. I love you, too."

Over the next couple of weeks I spend quite a bit of time with Pina and Ricky Nunez, explaining test results and trying to reassure them that they are in the best hands possible with the oncologist that I referred them to. Because of the potential aggressiveness of Ricky's cancer we've decided to hit it with chemo and radiation at the same time. He's young and strong; it seems the best option. But we're now at December 19, those departments run slowly over the holidays, and I don't want him in the hospital during what might be his last Christmas. They can start the treatments first thing in the new year.

I am a little bothered that I won't be here for his first round; Anna has our trip all booked. And it's not just Ricky. I hate to take off on my other patients, too. There are several of them who need ongoing follow-up.

I know they're in good hands with Mark and the others at the clinic, I just have this guilty feeling about leaving for a vacation. I know I shouldn't feel this way, and I've talked it through a million times with Anna, and I try to pretend with her that I'm fine with it, but I'm not. I use guilt, I always have, as a sort of backhanded way to wallow and punish myself. I'm not sure how a psychologist might clinically diagnose this but I don't need anyone to formally analyze it. I'm working on it … trying to, anyhow.

On the other hand, I am looking forward to the trip almost as much as Anna. She's got us booked for a week at an all-inclusive on Saint Martin, on the Dutch side, and then we'll stay for two more in a rented condo in Marigot, on the French side of the island. She says the first week will allow us to decompress without having to do anything or think about anything. Then the next two weeks we can both get back to practicing our French, which we haven't had much opportunity to use since leaving Paris sixteen years ago. I know that Anna, always a little more quixotic than me, is looking for a romantic distraction for us, however we can both most certainly use the three weeks to recharge.

The past nine months have been difficult: physically, mentally, on our relationship, on our jobs. We need a reset. I've always been the one more prone to burnout and flirting on the edge of depression while Anna is more able to let things go. She doesn't get bogged down worrying about the small stuff, she's much better than I about leaving work at work and not bringing it everywhere in her mind. But even these traits can only carry one so far during the sort of year we've had. Anna has arranged the three weeks off from work. She's paid by billable hours and they'll miss her, but they are as sympathetic to our situation as the staff at my clinic.

One of the things that first attracted Anna and me to each other was our view of the world and our desire to do our small part to make it a little better. We're both fortunate that we've been able to work ourselves into careers with firms that have philosophies similar to our own personal beliefs. Tierney, Thomas, and May are the legal equivalents to my medical clinic, the Sun Valley Family Health Center. Both firms are small and have developed niches in the Denver market. And both do a lot of pro bono work in the community, often with the immigrant population.

If things go well on the vacation I have been thinking I might try to broach the idea of us adopting. We wouldn't have to start over with a baby, there are plenty of older kids in Denver who need a home and family. Maybe we could even adopt two siblings and keep them from being separated. We tossed around the idea years ago but got busy raising Stephanie and growing our careers, and it all seemed to slip by the wayside. Neither of us has dared to raise the topic since Steph passed, and it might still be too early, but it might also be good for us. I'll see how it goes on the vacation. Anna might like the idea.

With less than a week left until Christmas I need to call Anna's mom, Ruth, and see what she wants us to bring. My agenda is full, trying to squeeze in all the extra patient visits before the holidays, but I'll have to make time to grab whatever she needs. Anna and I have kind of fallen into this routine over the years where I look after our share of the family dinners and Anna takes care of the other things like presents and scheduling. It's not going to be a particularly joyous Christmas, having just buried a daughter and granddaughter and niece, but it will be good for us all to be together to get through it. Anna's brother, Rob, will be there with his wife, Eva, and two kids, Sam and Eric. The boys will be missing their cousin, Stephanie. They've never known a Christmas without her. We'll all miss her.

Finding a few minutes between patients I squeeze in a call to Ruth.

"Hi, Mom."

"Alfred!" Ruth's always happy when I call. "How are you? We can't wait to see you."

"We're looking forward to seeing you guys, too, and having a bit of downtime," I say. "It's going to be different this year." This puts a bit of a downer on our conversation, so I add quickly, "What can we bring?"

"Nothing, we don't need anything." I knew she'd say this—she always does.

"You've probably already got the turkey?"

"Yes, we're fine. Really, we don't need anything."

"What about a ham? Can we bring a small ham?"

"No, nothing. Really, we're all covered. Just you and Anna. Bring you and Anna," she says.

"Okay. Don't buy any wine. We'll bring the wine … and rum for Eldon," I say. "How is Eldon? Store crazy busy?" Eldon and Ruth were once ranchers. Anna and her brother grew up in the countryside until Eldon injured his back in a machinery accident. After that he bought a small hardware store on the edge of town, and as the city grew, so did his business.

There's a pause in the conversation. I can sense emotion from Ruth through the cell.

"Oh, Alfred, he's not doing so great. You know how much he adored Stephie," Ruth says.

It's true, Steph was the apple of her grandpa's eye, his only granddaughter, his first grandchild. She was on his heels in the store every school holiday, and he just loved it. They spent a lot of time together.

"It'll be good for him to have you around," she says. "You're a calming influence on him."

"I might need *him* around more than he needs me," I say. We've only seen them a few times since the funeral, and Ruth doesn't realize the wreck that I've been for the last two months.

"You'll be good for each other," Ruth says. "We all need the time together, Alfred. Anna says you can stay until New Year's?"

"Yes, the whole week. It'll be nice. And then the day after we leave for Saint Martin."

"That'll be good for Anna. The vacation will be nice for her," Ruth says. "I don't know what she'd do without you. Thank you, for looking after our little girl, Alfred."

God, why do they all think I'm the rock? I need to move this conversation. "Hate to run, Mom, but I've got a patient. See you on Saturday, probably early afternoon if I can get Anna up by then. Love you, Mom."

It was natural for me to call Ruth "Mom" right from the beginning. It felt good to me, all my life without one, and then this woman opened her family and heart to me like I was her own child. I got along right away with Anna's dad, too. Eldon accepted me because his daughter did. He loved her and trusted her judgment, plain and simple. Still I could never bring myself to call him "Dad," even though he surely felt like one. I'd been around grown adult men for too long, ever since I was eight, and always called them by their names. Eldon and I, and Ruth for that matter, couldn't have been from worlds further apart, him from white-bread Middle America and me from the deepest jungle of Africa, but we had a mutual respect and a mutual bond—Anna. And that's exactly what we did, we bonded into one loving family.

Two days later, Thursday, just as I arrive at my office, Anna's brother calls me. It's technically the first day of winter, December 21, and we've been spared so far in Denver. Up until now only a few light flurries, but usually by this time of the year we'd have had a major dump or two of snow already.

"Bro," Rob says. "Just wanted to remind you to bring your racket down to Mom's. We can get a few games in."

"If you think you're up to it. We're there the whole week, so go ahead and book a couple of court times for us," I say.

Rob's a schoolteacher in the Springs, and he got me started playing squash with him years ago. It's our indoor winter activity together. Whenever Anna and I can get down to her parents' during the other months, Rob and I usually do a couple of long bike rides or backcountry hikes. I haven't played squash since last year; it'll be good to get on a court again. I'm sure he's been practicing with his other buddies at the Y.

"What about hiking shoes?" I ask. "Should I bring them?"

"Too late for that around here; you'd need snowshoes." He chuckles into the phone.

"How's school been? You must be ready for a break," I say.

"Big time," he replies, and then his tone turns somber and cautious. "How are you and Sis holding up?"

"We're doing okay, Rob. Thanks. Can hardly wait for this vacation though, especially now that it's almost here. We've got the whole week with Eldon and Mom and you guys, and then we're flying out on the second for three more weeks."

"You two deserve it."

"Anna deserves it."

"You both deserve it," Rob says. "Okay, I'll let you get to work, and we'll see you in two days. Don't forget the racket."

"Looking forward to it."

I set my cell on the desk and reach into the in-basket the girls have left for me. There's an especially big pile here this morning. With just two days left before the office closes for Christmas break everyone is trying to get things wrapped up. I've asked several of my patients whom I know will need special following while I'm away to come in over these last two days. I want to touch base with them and assure them that they will be in good hands while I'm gone. Ricky and Pina are among them, and this will be my last chance to see them.

The day is flying by, midafternoon already, when Abi slips into my exam room between patients.

"Dr. Olyontombo, there are two men from the Denver Police Department here to see you. I've told them you're really busy today, but they say it's important."

"That's okay, Abi. Ask them into my office. I'll be right there."

It's not common for police officers to ask to see me, but it's not exactly uncommon, either. It's usually to ask if I've had any contact with someone they are looking for. In this neighborhood the police and I often have mutual clients. Once in a while they'll show up with a warrant to collect a patient's records.

Entering my office I find the two gentlemen dressed in civilian clothes. Detectives, I assume. They haven't sat down and are actually facing the door waiting for me when I step in.

"Good afternoon, Officers," I say. "Please take a seat. What can I help you with?"

When neither of them makes any move to sit I am stalled from going around behind my desk.

"Dr. Olyontombo? Azikiwe Olyontombo?" one of them asks.

"Alfred Olyontombo," I say, offering a gentle correction.

"Azikiwe, alias Alfred Olyontombo." He reads from a paper he's holding. "We're here to place you under arrest. We have an arrest warrant from the office of the US Secretary of State. Would you please remove your lab coat and put your hands out in front of you, sir?"

I'm totally dumbfounded, shocked, too much so to even ask a question.

No one has called me Azikiwe for more than twenty years. I obediently do as he asked, and one of them clasps my wrists with a set of handcuffs. The other pats my torso, all around, my arms, my legs.

"Gentlemen, there must be some mistake," I say. "I haven't done anything wrong."

"We're sorry, sir. You'll have to come with us."

"I need to call my wife. My wife … she's a lawyer. There has to be some mistake."

"Sir, we're going to escort you out of your office. For your own good, please follow our instructions. Please step out, sir."

One of them opens the door and stands back for me to walk through. I'm trying to process what's going on, but I'm confused. It's all happened so suddenly. I step out into the hallway. Mark is there, having just come out of another doorway, and sees me. Bewilderment glazes his eyes.

"Alfred, what's going on?" he asks.

"I don't know, Mark. I have no idea." I can't think straight, I feel like I'm in a trance, and I keep walking ahead, stepping into the waiting room. I stop there. It's full, packed; all four of us doctors have complete schedules today. Looking around I can see that everyone has stopped what they were doing, and the babble of noise hushes to a few infants crying. They stare at me, asking me with their eyes, *What's going on?*

"Move ahead, sir." The order comes from behind me.

"Abi, would you please call Anna for me?" is all I can think to say, and I move ahead.

Ricky Nunez is there with his mother, and he jumps up and confronts the officer behind me. "What the fuck is this? Who are you?"

"Step back, son; the doctor is under arrest."

"Fuck you. That's Dr. Olyontombo. He hasn't done anything," Ricky shouts, too close in the officer's space.

The officer pushes Ricky roughly, and he falls backward onto the floor but springs up as quickly as a cat. I make an attempt to diffuse things. "It's okay, Ricky. There's some kind of misunderstanding. We'll figure it out."

The full, busy waiting room is suddenly entirely silent—even the babies fall mute—one of those surreal moments that simply stands still. Or perhaps my mind is just computing it that way; I know I am not thinking properly. They don't need to tell me, I just walk out of the office, one of them holding the door, the other behind me. They have their unmarked car parked right at the front step and I am put in the back. They both get into the front, separated from me by a metal screen.

Azikiwe? Azikiwe? I try to think of the last time that anyone called me that. I can't pin it down exactly, not since my youth anyhow. Have the sins of a past life finally caught up with me? It seems like the city is moving by our stationary car. I somehow know it is the other way around, but my brain is mixing it up at the moment. The confusion of the whole situation is rendering me dazed, and I let myself slip further into the trance. One part of my brain wants to just give in and be swallowed up, but another part is still operating on some intellectual plane and is trying to tell me to get control of myself. I'm torn between giving up on the situation and taking charge of it. *Azikiwe? Azikiwe?*

The car pulls up to a large gate at the back of what I recognize as the police station but I've never been here before. The gate opens automatically, and we drive into an enclosed parking area. Entering another, more secure area of the garage a second gate opens and then closes behind us. I am escorted out of the car to a windowless steel door. One of the officers looks into a camera, flashes his ID to the camera and speaks to it, "Prisoner transfer." He taps his ID on an electronic reader and the door gives a loud *click,* opening on its own. Once inside, the bright lights and activity wake me from the daze that I've allowed myself to settle into, and my conscious mind begins to finally take over again.

"Officers, can you please tell me what is happening?" I ask.

One of them says, "Doctor, we have an arrest warrant based on a federal extradition request instructing us to place you under immediate arrest. It's from the office of the US Secretary of State. It was faxed to us this morning, says that formal indictments will arrive later today. That's all we know, I'm afraid. We're to have you processed here and someone from the US Attorney's Office will take it from there."

"Should I have a lawyer?" I ask. "My wife will be coming soon. She's a lawyer. Can I see her?"

"We're sorry, Doctor. We really don't know any more than this. We're turning you over here for processing."

A uniformed policeman, one of half a dozen in the area, an older guy, limping, approaches us and takes the paper that the detective hands him. He looks at me and then the paper. "Azikiwe Olyontombo?"

"Alfred Olyontombo," I respond instinctively.

"Alias, Alfred Olyontombo," he says, reading from the paper. "Come with me."

He leads me into another room with no door, leaving the detectives behind. "Give me your hands."

No "Doctor," no "please." I suppose that to him I am just another black criminal for processing, one of a regular stream passing through. He takes my hands, still cuffed, and presses each finger individually to a scanner. I am reminded of the last, and only other time, that I was ever fingerprinted. That time an army officer was very gentle with me. He carefully took each of my small fingers and rolled them over a blotter of ink and then again onto little squares on an official form.

"Stand in front of that wall. Look straight into the camera. Lift your head a bit. Turn your whole body to the right. Look straight ahead at the square in front of you. Turn fully to the left. Look at the square. Over here. Open your mouth."

He puts on a rubber glove, looks in my mouth, and then wipes the inside with a swab, dropping it into a small plastic container, which he labels.

"Turn around." I am patted down again.

"Face me. Okay, I'm going to remove these handcuffs. Give me your hands. Now, empty your pockets. Put everything in this bag. Take off your belt. Shoes. Put them in here. All right, back out there and turn right, follow the blue line on the floor."

I do as he says and he follows behind me. The line takes me toward another door, which clicks open automatically as I approach. Looking around I see that there are cameras everywhere with no attempt to hide or disguise them. The blue line leads down a hallway with three doors, three rooms, three windows on each side.

"Last doorway on the left."

It's open, so I walk in. He shuts the door, leaving me alone. There's a single, solitary chair, and three cameras inside protective covers positioned in the corners of the ceiling. I take a seat in the chair, lean forward with my elbows on my knees, resting my forehead in my hands.

I have no idea how much time passes. Minutes? Hours? It's slow. At last I hear the door click and Anna comes in. I stand up but I am very heavy, hardly able to lift my own weight. Everything sags—my shoulders, my head, my face—I can feel it all weighed down.

"Alfred." Anna moves quickly to hug me, and I wrap my arms around her limply. Now that she's here I feel my eyes watering. She steps back. "Freddie, what kind of mistake is this? What's going on?"

I hang my head and shake it. "I don't know, Anna." I resort to my standard tactic, another lie of omission. I have a pretty good idea what's going on, I just don't want to admit it to Anna. At least not yet. I can barely admit it to myself.

"Well, they can't just arrest you for no reason," Anna says. "They must have told you something. What did they say? It's got to be a mistake."

"They said they have a federal extradition warrant. The US Attorney's Office is supposed to come or something. I don't understand any of it."

"A *federal* extradition warrant?" she repeats. "Something is badly mixed up here."

I sort of hope she's right, that it's a big mistake, but I also sort of hope she's wrong. This is my due, at long last, finally arrived.

Anna takes charge, and I remember that this is her element; she works in this stuff. "A federal extradition warrant," she says again. "I've got to get ahold of Steve. He'll get them at the US Attorney's Office, maybe tonight. My phone's at the desk. I've got to go call him."

Anna signals the camera facing her and the door clicks. She leaves me alone again. Steve is Steve May, one of the principals at her firm, a family friend, really. Anna's firm is small, like my practice. I feel terrible now that I start to think of my practice and Anna's firm. How is this going to impact them? And there are others: Anna's family, our friends … mostly though, Anna. What a mess.

Anna returns a few minutes later with a policeman. "Alfred, we're going to get a counsel room. Come on." She leads the way out and down the hall; she's been here before and knows her way around. She takes us to a room with a table and four chairs, and no cameras in it. She's all business and sits across the table from me. I'd like to have her right beside me, but somehow it's comforting to have her sitting across the table, taking charge. The situation feels a little more under control.

"Okay, Freddie," she begins. "They can't hear what we are saying in here. But here's the first thing, we shouldn't even be in here. The police don't realize what's going on. They're treating you like this is a state extradition warrant, but it's *federal* so you essentially don't have any rights, no Miranda rights, no indictment hearing, technically not even a right to counsel. Basically you lose all your constitutional rights once the State Department has signed the extradition warrant. But since they haven't given any details yet this is probably a provisional arrest. We've got to keep our fingers crossed and hope that this is just a major screwup by some bureaucrat.

"Once these cops here clue in, it's possible they'll throw us out of this room. They won't have to give me access to you.

"Steve's going to contact the US Attorney's Office directly. He's coming down here but he's going to try to find out what's going on first. If he can reach them, he might be able to work something out."

I'm only half listening to what she says. I cover my face with my hands and shake my head from side to side. "I'm so sorry, Anna."

"Don't be sorry, Alfred. This is just some kind of major screwup. Steve will sort it out. It's around four o'clock right now. I just hope he can get in touch with the office before the end of the day. He said he'd be here within thirty minutes, so it shouldn't be long. Now, while we wait, tell me what happened at the clinic. How did the arrest go down?"

I tell her exactly what I can remember, but already it seems fuzzy, like a dream. And then I ask her, "Anna, what if it's not a screwup?"

"That's impossible. Of course it's a screwup."

"But what if it's not?"

Anna narrows her eyes and looks hard at me. "Then it means you're a criminal felon in a foreign country." She goes on to add, "But that's not possible. You haven't even been out of the United States since you got citizenship. That was more than ten years ago." She stops to think for a moment. "It'd have to be something from France, or maybe Tanzania."

I just sit there dumbly, letting her puzzle over it all, adding nothing to help her connect the dots which I've already connected in my own mind.

There's a knock at the door and it opens. Steve May enters as both Anna and I stand up. He gives Anna a hug, and she thanks him for coming down so fast. Steve reaches over the table to shake my hand, but pauses and walks around the table, grabbing my hand and pulling me in for a hug. "Alfred," is all he says. I can tell he's at a bit of a loss, wavering between professionalism and informality. Professionalism wins out; he returns to the other side of the table and we all take seats.

"I spoke with Larry Jamieson on my way over here," Steve says. Jamieson is the US Attorney in Colorado. He's well known in the area and I've seen him at social events but never actually met him. "He's confirmed that this is a provisional arrest ordered through the US Department of State, but he doesn't know any more than that. He does say that they'll have to get you in front of a magistrate within twenty-four hours. Larry's promised to assign it to Laura Abroud. That's a big favor to us. She'll be reasonable at least, and Anna and I both have a good relationship with her. Larry said he'd have Laura get the indictments to us as soon as they have them. Let's see if we can figure out what's going on here. What can you tell me, Alfred?"

I shrug my shoulders.

Anna speaks up, trying to sound hopeful. "It's all got to be some mistake, Steve."

He looks at her and then back to me. His eyes narrow ever so slightly as he focuses in on me. I know he is preparing to read whatever body language and facial cues I might send out. He's an experienced lawyer, a good one. He's also a friend, but he's still much more objective than Anna could ever be.

"Okay." Steve starts over. "We know it's a federal extradition warrant. That means it's got to be a serious felony. Countries don't deal with each other over shoplifting infractions. And because they've ordered the provisional arrest without all the documentation in hand, it probably means they consider you a flight risk if you got wind of an arrest. Did you have any idea this was coming?" he asks.

I am truly perplexed and just shake my head.

"Have you any idea, any idea at all, what it could be about?"

I answer him honestly. "It's got to be Africa."

"What about France? Were you ever in any trouble there? Anything?"

"No, nothing. Nothing I can think of."

"What other countries have you been to?"

"Just France and the US. And Africa."

"Not Mexico? What about Canada? Ever vacation there?"

I shake my head.

"What about in Europe? Did you ever travel outside France?"

Again I shake my head. Steve is making notes, but I can't tell if they are about my answers or about me.

"All right. Could be France. But you think Africa. Where have you been in Africa? Which countries?"

"Tanzania—"

"When?"

"I left in 1998."

"Never been back?"

"No. Never. I've never been back to Africa since I left."

"Any other places in Africa? Any other countries?"

"Yes. Rwanda. Zaire, but it's the Congo now. Maybe Uganda."

"When?"

"Before Tanzania. Before 1994," I say.

Steve retrieves a paper from his briefcase and looks down it.

"The United States doesn't have extradition treaties with either Uganda or Rwanda, so it's got to be either the Congo or Tanzania. Or France, especially if it's some mistake."

"It's got to be France then," Anna interjects. "There's been a mistake in France." Anna is still clinging to a hope that I know is useless.

The three of us look at each other. There is no sense in holding back any longer. They must surely be able to read the guilt on my face.

"It's Africa," I state.

"How can you be sure?" Steve asks.

"Because things happened in Africa. It's Africa."

Anna recesses in thought. Steve looks at me as if trying to read more from my face. I want more words to come out. I want to explain more, but I am so ashamed I can't say them. I put my elbows on the table and sink my face into my hands. I don't want to look at them; I don't want to see their reactions to what I've just told them, especially Anna's. I don't want to look at her.

Steve is very logical, professional. "Alfred," he says. "How old were you when you left Africa?" His voice is steady, giving off no sign of judgment.

I don't even lift my face from my hands. "Twenty."

"Twenty when you left Tanzania?"

I nod a bit into my hands.

"How old when you entered Tanzania?"

"Almost sixteen."

Anna is a lawyer; she understands where Steve is going with this, but I haven't even tried to figure it out. She stands up and leans forward on the table. "That's right, Steve. He was a minor. He was a minor in Africa. The US won't extradite a minor."

"We won't extradite a minor, but I'll have to do some research on whether we can extradite for crimes committed as a minor," he says. "And again, it might depend on which country."

I'm not really paying a lot of attention to their exchange. I hear it, but don't want to think about it. I've started to drift back to events that I've spent two decades trying to erase, scrubbing hard over the years to expunge all memory. There's a battle going on in my mind as people and places begin to flash before me while I struggle to not see them, to continue to push them from my reality.

Steve asks another question, which jars me back to the present. "Alfred, who is Azikiwe? Who is Azikiwe Olyontombo?"

Anna hasn't seen the arrest warrant yet, so she is confused by the question and looks to Steve. "Who?"

He replies to her by reading directly from a copy of the arrest warrant. "Azikiwe Olyontombo. That's who's named here. It says 'Alfred' is an alias."

"Freddie?" Her look at me pleads for an explanation.

"I am Azikiwe," I say. "I *was* Azikiwe … once. I was born Azikiwe Olyontombo."

A slight lift of eyebrows asks me for more information.

"I changed my name to Alfred when I went to Tanzania."

"Why?" Anna asks.

"To escape."

Steve interjects. "To escape? The law?"

"No," I say. "To escape Azikiwe."

Anna is lost for words. Perhaps she is also lost for thoughts. I am sure Steve has more questions, but he must also be able to read the turmoil in me and perhaps the tension that is starting to build between Anna and me. "Look," he says. "It's almost five o'clock, that's the middle of the night in Africa. If the State Department doesn't have the full indictment by now they're not going to get it until tomorrow. I'll go do a little research. Anna, if we leave Alfred, they're probably going to put him in a lockup. You might want to stay here with him for a while. I'll have some food sent in. As long as he's with a lawyer they won't put him in a cell."

"What about bail?" Anna asks. "Can we get a hearing first thing in the morning?"

"I'm going to reach out to Laura Abroud and see what she might do. But technically there is no bail for federal extraditions."

"Shit," Anna says. "How long can all this take? How long can they keep him here?"

Steve shrugs. "Depends on the country and the treaties. Sometimes these things happen very fast. Could be right away or could be months." He stands and puts his notes into his briefcase. "Unfortunately, it isn't looking like much can happen before tomorrow. But if Laura has anything I'll get right back to you."

He extends his hand across the table, and I stand to shake it, still shamed, not wanting to look him in the eye. "Thanks, Steve," I mumble. "I'm sorry about this, Steve. I'm sorry, Anna." I reach out and pull her close, burying my face in her hair. My embrace of her is desperate, hers in return is soothing, comforting. Steve lays a hand on Anna's shoulder, giving her a firm squeeze and a nod before leaving.

It's awkward, alone here now with Anna. I am trying to think back, over the entire time of our knowing each other, to when such an awkwardness might have taken place between us. There hasn't been one, not for any reason, in the whole seventeen years. There have been times when Africa came up, but they were only moments, explained away by my careful sidestepping of the issue, telling only part of the story, conveniently leaving out those memories that I fought so hard to dismiss. I'd become somewhat expert at avoiding the past, burying it, omitting it, almost completely, by telling the truth but not the whole truth and justifying it all by never quite lying. My deceits have only been possible because of the pure virtue of Anna. She's known all along that I am hiding and avoiding the terrible things in my past. I think that her nature is too trusting to know how much I practice my avoidance of the whole truth. She believes me; she doesn't think I would lie to her. And I haven't. But she knows there are things I don't talk about, and she has never pushed me, never made them an issue. Now they have become an issue.

I never expected Africa to become a problem like this though, never expected the law to hunt me down and bring me to accounting. I always thought payback would come through karma, like the death of Stephanie, perhaps my failure as a doctor, perhaps the failure of my marriage. I've always harbored these fears of the good things in my life going bad. My ultimate payback would be for Anna to leave me. And she most certainly will, now that I have been found out. Even if she doesn't leave the law is going to separate us—by my incarceration and by the thousands of miles between here and Africa. Maybe even by death. Maybe they still have the death penalty in Africa. Of course they do; why wouldn't they? If America, the most advanced country on earth, has the death penalty, why wouldn't African nations? Worse for me than the death penalty would be the pain that this would inflict on Anna. My personal karma is about to be manifest through the pain and suffering of Anna.

I should have never let myself get involved with her; I am destroying her life. My karma has already taken her baby from her, and now it will take everything else.

With Steve gone we sit across the table from each other talking out logistics. Anna is hopeful that this mistake can be cleared up before Saturday, before we are due at her parents' place in Colorado Springs. Choosing to avoid creating more confrontation I don't bother to tell her that it won't be. She'll have to call Mark at the clinic and tell him that there was a huge mistake and that it should be cleared up soon, but I won't make it into the office tomorrow, Friday, the last day before the Christmas long weekend. She'll have to ask them if they would please cover my appointments for me. It dawns on me that my cell phone and laptop are still at my office and I meekly ask her if she could pick them up. And, I'll need clean clothes tomorrow. Anna reassuringly offers to look after everything.

Anna and I spend this last bit of time together trying to pretend that things are seminormal and we make attempts at small talk, but awkwardness pressurizes the room. We speak no more about the what-ifs of my situation, deciding to wait until we see the actual extradition orders and indictment. We deliberately and conveniently avoid talking about my past. Anna wants out, to go home, think things through on her own. I don't blame her; in fact I'd almost rather not have to face her anymore tonight. Neither of us eat any of the food that Steve sent in, and she leaves around six, telling me that everything will work out, but there is no certainty in her voice, and in a crazy twisted way I'm not sure that I want things to work out.

Once Anna's gone I am escorted to a spotless cell, cleaner than I would have imagined, fresh smelling even. A small stainless steel sink projects from the back wall, a one-piece stainless steel toilet sits beside it, and a molded stainless steel bed frame is anchored to the floor along another wall and topped with a heavy mattress. I lie down on the mattress and look up at the ceiling, contemplating my predicament, and then my marriage, and then my career, and then my life. I do this all night long, over and over again. I only know that the night has passed because at one point the lights dim from full brightness to half strength and then back up to full intensity. I start to hear the comings and goings of daytime but pay them no heed, preferring to burrow in my solitude.

After a sleepless night I've decided what I will do. I will excise Anna from all of this as quickly as I can. I owe it to her. It'll be difficult for her, I know, but it'll be the best thing. The sooner she is freed of my burdens the better. I'll suffer my fate alone, without dragging her in any deeper. Hopefully, she will have determined this same course of action on her own last night and we can get on with it smoothly. If she resists, I'll tell her the whole story. Surely that will convince her to just leave me to my own deserved fate. I feel good about this decision, owning up to things myself, taking responsibility for my actions the way that I should have years ago. I am energized by the fact that I have a plan.

My musings are interrupted by a guard. "Your lawyer, Mrs. Fraser, is here for you. Let's go."

I follow the blue line back to where I came from last evening, entering another counsel room, this one the exact same as yesterday, except the table has a tray of sandwiches and muffins with some fruit and two large paper cups of coffee.

"I have your clothes in the car," Anna says, surprisingly perky. "And your phone and laptop. I stopped at the clinic on the way here and picked them up. Steve's talking to the US Attorney's Office this morning, and he's going to call the State Department. He'll petition the court as soon as it opens for a writ of habeas corpus. That'll at least get you in front of a judge, and hopefully get you out of here."

"I thought there was no bail for these kinds of things?" I say.

"There is no bail in extradition cases, but they still have to show some cause for holding you. They still have to show an indictment, and they haven't done that yet. If they don't by the end of the day, we'll argue that there is some mistake. Maybe get them to drop the provisional arrest."

"Thank you for the food, Anna. I'm starved." I haven't eaten since a quick lunch in my office yesterday. Taking the lid off one of the cups of coffee, I inhale the aroma and take a sip.

"Mark left a dozen messages yesterday," Anna says. "So, I called him at home last night and told him we think there is a big misunderstanding. I saw him at the clinic this morning, and he said not to worry about your appointments. They'll take care of them."

I nod my head as Anna continues. "He also mentioned that someone from the *Sun Valley Herald* had already been in this morning to ask them what happened there yesterday."

"Nothing goes down in that neighborhood without everyone knowing about it," I say. "What did he tell them?"

"Just what I told him last night. That there was a big mistake and it would be taken care of today."

Trying to summon the resolution I had come to in my cell I take a deep breath. "There's no mistake, Anna. I have been arrested, I will be tried, and I am guilty." I want this to sink in so that's all I say.

"No," she says, dismissing my statement firmly. She is defiant and stares me in the eye.

"Anna, I have done terrible things, things you know nothing about. Perhaps I should have told you before. No, that's wrong—I *definitely* should have told you before. I accept all the blame for hiding these things from you. I won't hide anything anymore. But I don't want you involved in it. I don't want your life ruined any more than it already has been. I've fucked things up for you already. I will go back to Africa and face this like I need to. But you need to understand, I—"

Spontaneously, out of the blue, she slaps me hard across the side of my face. "Shut up! Shut the fuck up!" she screams, stunning me to speechlessness. I'm stunned that she has screamed at me; she almost never does that. Shocked that she swore; I've seldom heard that from her. And dumbfounded that she has hit me; she has never done that before—ever.

"Quit being so fucking pitiful," she says. "Whatever these things are that you might have done, you were a child—a minor. You're not guilty. You're not going anywhere. And I *am* involved in it. I'm your wife. We're in it together and we'll get through it together."

Tears run down my cheeks. I am humiliated and small, even as I stand over her, looking down to her. I'm not sure what to say. "I'm sorry, Anna. I'm sorry. I'm sorry for the way I am. Sorry for the things I've done. I never wanted to hurt you, Anna. I'm sorry."

Leaning into my chest, she begins to sob and reaches around me, holding on to me tightly.

"I know you'd never hurt me, Freddie. You never have. Whoever you were as Azikiwe, I don't care. I married Alfred. Alfred is all I know. You're not Azikiwe. You're the kindest person I've ever known. You're a doctor. You heal people. You save people. That's the only truth I've ever needed." She steps back from me and reaches up with her hand, wiping the tears from my cheek, and then very tenderly traces the line of my scar down across my forehead. "We'll get through this, Alfred. We'll get through it together."

There's a knock and Steve May steps in, closing the door behind him. Seeing us, distraught as we are, he asks if we'd like him to come back.

Anna wipes her eyes with her sleeve. "No, it's fine, Steve."

He suggests we sit, and Anna and I each take a chair close beside one another, holding hands. Steve sits across the table. "Okay, State Department says they're expecting to have everything formalized by this afternoon. We'll know exactly what we're up against then. We've got a judge at three-thirty today. I've talked to the US Attorney's Office and one way or another we'll get you out of here today. Depending on what State sends over we can argue for improper confinement. If that doesn't work, Laura Abroud has agreed to electronic monitoring. We'll ask the judge to authorize that, and you can be at home for Christmas.

"Is there anything you need to know, Alfred? Any questions?"

I'm only half paying attention to Steve. I just want to get this whole thing over. "No. I can't think of anything. Thanks, Steve."

"Anything *I* should know?" he asks. "Anything you might have thought of since last night?"

"Steve, I've made a decision. I don't want to fight. I've decided to own up to things and face my consequences."

Steve looks at Anna, and I can see out of the corner of my eye that she is shaking her head, "no."

"What do you mean?" he asks. "Go to the Congo or Tanzania to face some kangaroo court? Bullshit. Of course you're going to fight."

I sit silently, but Anna responds. "Thanks, Steve. Let us know if you hear anything, and we'll see you this afternoon."

As soon as Steve leaves Anna turns to me. "He's right, Freddie. You can't let yourself be crucified in some place where we have no idea what their laws even are—or how fair their courts are." She knows that she hasn't convinced me, and I can see she is trying another tack when she adds, "Some of this is my fault."

"Don't be silly, Anna. None of this is your fault. This is me. It's all my doing."

"No," she says. "I shouldn't have let it go this far. I knew you were suffering. We should've gotten you help long ago. *I* let this go on too long."

"That wouldn't have made a bit of difference, Anna. The things I did twenty-five years ago, I did. *I* did them. No one else. It wouldn't have mattered if I'd gone to a shrink or a thousand shrinks. It wouldn't have mattered if they waved a magic wand and cured me. I still did those things. I'd still have a warrant for my arrest, and I'd still be going back to Africa for my accounting."

This makes Anna pause. "All right. I'm sorry, Freddie. We'll do whatever you think is right. But *we* will do it together. I'm going with you wherever you go."

"Thank you, Anna. Truly. But I've caused you enough trouble, enough pain already."

"Would you fucking stop that!" she erupts again. "Quit pitying yourself. We're in this together. *We.* Do you understand? *We! You* and *me.* You're my husband, and I'm your wife. Without Stephanie, what else do we have? Nothing. And nothing is going to come between us."

How can I not weep at this undeserved love that Anna just keeps giving me? I do, I weep without tears, from every pore of my soul.

We're silent for a long time, when Anna finally asks if there's anything I want to talk about.

"Yes, Anna. I want to talk about it all. If you'll listen, I want you to know it all. Please."

I close my eyes, thinking how I should begin, trying to conjure up the memories that I have spent most of my life trying to erase. I've done everything I could for more than twenty years to hide these memories, bury them, pretend they didn't happen, ignore them, and deny them. And, as a testament to how utterly unsuccessful I have been at this, they come flooding back in an instant, all as vivid as I see them in the nightmares that have awakened me many times over the years, leaving me sweating profusely and crying like a baby in Anna's arms.

I had, of course, told Anna over the years that I was an orphan, but as was typical I didn't tell her the entire truth. She knew that my parents died when I was young and that I was largely schooled by missionaries in Kigali, but I never told her that I was twice orphaned, that Uncle Dzigbote and Auntie Nyaka were my adopted parents. So, I begin by telling her of my life in the village with them, how in my childhood innocence I had no concept of poverty and felt that I lived as well as any other human on the planet. And because I knew no differently, I was perfectly happy and secure.

At first it is difficult to verbalize the scene, to explain to Anna what I felt as my aunt and uncle were murdered while I was helplessly restrained nearby. The sight has played out countless times in my mind, but I've never put it into words before. Still, the initial challenge quickly dissolves, and I become caught up in unloading the burden that I have been carrying.

I spew out the story of Uncle Dzigbote's killing and then how all four of my captors first raped Auntie Nyaka before also killing her and sending her lifeless body away in the current. I try to explain to Anna how I think that I was too young at the time to process much of what was happening around me, telling her I am not sure if I was at fault at that young age for not having resisted my captors more. As I look back, I realize that from the moment I witnessed those first two deaths I had begun to succumb to the depravity of humanity's lowest common denominators: slavery, poverty, hopelessness, and despair. I had been plucked from the comfort and innocence of a happy childhood and dumped into a cesspool.

As much as I may wish *now* that I had fought harder to escape the situation, as a young boy I somehow resigned myself to it. I wish I could explain why, but the best I've come up with over the years is that I was reacting to some innate instinct to simply survive—and doing it by the path of least resistance.

Africa

After they rolled Auntie Nyaka's lifeless, naked body into the river and made sure that it caught in the current, the four men stepped onto their flat-deck boat. They shoved it back into the stream, and with two hands the boat driver pulled on a cord, bringing the motor to life. He steered it upstream, *pud, pud, pud.* My wrists were bound in front of me, and the other end of the ten-foot rope was tied to the boat deck. They had stuffed my mouth with a section of Auntie Nyaka's bolt, which prevented me from making more than a whimper, but I cried—as any other child would, having just witnessed the deaths of his parents.

The man with the gun, the fat one, said in Swahili, "Let's kill the boy. Dump him now."

One of the others responded, "We'll take him with us. We can sell him at the mine."

"No, Idi. He'll be nothing but trouble," the fat man said.

The one called Idi turned to me and asked in Swahili, "Do you understand me? Shake your head yes or no." The cloth in my mouth stopped me from speaking but I refused to even shake my head for him. I glared at him through my tears. "These other men want to kill you," he said. "Answer me, or we will have to." I really didn't care if they killed me, I was too young and too shocked to be deciding between life and death. Idi pulled the cloth out of my mouth. "What language do you speak? Do you speak Swahili?"

I looked at them but said nothing. The fat one with the gun took four long steps in the boat, back toward me. I expected him to shoot me, but he grabbed me by one arm and one leg and lifted me up as he shouted at me, "You little fucker. If the crocodiles don't eat you, we'll give you one more chance to speak. One more, and then I'll kill you."

And with a single swing he tossed me off the back of the boat. The rope sprung taut as soon as I hit the water, my arms jerked forward, and I instinctively stuck my head high searching for air. But my face was plowing the surface, and I couldn't breathe. I rolled onto my back and was able to suck a gasp of air in through my mouth. With my arms extended over my head and the rope tied to my wrists, they towed me through the water. Until I was able to find the right position, water kept rolling over my face not allowing me to breathe without also sucking water into my lungs. Eventually I settled with my head above water and the backs of my shoulders breaking the water, acting as a prow, and the boat *pudded* along. It wasn't comfortable, but it was preferable to being in the boat with those men—until I noticed the yellow eyes and brown snouts of the crocodiles floating by the river's edge. This brought a terror to me. I had seen what the crocodiles could do to animals much bigger than me.

Death by gunshot suddenly seemed the better option, and I tried to wriggle the rope to signal the men in the boat. But the more I struggled with the rope to attract their attention the more I was also attracting the crocodiles. One large beast basking on the shore took note of me and with surprising speed sprang into the water. I watched its powerful tail whip side to side as it propelled itself toward me. I thrashed harder and shouted, "Swahili, I speak Swahili! And Kinyarwanda."

Just as I was about to be taken by the crocodile I was jerked straight up in the air and hoisted onto the back of the boat. I gasped for air while Idi pushed his face within inches of mine and laughed hard.

"So, you speak Swahili and Kinyarwanda? That's good." He turned to the others and said, "See? He might be useful to us."

"You should have left him in the water, and we wouldn't have had to waste a bullet on him," said the first man with the gun. He was the one who had shot Uncle Dzigbote and Auntie Nyaka.

"You see how easily Kakengo will kill you?" Idi asked me. "You be a good boy, or I'll have to let him. What's your name?"

I just stared at him, determined to show defiance.

Kakengo didn't waste any time. He kicked me hard, and I tumbled back into the water. In a second the rope was stretched back out and I was gasping for breath again.

"Azikiwe. I am Azikiwe."

"Azikiwe?" Idi fished me out again. "They call you Azikiwe?"

Once I had caught my breath I said, "I am Azikiwe. But they call me Azi."

"That's a good boy. I am Idi. You can speak Swahili and Kinyarwanda, Azi?"

I nodded.

"Good," he replied and left me sitting there while he stood to talk to the others.

The boat continued to *pud* along for the rest of the afternoon. I sat naked on the flat deck with the men paying little attention to me. Three of them, Idi, Kakengo, and the other one, lay on the deck, dozing frequently. Only the boat driver stayed awake. Four large chests were welded to the metal deck of the boat, two on each side. These doubled as seats, and every once in a while the men would wake, stretch out, and then take a seat. From a tin canister they would pull out wads of tobacco, rolling themselves cigarettes by wrapping the tobacco in banana leaves.

I'd never been this far upstream on our river. The waterway didn't seem to get much wider or much narrower; it just meandered along for miles and miles. When the sun started to dip below the treetops the driver found a shallow shore where he steered the boat up until it was grounded. The men opened one of the large chests and took out some cooking gear and food and built a small fire on the shore. They continued to ignore or forget me while I watched them eat. I was hungry but wasn't about to grovel to them for anything. In fact, when they finished and Idi finally came to me with a small bowl of millet meal I pushed it away, intent on demonstrating defiance. It didn't seem to bother him, he simply shrugged and took away the bowl.

They cinched my rope shorter and left me tied on the deck like that all night, totally naked with no bedding. I watched them lay out their bedrolls on the flat deck and then fall asleep. I was afraid in the open like this. I'd never slept outside of our mud house. Uncle Dzigbote had often warned me of the creatures that came out in the night in the jungle. Shivering and afraid, I searched the shoreline, picking out eyes that reflected in different colors in the moonlight. I wasn't sure to which animals they belonged, as they appeared only intermittently and for short periods of time from behind the bushes or rising above the water's surface. Eventually even the cold and the fear couldn't keep me awake, and my eyes closed until a light kick in my ribs got my attention.

It took me a few moments to get my bearings, woken in the damp darkness like that. The despair that I had fallen asleep with returned in a wave.

"Eat this," Idi said as he handed me plantain, cooked and mashed and served on a banana leaf. But the same defiance from yesterday was back with me and I just shook my head.

"Fine," was all he said.

By the time dawn started to show the camp had been cleaned up and the boat driver steered the craft back upriver, *pud, pud, pud*. I was glad to see the sun break the treetops an hour later because I shivered in the cool dew that had settled on me during the night. We continued upriver for hours while the men trawled lines from the boat. They managed to catch enough fish by midday for us to stop and make a fire to cook them. As much as I wanted to be strong, my sunken belly out-willed my stubbornness and I accepted the food at this meal.

"That's good," said Idi. "No sense in being stupid. You're a smart boy.

You know that you need to eat, and you know that we'll not hurt you if you do as you're told."

The nourishment did bring some sense back to me, and I began to think a little more clearly. I set my mind to devising my escape. A short while later it seemed I was about to get some help with my scheming when Idi came to address me. "Azi, I'm going to cut your hands free. You'll do as we say?"

I nodded and then said, "My shorts are gone."

"Yes," said Idi. "You won't want to run away too far. If you do try to run, I'll tie you by your pecker next time." He let out a big laugh like he had just made a funny joke.

Late that afternoon we came to a place where a bridge crossed the river and the boat driver pulled us into shore directly beneath it. I heard Kakengo say to Idi, "We should kill that kid. He's just going to be trouble for us."

Idi came back to me. "You heard what Kakengo says, he wants to kill you. If you do what I say we won't kill you. But if you cause us any trouble, we will. Do you understand?"

I nodded.

"We're going to meet some people here. If they don't speak Swahili you're going to speak to them in Kinyarwanda for me. Do you know what I mean?"

I nodded again.

"Good." He took a shirt from one of the boxes and tore it for me so that I could wrap it around my waist like a loincloth.

And then we waited. No one showed by sundown, so the men made a small camp under the bridge, but they made no fire that night. Taking no chances, they retied me to the boat. I slept better that second night with food in my stomach and the bridge above to keep the dew off. Having learned I was better off staying quiet and obedient, I did just that and was rewarded by them untying me again during the daytime. We waited in the shade under the bridge all the next day and it was late in the afternoon before we heard a convoy of trucks coming along the roadway.

The three men, Idi, Kakengo, and the third, opened one of the chests and pulled out holsters with pistols in them and then they sent the boat driver up top on the bridge. Idi came over to me, knelt down, and looked me straight in the eye.

"Azi," he said. "We're going to meet some men. If I need you to, you will speak for me to the other men. But you're not to say a word unless I tell you to. Do you understand?"

Kakengo was standing over us and pulled his gun from its holster. Holding it out straight-armed, he firmly ground the muzzle into my skull.

"Do you understand?" Idi repeated.

I nodded my head.

We could hear the convoy of vehicles up top pulling to a stop as the boat driver flagged them down. A few minutes later eight or nine soldiers carrying machine guns escorted the boat driver down the embankment to where we were. The boat driver had his arms raised over his head, and one of the soldiers had a gun pointed into his back. Trailing them all was an officer. He carried no weapons except his pistol, still holstered. I felt a wave of relief with my rescue imminent.

The officer walked past his men and stepped onto the boat deck.

"Good day, gentlemen," he said, addressing my captors in Kinyarwanda. I was joyed to hear the sound of the language that I knew my captors could not understand. My hopes soared.

Idi spoke in Swahili. "Captain, thank you for meeting us."

The officer switched to Swahili. "*Major ... Major* Ntagura. You have something for me?"

Kakengo nodded to the boat captain who went to one of the chests that were locked with large padlocks. He spun off a combination, flipped up the lid, and removed a small but obviously very heavy sack. He set it on the deck and untied the top. Major Ntagura went over to the sack and scooped into it with cupped hands, letting the contents, small black nuggets, dribble back into the bag.

"Very nice," Major Ntagura said, nodding his head with a big smile.

"No, *excellent*," Idi said. "Guaranteed over thirty percent. You won't find this purity anywhere else."

"How much do you have?" the major asked.

"We have eighty kilos here."

"How much can you get?"

"The same, every two weeks."

"Twenty-five hundred francs a kilo," the major said.

Idi smiled. "American. US dollars. And a special price for you, Major. Ten US a kilo, eight hundred dollars for this. The rest in hardware."

The majored nodded to him.

"And," Idi added, "safe passage on the roads from the border to here, every second week."

"Don't you ever fuck me, or I'll give you safe passage to hell," the major replied before instructing his men to take the sack, along with the three others that remained in the chest. Four men threw the sacks over their shoulders and lugged them up the embankment. A few minutes later they returned carrying six rifles, two machine guns, and two heavy boxes of ammunition. The major indicated for them to set the boxes on the deck, and one of the men handed the major a pouch from which he counted eight hundred strange bills. As he went to hand it to Idi, Kakengo stepped forward and snatched the cash. The major looked from Kakengo to Idi and then shrugged his eyes.

If I was going to have any chance of escaping I was going to have to do it now. Until now, not one of them had paid me the slightest attention. As the major turned to leave I dashed toward him, fell to my knees at his feet, and grabbed him by the leg, hugging tightly.

"What's this?" asked the major.

"My nephew," Idi responded quickly. "He's with us for the ride."

I looked up at the major and spoke quickly and imploringly to him in Kinyarwanda. "Sir, please, he's not my uncle. These men killed my uncle and aunt. They have taken me. Please help me."

The major looked down on me with a serious face and picked me up in his arms. He held me to his chest and I wrapped my arms around his neck, embracing him snugly.

Idi glanced nervously at his comrades. "What does he say to you, Major?"

The major pried me off and held me out for Idi to take. "He says that you're his favorite uncle and he loves you."

With that he walked off the boat and his men followed him up to the bridge. Idi set me down on the deck and I started to sob. Kakengo took two steps toward me and swatted me with a large hand across the side of my head. He turned to walk away but then abruptly came back and kicked me in the ribs. I coughed and sputtered and cried like the child I was, alone, without hope. Once again, Idi tied me by my wrists to the length of rope again.

While I whimpered in my corner of the boat the men were in a jovial mood. They set camp in good spirits, enhanced by the homemade booze that they retrieved from their supplies. Emboldened, they built a large fire and laughed. Examining the new weapons that they'd received, they tested each of them by firing rounds into the sky. They cooked a large meal but offered me none. In fact, they paid me no attention; they'd forgotten me again, or so I thought.

Well after dark, when all but Kakengo had drunkenly fallen asleep, he called me over to where he sat on one of the chests. I looked at him, afraid to venture close. He pointed a pistol at me and said, "Get over here right now, you fucker."

I crawled across the deck to him and he reached down with his big meaty left hand, clamping it around my small ankle. Holding me like that, with one foot up in the air, he casually took a long puff on his homemade cigarette. He then took the cigarette from his mouth between his finger and thumb and held the lit end to the bottom of my foot. I wailed in pain while he held it there, searing me. My screams woke the others but only enough to have them grunt for me to be quiet. Kakengo put down the cigarette and transferred his grip to my throat, squeezing it with one big hand. He drew me close to his face, his steamy breath stinking. He looked at me for a long moment before spitting in my eyes.

"Fucker." He dropped me to the deck, and I scampered as quickly as I could to my corner of the boat.

I hated that man with every bit of my being.

The trip back downriver was swifter; we had the current behind us and were able to make better time. The men remained in high spirits, likely encouraged by their new arrangement with Major Ntagura. Their chests puffed out with their new stature, and it was manifest toward me in two very different ways. Idi used his newfound importance and doled a small level of benevolence to me while Kakengo demanded I demonstrate total subservience to him. Idi fed me; Kakengo insulted me and whacked me whenever he felt inclined. On the first day heading downriver Kakengo insisted on keeping me tied by my length of rope. Whenever he saw an area of crocodile infestation he would kick me overboard, taking pleasure in my terror. Idi fished me out several times before standing up to Kakengo.

"That's enough, Kakengo. Don't do it again."

"The boy will develop courage," Kakengo said.

"The boy will be dead, and then he's worth nothing," Idi countered. "He's worth two thousand francs at the mine, but I might keep this one myself."

They kept me tied up the entire first day and night of our journey back downriver, until we were well past the area of my village. Our stop the first night was only a little way past the place where Kakengo had killed Uncle Dzigbote and Auntie Nyaka. I hardly slept at all that night, thinking about them both. Uncle Dzigbote had taken me into his home when I was two. My father had been killed by the same sort of thugs who now held me and had only a few days ago killed my aunt and uncle. Uncle Dzigbote took both my mother and me into his care and his home to live with him and his wife, Auntie Nyaka. My mother died very soon after that when she contracted the sleeping fever that seemed to curse many of the pregnant women in our village. Auntie Nyaka told me this family history because at that age I had no memories of what had happened to either my father or mother. Nyaka, "precious" in our language, and Dzigbote, "patience," became my mother and father. They were each both precious and patient. They, having no children of their own, and I, an orphan, became a family. They were the only family I had ever known, and at that young age I was oblivious to the facts of orphanhood and hardship.

I have many memories of my childhood, many pleasant memories, before they killed Uncle Dzigbote and Auntie Nyaka. Most of these involved the comforting smotherings and gentle smiles of Auntie Nyaka. Rarely would I look for her and not see her eyes already focused my way. Or if she were busy with some task, she was never so busy that she wasn't regularly finding me with those deep dark pools of envelopment. The love and affection that Auntie Nyaka endlessly showed me gave me a sense of security and happiness that I just assumed would always be there. And then, when it was gone, I was certain that I would never again find someone who loved me in such a wholesome, all-encompassing outpouring.

On the second day downriver Idi untied my wrists, but I might as well have still been shackled. I was too afraid of any of them to venture near them and I stayed in my corner at the back of the boat. I thought of jumping off and swimming to shore but knew I'd be an easy target for them in the water. Even on shore, I could not survive alone in the jungle long enough to find my way back to the village. After lunch on this day the men unloaded everything from the chest where they stored the guns. They laid it all out on the deck, and Idi gave me two rags and poured some oil into a tin can. One at a time he brought the guns over to me and slipped the bolts open to show me that they were empty of cartridges. He showed me how to use just the right amount of oil on a rag to scrub the dirty and rusty spots, cleaning and lubricating the entire weapon. The second rag I used to wipe off the excess oil and to polish a dull gleam into the guns. The work helped take my mind off my plight.

I was surprised at the number of parts to each gun. With Idi inspecting each one when I handed it back to him, I was diligent in cleaning every crevice. Some of the rifles were almost too heavy for me to lift—they were longer than I was, and I manipulated them by working on one end at a time. Even some of the handguns were too heavy for me to hold steady, but there was one that was smaller. I picked it up with both hands and extended it out like I had seen done, my forefinger braced around the trigger. Kakengo was snoozing on the front of the boat with his eyes closed. I swiveled the gun around in his direction and looked down the barrel, setting him up in my sights. With great care and calculation I squeezed the trigger. When I looked toward Idi I saw that he was watching me, staring straight at me. As our eyes met, the corners of his mouth curled up ever so slightly. He came over and took the gun from me, replacing it with a machine gun.

I was surprised at its modest weight. "It's not so heavy," I said.

He picked a full magazine out from the ammunition stash, flipped the catch, and shoved it into place. The weight unexpectedly doubled in my hands, and I held the gun with my arms hung down, fully extended. I went to rest my finger on the trigger, and before I even felt it the gun exploded, *ratttattaattattataatatt*, jerking my arms back and pulling me to the deck with it. Almost as quickly as the gun had fired, Kakengo was across the deck. He grabbed the gun and dropped on me with one knee in my chest. I couldn't breathe with his full fat weight on me.

"What the fuck are you doing?" he screamed. "What the fuck is he doing with ammo, Idi? Are you fucking nuts?"

Idi started laughing hard. "I told him to wake you up."

"Are you fucking crazy?" Kakengo shouted. "I should shoot both you fuckers."

"The kid needs to learn how to use a gun," Idi said.

"Not a fucking machine gun."

Kakengo stood while Idi continued laughing. I didn't think it was the least bit funny. I could have been killed the way Kakengo had dropped his knee onto me. I tried to catch my breath as I watched Kakengo move his face close to Idi's. Idi's laughter died and he bored into Kakengo's eyes. The coiled vipers faced each other for a slow moment—but neither of them struck. Kakengo finally sneered, picked up the machine gun, and released the catch, allowing the magazine to fall to the deck with a loud clang.

The next day the slow river of my village emptied itself into a much larger one, and our boat *pudded* out into it, moving even faster with the stronger current. After the incident with the gun Idi made sure that both he and I gave some space to Kakengo and stayed out of his way for the rest of the journey. On the fourth day after selling the heavy sacks to the major, our boat driver steered us up a small creek. He angled the motor up to the surface of the water because the creek was so shallow it couldn't take the full depth. At some places it was also barely wide enough for the boat to slip through; thick lush jungle in a thousand different shades of green reached out over the banks, stretching to find sunlight. Suddenly, without warning Idi pointed his pistol in the air and shot off two quick rounds, paused just a second, and fired a third. A few moments after this we came to a spot where the boat just couldn't go any farther. A giant of a man stood on the shore, pointed his rifle overhead, fired off two shots in succession, paused, and let a third one go, and then reached out and tied our boat to some trees.

Once our motor was shut off, I could hear a commotion of other sounds in the distance, farther upstream. The sound of another motor droning competed with running water, the clinks and clanks of machines and equipment, and the murmuring babel of many voices. The men began to unload our empty fuel cans and the weapons and gear from the chests on the boat. Idi directed me to jump to the shore to help with the task. Within minutes six others, armed with rifles and pistols, broke from a path in the bush. They were boys, much older than me, but not yet men. Some had the patchy whiskers of almost being there, and muscles tough and stringy, but not quite the full bulk of manhood. These six and the four from our boat easily hauled the entire load we had to carry. Kakengo led the way on the path back into the bush and Idi brought up the rear, with me just in front of him, limping to take some of the weight off my foot that Kakengo had burned. Idi tapped me from behind on the shoulder and handed me part of his load, weighing me down with as much as I could handle.

The path into the bush did not go far before it led us through a narrow crevice in a small escarpment. The other side of the bluff opened to a large clearing, perhaps fifty yards wide by a hundred and fifty long, where the jungle was missing, replaced by red-brown muck. The far side of the clearing was separated from the jungle by strands of razor wire coiling the entire perimeter. On this side of the clearing the rock ledge made a natural barrier, but in spacing along the top of it, guards sat with rifles or machine guns leaning against their shoulders. The creek we had been following ran through the muck field but was barely identifiable, having been dammed and diverted through at least a dozen different sluiceways. Seventy or eighty people, all colored the same red-brown from their necks down, toiled in the muck. Some of these were men, some boys, others in between.

At the farthest end from us a large wooden cabin sat surrounded by a haphazard group of plank sheds. Off to one side a small village of tents, everything the same mucky red-brown color, peppered a patch of muddy ground. We trudged a path along the bluff toward the cabin and sheds. As we continued around to the far side of the cabin, a green lawn, manicured with gardens, surprised me. A table was set with fruit, a platter of fried fish, and a large bowl of rice. A tall thin man, black but not black like the rest of us, dressed in a clean and pressed safari suit rose from his seat at the table.

"I thought perhaps you'd decided to take off with my coltan," he said, looking first at Idi and then at Kakengo, deadly serious.

"We'll wait for a bigger load than that. Then we'll steal it," Kakengo replied, and laughed at his own joke.

The man in the suit didn't laugh. "Did you find them?"

"We did. I think we can trust him. He looked greedy. Said he'd take a load every two weeks."

"What did he pay?"

Idi spoke up, "For the eighty kilos we delivered we got nine dollars a kilo from him, seven hundred and twenty dollars US." Idi pulled the pouch of money out and began to count it out. "Fifty for Kakengo and me for arranging it and one hundred for our twelve men for the last month. Five hundred US dollars for you, Gregoire." Idi handed it to him.

"When I find out what he really paid you, I'll take it off your fees," Gregoire said. "How much for the boy? I'll give you five dollars for him." I was surprised he'd even noticed me.

"I'll keep this one for myself," Idi said. "He's already pretty good with a machine gun."

Kakengo glared at Idi. "Take the money," he said. "The fucking boy's not worth five dollars."

"I'll keep him," Idi responded firmly.

"Then pay me for half. Two dollars and fifty cents," Kakengo said.

But before Idi had a chance to respond two mud-brown skeletons appeared, whimpering indecipherably and prodded ahead by the barrel of an automatic rifle. The lighter-skinned man dressed in the suit, Gregoire, barked at the owner of the weapon, "What's the problem?"

"Master Gobeni, these two were caught on the path to the boats," the captor said.

Both men had already dropped to their knees and were groveling at the same time. I could see the pleading in their eyes, and although their speech was unintelligible through their stammering it was unmistakably a piteous beseeching for mercy. I could not make out whether they were old or young men, so weathered was the bit of skin that showed through the caking of red-brown mud that coated most of their bodies. I had seen hungry people, but I had never seen the effects of real starvation on a man's body until these two dropped in front of us. Neither of them had any meat covering their bones, and when they bent over in pathetic supplication to the man in the suit, every vertebra in their back and each rib stood out, clearly identifiable.

"Take these two to the sluicing wash," Gregoire Gobeni said.

It was obvious who was in command of this place. Even Idi and Kakengo jumped at the direction issued by Gobeni, and when neither of the two prisoners made any move to get up from their knees, Idi ordered two of the others with us to take them by their legs. The skeletons clawed at the ground desperately as they were dragged around the cabin and out to the center of the cleared work area through which we had just arrived. We followed, creating a procession that demanded the attention of nearly all the other men working on the site. The sluice wash seemed to be the center of the entire operation, and the several channels of water that had been ditched out through the site were all diverted to this one area where a team of two men sat, continuously cranking around large handles in unison, which in turn propelled an upright waterwheel, lifting the water up in its paddle buckets and dumping it into an angled wooden trough. When we arrived at the sluice, Gobeni blew on a shrill whistle that brought the entire site to a standstill. A second blow beckoned virtually everyone within hearing distance to leave what they were doing and gather around.

This was the first time that I had noticed that there were not just men and boys on the site but that there were also several girls and women who emerged from the small village of tents on the far side of the clearing. Like the men and boys, they too were coated in the same red-brown dried muck. Even the few clothes which they wore were similarly soiled the same color as their bare skin. None of them, not one of the males nor any of the females, had any extra flesh on their bodies. The same could not be said for Gobeni or Idi or Kakengo, or any of the men that carried weapons. In fact, Kakengo was corpulent and powerful, with a fleshiness that stood out even more when viewed beside the laborers in this place.

The two men who had been dragged by their legs once again hunched over on their knees at Gobeni's feet and whimpered. Gobeni had brought a machete with him and he patted the flat edge of it in the palm of one hand as he waited for everyone to gather. No one spoke a word, save the two groveling souls on the ground. Once we were assembled Gobeni nodded to Kakengo who silenced the two men by kicking them hard several times in the sides of their heads. The motor and machinery that I'd heard when we arrived had been shut down, and now even the two men turning the sluice crank stopped working. The quiet itself was frightening.

Gobeni broke the silence by speaking to the crowd in a calm and measured tone. "It seems that, in spite of the fact that everyone here has a roof over his head and food for his belly each day, there are some who are so ungrateful they choose to leave." Then, speaking directly to the two men at his feet, he said, "Straighten up on your knees."

Both men feebly obeyed but hung their heads in resignation. Gobeni walked behind the men and lifted the machete high above his head in show. My stomach churned, and I felt I might vomit as I waited for the first man's head to be lopped off. But in a quick move Gobeni lowered the machete, and with one long swift slice he severed the tendons in the backs of all four ankles of both men. The two men screamed in agony and fell face forward into the mud. Their feet drooped limply from where they remained attached to the bottoms of their legs, and blood flowed freely from the wounds, turning black as it pooled in the mud around it.

Gobeni blew on his whistle and the crowd began to disperse, the waterwheel started up again, and the din of the worksite began to rise to its previous clamor. A few of the other men picked up their punished comrades, removing them to the tented village. I had been so aghast at what had just happened that I didn't realize I was the only one not moving until Kakengo swatted me on the side of the head.

"A good lesson for you on your first day, you little fucker—the slash of the elephant hunters."

I later learned that the severing of the back ankle of an elephant is an ancient method used by hunters for eons to down the great beasts.

"What'll happen to them now?" I asked.

"They won't run away again, that's for sure." Kakengo laughed.

"Will they die?"

"Maybe. But probably not," he said. "They'll be well enough in a few days to turn this waterwheel."

As I started to limp away, still smarting from the cigarette burn Kakengo had put on the bottom of my foot a few days earlier, and following in the direction that Idi had gone, I heard a soft whisper from Kakengo behind me, "Azi ..."

I froze in my tracks as I felt the metal of his machete blade slide across the Achilles tendon of my trailing foot. I was afraid to look down at the damage I feared I would find, and the terror he instilled in me wouldn't allow me to think coherently. I remained stalled in my tracks with tears running down my cheeks until he whacked me on my backside with the flat edge of his machete and laughed uproariously while warning me, "You even think about sneaking away and I'll use the sharp edge the next time, you fucker."

One of those two men must have died because I never saw him again, but the other one did survive, and I saw him often in the camp. Each morning when the sun came up he crawled to his spot at the waterwheel where he sat all day, incessantly turning the crank handle until the sun went down at night, whence he crawled back to the tents. It was too much effort for him to get back and forth at the lunch break, so one of the camp women brought his gruel to him. Similarly, it was too much for him to drag himself to the latrines and several times I witnessed him simply relieving himself right where he sat at his wheel. This went on for many months until one day there was nothing left in the man and he quietly expired as the sun was coming up and he was halfway across the camp to his station. He just quit crawling and lay in the mud.

But Kakengo was right. That was a good lesson for me that first day. It scared me into total resignation, as I'm sure it did any of the others in the camp who might have harbored any thoughts of leaving, or rather escaping. And even though I was Idi's property, not Gobeni's, I did not want to test the limits of any of them.

I have no idea why Idi kept me rather than selling me to Gregoire Gobeni, but as much as I hated him then, and continue to hate him to this day, it probably saved my life. I don't think that I could have survived in that camp alone at that age. It's true, there were a few other younger boys who worked as slaves doing a variety of jobs, but they all had some family confined there with them. They were able to treat and feed each other and tend to the basic human needs of one another. I am sure that alone I would have perished. Indeed, there were many who did succumb to the overwork and undernourishment. I can't count the number of pitiable bodies I saw just drop at their work stations only to be dragged away and left to slowly die in the scorching sun. And there must have been many others who died in their tents during the nights because often I noticed that someone who had been wasting away simply would stop appearing for work.

As quickly as the emaciated workers died they were replaced by healthy, if often terrified, individuals. They came from a variety of sources. Sometimes men and older teenage boys would show up at the camp looking for work. These were never turned away. They were promised wages that never materialized and given just enough food to keep them hungry, but not starved, until eventually even these small food rations were cut. But by that time their wills had been broken, and they had become resigned to the same heartrending fate as everyone else. Sometimes, when more bodies were needed, Idi and his men went on recruiting drives to villages with promises of a better life at the camp. Whole families were sometimes lured into slavery with dreams of making a better life than they were currently eking out. And when this tactic didn't entice enough unwitting workers to fill the constant vacancies created by death, replacements were taken by force. I saw this several times, especially with the girls and women who were brought to the camp. Constant supplies of females were required to do the household chores of cooking and tending to the sick. Looking back, I now also realize that many women were brought into the camp to satisfy the sexual desires of Gobeni, Kakengo, Idi, and their men.

It took me several months to figure out the structure and workings of

the camp, and several more before I began to understand the business of
what was going on. After the fright I received on my first day in camp I
rarely spoke, except when spoken to, and I made myself as useful to Idi
as I could. At that young age I wasn't all that valuable, but I was quick to
learn the menial tasks he set me to. Much of what he had me do probably
wasn't even necessary, but it kept me busy. I was more like a pet monkey
to Idi than anything else. I slept at the foot of his bed and hung around
him constantly, waiting to be ordered to run some small errand. All the
while I tried to keep as much distance as I could between Kakengo and
myself. This was no easy task in the confines of the camp, and Kakengo
often found opportunities to make my life difficult.

It was a stroke of luck that Idi decided to keep me as his pet rather
than sell me to Gobeni, because Idi and his men, me included, never
went hungry. While dozens around us were starving, literally to death, we
ate well with a regular supply of hunted meat and fresh fish. And while
the workers in the camp were paid nothing other than subsistence food
rations, Idi's men were paid a monthly salary on top of their healthy food
allotments. When I first went to the camp I was glad just to receive food
to put in my belly, but gradually, over time, as I became more useful, Idi
started to pay me a small allowance. I now realize that this wage was Idi's
way of cunningly winning over my allegiance to him, and the wages paid
to the others were used as bribes to maintain their blind loyalty.

When I first arrived, Idi and Kakengo seemed to control about a dozen
of the armed guards, whose job it was to keep the work crews confined to
the site as well as to keep possible intruders out. At times they also acted
as bodyguards for Gregoire Gobeni, especially when he wanted to impress
any of the guests that he hosted in his cabin. Sometimes these guests
were important-looking men in suits and other times they were beautiful
women who would arrive and stay for three or four days. Whenever any
of these people were around, a great show of chest pounding went on,
augmented by a show of Idi's security team.

One night, several months after my arrival, while Gobeni was
entertaining two beautiful women in his cabin and Idi was away, I was
able to learn the true business of the camp. Up until then I had assumed

that the black pellets that Idi was shipping for Gobeni to Major Ntagura were gold. This just shows my naïveté at that age. I somehow knew that gold was a valuable commodity, but I had no idea what it looked like. In my mind there was no reason it couldn't be black, like the nuggets in the sacks. I discovered the difference on the same night I caught one of the guards peeping through the window into Gobeni's cabin.

With Idi gone, and little for me to do, I walked around to the manicured side of Gregoire Gobeni's cabin, the side with gardens and paint. It would not be uncommon to see a guard stationed at the front stoop, but this particular night I found the guard in a shadowed corner of the cabin with his pants down. He was so preoccupied peering over the windowsill into the lit room that he never heard me approach. When I looked over his shoulder and into the room I saw that Gobeni was naked with his two female guests. He was doing to them what I had seen Kakengo and the others do to Auntie Nyaka before they killed her. The guard with his pants down was himself panting and rubbing on his private parts hard and fast. This whole scene went on for several minutes until the guard finished his business with a loud grunt. I thought it was surely enough to alert Gobeni, but he was so engrossed in his own activities that he never noticed. I ventured closer to the guard. He was breathing heavily, and his pants were still at his ankles.

"Will he kill them?" I asked. The guard, thoroughly startled, scrambled to pull up his pants before reaching for his rifle and pointing it at me.

I don't think he could see me very well because he had to ask, "Who's there?" By that point, all of Idi's men knew me.

"It's me, Azi," I replied.

"Shhh …" he whispered and motioned toward the front stoop. We crept over there and sat on the step.

"Azi, what the fuck are you doing out here?"

I ignored his question and repeated my own. "Will he kill the two ladies?"

"Of course he won't kill them. What are you talking about?"

"After Kakengo put his man parts inside Auntie Nyaka he killed her," I said

The guard chuckled. "No, Master Gobeni likes these two. He wants to

fuck them again. We only kill the *bitches* after we fuck them. These aren't bitches."

This guard was somewhere between boyhood and manhood, and I could tell by his bravado that he was trying to impress me. His answer, however, was confusing because I didn't know if Auntie Nyaka was a bitch or not, but they'd certainly killed her.

Seeing that I wasn't interested in playing along with his bragging he asked me again, "What are you doing out here?"

"Idi's gone to deliver the gold," I replied, trying to sound important myself.

"What gold?"

"The gold in the sacks … to Major Ntagura." I spoke with authority.

The guard opened a small tin of hand-rolled cigarettes and pointed to it with his eyes. "Do you want one?"

"Sure." I took it and put it in my mouth, waiting for him to light it. I'd seen this done a million times, but I had never been offered one before. "What's your name?" I asked.

"Mamba." He held a match to the end of the cigarette which hung from my lips, but it didn't light. "Suck in, you dumb fuck, suck in."

I had seen that a million times too, I just forgot to do it. I pulled in a heavy breath and watched the end glow brightly before I promptly coughed, choked, and spit it on the ground. Mamba laughed and picked it up and drew a long puff on it himself before handing it back to me. "Start with a little puff, slowly."

"Mamba's a snake," I said. "Why did your mama name you after a snake?"

"Mama named me Antoine. Do I look like a fucking Antoine? I'm Mamba," he stated. "What's that about the gold? What gold are you talking about?"

"The gold we find in the water," I said as I tried to master a second puff.

"There's no gold here." Mamba laughed again. "That's coltan. It's much more valuable than gold. Gold is gold—it's yellow. Can't you see that's coltan? It's black as your ass. And we don't find it *in* the water, we just wash it out of the dirt *with* the water."

Now it made a bit more sense to me. That was why the workers spent all day digging the earth into baskets and carrying it to the water wheel.

"But it just looks like black pebbles to me," I said.

"Them pebbles worth a lot of money. 'Mericans and Chinese pay dearly for it."

I didn't know what a 'Merican or a Chinese was or what they did with it, and Mamba didn't know either. Mamba became my first quasi friend in the mine camp. If no one else was around he would acknowledge me, and we'd sometimes sit and have a smoke together. He was my main source of information about everything for the next few years. He seemed to enjoy imparting his worldly wisdom to me, so long as none of the other guards his age knew he was doing it. In exchange for answering my questions I think that he figured he was gaining some slight advantage with Idi by treating me well.

I later learned that the coltan we were mining was a shortened form of its real name, columbite-tantalite. Years later, through my own curious research, I discovered that coltan is a black metallic ore from which the Chinese and Americans extracted the rare element tantalum. Tantalum in turn was, and still is, used in the manufacture of components for cell phones, laptops, and other electronic devices. Back in the 1980s, it was only found in very few places in the world, primarily in our region of Zaire and Rwanda. With the explosion of consumer electronic devices at that time the prices for tantalum shot up, making it worth much more than gold. Mining operations in the remote jungle areas became very lucrative, especially with the use of slave labor. To avoid government interference with the slave camps, 90 percent of the coltan mined and sold in the world was funneled through the Rwandan army to outside sources in China, America, and Europe. None of this mattered to me at the time; back then it was all about day-to-day survival.

One of the other reasons Mamba enjoyed my company, after he got me hooked on smoking, was that I had easy access to Kakengo's supply of bulk tobacco, and I wasn't beyond snitching a handful every now and then. One afternoon while Mamba and I sat at his post puffing on some of this pilfered lot, Kakengo came along and found us. I suppose he had noticed some of his stash missing—at just eight years old I wasn't much of a crook yet—because when he saw us enjoying our smokes he knew immediately where the tobacco came from. He went straight for me, totally ignoring the fact that Mamba was puffing away along with me. It was clear that this was the excuse he had been waiting for.

I had seen Kakengo's temper before, and when he drew his pistol and aimed it directly at my forehead I began to shake. I wanted to be brave and stare him down, but I couldn't. I was too afraid to even raise my eyes to look at him.

"Mamba, get me a cane of bamboo. Green," Kakengo said. Mamba ran off quickly, returning moments later with the staff. A few others had seen Mamba returning with the fresh cane and followed him back, hoping to see what was happening.

"Take off your clothes, Azi," Kakengo said.

I did as I was told, grateful to receive only a caning rather than a bullet. But as I stripped, Kakengo took his machete and chopped the bamboo into a three-foot length and then proceeded to split the green wood from the end. He drew his machete two-thirds the length of the cane several times until one whole end of the cane was shredded into a dozen pliable razor-sharp lashes. More of a crowd gathered, slaves and guards both.

"Get on your hands and knees," he ordered me.

I had no alternative but to obey. The whip came down hard on my small back twice in succession before I collapsed, prone on the ground. I know he hit me several more times, but I was too agonized to count. When I heard a single gunshot ring out loudly, I was relieved that he was going to put me out of my misery. Blood ran around my sides and coated my whole torso, pooling in the dirt below me. The whipping had stopped, and I thought to lift myself to my knees, but my body just wouldn't move like my mind wanted it to.

I lay on my stomach for the next three weeks in the tent of one of the camp women, wavering between excruciating pain and unconsciousness. My back festered with infection, and I burned with fever. There were no antibiotics, and I relied completely on the poultice that the woman made from roots of reeds in the creek. Whether it helped or not, I don't know.

But I did slowly get better. I remember Idi and Mamba both coming in to see me several times during my recovery, and when I was finally able to sit upright Mamba visited and filled me in on what had happened.

Idi had fired his gun in the air, causing Kakengo to stop.

"What is going on here?" Idi asked.

"Your little fucker stole my tobacco," Kakengo replied.

"He's a baby, Kakengo. You're whipping him like a grown man."

"If he was a grown man, I'd have cut off his hands, Idi."

Idi lowered his gun and pointed it directly at Kakengo's face. This was in front of a large crowd of their own men. "Kakengo," he said, "if you ever touch that boy again I will kill you."

As Idi turned to walk away, Kakengo pulled his own revolver from his belt and raised it to Idi's back.

"I was sure the fat man was going to shoot him," Mamba reported to me. "I was sure of it."

But Idi swung around and marched right back to Kakengo, straight up to him with the gun coming closer and closer to his face, until it touched his nose. Stalemated like this for a few moments, Idi finally broke the tension, laughed, and slapped Kakengo on the shoulder saying, "Partner."

I didn't think I could hate Kakengo any more than I already did until he nearly killed me with that whipping, scarring my back and rump for the rest of my life with deeply cut wounds. But now I hated him with every speck of my being. I pledged to get my revenge someday, and I thought of myself, even at that young age, as a man for making such a vow. On the other hand, I was impressed that Idi had stuck up for me, and in such a public way, right in front of their men. And he had come to check on me while I was recovering. As much as I resented him for having been part of the killing of Uncle Dzigbote and Auntie Nyaka, at that point in time, I was developing a perverse allegiance to him.

This incident didn't move just me toward a closer commitment to Idi. Several of the other men, especially Mamba, elevated their respect for him. They already followed him and Kakengo with the sad naïveté of the uneducated and the desperate—those caught in the circumstances of life from which they saw no way out, no way ahead, other than blindly following the leadership of the semicharismatic despots offering them short-term gratification. Our two oppressors jousted for their little slice of power in the world, taking advantage of us by offering a wage, food, camaraderie, and immunity from justice.

The men recognized that while both Idi and Kakengo were vicious leaders, Idi was less likely to turn that brutality on them. That extra bit of security inspired all but the most depraved to favor Idi over Kakengo. Idi sensed the newfound respect from many of the troops, and he began to carry himself with a slightly different air. Of course, Kakengo sensed the same thing and his response, the only one he knew, was to react with even more intimidating barbarity.

Mamba's misguided loyalty to Idi was further inflated when he watched the tyrant stand up to Kakengo. He was rewarded for it by Idi entrusting him with increasingly more sensitive duties. This, in turn, cemented the follower to the leader even more tightly. And I am as guilty as any of the rest of them for succumbing to the same entanglement. Mamba was the closest thing I had to a friend in the world. He was eight years older than me, a man in my eyes. And I followed his lead, gravitating along with him, placing my blind trust in Idi.

Even after I had seen both Mamba and Idi, several times, mounting from behind the woman who was nursing my flogging wounds, it didn't occur to me that there were ulterior motives to their many visits to me. I believed what I wanted to believe, that someone, anyone, these two men, cared about me. Just as all humans do, I needed to be needed, and I desperately craved any affection I could find. Looking back, I suppose even that woman, whom I thought at the time was caring for me out of the goodness of her heart, was just doing whatever she needed to do to survive. Whether the sexual satisfaction was necessary to her or not, I don't know, but in giving it to Mamba and Idi she raised her own stature ever so modestly. In the situation we were all in, every little bit counted toward surviving. No one could begrudge her since even her tending to me bought her some extra bit of relevance in the camp, particularly in Idi's regard.

After a month, I was well enough to get up and move around again, but several of the slashes into my back remained infected and festered for many more months, taking more than a year before I could say that I was totally healed. As soon as I was able, the pet monkey I was, I became ever more securely attached to my master, closely tethered to Idi nearly all the time. Mamba became his most trusted lieutenant and, thanks to this, he and I ended up spending even more time together. I was able to pick up the dialect that was Mamba's first language, and while many of the slaves spoke it, none of Idi's other men did, so it gave us an advantage in being able to converse together safely. Idi took note of this and, seeing an opportunity for himself, encouraged me to learn the dialects of his other men. One of the original reasons he had kept me alive after he killed Uncle Dzigbote and Auntie Nyaka was because I spoke Kinyarwanda; he assumed that he might need me as a translator between him and Major Ntagura. That ended up not being the case when Ntagura spoke Swahili, but Idi saw how easily I picked up Mamba's dialect and knew that if I could speak the languages of the other men, he would have a spy in their midst that would keep them all on their toes.

This area of Central Africa contained almost as many languages as villages, each of them having some variations from the languages of the greater neighborhood. When Idi first encouraged me to learn the tongues of the others in our motley band, I was unaware of his use of me as his ears among the others. I took up the challenge with vigor, both to give myself something to do and to impress him, but equally important, it gave me license to circulate and socialize with the others. This became my schooling, and my intrinsic curiosity provoked questions, stimulating speech, allowing me to learn the languages, but also allowing me to learn about the world around me. The men we were dealing with were not stupid. They were uneducated and desperate, but not stupid. They had all sorts of knowledge about all sorts of things that might not be important to getting ahead in Western society, but they were vital to survive in our African environment. My inquisitiveness and willingness to converse in their own languages and dialects inspired a sense of trust and acceptance of me, even though I was the youngest by far. Another curious thing happened—it gave the men a feeling of self-importance to be able to impart their knowledge to me. Suddenly they were satisfying their own need to be needed, and they enjoyed the respect I gave them and the feeling of extra worth that they suddenly had. As small as it might have been, it was probably more than they'd ever experienced before. I might even say that this whole dynamic contributed to the group developing a cohesiveness that would serve us well when, several months later, we split away from the mining camp as a misguided militia.

All this is not to imply that there was any nobility to our little society, because there is no way that we could have been described as civil. We were a despicable lot of misled creatures, following a despicable leader down a dead-end path.

Once my back was healed enough and Idi began keeping me closer, he also started taking me with him on his bimonthly deliveries of Gobeni's coltan to Major Ntagura. Kakengo always went with us, as well as four or five others, who were charged with providing protection for the valuable shipment. Instead of taking the four-day trip upriver and then back again, we were able to go downriver by boat for a short distance, and then make the complete trip by road in an open-back truck within a day. We had the guarantee of safe passage from Ntagura, and mention of his name allowed us to cross the border checkpoint between Zaire and Rwanda without problems, and then safely navigate the several other army checkpoints along the way. We seldom did it in a single day though, almost always making a stop overnight on our way back to purchase supplies and gather new workers for the mine and recruits for Idi and Kakengo's band.

We constantly needed new people for the mine and for the security group. Once the arrangement with Ntagura had been worked out, the mine was continually expanding, and it took more and more workers to operate it, not to mention replacing the ones who succumbed to starvation, overwork, and illness. And as the slave contingent grew, Idi and Kakengo needed more and more men to guard the mine and keep the slaves under control. The eighty or so workers who were at the mine when I arrived grew to at least a hundred and twenty by the time a year passed, and Idi's group had grown from twelve to twenty-five.

The trips to sell Gobeni's coltan to Ntagura also included time for the men to drink and purchase sex from local women willing to earn a bit of extra money. It was on one of these trips that we stopped and picked up four young men to take back to the mine with us. That was when I was baptized into a role that I would forever regret. We traveled with the four men for a few more hours to a large town along the Walunga road. It was one of Idi's favorite places to stop. He paid each of the new men a small amount in US dollars and instructed them to be back at the truck by dusk. Mamba and I were left at the truck to watch over our supplies while Idi, Kakengo, and the others went into town looking for their favorite women, but not before leaving us some orders.

"Azi," Idi said, "make sure that the new men don't leave the truck after dark. The two big ones are for Kakengo and me, not Gobeni. Do you understand? And don't let Mamba get so drunk that he can't watch our things."

Eager to impress, I nodded and made a show of gripping my machete firmly.

As dusk was settling Mamba and I made a fire beside the truck, which we'd use to heat our food and to keep us warm through the night. None of the four new recruits had yet returned and I began to fret, but Mamba was unconcerned.

"Don't worry," he said. "They'll be back soon. They always come back because they want the jobs. Take some of this." He handed me his jar of cane whiskey, and we sat down by the fire for a smoke, taking frequent gulps of the homemade liquor. It didn't take much of the alcohol for it to have an effect on me. I was nine and a half, couldn't have weighed more than thirty kilos, and wasn't used to drinking alcohol. When the four men eventually returned to our truck, themselves clearly under the influence, I took it upon myself to exert my authority.

"You two ... you big ones ... Idi wants you for himself. Sit here," I stammered.

"Fuck off, you punk, we don't need to stay here," one of them replied. He could have swatted me away as easily as a fly. I was less than half his weight and more affected by the alcohol than he, but Mamba came to my aid.

"Azi says to sit here. You sit here." He cocked his revolver, pointing it at the one who had spoken.

Feeling emboldened I grabbed my machete and brandished it as if I knew what I was doing. "Kneel here, you two pricks. Face the fire."

"You heard Azi. Kneel in front of the fire, you pricks," Mamba drunkenly parroted.

Since Mamba was the one with the gun, the other two did as they were told.

"Don't think you'll leave here when Idi has put me in charge," I said, and then, as deftly as if I had been stone sober, I smoothly drew my machete across the backs of both of their ankles causing them to scream in agony. They rolled onto their sides beside the fire, writhing in their own blood, which spurted and ran freely from their partially severed limbs. The screeching wails had an instant effect on all of us. The other two recruits ran away as quickly as they could, fearing my machete more than Mamba's gun. Mamba himself just stared incredulously at the brutal mess I had caused. And I, both queasy and goaded from the booze, passed into a trancelike state, aware of what I had done, but feeling no remorse. In fact, I proceeded in the exact opposite fashion by laying my machete across the throat of one of the men while reminding him, "You won't leave here when Idi has put me in charge."

The two men lay on the ground trying to hold their feet to the bottom of their legs in a useless attempt to stop the bleeding. They implored us to go for help, but neither Mamba nor I was about leave. After a few more hours, Kakengo returned to find the two injured men delirious by the fireside, and Mamba and I even more inebriated after having further stoked our courage with more booze. But it wasn't nearly enough to douse the fear that we felt when Kakengo began yelling at us, demanding to know what had happened.

"These two were going to leave," I slurred. "Idi told me to keep them here and that's what I did."

"You bratty little fucker." Kakengo grabbed me by the same ankle he had grabbed on the boat a year and a half earlier, and lifted me upside down the same way. But this time, instead of burning my foot with a cigarette, he pulled his hunting knife from his belt and sliced it across the sole of my foot. The blood spouted profusely, and the pain rivaled the beating he had given me on my back the year before. He dropped me on my head, and I crumpled into a mass, a third bloody body by the campfire.

Mamba cowered back, not willing to make any move to help me for at least an hour. By that time Kakengo had drunk himself into his own stupor and Mamba felt safe enough to wrap my foot in a rag. As I lay there sobering up, I watched Kakengo get more and more drunk, until he eventually slumped against a wheel of the truck and passed out. Still under the effects of the alcohol, and fueled by my total hatred for him, I crawled over to where Kakengo snored like a wild boar. He wore no shirt, and his fat belly gathered up and spilled out over his legs. Sweat pooled in his navel and ran in a stream from it. I looked with disgust at the great mass of black blubber, sharply coiled black hairs matted to the wet skin. Carefully withdrawing from his belt the same knife that he had sliced my sole with, I gripped its ivory hilt with both hands, raised it over my head, and at the last minute changed my mind about plunging it into his fat belly, and instead made a hacking slash across his throat.

The wound was neither deep nor clean, but it was sufficient to tear a hole in his windpipe. I knew this because the air in his lungs expelled out the hole in a single large puff. His hands came up reflexively to the laceration and his body spasmed as it futilely tried to suck in another breath. There was remarkably little blood since I had missed the main artery and only a few small trickles ran over his hands. I sat myself on his fat stomach and pried his hands away from his throat, holding them helpless as the life left him. When I thought he was dead, I beat on his face with my small fists until I was too tired to hit anymore. Mamba came and lifted me off the dead body, and I cried in Mamba's embrace like he was my mother.

One by one, through the night, the rest of our men returned to the camp and found the carnage. The last to arrive was Idi, showing up just as dawn was breaking. "What happened?"

Mamba spoke up for us. "Those two were going to leave and Kakengo gave them the slash of the elephant hunters. Azi argued with Kakengo and at first he threatened to do the same to Azi, but instead sliced the bottom of his foot."

"And Kakengo?" he asked. "What happened to him?"

Fearing Mamba might get the blame I spoke up. "I killed him."

"You?"

I nodded.

"How could you kill Kakengo?"

"I slit his throat with his own knife." I was terrified at my punishment to come from Idi for having killed his partner.

"You did?" He knelt down by Kakengo's dead body and pulled the head back exposing the hole in the larynx.

"Well done, Azi. Well done." He nodded affirmatively, and then smiled at me. "Well done."

Reaching into Kakengo's pockets, Idi took out what money there was, threw the identification papers into the fire, and then picked up the eight-inch ivory-handled knife from beside the body. "This is yours, Azi. Keep it."

To the others he ordered, "Kill the two with the elephant slash. They're no good to us now. Put them all in the bush."

I remained wary of Idi's simmering wrath for several days, but it never came. On the contrary, Idi demonstrated joviality to me and kept me close by his side. It took an explanation from Mamba before I was finally able to relax. "Azi, you did Idi a favor. He had no love for that fat bastard. He was probably looking for the chance to kill Kakengo himself. You saved him the trouble."

I had no regrets whatsoever about killing Kakengo. Any morals that Uncle Dzigbote and Auntie Nyaka might have instilled in me seemed long lost by that time. I'd witnessed so much misery and death in the mining camp that my killing of Kakengo just seemed the logical thing to do to survive my situation. Similarly, that I had maimed those other two young men, leading to their deaths, bothered me not a bit. My actions on that day, and Idi's tolerance of them, further emboldened me to puff out my tiny chest and seek even more ways to prove my worth to Idi.

Kakengo's knife, which Idi had given me as a sort of reward for my actions, became for me an honored symbol of my manhood. I cherished it as one of my few possessions and carried it proudly. I was never without it for the next years of my life. It was my weapon and tool, and I displayed it prominently whenever I was around Idi, letting him know that I cherished the gift, and hoped he would see it as a sign of my conviction and loyalty to him. I spent many hours over the course of several evenings sitting by the fire and using Mamba's knife, carefully and clearly chiseling my name, "Azi O," into the ivory handle.

* * *

Several months later I was with Idi when he confronted Gregoire Gobeni in the gardens at the mining camp. "Gregoire, your last shipment of coltan that we delivered to Ntagura didn't even bring enough for me to cover the expenses of my men," Idi said. "I'll take them elsewhere if you can't keep up your payments to me."

"Where would you go?" Gobeni mocked Idi as he sucked on his large cigar. "What could you possibly do with a shoddy band like this? You're lucky I pay you anything."

I could see that this infuriated Idi since he knew that Gobeni was probably right—that he didn't have a lot of options. I had noticed that the shipments we had been taking to Major Ntagura had been decreasing in size, in spite of the fact that the mining operations had grown substantially. It seemed that the harder the workers were driven, and the more dirt they washed, the less coltan they found. So, while the mine's expenses increased, the revenue was decreasing. Idi's men now numbered around thirty, and all of them had to be paid something to keep them loyal. Then there was also the cost of weapons and ammunition for our band. The guns that Idi provided each of the men were a key incentive to keeping them happy. We had less and less money to buy food, and our rations began to dwindle. Idi realized it wasn't sustainable. But he was an entrepreneur, so he gathered his men one day to try to rally them.

"This shit hole of Gobeni's is just about worn out." He addressed the band like a preacher rallying his congregation. "We're going to leave here and live like we should be living. And be rewarded like we deserve."

A cheer went up from the men even before they heard what he was proposing.

"We'll go north to the mountains where the NRA wants us and needs us," Idi shouted.

The NRA was the National Resistance Army, a loosely organized group of freedom fighters who numbered in the thousands and were steadily growing. They were well financed and supplied with modern weapons. The group began as a Rwandan political party representing expelled refugees from Rwanda who were living in the mountainous borders of Uganda and Zaire, but it had morphed into a fighting force intent on terrorizing the Rwandan citizenry. Money flowed from the governments of both Uganda and Zaire, as it was in their interests to move the tens of thousands of Rwandan refugees back to their own homelands. None of this was known to us at the time, and probably Idi didn't even know it. All that we knew and cared about was the fact that we had a cause to rally around, the cause could pay us well, and we were on an adventure of plunder.

Using the guarantee of safe passage through the roads of Rwanda that Major Ntagura had bestowed on us, we set out on a march, first going east into Rwanda and then north along Lake Kivu and finally high in the mountain areas near the northern borders. It was a complete abuse of Ntagura's deal, since we were on our way to fight him as the enemy of the NRA. For me it was a fantastical adventure, and I blindly followed, oblivious to the politics.

When our supplies and cash ran out we simply helped ourselves to whatever we could find in any of the villages we passed through. Food, shelter, weapons, women for the men—they were all fair game and spoils just waiting for the taking. Our numbers actually grew over the month-long march as we added other impressionable young men to the group. Idi began to see himself as a military leader and tried to train and drill us into some sense of formation. But he knew nothing of organized armed conflict and we remained little more than a band of murderers and thugs.

Eventually we made our way to one of the NRA camps where Idi negotiated tents and supplies in exchange for our loyalty. We lived as relative princes compared to what we were used to. Everyone was issued new weapons—rifles and machine guns—and some of the men were trained in the use of mortars and shoulder-mounted bazookas. I hadn't yet turned ten years of age, but I was given my first gun, a small automatic rifle. From the main camp we were dispatched on several different missions, sometimes riding the roads in open-backed trucks, other times marching through the mountainous jungle trails.

Engagement with the Rwandan army was the most serious of our missions, but usually we were simply sent to terrorize the populace. This intimidation took many forms, and I not only witnessed the brutal tactics of the NRA's terror warfare, I actively sought it out, wanting to prove my worth and bolster my status with Idi. Likewise, Idi wanted to prove his worth to the leaders of the NRA and in doing so he took on an ever more savage character, referring to himself as *Mwisho Simba,* Swahili for "the last great lion." It became common for us to refer to him as "Simba," and he liked it when we did so. As Idi became increasingly ruthless, it meant nothing to him to enter a village and have his men rape the women, some as young as me, and then leave them all dead as a message to those village men who thought they might resist us.

On one particularly violent spree, we rounded up eight men in one village that, even though they dared not raise a weapon against us, refused to help us locate the Rwandan army patrols in the neighborhood. Idi ordered that all eight men be shot, and I volunteered as the executioner. It became a joke to the rest of our group that a small boy like me would do this job, and they prepared a grand ceremony of it in the town square. Their ridicule made me all the more determined to see the job through.

The townspeople were forced to gather for the executions, but every one of them closed their eyes and turned away as I emptied my weapon into the backs of the eight men. As each one fell, our own men cheered louder and louder, encouraging me on. I became caught up in the frenzy and made a flamboyant show of taking the innocent lives of the last of the eight. When they all lay crumpled on the ground, Idi ordered their heads removed, and I took my ivory-handled hunting knife and did my part by hacking through flesh and bone until I had a trophy to dangle by the dirty bloodied hair. We then took all eight of the heads and mounted them on the four canopy posts of two jeeps, where they remained for many months to come. Maggoted and rotting, pecked by birds, the innocent former sons and fathers and brothers and husbands became warnings to others when we drove into their villages.

When we arrived back at the main camp of the NRA for the first time with the decapitated heads affixed to our jeeps, the other troops cheered, and we gave our small band the title, "the Heads of State." We became known throughout the north of the country by this name, and even the Rwandan army, who hunted us, referred to us by it.

At one point we were able to add to our collection. While away from the main camp we often had to provide for ourselves, hunting food where we could. But game was rare in the lush misty mountains where we were operating, and the most we could hope to find in these parts were several different species of small monkeys. However, one day as we traipsed through the jungle Idi stopped suddenly and motioned for silence from the four of us behind him. Creeping cautiously ahead, we peered from the underbrush out into a small grassy clearing where a clan of mountain gorillas lounged and chewed casually on bamboo shoots. Several large females were harassed by just as many youngsters, and to one side a massive silverback minded his own business.

As Idi silently motioned for each of the other men to aim their rifles at one of the females and indicated that he would himself shoot the great male, a flush of sadness went through me. It felt odd how, after becoming immune to the killing of human beings, I was moved to care about the deaths of these wild animals. But I didn't have much time to think about it as four triggers were pulled in synchronization. The entire clan darted for the bush, scurrying in different directions. It took us most of the day but, eventually, we tracked three of the injured gorillas, including the silverback. When we found him he had already died from Idi's well-placed shot through the lungs. But the other two females were panting and near death when we came upon them. They both looked us all right in the eyes, urgently appealing for something more from humanity.

After we dispatched them with bullets through the hearts, we had to contend with three young babies no bigger than monkeys that clung to the bodies of their dead mothers. One of the youngsters even climbed from the mother to me and clutched me as I used to hang on to Auntie

Nyaka for security. It was desperate, terrified, pleading to me when Idi stripped it from the cradle of my arms and with one sharp blow with the handle of his machete to its head rendered the baby dead.

Our haul was impressive, several hundred pounds of meat that took us numerous trips back into the bush to carry out. And more importantly, according to Mamba, several organs which would command a good price in the black markets of Kigali, twelve severed paws representing well over a thousand US dollars when properly cured and sold, and three more nice severed head trophies for another vehicle belonging to the Heads of State.

Our unfettered reign of terror carried on for two full years in the mountains of northern Rwanda until just after the New Year's celebration of 1990, when a group of twenty-four of us Heads of State, Mamba and Idi included, along with me, rode our jeeps into a village in search of Rwandan army patrols that we knew were operating in the area. But instead of finding a cowering populace, as we had become accustomed to, we were caught unawares in an ambush by the army forces.

I lay flat in the back of the jeep and covered my head with a sack of beans as bullets whizzed by. Several tore through the metal walls leaving star-shaped holes just inches from my face. The tides of terror had turned, and I was frightened for my life. I wasn't used to such situations. Until then I'd been riding a wave of cockiness, gleefully following Idi as we easily bullied our way through the countryside. But suddenly we faced real weapons and real trained forces—a lot of them.

After a few frighteningly long minutes the barrage finally stopped. I lay silent where I was; the bag of beans still covered my head. A body had fallen on top of the rest of me. The soldiers shouted in Kinyarwanda and then in Swahili for us to drop our weapons and stand up. I clambered out from beneath the bag and the body and carefully raised my hands in the air, lifting myself up to my knees and looking around. Several weapons pointed in my direction and when I looked to the other jeeps I saw only two others of our group moving, both of them with bloody injuries. Looking down at the body I had just rolled off me, I saw Mamba, a gangly heap with at least two dozen bullet wounds to his body, several of them in his head. It dawned on me that he had saved

my life by falling on me and taking the bullets that would have surely hit me in that spot in the truck.

I began to weep for the only real friend I had in the world. I wanted to reach down and touch him, but a rifle muzzle was shoved firmly to the back of my head and a voice said from behind me, "If you move one inch, I'll kill you."

We had brazenly gone into the town as a group of twenty-four. I counted sixteen dead bodies that were pulled from the three jeeps and piled on the side of the street. Four others emerged with various wounds and were being tended to by the Rwandan army medics. That meant that three others had survived the short battle and escaped. I couldn't make out Idi among the dead and I hoped he was safe.

The soldiers took me inside one of the small homes that they had commandeered as a command post and offered me an ice-cold can of Coca-Cola. The can sat on a table in front of me, condensation beading on the outside and dripping down, pooling on the table around it. I had tasted Coke before, but never cold. One of soldiers broke open a bag of potato chips and dumped it into a bowl beside the Coke.

"Go ahead." He motioned toward the offerings. I wanted to drink that Coke so badly but resisted as a petty stand of defiance.

He took a handful of chips and began to munch on them. "Suit yourself," he said. "I'm First Lieutenant Paul Rwigyema. My men call me Wigy. You can call me that, or Paul, or Lieutenant. What should I call you?"

I looked at him as boldly as I could, but it didn't seem to faze him. He took another handful of chips and pushed the bowl closer to me.

"I'm not going to hurt you. I just want to talk with you. Can you please tell me a name I can call you?"

When I didn't answer he picked up the Coca-Cola, snapped it open, and took a long guzzle from the can.

"Should I call you Azi?" he asked. I wondered how he could have known this.

"I am Mwisho Simba," I said, puffing out my chest and raising my chin.

He tried to remain professional but couldn't stop himself from smiling. "You're not Mwisho Simba. You're barely a little kitty."

This insulted me tremendously but, admittedly, it gave me an opening to back down my bluster. He must have sensed it and he retrieved another can of Coca-Cola from the other room, setting it before me.

"Do you know where Mwisho Simba is? Do you know where he would have gone?"

"You'll never find him."

"Mwisho Simba." The lieutenant laughed. "The last great lion. Do you know how many lions are left in this part of Africa, Azi? None. We will hunt him down like every other lion that ever lived in these parts and we'll kill him." He paused for a few moments and pointed to the new Coke can, which had started to sweat. "Do you know how many of your friends died today, Azi? Eighteen. Two more have died just since we came inside here. Do you know how many have died this week? Sixty-seven. One hundred and eighty-two last week. So far this month? Two hundred and ninety. Do you know how many have lived? You ... maybe a handful of others. Drink the Coke. It's all over, Azi. They're all dying." He paused for a moment to let me think about this. "How many will be left six months from now? Can you multiply two hundred and ninety times six? Have you ever been to school?"

I was insulted again. Of course I'd been to school. I'd attended the village school, four years earlier. I could count to two hundred and ninety, but I couldn't multiply two times nine. I felt the sting, or perhaps it was shame.

"How old are you, Azi?"

"How do you know my name?"

"It was on the knife we took from you. What is your full name?" He pushed the bowl of chips a little closer, and I took a few, ignoring his question.

"How old are you, Azi O?"

I wanted to exert what little audacity I had left so I answered him. "I'm sixteen. I am a full man."

Once again, he couldn't keep himself from chuckling at my answer. "You're barely a little kitty. How old are you really, Azi?"

"Fourteen."

"You're not fourteen. You haven't even got a lick of fuzz on your face. What's your birth date?"

"May 3, 1977." I lied by a year, trying to preserve some last bit of dignity for myself.

He looked at me for a long minute, trying to decide whether I was telling the truth.

I relented and pried open the can of Coke. It was one of the nicest things I had ever tasted.

"Okay, that makes you twelve, Azi." He let me maintain my little lie.

By the time I was shipped south two weeks later, Wigy had coyly broken me down with patience, respect, and kindness, all traits that I had vaguely recognized from another life a long time ago. I gave nothing away about where I thought Idi might be or where the NRA's camps were, but I had conceded, to Wigy and to myself, that my life was headed toward sure and soon death. I had to admit that I had no idea why I was fighting the Rwandan army or any of the villagers. I never admitted to ever killing anyone and Wigy never asked me. But he certainly must have known. There were many witnesses to the atrocities that I had publicly committed and, although there were many youths in the ranks of the NRA, there were no other children my age. I was considerably younger than the others and would be easily identified. But instead of threatening me with punishments for my crimes, Wigy spent the time convincing me of the possibility of a future.

At that time I had no sense of contrition for the crimes I had committed, no feelings of guilt. If they had put me in front of a psychologist, I might have been diagnosed as a psychopath. But the corruption I had undergone over the previous four years was not a matter of the wiring in my brain or the genes that controlled it, rather it was the result of an assimilation into a culture of lawlessness and savagery. Surely some of those around me must have been true psychopaths—probably Idi and several of the other leaders. And they attracted many other like-minded miscreants. But I now know, in my heart, that I was never really like them.

And even though in those first few days around Lieutenant Wigy I wasn't yet experiencing remorse, I must have felt the first caresses of it because I distinctly remember trying to make sense of what Mamba had done for me. He had saved my life by lying down on top of me and giving up his own life—or perhaps that's just what I wanted to believe, so I did. It was a concept that was foreign to our group. For us, it was every man for himself, survival of the fittest at all costs. The kindness of the army toward me, particularly Wigy, edged me to begin reassessing my belief that there were no good people left in the world. *These* were good people. And beyond that, just a few days in the army camp—sleeping on a real mattress, eating healthy rations of food, bathing in a tub of hot water, and eating potato chips and drinking Coke—made me realize how miserable my life had been with Idi.

The army took me to a detention center north of Kigali, a city I had only heard rumors of. There they processed me by taking my photo and rolling my small fingers over an ink pad, one by one, and then rolling them again on the official form containing all my statistics.

NAME: Azikiwe Olyontombo
AGE: 12
HEIGHT: 147 cm
WEIGHT: 41 kg
EYE COLOR: Black
IDENTIFYING MARKS: Numerous scars on back, several scars on both arms, multiple scars on buttocks, one long scar and one circular scar on sole of left foot

A week later I was driven through the city, seeing for the first time concrete towers that stretched ten stories or more in the air, smooth paved roads, homes with solid roofs, and stores with goods in them. The soldier took me to the southern edge of the city, to a calm-looking compound surrounded by a hedge of azalea shrubs. The center of the grounds was dominated by a rectangular one-story church in a typical Central-African style, with a sloping roof of corrugated steel and a simple cross affixed to the apex on the near gable end. On one side of the church sprawled four low-rise dormitories and an administrative building. On the other side were four more single-story school buildings with windows thrown wide open to let the breeze inside.

I had been given clean pants by the soldiers, a shirt that buttoned up the front, socks, and shoes, all of them new and even the correct size. They also gave me a rucksack, two bars of soap, enough head powder to treat my lice for another two weeks, a toothbrush with toothpaste, an extra pair of socks, and two pairs of underwear, something I had never worn in my life. These sundries were stowed inside the rucksack along with my ivory-handled knife, which Wigy had kindly realized was my only possession in the world. This was how I was when the soldier left me in the office of the convent school.

The white priest spoke to me at first in French. I stared back at him quizzically, and when he realized that I didn't speak the language he repeated it in Kinyarwanda. "Welcome to Notre Dame de la Paix, Azi. I am Father Michel Savard. You may call me Father Michel." This time I nodded.

"Your lessons here will be taught in French, and you'll be expected to learn the language quickly," he said.

I had started to learn a few words as a small child when I was first sent to school in my village, but I couldn't recall any of it. I hoped they would come back to me.

"How old are you, Azi?" he asked.

"Twelve." I perpetuated my lie, somehow making me feel a bit more important.

"Twelve?" He looked me up and down. "You don't look that old. You've been to school before. What grade have you completed?"

"Several," I answered.

"Can you spell *Christian*?"

I looked blankly at him. He handed me a paper and pencil. "Can you spell your name?"

I carefully and rather proudly wrote out *A-z-i O-l-y-o-n-t-o-m-b-o.*

"Your village ... where you're from? Can you spell it out, please?"

This was a stickler. I shook my head.

"What is nineteen plus twelve?"

I looked down to my hands, opening one finger at a time, counting them until I ran out of fingers, and then without looking up at him, just shook my head again.

"We'll put you in the first grade, Azi. Congratulations. You'll be taught by Sister Marie until you complete the third grade. Come with me and I'll show you where to put your things."

I followed him outside, and we stopped beside the church. "Have you been baptized, Azi?"

I shrugged my shoulders, giving him an honest answer.

"No need to worry. We'll take care of that."

He led me into one of the dormitories and showed me to a single bed. "This will be yours," he said. "You can put your things in here." He pointed to a small chest, a footlocker at the end of the bed. "When you turn fifteen you can move to the seniors' dorm. The other one is the sisters' quarters. You're not to enter there. If you need them, there is a bell outside their door. My rooms are by the office, and my doors are always open to you. You can come to me for anything." He smiled, friendly and inviting. "It's near lunchtime. I'll introduce you to the sisters in the cafeteria, and they'll present you to the boys."

He left me alone in the cafeteria, an open-air arrangement with rows of tables under a roof for shelter. I sat there alone, thinking about my predicament, weighing the options of either staying or bolting right then, when a bell rang, startling me. Within minutes the room filled with boys. Children, not the men I was accustomed to being around. These were kids, some younger, some older, some my age. They surrounded me as the tables filled up, and they laughed and playfully swatted at each other, teasing one another. They bantered among each other in a mixture of Kinyarwanda, French, and Swahili. Several of them opened satchels and pulled out their lunch while others formed up in a line with trays.

Father Michel had returned. "Take a tray, Azi," he said. "Get in line and come back to sit here. I'll get you introduced."

I took to that school like a bird freed from its cage. I soared almost from the moment I arrived, seeing the world from new heights, swooping in and exploring from one horizon to another. At first I was limited by the language barrier, but I quickly mastered French and then was limited only by the hours of the day. Learning was not a challenge for me, it was an experience, a satisfaction, and the nuns were more than happy to have a student who relished being in school. I quickly found out that this was far from the norm and couldn't grasp how most of the other boys resented having to go to school. For me it was an opportunity I had never even dreamed of, a life so completely different from the one I had led the previous four years.

This isn't to say that everything was easy, especially the first year. Initially, my lack of French significantly slowed my progress, and I was often embarrassed at being the oldest in my early classes. I was much bigger than the younger boys that I was placed with. But this only lasted awhile. The sisters had established a mentoring system at the school whereby the older boys spent time tutoring the younger ones, and it was a big help in getting me caught up. By the second year I had caught up with the boys my own age.

More troubling for me in that first year were the many nights I'd wake in fright, hearing the bullets whizzing by, feeling the weight of Mamba lying on top of me, his blood running down over my face and body, only to realize it was my own sweat, a product of the memories I couldn't shake. Sometimes when this would happen I'd lay awake for hours listening to the sounds of the boys around me sleeping, perversely missing the grunts and snores of the men I'd camped with for the past years. It was an odd mixture of knowing I was in a safe and better place, but somehow yearning for the harsh, yet still more familiar, life I had come from.

There is no denying, however, that the instinct for survival is primal and strong. And when survival is a daily challenge, one quickly learns to sense the paths that are smoother and more secure. I, an orphan who had honed this sense of survival, had no trouble choosing between the comforts of my new school and the dead end of my previous life.

I made numerous friends, some of them very close, and I enjoyed hearing about their families. The school was made up of two groups of students, those of us who lived in the dorms, and the majority, who walked from home to attend six days a week. A few of the others who lived in the dorm with me were also orphans, but none had come from the life that I had. It didn't take me long to start to recognize the deviance of my past life, and I became ashamed of it, never uttering a word about it to any of the others. This was when I first began to shape my truth by omitting those details which I wanted to bury. The students and the nuns had no reason to doubt my tales when I told them of living at a mine in the jungles. The details that I offered made it believable that I hadn't yet been to school. It served no purpose to tell anyone of my crimes.

As much as I loved and appreciated the school, there was one aspect that I didn't care for. Notre Dame de la Paix, Our Lady of Peace, was a Catholic missionary school. I'm not sure of the exact sources of funding, but it was one of several schools in Rwanda run by religious orders based in Europe. Father Michel acted as the school administrator, headmaster, and chief spiritual force. He was aided in shepherding the young flock by a cadre of four white nuns from Europe and several locals who filled teaching positions and housekeeping duties. The four nuns, Sisters Marie, Geraldine, and Brigit, and Mother Katherine, as we knew them, were responsible for ensuring all students received adequate indoctrination through twice-weekly catechism classes. I had no use for this gibberish, but put up with it as a small price to pay for receiving the rest of my education, courtesy of the generous support of donors in faraway countries and the volunteer efforts of the four sisters and Father Michel. It didn't take me long to recognize the selflessness and true generosity of these kind women. They cared for our well-being in a way that I'm sure many mothers couldn't even offer to their children. And Father Michel, though often firm and sometimes stern, would make the effort to spend one-on-one time with many of the boys, particularly the younger ones who needed extra help or a fatherly presence in their lives.

One day, after I had become comfortable in the school and, according to Sister Marie, been adequately prepared "to be welcomed into the family of Christ," Father Michel approached me.

"Azi," he said. "I'm sure that you've been anxiously awaiting your baptism into the Holy Catholic Church."

I knew what he was talking about because Sister Marie had been tutoring me toward it, but "anxiously awaiting" was far from accurate. I'd have preferred to skip the whole nonsense but dared not jeopardize my place at the school since it mattered a lot to the sisters, and obviously to Father Michel.

"Once baptized," he said, "you'll be able to receive Holy Communion with the rest of the boys at the school. We can do the baptism and your First Communion next Sunday."

"I'd like that, Father."

"Have you thought of a Christian name you'd like to be baptized under?" he asked.

I really didn't care. As far as I could tell it was just a formality and I would still be called Azi by my friends. "Sister Marie has suggested Alfred," I said.

"Ah, St. Alfred. An excellent choice, Azi. One of the greatest scholars in the history of the church—and a fluent linguist, like you. It'll bode well for you in your studies. St. Alfred will make a superb role model for you."

I was unaware of this. I thought that Sister Marie had recommended it because that was her father's name.

"You'll need to make your first confession sometime before that," Father Michel added. "You're welcome to come to my rooms this week, anytime you like."

When we were seated across from each other in his sitting room two nights later he began by saying, "Azi, I know that this may not be easy for you. And although you've been very private about your past, I am aware from the soldier who dropped you off that you've been through some very troubling times. You can feel free to talk about any of these things with me. You understand that, don't you?"

I nodded, still not yet sure what I was going to confess. Sister Marie had taught me all about the Ten Commandments and the sins according to the church. I became lost in the thoughts of my dilemma, either opening wounds that had barely begun to heal or ignoring them and risking not gaining entry into heaven—on the off chance that there was something to this forgiveness stuff. Actually, before Father Michel informed me that he knew more of my past than I thought, I had been prepared to ignore the brutal sins of my previous life and keep my confession to a few lies and lascivious fantasies. But now that I knew he knew some of the truth, and I wasn't sure exactly how much, I had to make a decision. And it wasn't just about my everlasting salvation, it was about imperiling my standing and my relationship with him and the sisters.

My lips tightened and began to quiver as I weighed it out. Father Michel saw my turmoil and responded by leaning forward and putting a firm hand on my shoulder. The human touch caused a tear to form, and I could feel it dribbling down my cheek.

"It's okay, Azi. It's what's in your heart, what you confess to God, that matters. If it's too difficult for you to say to me, just say it to our Lord."

"Thank you, Father," I whispered.

"Let's begin, shall we?"

And I did. "Bless me, Father, for I have sinned, in the name of the Father and the Son and the Holy Spirit, Amen. Father, I have sinned. I have done many things that I know are wrong and I hope you can forgive me. That's all, Father."

I sniffled, not because of my sins, but because of my cowardice in not being able to face them. Father Michel, trying comfort me, moved across and sat beside me, putting his arm around my shoulders until I straightened up.

"I'm sorry, Father."

"It's quite all right, Azi. No need to be sorry." And then he dropped his hand to my knee giving it a fatherly pat. "Don't be sorry. You can come to me anytime you like." His hand stroked my thigh. I sat frozen, not knowing if this was part of the sacrament or him just being fatherly. Eventually he broke the spell and said, "You're a good boy, Azi. No need for penance."

When I returned to the dorm that night some of the boys asked me how my time with Father *Gushyukwa* was. I was familiar with the term, it meant "erection" in Kinyarwanda, but I hadn't heard it used in conjunction with Father Michel. It seemed to be a joke among some of the older boys that the priest would often be seen with an erection, especially when he was alone with any of them. Once I was let in on the secret, it became a frequent topic of conversation around the school for me. Some of the boys claimed that Father would rub his *gushyukwa* up against them, some made claims of him exposing it, others said that he had fondled them, and the most outrageous claims were that he had made some of the boys suck on his *gushyukwa*.

I wondered for months whether they were just playing a joke on me or if some of these claims could be true. The sisters had never told me anything about these types of activities being a sin, but I already had a firmly entrenched belief of what I thought about them. Among the men that I had spent those horrible four years with, homosexuality was despised, and even though they would joke about it, such proclivities were taboo. But even more reviled was the practice of men playing with boys. This was such a serious crime, even among the despotic criminals I had lived with, that offenders were subject to the most severe of punishments. I witnessed it more than once—a man disemboweled alive, his belly slit open, and then his genitals severed and stuffed into his mouth before he died. I can't say with certainty that all of the men I watched suffer this punishment were true pedophiles. I suspect that the accusations against these men were frequently false, used to justify their savage murders. Nonetheless, I understood that what the boys at Notre Dame de la Paix were alleging of Father Michel was very serious.

Even though the rumors about our headmaster persisted for the next two years, I had no firsthand experience of such behavior. I did keep my distance somewhat, avoiding being alone with him whenever possible, so I wouldn't have to find out the truth for myself. I did notice what I thought was Father Michel's *gushyukwa* on many occasions, but it was possible that I was mistaken and just susceptible to the power of persuasion. And even if it was, that in and of itself wasn't necessarily a bad thing. We were all boys, most of us either approaching or going through puberty, and we all often sported a healthy turgidness. Why should we expect any different from Father Michel?

It seemed that the completion of my First Confession that night had sealed the deal and the following Sunday I was baptized into the Holy Catholic Church as Alfred Olyontombo. Father Michel printed me a certificate saying as much, also showing the false birth date I had given and my baptismal date.

During the first couple of years at the school I grew quickly, and when I entered puberty I began to fill out with the muscles I had coveted from the time I was young. On my first birthday at the school I turned twelve but continued to feign my age as being one year older. Now I even had a baptismal certificate, officially signed by Father Michel, offering proof. It had been a matter of chest puffing when I had first begun the deception by telling Lieutenant Wigy the lie, and then it evolved into a matter of personal pride. Eventually, I became so caught up in the lie that I began to believe it myself. Fortunately for me, I was growing faster and taller than most of the other boys and no one ever challenged me on my claim. And by the time I reached fourteen, after just two years at the school, I had caught up in my studies with the others of the same age. Sister Geraldine, who was now teaching me, was as proud as my own mother might have been at how well I was doing.

The sisters gave me my first responsibility in the homework program, assigning to me one of the younger boys who had come to the school shortly after I arrived. Gabriel—Little Gabe, as we all affectionately called him because of his diminutive size—was, like me, an orphan and he lived in the dorms with us. But unlike me, he had a cheerful and bubbly disposition. Whatever hardships he had endured in his short life were either put well behind him or carefully disguised. He was always full of exuberance and pep, and he endeared himself to all of us at the school.

Perhaps in the way that opposites attract, Gabe and I began to spend quite a bit of time together, originally through my good fortune of having been assigned as his homework mentor, but increasingly by what each had to offer the other. I think Gabe looked up to me as a big brother— the serious and stalwart figure he could rely on for advice and security. And I, in response, enjoyed the role of being respected and relied upon. Gabe's carefree, jovial attitude inspired me to enjoy my own good fortune at having escaped my previous life of destitution. Gabe seemed proud of the attention and care I showed him. He hung around me constantly, and I didn't mind one bit. Then, the cord that bound us cinched even tighter.

Sunday mornings at the school were reserved for attending Mass, but the afternoons were free time and most of us spent it playing football in the large open field at the back of the compound. Father Michel often joined us, and even opened the field to other boys in the neighborhood. We split ourselves into teams based on ages and abilities, usually playing three games side by side. One Sunday afternoon, in the midst of play, I caught sight of Gabe running as hard as he could, laughing and taunting a much bigger boy who chased him. What I first thought was horseplay between the two turned serious when the bigger lad finally caught him and violently threw him to the ground. I ran from my own game and grabbed the one on top by his shoulders, pulling him off, but not before he landed a series of solid blows to Little Gabe's face. When the assailant turned on me, I let my fists fly in a flurry of punches that quickly brought him to his knees.

Father Michel parted the crowd that had formed and stepped between me and the neighborhood boy, thinking that I might lay more wrath on him. But he need not have worried; I wasn't a fighter. I was only acting on impulse, only doing enough to save Gabe from his beating and then defending myself. Father Michel sent the other boy away, banning him from the school grounds, and he ordered Gabe and me to the dorm, to "be dealt with later."

I helped Gabe from the ground. He was crying from the punches, and I suppose from the fear of punishment to come from Father Michel.

"C'mon, Gabe. You'll be all right." We walked toward the dorm. "What happened? How did that start?"

"I was just having fun and then he jumped me," Gabe said.

"There must have been more to it than that. What did you do to him?" I asked.

Gabe looked at the ground. "I narrowed their goalposts when the goalie wasn't looking. I guess he saw me. But it was just for fun." He looked up at me as we walked and cracked a smile through the tears, and then he began to laugh. Throwing my arm over his shoulders, I shook my head and couldn't help but smile back at him. That was Gabe, a goofy practical joker. The boys from our school all knew him and often put up with such antics, recognizing it all as good fun. But the neighborhood boys, those unfamiliar with Gabe, took moving the goalposts as a severe offense.

Once in the dorm, laid out on our beds, staring at the ceiling, Gabe turned uncharacteristically serious. "Azi, thank you for helping me." I shrugged my shoulders as if to say, *no big deal.* We were silent for a long moment before he spoke again. "Nobody else helps me."

I turned my head to the side to look at him and noticed tears running down his face. Throwing my legs over the side, I went to sit on the edge of his bed. "What's wrong, Gabe?"

He rolled his head side to side and more tears flowed. "I'm all alone, Azi. I'm all alone."

"You're not alone, Gabe. I'm here."

"I miss my mom and dad," he said.

I nodded quietly, understanding how he felt. Orphanhood was a kinship we shared but never spoke of. It began to dawn on me that the outward facade of joy that Gabe wore was a well-crafted disguise for his own inner turmoil.

"Do you want to tell me about your parents?" I asked.

He wiped his tears on his arm and sat up.

"The rebels in the north killed them." The words made me slump as I thought of my own participation with such rebels.

"First my mother, when I was very young," he said. "And then my father about three years ago."

I sucked in a slow deep breath and my heart thumped. Three years ago *I* was running with the despots in the north. But I said nothing, letting him continue.

"They made us all gather to watch, and then they made a boy, just a little boy, just ten or eleven, shoot them all. He did it. How could a boy do something like that, Azi? He killed my father. I ran away, but when I went back to see my father's body, they had cut off his head. How could they do that, Azi? How could they? My father, Azi. My father." Gabe was sobbing, and he buried his head in my chest.

I wrapped my arms tightly around his small body, shamed, nauseated by his revelation, and I sobbed uncontrollably along with him.

From that moment, I felt I owed Gabe my own life. And I might have. I asked him no further details of the death of his father or the town he was from, unable to deal with the possible reality of it all. I forced the thoughts from my mind, crowding them out with a vow to myself to keep Little Gabe safe.

Outside of our sheltered school environment, the situation in our country was rapidly deteriorating, and we couldn't ignore the political and cultural upheaval taking place. The battles of the insurgents in the northern mountains were creeping farther and farther south, embroiling more of Rwanda. The NRA had been replaced by the Rwandan Patriotic Front as the leading militant group. The RPF was far better organized and financed than the old NRA, and the political conflicts were becoming race conflicts as the minority Tutsi population sought to reestablish its hold on power over the majority Hutus. A couple of the older boys at the school began openly touting their support for the Patriot Front, and Father Savard stepped in immediately and expelled the two students. Neither he nor the nuns wanted any part of the greater racism issues polluting our Catholic school environment.

We discovered that the outside world was taking some notice of the near civil war situation that was brewing in Rwanda when a BBC news crew showed up one day. Our school was much appreciated and respected in the local community, and indeed the entire city of Kigali, and it must have also had some reputation abroad. The BBC wanted to interview Father Michel and the nuns and even some of the students about our island of neutrality in the center of the sharply drawn lines between factions. Father Michel thought that I would be a good example to parade out, especially with my previous history of being right on the front lines in the guerrilla battles. I reluctantly agreed to help him, but I had no intention of speaking about the things that I had seen and done.

I tagged along with Father Michel and Mother Katherine for several hours as they showed the reporter and camera people around the school and answered their various questions.

At one point the interviewer turned to Father Michel. "Father Michel, what is it that draws a priest from the safety and comfort of parish work in France to come down here to a country teetering on the brink of war?"

Father replied, "We all have our reasons—I suppose."

"But what about you, Father?" the interviewer persisted. "What about you personally? What are your reasons?"

Father Michel's eyes made an involuntary glance my way as he answered, "Opportunity. Opportunity to do God's work."

Later, just before the crew was about to leave, the interviewer asked another interesting question of Father Michel. "Father, as a current outsider, someone who can observe from afar but has an understanding of such things, what is your opinion of the sex abuse scandals that are currently plaguing the clergy across much of Europe and North America?"

He didn't even flinch. "Let he among us who hath no sin cast the first stone."

I was glad that I was not asked too much during the visit. When they did question me about whether I had any idea what armed conflict might look like if it came to that point, I simply responded, "We can only pray that it doesn't."

I think this must have been an answer that very much pleased Father Michel because I remember him smiling proudly when I made the statement. After the crew left, Father was gushing about what an excellent job I did.

"Come see me in half an hour, Azi," he said. "Come to my office, we'll celebrate."

I wasn't sure what we had to celebrate but I knocked on the door to his office as instructed. This was when I was first exposed to the truth of another rumor that circulated among the boys as he pulled from his desk drawer a flask of liquor.

"Sit down, Azi. Gin only on the most special of occasions." He raised the flask in a toast before taking a hearty swallow. "This interview could mean great things for the school's funding. You did an excellent job answering their questions. Thank you, Azi. We're blessed to have you at the school. You do like it here, don't you? I can see you appreciate all we've done for you. You're comfortable here, aren't you? I mean, you were exposed to a lot where you came from."

I could tell by the way he rambled on that he had been drinking before I arrived. He took another swig and stepped around behind my chair, continuing to yak away. I felt him place one hand on my shoulder, and I let him blather on about what a great school we had, and how difficult it was for him to work in this secluded environment so far away from his home in France, and what a great pleasure it was to have a student like me at his school. I was getting more uncomfortable the longer it went on, and I swiveled around in my chair to see him, but was confronted, right at face height, with his *gushyukwa*. He was stroking it and didn't bother to stop even as I pulled back and stood up.

"You've seen this before, haven't you, Azi—living in isolation with men as you have all your life?"

Unsure how to respond, I just nodded.

"You know how men sometimes need … relief, don't you?" he continued to prattle on. "Did you ever … help the men? Relieve them, I mean. Would you like to help relieve me, Azi?"

I felt like taking his pathetic little pink dick and cutting it off right there, but instead just shook my head and left his office, slamming the door behind me.

That was the turning point in my relationship with the priest. The worst of the school's rumors were now confirmed, and I had not a shred of respect left for the man. I could no longer bring myself to afford him the deference of calling him "Father" and began to avoid addressing him directly. In my mind, I thought of him only as Savard or "the sick priest." I contemplated walking away from the school, but even if I had had somewhere to go, I didn't want to leave. Despite Savard, there was too much good about the school. I had become very close to some of the boys, especially Little Gabe, to whom I now had a self-imposed responsibility. And I adored the nuns. They weren't just superb teachers, they were among the best of humanity. Their examples of kindness and selflessness were ones which, by then, I strove to emulate. They were the only female influences I'd had in my life since Auntie Nyaka was killed. They became more than teachers; they were mothers and grandmothers and sisters and aunts and friends. And I loved learning. I craved the new knowledge and soaked it up with a passion. All things weighed out, I could work around the sick bastard.

By my third year at the school I was assumed to be fifteen, and I was indeed physically big enough to easily pass for that age. I was moved to the older boys' dorm. It was a proud rite of passage for all of us when we moved from being with the youngsters in the group into the smaller, but more prestigious, seniors' house. Those of us who lived in the seniors' dorm also received the extra privilege of being able to go off-campus on our own, as long as we were back by study curfew at seven in the evening.

I had accumulated a few extra trinkets over the three years since arriving at the school, but there wasn't all that much for me to pack for the move. I took my most prized possession, the ivory-handled knife, which I still cherished, from its hiding place under my mattress and threw it in a cardboard box. As I emptied my few belongings from my footlocker into the box, Little Gabe came along and sat on my bed.

"I don't want you to go, Azi," he said.

"Gabe, I'm just going next door to the seniors'," I said. Our bond was so close that I'd expected this would upset him.

"I don't want you to go," Gabe said again, this time with his body tensing and his chin trembling.

"Is something wrong, Gabe?" I asked.

He shook his head "no," and nodded then "yes," and then shook "no" again.

"What's wrong, Gabe?"

Again he silently shook his head, this time unable to stop tears from forming. He fell forward into me, wrapping his arms tightly around me and burying his face between my shoulder and chest. He clung to me. I sensed there might be more upsetting him than my changing dorms, and I tried to get him to open up. "Gabe, are you thinking about your parents again?"

He shook his head in my chest.

"What then?" I asked.

He took his time before saying anything. "Do you think it could be true what they say about Father *Gushyukwa*?"

"That bastard. Has he done something to you, Gabe?"

He shook his head again, before feebly managing a mumbled, "No."

"He's done something to you, hasn't he, Gabe?" I pushed him away and held him squarely by his shoulders. He gave a small shake of his head, "no."

"You're sure? You're telling me the truth? Are you, Gabe?" He looked down and gave a small nod.

"You'll tell me, you'll tell me if he ever touches you. Promise?"

He nodded again but refused to speak. I could tell he wasn't going to say any more, so I pulled him back in tight, cuddling him close, holding

him for a long while. Eventually, he stemmed his tears and bravely picked up my box of belongings, carrying it next door to the seniors' dorm.

By the fall of 1993, the situation in Rwanda had deteriorated substantially from the previous year when the BBC had come to the school to do their interviews. The predictions of the reporter were coming true around us. Several bombings had occurred right in downtown Kigali, and patrols of soldiers and artillery on the streets were commonplace. Demagogues abounded, spewing racist rhetoric and inciting hatred among even the most peaceable of peoples. Everyone was lining up on one side or the other, with moderates caught up in the spreading flames of the hardliners. Several militia groups had spawned and were being openly supported by the government with guns and money and the RPF was brazenly recruiting right off the streets. No one trusted anyone, everyone suspicious of the other, neighbors turned against neighbors.

One evening, as I left the school compound, I heard a familiar voice behind me. "Azi. You're a man now." I turned to find Idi smiling at me. "Look at you. I'm proud of you."

I didn't say anything.

"You've stayed in school all these years?" he asked.

I nodded.

"Good, good. We need smart men," he said. "We need smart men now, and we'll need you after. Good, smart men to run this country. I want you to come with me. We've got important work to do."

"Idi, I don't do that anymore," I said. "I can't go with you."

"You have to, Azi. Everyone is going to be in this fight. You have to pick a side. Sooner or later you have to choose."

"I'm not a fighter, Idi," I said. "I never was. Not really."

"You were a good fighter, Azi. You still are. Look at you. Look at the size of you. You're a man now. You were a good fighter as a boy, and you'll be a better fighter as a man. Come on. Most of these pussies don't know how to kill. You've killed. You're the kind of man we need. You'll be great, Azi."

The more he spoke about killing the more negative effect it had on me. I'd spent three and a half years trying to forget the killings and now this beast was back trying to glorify them.

"No, Idi." I looked him in the eye. "You stole my childhood from me; you won't steal my manhood."

We stood there, each waiting for the other to make a move. Finally he shook his head. "Fine. Fine, Azi. But mark my words: a time will come when you will have to choose. You might as well choose the side that'll reward you the most. I'll wait for you. I want you on my side, Azi. Come to me when you choose. Major Ntagura. You remember him? Ask for him at the army headquarters, and he'll know where you can find me."

I just shook my head "no" until he had walked away and turned the corner.

Around this time, we'd started to see armored convoys from the United Nations patrolling the streets. Evidently the world had taken notice of things in Rwanda and had come to try to help us. But even as the numbers of UN peacekeepers increased in Kigali, the bombings continued, and eventually street battles were breaking out between the militia factions. The priest and the nuns tried to keep the school operating as best they could, but most of the parents quit sending their boys, fearing the streets too dangerous. For most of us who lived at the school there wasn't an option, since several, like me, were orphans with nowhere else to go. Those of us who remained living at the school compound became an even closer-knit little family, relying on each other for support.

Little Gabe was one of those who was still left at Notre Dame de la Paix. I had noticed that since I'd moved to the seniors' dorm he had changed a bit, becoming more introverted and quieter. He wasn't quite his same jovial self, but I assumed that was just Gabe's way of dealing with all the distractions and disruption around us. As the wars of the north moved closer it was bound to bring back memories for him. Also, several of his other friends no longer attended the school. Finally, it didn't help that I was in the other dorm, which meant we weren't spending quite as much time together. Fortunately, as our numbers at the school continued to shrink, all the remaining boys were eventually moved into the seniors' dorm. Gabe selected a bunk right next to mine, and for the first few days after moving in his disposition perked up.

One day, while sitting on the lawn in the shade of the azalea shrubs helping Gabe with his studies, he suddenly closed his books and laid back on the grass. He looked straight up into the yellow-gray haze that tented the sky.

"Azi, why is all this happening?"

I laid back beside him, took his hand in mine, and searched the haze myself for some suitable answer.

All I could come up with was a small unknowing roll of my head.

"But why are there so many bad people in the world, Azi?"

"They're not all bad, Gabe." It was hard for me to speak convincingly since I knew that there was far more bad than good around us. But the few good people in my life had been really good to me: a long time ago Nyaka and Dzigbote, and now, the four sisters, Wigy, and Mamba. I wanted to be good like them for Gabe.

"You're the only one, Azi. You're the only good person I know." I rolled toward him and cuddled myself around him, both of us finding security in our brotherhood.

It was hard to find true happiness in those days in Kigali. The mood of the city was gloom, and it pervaded the very air we breathed. The bond between Gabe and me gave each of us a small bit of respite, but it wasn't enough to halt Gabe's deteriorating mood and increasing reclusiveness.

Then one morning in early March I awoke to find that Gabe had already risen from the bed beside me. I made my way to the bathroom, and I pulled the shower curtain open to step in. I was stalled in midstride by the sight of Little Gabe hanging from a rope around his neck which had been fastened to the showerhead, a chair knocked over beside him. I gagged, and at first couldn't even find enough air in my throat to scream. Wrapping my arms around his little body, I lifted him up, taking the weight off the rope, and shouted for help.

The authorities were far too busy trying to avert warfare in the streets to attend to the suicide of an orphaned schoolboy. Savard arranged a funeral mass for the next day in the chapel at the school, and we buried Gabe in the new parish cemetery on the outskirts of the city. Upon returning, I found Gabe's bed still rumpled, just as he'd left it the night before. The sisters said they would tidy up his things, but I insisted on doing it myself.

I stewed for another two days, not wanting to disturb what little was left of Gabe's tiny imprint on this screwed-up world. Everyone assumed that he had killed himself in response to the growing violence in our city and the stress of living in a semi–war zone. Still, his death was hard on all of us, the boys as well as the nuns. In spite of all the deaths I had seen, some I had even caused, this one was truly traumatic for me. It was the only one for which I felt instantaneous guilt. I had vowed to myself to look after Gabe, and I hadn't.

Finally, I forced myself to get on with tidying up Gabe's meager possessions. I pulled the entire drawer from the locker at the foot of his bed and, with reverence, I placed it beside me where I could examine the contents. I knew there wouldn't be much to go through since he had come to the school with almost nothing. On one side of the drawer, his spare clothes were neatly folded, and on the other, two battered primers and a half-dozen dog-eared notebooks made a tidy stack. The small Bible he'd been issued when he arrived at Notre Dame de la Paix sat prominently on top. A sheet of lined paper, torn from one of the notebooks and folded in half, was tucked into it. As I lifted the Bible it naturally fell open to the page where the paper lay. I unfolded the single page, easily recognizing the clean script as Gabe's. A short note, printed in red pencil, addressed to Father Savard. It read,

You have made your sins my sins. No more. I will go now to find Jesus and tell Him my side of the story first.

I read it several times, and then folded the paper along its crease, halving it twice more, repeating the words to myself each time, before shoving it into my pocket. I would hand deliver Gabe's final note to the bastard priest myself.

The Bible lay open on my lap, and I saw where Gabe had underlined a section of text with the same red pencil. It was a passage from Paul's Second Letter to the Corinthians, Chapter 5, Verse 10:

For we must all appear before the judgment seat of Christ, so that each one may receive what is due for what he has done in the body, whether good or evil.

I was unfamiliar with the passage, and I reread it several times. It was obvious that Gabe had been thinking of the bastard priest when he'd marked the scripture, but I couldn't help contemplating the entries that God must have surely already inscribed beside my name in the eternal ledger. I wished Gabe a better hearing in his appearance before that judgment seat than I expected to receive myself.

The next day I went to the army headquarters and asked for Major Ntagura. "I've made some decisions," I said. "Can you get in touch with Idi and ask him to come and see me at Notre Dame de la Paix tomorrow after dark?"

"Does Lieutenant Wigy's little kitty finally want to roar like a lion?" He laughed.

I ignored his mocking. "I've made my decision. Ask him to come for me," I said.

The next day, as the sun was setting, I knocked on Savard's door. "May I come in?"

"Certainly, Azi." He was surprised to see me at his doorstep since we had warily been keeping our distance for nearly two years. "What can I do for you?" He indicated a chair, but I remained standing in front of him.

"I'd like to make a confession."

"Of course, Azi."

He surely heard the trembling in my voice and must have seen me quaking. "Are you sure you wouldn't like a seat?"

"No, Father. I want to look you right in the eye."

"What is it that's troubling you, son?"

"Will your god forgive me for *all* my sins?"

"You've only to ask, my son. What is it you need forgiveness for?"

Steeling my nerve, I withdrew my knife from under my jacket and pushed my face up close to his. "For all the deaths I've caused." And I stuck the full eight inches of the blade into his soft belly. He toppled forward, coughing and sputtering, and I let him slip from the blade of the knife and slump to the floor. His eyes remained focused on me while I tore open his shirt and then put the knife back in just under his skin and sliced open his belly from his belt to his sternum. With my bare hand

I reached in, grabbed his innards, and pulled them out so that he could see them. Unbuckling his pants, I drew them down and prepared to sever his genitals and stuff them in his mouth while he was still alive, a small retribution for Little Gabe. But I couldn't bring myself to even touch the filthy organs. Instead, I retrieved Gabe's folded note from my pocket and stuffed it deep into his throat. I left the bastard there, gagging on Gabe's last words to him and futilely trying to gather his spilled entrails.

Christmas

Anna now knows it all, everything of my childhood in Africa, right up until the time I committed my last murder. I am feeling tremendously unburdened after having just confessed to her. She finally knows the real me, for good and for bad, it is all out there, all the things I have never told anyone before. Anna listened for hours, often looking sad but never condescending. She wiped my tears, and she hugged me when I began to shake uncontrollably, rocking me like a baby until I was able to continue again. We're now sitting quietly. Anna is lost in the things I have just told her. She's biting her lip and slowly shaking her head side to side. "I had no idea, Alfred. No idea. I'm so sorry." It's her turn to cry and mine to comfort. With her leaning against me, I gently stroke the back of her head. But as more silence passes between us, I sober up to the present situation, and my thoughts turn to my current predicament.

I know the extradition warrant that is coming concerns the time I spent in either Zaire or Rwanda with Idi and his band of thugs. Steve said that Zaire, now known as the Democratic Republic of the Congo, has an extradition treaty with the United States and that Rwanda doesn't. So that makes it most likely that it was something from those very early days with Idi, rather than Rwanda. However, I also know that the United Nations held war crimes trials several years ago for the conflict and genocide that took place in Rwanda during the years I was there. But I haven't seen it in the news recently, so I assumed that those trials were over. Perhaps they're not. Maybe this is an extradition by the United Nations for war crimes. That priest, Savard, was my most probable guess, but how could they know about that? How could they know I was the one who'd dispatched him to the judgment of his god?

My guessing is interrupted when Steve arrives around two thirty. There is a perfunctory knock on the door and the senior partner at Anna's firm, our good family friend, and my lawyer as of the past twenty-four hours, comes back into the counsel room where Anna and I have spent most of the day.

"Okay, sit down." He's brisk and all business. "We've got the warrant with the indictment. We'll have to talk about this because we're up in front of a judge in one hour. Alfred, what the hell happened in Belgium?"

I have no idea what he is talking about. "Belgium? Nothing. I have never been to Belgium."

"Something happened in Belgium. This extradition warrant is from Belgium." He reads directly from it. "'Azikiwe Olyontombo, alias Alfred Olyontombo, currently known to reside in the United States of America, formerly of the Republic of France, formerly of Tanzania, formerly of Rwanda, having caused the premeditated deaths by his hands of Geert Grennerat, Marjon van den Bosche, Kaatje Simmons, Brechtie van Huejten, all citizens of the Kingdom of Belgium.'"

"May I see that?"

He hands the warrant across the table, and Anna leans in to read with me. I shake my head, perplexed. "I don't know these people. I have no idea who they are. And I've never been to Belgium."

"Are you sure, Alfred?" Steve asks.

"I'm positive."

"This is good." There's excitement in Anna's voice. "This means that somehow there is a mistake. This is all some kind of mistake. Mistaken identity perhaps. Or someone else with the same name."

"With the name Azikiwe Olyontombo, who also, coincidentally, changed his name to Alfred Olyontombo? Maybe a mistake, but not mistaken identity," Steve says.

"Can we challenge this with the judge this afternoon?" Anna asks.

"Anna, it's an extradition warrant." Steve looks directly at her. "There are almost no challenges available to an extradition warrant. You know that. But before they extradite they do have to present the bare bones of the charges and the case. They'll have to show us that at some point."

"We have to try *something* now," Anna says.

"We're really, really limited with this. Let's see what the US Attorney's Office has to say. In the meantime, our first priority is to get Alfred out of custody. The marshals will be here soon for transport to the courthouse."

"What if they keep him in custody?" Anna asks. "We know bail is unlikely."

"Bail is almost impossible. It's just not applicable in foreign extraditions. The best we can hope for is electronic monitoring, and that's only if the attorney is feeling generous."

"What if we don't get that?"

"That's why the Marshals Service is coming. They'll take Alfred out of Denver PD's hands and put him in federal custody for holding until transfer is arranged with Belgium."

I hear this exchange between Anna and Steve, but it barely registers. I am trying to think of Belgium. I had absolutely no connection with Belgium. Nothing. These four people who were murdered, if they were Belgian, were most likely white. Not necessarily for certain, but likely. I think back through those I had killed and conclude that the only white man I ever killed was Savard. That I am sure of.

None of it fits, but none of it matters. Whatever is happening, whether a mistake, or right or wrong, this is my comeuppance, my rightful due for having taken the lives of others, innocent others. Unlike Anna, I am not looking for an angle to escape. On the contrary, I am feeling a strange sense of relief at having been found out. The opportunity to confess my sins and accept whatever penance a court wants to impose on me lessens the load I have been bearing all my life. It really doesn't matter to me if it is Belgium or the United States or the Congo or Tanzania; I don't care.

The marshals show up, two of them, looking much like the Denver police with different insignias. It's humiliating to be put in handcuffs again, especially in front of my wife, but I revert to thinking of the crimes I have committed and decide it is a small, well-deserved punishment. They transport me in the back of a van, securing me to a seat by waist and shoulder straps, and then shackling my ankles to the posts of the bench. They handle me roughly, like they would any other common criminal. When the police came to arrest me at my office they showed some modicum of esteem; they knew I was a well-respected doctor in the local community and the husband of a well-respected lawyer. But these officers know nothing of me. To them I am just another black man who committed another crime. And that actually makes me feel good, to be treated with some roughness, because I am more despicable than any of the other prisoners they've ever dealt with.

I'm delivered through the prisoners' dock and escorted to the fourth floor of the US District Court on 19th Street where I join Anna, Steve, and a third person, whom they introduce as Laura Abroud, the Assistant US Attorney. We're in a small room, not the grand courtroom that I expected. Within moments we're joined by Judge Coleen Cain, who officiously takes a seat on one side of a large desk while the rest of us stand.

"What have we got here, Ms. Abroud?" the judge asks.

"Your Honor, this is Alfred Olyontombo. Dr. Olyontombo," Laura Abroud says. "We have a federal warrant from the State Department in response to a request to extradite from the country of Belgium."

"On what charges?"

"Four counts of murder."

"What do you need from me?" the judge asks.

Steve interrupts. "Your Honor, we'd like a writ of habeas corpus."

"On what grounds?"

"We believe that there has been a mistake in arresting my client. Dr. Olyontombo has never even been to Belgium," Steve replies.

"He's never been there, or he *says* he's never been there?" Judge Cain asks. "Mr. May, you know full well that there is no challenge to this federal warrant. Our international treaties only mean anything if both parties respect them. If the crime in Belgium is a crime in the United States, we have to honor the request. And I think that murder is still a crime here. This court has no authority to litigate a case before the courts in Belgium. I presume the documentation is here, Ms. Abroud?"

"Not all of it. Not yet. The arrest is provisional, and we expect to have the detailed indictments within a few days."

"Then, Your Honor, we'd request house arrest," Steve says. "Dr. Olyontombo is a well-respected member of our community—a doctor— and would like to be home with his family over Christmas. He poses no flight risk."

Laura Abroud speaks up. "Your Honor, the government doesn't consider Dr. Olyontombo as a flight risk and would have no objections to house arrest."

"Very well," says the judge. "House arrest with electronic monitor and surrender of all passports, confined to residence only, no internet use, transportation only by the marshals. Anything else?"

The marshals take me to a room near the prisoner docks and fit me with a bracelet around my ankle, testing the small electronic lock a few times, before driving me all the way home to Boulder, strapped and shackled in the back of their van. One of my elderly neighbors is unloading groceries from her car and stops to watch as the marshals remove me from their van, conspicuously marked with large lettering, US MARSHALS SERVICE. I can see her staring as they escort me up the driveway, up our steps, right to the front door. I deserve the humiliation but I am wounded for Anna, she doesn't deserve any of this. And there are so many others that I've let down. I'm sorry, deeply sorry for having brought this on them—especially Anna. And oddly, I feel that even in her death, I've let down our baby girl, Stephanie. Thank the gods she's not here to see this. The marshals take me inside my house before removing the handcuffs, as if I would have broken free and run had they taken them off in the van and spared Anna the disgrace in front of our neighbors.

Anna and I haven't spoken since the marshals left. She's made tea, and we're both sitting on stools at the island. I suppose we're both thinking the same thing: *What a dizzying twenty-four hours.* Yesterday, around this time, I was concerned only about getting to see all of my patients before time ran out and the Christmas holiday started. I was looking forward to moving on, spending time with Anna's family, chats with her father by his fireplace, Mom's home cooking, too many cookies and chocolates, some good games of squash with her brother and the giggles and joy of his kids on Christmas morning. Of course, this would all have been bittersweet, as it was also our first Christmas without Stephanie, but I tried to focus on the good: three weeks of vacation right after New Year's, our long-delayed honeymoon in Saint Martin, time for Anna and me to reconnect after the strain of Steph's illness and death. But that was yesterday. Now I don't know what I'm facing. We sip our tea quietly.

The silence is suddenly broken by the chime of the doorbell. Neither of us really wants to move but I get up and open the door.

"Excuse me. Dr. Olyontombo?" A young man is on the step with a small recorder.

"Yes."

"Dr. Olyontombo, my name is Kelly Aubry. I work for the *Sun Valley Herald,* and I have a few questions. Some of your patients told us that you were arrested at your office yesterday. And this afternoon we found an extradition warrant with your name on it. Do you have any comment?"

I'm not sure what to say, but Anna answers from behind me. "He has no comment. You'll have to leave, please." With that she steps around me and closes the door.

Anna sighs, returns to the kitchen, and sits back down on her stool.

Suddenly she looks like an old woman, not the vibrant thirty-seven-year-old that she was just a few months ago, before Stephanie got sick, before yesterday. Her face looks heavy, it's puffy; her eyes have gone from blue to gray.

"I'm sorry, Anna."

"We don't have time for that, Alfred. We don't have time to be sorry."

As useless as it makes me feel, I'm glad she has taken charge again.

"What do we do now?" I ask. "What's going to happen?"

"There are a couple of things for us to think about," she says. "Steve says we have to prepare for the worst; that they could show up from Belgium any day to take you away."

"How soon?"

"Who knows. Not likely over the Christmas break, but it's within their rights to come any time after they produce a full indictment and get it signed off. If they want to, they could show up tomorrow with it—this afternoon even—but they still have to show some validation of the charges."

Steve has advised Anna to have a bag packed in case things happen quickly. He's going to try to get in touch with some of his contacts in New York in an effort to get referrals for attorneys in Belgium, but he's not sure if he'll be able to reach anyone with the Christmas holidays just starting.

I don't know if I even want an attorney in Belgium—if I want to fight this—but I don't want to upset Anna any more than she is already, so I don't mention it, saving that battle for later.

"Alfred, I'm not sure what to do about Christmas. Obviously, we're not going, but I don't know what to tell Mom and Dad. I'd rather not say anything about any of this until we have to. It *has* to be some kind of mistake. I don't want to upset them. Let's just say we're sick and can't make it."

I can imagine how much all of this hurts Anna, made even worse by the prospect of having to tell her parents. "I'm sorry, Anna."

"Stop that!" She startles me with her shout and jumps up quickly from her stool. "Stop saying you're sorry. Stop it!"

In response to this I just want to apologize more. I *am* sorry, very sorry. It is a terrible feeling to have no way at all to adequately express regret or be able to do anything toward redemption.

Anna begins pacing in the kitchen while I sit silently. After a few moments of calming down she says, "I'm sorry, Freddie. I'm sorry myself. Not for the situation, but for shouting at you. I'll call Mom and tell her you're sick—we're sick—we can't make it. It'll buy us some time."

I simply nod in agreement while she continues to pace.

Eventually I venture to speak. "Do you want me to call them?"

"No. I'll do it. I might as well do it now and get it over with."

She grabs her cell and leaves the kitchen. The conversation is short and when she returns, I ask her what her mom had to say.

"She said she hopes we get well soon, that they'll miss us, and that they'll probably come up here the day after Christmas. She wanted to know if we were avoiding Christmas because of anything to do with Stephanie. I told her definitely not. That we'd been looking forward to being with them."

I checked my messages while Anna was on the phone and found more than a dozen, at least six from Mark Su at the clinic.

"Mark left me a bunch of messages."

"He's been calling me all day, too," Anna says. "I just haven't bothered to answer him."

"I guess I'll have to call him and say something. Any ideas?"

"Don't say anything for now," Anna says. "Tell him you're home and we'll have everything sorted out soon. They're not expecting you back at the clinic for four weeks anyhow."

I'm lucky and get Mark's voice mail, so I don't actually have to talk to him. I try to sound as upbeat as I can, but I am pretty certain he'll be able to read my voice.

Anna goes to the sideboard where we keep the booze, pulls out a bottle of gin, and takes a glass from the cupboard. "Do you want one?"

Neither of us are big drinkers. "Please," I say. "No ice. Do you want me to make us some food?"

"I couldn't eat anything, Freddie."

I'm not really hungry either, I was just trying to do something, anything, for Anna. She leaves my drink on the counter and moves into the den where she slouches onto the sofa. By the time I take a seat in my favorite armchair she has half finished her drink, so I get up and bring back the gin and a full bottle of tonic, setting them on the coffee table. The room is fairly dark, and through the windows I can see some blowing snowflakes. The sun is just beginning to set.

I try to distract us both from the nightmare. "Are we going to have snow for Christmas?"

"Don't know," she responds. "I haven't checked the weather today."

Anna picks up the remote from the coffee table, points it at the TV, and clicks to the Weather Channel. A strip across the bottom of the screen that shows the seven-day forecast tells us that we will indeed have snow, beginning tonight and lasting all day tomorrow.

Without rising from our seats we take turns pouring drinks, a couple of them, a few more; we watch the weather for Denver, the region, the country, several times. As hard as I try to focus on the TV the gin is blurring my retentiveness, but between the two of them, the gin and the weather, I have forgotten, for a while at least, that I am an arrested murderer. Sleep comes to me, right there in my chair, in the form of a clipper that's racing across the northeast carrying freezing rain to Washington and Baltimore.

Waking with a kink in my neck and the Weather Channel frozen on the local seven-day forecast, I can see that Anna is likely to have a worse kink if she doesn't get straightened out. I also see by what's left in the gin bottle that she didn't fall asleep as soon as I did. Reaching under her with both arms, I lift her and take her to our bedroom, carrying her like I used to carry a sleeping Stephanie. Gently, I lay her on the bed, as I often did with Steph. For a few moments I feel like a knight, doing something good for Anna, doing the right thing. But only for a few moments because, as I take off my clothes, I notice the bracelet on my ankle and am reminded of all the unknightly things I have done.

Sitting on the edge of the bed, I pull up my knee and fondle the bracelet. What could I have done differently to change this? Where would I have had to start? For twenty-five years now I have done everything in my power to even the ledger. I work at saving lives, giving people hope, helping them overcome illness. I go out of my way to volunteer in the community. I obey every law of this country; I don't even speed on the roads. So what could I have done differently? I should have run away that day they took me on the riverbank. I should have run any of the many other times I could have. Why didn't I? Because I'm not a knight, I'm a phony. I'm not a good person; I'm not a good doctor, a good husband. I'm a fraud.

There's a bottle of sleeping pills in the medicine cabinet. I got them when Steph was sick, for those times when we were so backed up on our sleep that we couldn't function. I know what these can do. I take one, two, three. I'm going to sleep.

* * *

Waking is slow, very slow—very unusual for me. There are several layers of waking that I have to work through before comprehension. Sounds. Music. Christmas music. My bed, my own house. This is good. I lay there, listening to the music in the other room, enjoying my bed. Feeling beside me, I realize Anna's not here. It's dark. Pushing through another layer of fog, I focus my eyes. It's not nighttime dark, but the curtains are closed tight and the door is shut. Still, there's laser-bright light around their edges. The clock reads 11:33. Impossible. I sit up and even though I'd rather lie back down, I will myself to my feet and move toward the door. When I open it, my eyes sting from the brightness. But the Christmas music is louder and feels so good it helps me find another level of waking.

"I thought that I drank more than you last night, but I guess not," Anna says, by way of greeting. She is in a nightgown, and it dances lightly around her body. It's almost sheer and there's nothing underneath, her long blond hair is freshly washed and blown. She has no makeup on, but God, she is beautiful.

"Do you like it?" She points into the living room.

All our Christmas decorations are up. "You did all this this morning?" I ask. The artificial tree, which we haven't used for years and was stuck in the back of the storage room in the basement, is fully decorated in the front window. Everything looks just the way it used to look with Stephanie. We weren't going to decorate this year since Steph's not here and we weren't going to be here, either. But the reality sets in—we are here.

"I need this, Freddie," Anna says.

"Me too. Thank you, Anna. Thank you." I give her a kiss, and she wraps her arms around me, pressing her cheek to my chest. "Is it really eleven thirty?"

She nods. "You must have needed it. How do you feel?"

"I feel fine. A little groggy, but fine. Good actually."

"I'll make breakfast—or brunch," Anna says. "What would you like?"

My long refreshing sleep, her kiss, her hugging me tight, her sheer gown, has aroused me and I rub in close to her. No more of an answer is required. She begins to melt, purring in my embrace. Anna places both hands on my chest, under my T-shirt, and plays with my nipples. I lift the shirt over my head and palm her breasts through the filmy gown, returning the playful pinching and touching. She slides into the living room and slips out of her gown before laying back on the sofa while I step out of my pajama pants, fumbling as I draw them over the ankle bracelet. Feeling the immediate wetness of her arousal, I skip any foreplay and I push deeply, fully inside her. Anna responds by arching her hips off the couch, and we thrust wildly at each other for less than a minute, both of us climaxing with a scream at the same time. I have to lay my weight half on her to catch my breath and then withdraw, standing and pulling her up with me, leading her to the bedroom.

Anna lays down on the bed, gorgeous in her nakedness and flushed from the frenzy of a moment ago. I want to take her again, but I want to see all of her, so I draw open the curtains letting the natural light flood in, making her even more attractive. This time we make love, spending an hour pleasuring each other in all our special and private ways. When we finally tire and lay together, side by side, Anna runs her fingers softly along the contours of my scars as has become our habit. But this time there is a new meaning to these puckered, purplish blemishes. They are linked to the ankle bracelet, which is the only thing either of us is wearing.

"I'm glad you told me yesterday—about Africa—about these," Anna whispers.

I roll my head to the side and throw an arm over my face, burying myself in the sand of a nonresponse.

She props herself on an elbow beside me and, ever so gently, pries the arm away. But I keep my eyes shut tight. "You were a child, Alfred. There are reasons we don't prosecute children. Yours is a perfect case why we don't. You weren't responsible for those things."

That's the wrong thing to say, and I throw my arm off my face and turn to look her in the eye. "No, Anna! I was responsible. I killed innocent people. Maybe that fucking priest deserved it, but don't you see? There were others, and I killed them. I knew what I was doing when I pulled the trigger. Whatever is coming … I deserve it."

Anna hangs her head and runs her fingers through her hair, pausing, diffusing, giving me time to calm down before I admit to her my real fear. "They're going to take me away, Anna." My voice cracks. "They're going to lock me in a cage, away from you. Far away."

"No, Freddie. They're not. You were a child when you did those things. They can't."

"But these charges of killing those four men … I don't even know those people."

The intimacy of just a few moments ago has slipped away, and reality is flooding in, quickly replacing it. Anna sits up fully and looks down at me. "That's why we have to wait and see. Maybe there's a mistake. Even if they extradite, they have to give you a fair and full trial in Belgium. They can't convict you for crimes committed as a child. Belgium doesn't do that."

"They're going to separate us, Anna." The thought of this makes me tear up.

"No, they won't. I'll go with you. Don't worry, Freddie. I'm not going to leave you alone."

The rest of the day passes slowly but pleasurably enough under the circumstances. Anna and I try to avoid any more talk of my plight, but it's difficult. Anna means well, and several times mentions that whatever happens, she will be by my side. She is insistent that she is coming with me, and there is no sense in trying to dissuade her. In truth, I want her with me for as long as possible. I don't know if I could bear to lose another angel. To banish these thoughts I go to bed early, alone, and an hour later I make a trip to the medicine cabinet.

I awake the next morning to heavy wet snowflakes, which continue to fall all day, ensuring that Boulder will have a white Christmas tomorrow. Several calls come in. Steve checks on us, all three partners from my work call, trying to get more information, but also sounding genuinely concerned. Anna's brother, Rob, calls to see how we are feeling and to say how they'll miss us at Christmas, but maybe we can all get together before we leave for Saint Martin. Anna's mom also calls to see how we are feeling, hopeful that we might be well enough to make the drive down after all. She tells us that she and Eldon are going to spend Christmas Day with their grandchildren in the Springs, but they are coming right after that to see us, even if they catch whatever it is we have. As has been the custom of family Christmas Eves at her parents' over the years, we sip on rum all day long, just enough to keep us in a bit of good cheer. It's a forced and false mirth, and we both know it, yet each of us does our best to play along with the charade. But it's too draining to last.

After the sun sets and the inside of the house is lit by the dimmed lights and the sparkling colors from the Christmas tree, the double yoke of the warrant and the absence of our precious little Stephanie has us both drinking heavily; all good cheer is lost. We spend the evening in morose conversation and attempt to extinguish it by retiring early. Aided by the rum, Anna falls right to sleep but my mind jumps from one negative thought to another until I end it by making yet another trip to the medicine cabinet.

I can't imagine awakening to a more bleak situation on Christmas morning. Still, we set about making it as normal as possible. Anna prepares a full breakfast and fills the house with smells of cooking and baking. But, once again, we can only play the game so long and by dinnertime the stark truth confronts us when the two of us sit down to eat alone. We drink more than we eat.

Several calls had come over the day, all the expected ones, and some from friends wishing us well knowing we would be missing Steph, but totally oblivious to the new problem in our lives.

The day after Christmas both Anna and I are experiencing the dread of having her parents visit, but there is no way to put them off. Her mother calls to say that they will leave by midmorning; her dad wants to go into his store to make sure everything is fine before they drive up to Boulder. We've always enjoyed having them around, but we don't want to give them the news about the extradition. If we can put off telling them, perhaps it will somehow miraculously clear itself up. We'd like to spare them any unnecessary grief so we agree to be very careful about not letting anything spill. I take the bracelet around my ankle and pull it up on my calf as high as I can, wrapping it in place with a tensor bandage to keep it out of sight should my pants leg slip up when I sit.

Ruth and Eldon arrive in the early afternoon, carrying their overnight bags and Christmas presents. They make another trip to the car to carry in the leftovers from yesterday's Christmas feast. Surprisingly, it turns out to be a big comfort to have them here. I can't imagine a more wholesome, nicer family than Anna's. They've supported Anna and me from the time we arrived back in the US from Paris. They sent care packages for both of us during our years at school in Pittsburgh and flew out there a few times each year to visit us. They paid for both Anna and me to fly to Colorado to be with them and Rob during holidays. And they lent us money several times when we were tight during my residency. They were both extremely proud of us for putting ourselves through school and ending up as respected, working professionals.

Eldon graduated high school but never had a chance to go to college, so he was especially proud to introduce me as his "son-in-law, the doctor," oblivious to the unspoken thoughts and raised eyebrows at the fact that an onyx-black man from Africa with a glaring scar cutting across his face was married to his wholesome, white, mid-American daughter. I had desperately needed someone like Eldon: someone I could look up to, someone who would show such pride in me. Without Vincent around, as he had been for six formative years of my life in Tanzania and then when I first went to France, Eldon filled that void. He wasn't just a father figure, he *was* my father.

At the first chance to be alone Eldon asked me, "Alfred, are you two all right?"

"We're okay, Eldon. Thanks."

"You weren't sick the last few days, were you?"

I don't want to lie, but I don't feel like speaking either, so I give a small shake of my head.

"I didn't think so. You thought it better to be alone? That's fine, if that's what you wanted. We totally understand. But if there is anything we can do to help …"

"Thanks, Eldon, we know."

"Alfred, I don't want to say that we can pretend to know what you and Anna are going through, because none of us has ever lost a child; I can't even really imagine it." He embraces me in a big, generous hug. Loosening his grip and leaning back, he looks softly all around my eyes. I imagine this must be the warm affection that every good father enjoys imparting on his dearly loved son. And surely every appreciative son must relish these moments with his father. I do. I bask in these moments that I missed during my own childhood. Drawing me in tight again, Eldon speaks softly into my ear. "I love you, son. You'll get through this; we all will. We'll always be here for each other." Suddenly, I am embarrassed as I cling to him, not wanting to let go of him. I'm not embarrassed of the hug; I'm embarrassed at not being able to fess up to him about my predicament.

The afternoon is spent with Ruth and Eldon in family conversation, nursing rum and eggnog, and sampling from the mountain of squares and cookies that Ruth has brought. Time passes pleasantly and fairly quickly, allowing me to forget my situation, even if only for a while. As the sun starts to go down, Anna and I head to the kitchen to prepare dinner, leaving Ruth and Eldon in the den to kill a bit of time flicking through the college football games. At one point the background noise of the television goes silent and the two of them appear in the kitchen, looking serious and perplexed.

"Anna, Alfred." Eldon has his eyes narrowed and forehead tensed in puzzlement. "We've just been watching the six o'clock news …" He leaves the sentence dangling, waiting for a reaction from us.

Looking to Anna I see guilt painted across her face and expect mine must look the same.

"What did it say?" she asks.

Eldon responds in a slow cadence of words. "It said that Alfred was arrested on Thursday."

He knows right away it's true by the way we hang our heads, unable to address the accusation.

"What's going on?"

"Daddy, it's a huge mistake." Anna is pleading for that to be true and for her father to believe it. "For some reason—we don't know why—they arrested Alfred. But it's a mistake."

"What kind of mistake? They had to give a reason. You can't just be arrested without a reason. This is the United States of America, for God's sake."

"It's an extradition warrant," Anna says. "And you can be arrested without a full indictment in these cases. We're waiting on someone to give us that. That's why we just don't know how this mistake could have been made."

"You have no idea what this is about?"

"No," Anna responds quickly, lying outright.

"Alfred, you must know something. You have no idea?"

I look at Anna, giving away the conspiracy, and answer lamely, "No. No, Eldon, I have no idea."

I can tell he doesn't believe us by the way he shakes his head and turns sharply, leaving the room with Ruth in tow.

"Anna, shouldn't we tell him what little we know?"

"No." She is firm. "The less they know now the better. When we get it cleared up, none of the rest will even matter."

Dinner couldn't be more awkward. There is a lot of silence, occasionally broken by a question from Eldon trying to pry some additional small morsel of information from us. He knows that we know more than we are letting on, but Anna remains firm, not letting any more out of the bag. Occassionally one of us makes an attempt at starting common conversation, but it goes nowhere. Anna and I clean up while Eldon goes back to the TV in the den, watching more news than football, and we all go to bed early.

My mind is cycling around and around as I layer guilt on top of guilt. I work hard to find some fleck of memory about Belgians, but all of the men I killed were Africans, except for Savard. I'm positive. At least, I think I'm positive. Maybe not. I don't know. And now Anna's parents are dragged into it. It'll be a relief to have them go home tomorrow. I need a couple of pills. I need some escape from this. Sleep comes within moments of swallowing, but so, it seems, does morning, when Anna's phone rings on the night table beside her. She checks first to see who's calling, and then answers. "Steve. It's early; this can't be good news." After listening for just a few seconds she says, "Okay, Steve, start over. I've just put you on speaker. Alfred's here with me."

"Good morning, Alfred," he says. "I've just gotten a copy of the full indictment, and this doesn't look good. The US Attorney's office is trying to get back in front of Judge Cain sometime this afternoon."

"What do you mean, 'It doesn't look good,' Steve?" Anna asks.

"The charge is four counts. We already knew that. It's from a multiple murder in Rwanda in 1994. Belgium has claimed jurisdiction since they were all Belgian citizens and Rwanda had no functioning government at the time to be able to prosecute."

"That's bullshit," Anna says. "They have a government now, and they could prosecute now if they wanted to. It's Rwandan jurisdiction."

"Not quite. This was during the time of the Rwandan uprising and genocide. Rwanda refuses to prosecute any crimes from those years that have not already been litigated by the international war crimes tribunals. It's part of Rwanda's official attempt at national reconciliation. But Belgium isn't recognizing it."

"Well, it's still bullshit. We can challenge that," Anna says.

"Not here we can't. Maybe in Belgium," Steve says.

"Why Alfred? How does he fit into this? In 1994 he was just sixteen or seventeen. Is there any more information?"

"There is, Anna. And this is the worst part—they have a corroborating witness."

"A corroborating witness? Witnesses lie. We both know that."

"There's more, Anna. They've got Alfred's fingerprints on the murder weapon."

"What? That's impossible."

"No," says Steve. "Double verified. Denver police have confirmed that the prints the Belgians sent here are Alfred's. And the prints Denver sent to Brussels were positively matched to the weapon they have there."

"The weapon … a gun?"

"A knife."

"A knife?" Anna repeats Steve's answer, clearly lost in thought.

I'm sure she's thinking the same as I am, *It has to be something to do with the murder of the priest.* But Anna's also a lawyer, and she knows not to panic, not to be alarmist, especially in front of the client. After a deep breath she asks, "So what do we do now?"

"I'll go to the hearing this afternoon. I'll ask for a writ of habeas corpus again, but it's not likely it'll be granted. With what I've seen so far it looks like the case is solid for extradition. Not necessarily solid to *convict*, but enough that they can at least extradite to Belgium. I've got a few recommendations for counsel there, so I'll make the initial contacts today in case things move quickly. I have a feeling Brussels is going to want it done soon."

"Is there anything we should do here?" Anna asks.

"Yes," says Steve. "Brace yourself ..."

"For the worst?" Anna says, finishing his sentence.

"For the worst, and for the media. The locals have been all over this already. They're running stories now."

"Shit," Anna says. "Thanks, Steve. Let us know what happens as soon as you finish with the judge."

Sitting in the bed in her pajamas Anna is all business. "Alfred, what happened in 1994? Think about it. Try to remember everything—or anything."

"Anna, I remember 1994 very well. It's the year I left Rwanda. I left early in the year to get away from the killings. I spent most of that year in the Nkwenda refugee camp in Tanzania. I've already told you: I killed *one* man that year—the priest, Savard. There was no one else. You have to believe me, Anna."

"Of course I believe you, Freddie. It's just that we have to figure out what's going on. How could this mistake be happening? Fingerprint evidence is tough to refute. Where the hell would they have ever gotten your prints—twenty-two years ago—in a place like that?"

I am just as lost for words and ideas as Anna is when she changes directions. "We have other things to deal with here, too. Mom and Dad are up already. We are going to have to say something to them if this is going to come out in the media. And your clinic … we might as well call Mark before everything hits the fan."

We're a few minutes too late. By the time we dress and go out to own up to Anna's parents, they are already glued to the television in the den. We're greeted somberly with, "Why didn't you tell us the truth?"

"Dad, we didn't know the truth. We only heard this morning, and we've just come out to tell you everything we know, right now."

"We've already heard quite a bit on the news," says Eldon. "I hope you're going to tell us that it's all wrong."

"Dad, this is Alfred we're talking about. Of course it's wrong. Are you going to believe the news over Alfred?" She has started to raise her voice.

"You know I want to believe you, Alfred." Eldon addresses me directly. "But you know what they're saying on the news? It sounds pretty convincing. We've always trusted you, but this? This is hard to take."

Ruth interrupts. "Eldon, please. Alfred, of course we trust you. We just need to hear your side of the story."

"What are they saying on the news, Mom?" Anna asks.

"Here …" Eldon points the clicker at the television and presses the unmute button.

A perky young morning anchor dominates the TV screen and a small insert photo of me looks back at us:

"KCBC 6 has been able to confirm several new details of the story that we first reported to you yesterday. Respected Denver family physician, Dr. Alfred Olyontombo, a Rwandan immigrant and US resident citizen for the past ten years, is currently under house arrest after the US State Department acted on a request by the Belgian government to have him extradited for the murders of four Belgian citizens in Rwanda in 1994. Our sources in Belgium say that the four victims were all nuns teaching at a missionary school at the time. The savage murders drew national outrage in Belgium in 1994 when they happened only a few days after ten Belgian UN peacekeepers were slaughtered. At that time, Rwanda was in the midst of a bloody civil war and until now, no one has been held accountable for the crimes which shocked the Belgian nation twenty-three years ago."

There is new information here that even Steve had not told us. Probably because he didn't know. The four of us are riveted to the television screen as the news anchor continues:

"KCBC 6 has been able to confirm that Dr. Olyontombo was arrested this past Thursday at his clinic in downtown Denver. Neighbors near his home in Boulder, and patients that we have been able to speak with, are in shock. Dr. Olyontombo is married to Colorado-native Anna Fraser, an immigration lawyer at the firm of Tierney, Thomas, and May. KCBC 6 will be following this story and will bring you updates as they become available."

Eldon clicks the power button, and the TV screen goes black. I know that the other three are all looking at me, but I pay them no attention. I'm stunned by this news, and I move to sit down in my large armchair. I feel like my stomach has been punched hard, the wind knocked out of me. I am slightly dizzy and almost miss the chair, sitting on the arm before sliding into it. A vague memory seeps into my head, something that I had never thought about before. I try to picture it more clearly in my mind, something one of the refugees at the Nkwenda camp had said to me: "The depravity of some men knows no lows. They closed the school."

For a while after I left Notre Dame de la Paix, I would ask new arrivals from Kigali who came into the camp if they had any news of the school and the good sisters. Finally one of them told me that the school had closed. I didn't pay any heed at the time to his comment, "The depravity of some men knows no lows," thinking that it was a general reference to the sad state of the genocide that was taking place in our country. Now it made sense; they had killed the sisters.

I must have been thinking out loud because I hear Anna addressing me: "Alfred, what do you mean, 'they had killed the sisters'?" she asks. "Do you know something about this?"

I look up and toward Anna, but my gaze goes right through her.

"Alfred? Alfred, what do you know about this?"

"Nothing, Anna. I knew nothing about this," I mutter.

My thoughts go back to the convent and the last encounter I had with the nuns. I hadn't wanted to leave the school, to leave them alone there. I thought that if I stayed I might be able to protect them, but they insisted that I go. Kigali was a chaotic mess, indiscriminate murders and slaughters were becoming the norm. Friend had turned against friend, and old neighbors against old neighbors as the viciousness of zealous racism spread like a plague. The sisters were emphatic that they would be safe; they had no part in this race war, they weren't even black. They knew that those of us that were black could never be certain of escaping the violence. I tried to convince them that if it hadn't been safe for a priest it wouldn't be safe for them. They firmly believed that no one would harm them—women, women of the church no less, and not politically active like Savard. They were sure they would be fine, but they could do little if the mobs came looking for me or others like me, others that might be hiding out under the skirts of the church. They made the last of us students leave, for our own protection.

* * *

"Azi, you have to go with the rest of them," Sister Brigit said. "It's too dangerous here, Azi."

"All the more reason for me to stay," I said. "I'll stay with you and the others—to help protect you."

"We're fine. They won't do anything to us. But it's not safe for you. Even in here. You have to go to one of the camps. And you have to go soon," she said.

Mother Katherine spoke up, "You cannot stay here, Azikiwe."

"Mother, I'm not one of them. I'm neither Hutu nor Tutsi."

"Neither side knows that. And they won't care anyhow. I am ordering you to go to one of the camps. Go to Zaire. We will give you what money we can spare, and you can take some food from the kitchen. You can come back when it is safe. But you have to go tonight—in the early hours before dawn. That will be the safest."

I went to the kitchen and packed my small rucksack with fruit and a bit of cheese and bread. The four sisters were in discussion when I went back to say goodbye. I hugged them all, one at a time—Sister Marie, Sister Geraldine, Sister Brigit, and Mother Katherine. Mother Katherine offered a blessing on me and handed me two thousand francs, urging me not to hide it all in one place.

I returned to the dorm to wait out more of the night before leaving. I thought about what else I should take with me and then decided to leave whatever meager possessions that I owned in the little drawer at the foot of my bed. I was sure I'd be back within a week or two, a month at the most. I left it all—my books, my notebooks, my change of clothes—taking only my single piece of identification: my baptismal certificate. As Mother Katherine had advised, I split up my two thousand francs, hiding five hundred in my shoes, five hundred each in two different places in my rucksack, and kept just five hundred in my pocket.

* * *

"Alfred? Alfred?" Anna has raised her voice to get my attention, and it brings me back to the present. "You know *something* about this." The way she says it as a statement tells me that she can almost read my thoughts.

"Not about the murders," I reply. "But I think I knew those nuns."

Eldon and Ruth are watching the two of us, me particularly, searching for my reactions. And why shouldn't they? The whole situation is as big a blow to them as to Anna and me, only they haven't had the few extra days to mull on it. I contemplate my options, deciding between defending myself against the charges we have just heard on the television and confessing all the other sins of my past. I settle for a mix of the two.

"Mom, Eldon, there are a lot of things that I've never told you about myself. Evil things. Things I have spent decades trying to erase. I wish these things never happened, that I never did them. But I am guilty, without excuse."

Anna stops me. "Freddie, you were a child. It was a horrible world you lived in."

"Nonetheless, I did them, Anna. Others lived in the same horrible world and didn't do what I did."

"That's nonsense, Freddie. You were forced to. *You'd* be dead if you hadn't."

"What are you talking about?" Eldon asks. "What kinds of things, Alfred? Did you kill those nuns?"

"Stop it, Daddy." Anna jumps between her father and me. "It's Alfred. Of course he didn't kill them."

"I haven't heard him say it yet. I want to hear it from *him*." Eldon steps around Anna, looking directly into my eyes, trying to find the truth from my words. "I want to hear you say it, Alfred. I want to hear you say that you didn't kill those nuns."

Shaking my head infinitesimally side to side, I respond firmly, "No, Eldon. No, Ruth. I did not kill those nuns. I loved them. I never would have hurt them." After pausing, I venture to continue. "But if you want the rest of the truth, I did kill others. So, while I am not guilty of the murders they want to hang me for, I am guilty of many others."

Anna starts to cry; so does her mother. Eldon clamps his lips shut tightly and nods to himself. He's struggled with his own war demons, having lived through Vietnam, and seems to comprehend that war comes with many shades of righteousness. Despite my stoic resolve to be strong, I feel my eyes welling with tears—not tears for my present situation or for what I have done in my past, but tears for what I have done to Anna and Eldon and Ruth. Tears for having let them down, tears for the shame they will now have to endure.

Right at this moment the doorbell chimes. None of us move; we all know who it is.

It rings a second time. "I'll get it," I say. "It's me they want."

"No." Anna is firm and quickly steps between me and the front hall. "I'll get it. You don't say a word to them."

I can see over her shoulder when she opens the door, and the scene is worse than I expected. Two news trucks are parked on the street along with a couple more cars splashed in the colors of daily newspapers. A gaggle of reporters stands at the step. They all start to talk at the same time, throwing out questions. Anna raises her hand, as a teacher in a noisy classroom might, and is able to silence them in unison. I hear Anna's warning in my head, *Don't say a word,* and I momentarily weigh that against going out and offering up the total confession that is bursting to get out of me. They are asking for me, asking who Anna is, launching questions at her.

"Did he kill the nuns in Rwanda?"

"No, he did not. Absolutely not."

"Did he know them? Was he there? Was he at that school? How is it his prints were found on the murder weapon?"

"I'm sorry. We have nothing else to say. But I ask you all to please respect the privacy of our family in my home. Please."

Anna closes the door behind her and slumps back up against it, closing her eyes and taking in a deep breath.

"Thank you," I mutter.

Anna rubs her forehead and tries to smile.

I feel helpless. "I'll put a pot of coffee on. You better see if your parents are okay."

Before entering the den I pause to listen to the conversation that they are having.

Eldon: "Have you considered that it's possible he might be guilty?"

Anna: "Don't even say that. It's Alfred. He's not guilty."

Eldon: "Anna, get your head out of the sand. He just told us he's guilty of *many* other murders. Why wouldn't he be guilty of these too? Because they have caught him and want to hang him, that's why. He's not admitting to these. It doesn't mean he didn't do it."

Anna: "Stop it, Daddy!"

Eldon: "Think about it, Anna. What if they convict him? Do you want to be married to someone locked up five thousand miles away? And even if they don't convict him, he's a murderer. Do you want to be married to a murderer for the rest of your life?"

Anna: "Yes … I don't know. Please stop, Daddy. I need to think."

Eldon: "You need to open your eyes, honey. They wouldn't be bringing charges twenty years later if they didn't have a damn good case."

So, it's already begun, the public trial by family and peers, and it hasn't taken long to reach a verdict. A guilty plea would speed things up and spare Anna some of the humiliation that is coming. Eldon is right: I am a murderer. Why shouldn't I be punished for murder? Does it matter that these are the wrong murders? Does anyone care, as long as justice is meted out?

Anna bursts from the room before I have a chance to contemplate these questions. She bumps into me and roughly pushes away my attempt to wrap my arms around her.

"Please, Alfred. Give me some space."

It takes a lot to rattle Anna, and her father seems to have managed it this morning. That in and of itself is uncharacteristic. Eldon is not usually one to upset others. He's rational and thoughtful, the one who calms nerves and finds sensible common ground. His natural tendency to get all the facts and not prejudge has clearly been pushed to its limits this morning.

"Eldon, Ruth, I'm terribly sorry about all of this. I don't know what else to say. And you're right not to trust me. I've misled you all these years. Not because I wanted to, but because I just haven't been able to admit things, even to myself."

"Alfred," Eldon says. "We'll give you the benefit of the doubt, for now. You're our son-in-law. We love you because you're married to our daughter. And we'll do what it takes to get her through this."

These statements hit me like a speeding truck. "We love you because you're married to our daughter." I've never, ever heard any qualification of their love like this before. Their love has always come free of conditions. Now, however, all of a sudden, things are different. And they'll do what it takes to get *her* through this? Nothing about getting *us* through it.

Eldon and Ruth make a perfunctory offer to stay and help Anna, but both Anna and I read it for what it is: they'd rather be out of this situation, away from the media and away from the volcanic rift that is growing between Anna and them, and me and them. Anna doesn't need the distraction they pose. She knows she needs to focus on the situation, both as a wife and professionally, and I'd just prefer to be left alone to wallow in my misery. We all agree it is better for them to go home. Eldon and Ruth promise to break the news to Anna's brother and his family before they hear it elsewhere—if they haven't already. That'll save Anna and me one phone call we'd rather not make.

Within a few hours we are inundated with calls, most of them media inquiries, but some are from the more gossipy and nosy of our friends. By noon we unplug the landline and I turn off my cell. We leave Anna's phone on because we need to be able to hear from Steve.

Alone in the house, stuck here, Anna and I wait out the day in agitated irritableness. Anna is doing her best to be professional and logical, but my attempts to converse with or touch her are met by snaps and a coldness that is foreign to our relationship. I can feel things changing. I sense it all around me, not just here in this house with Anna—everywhere. A call from Mark at the clinic, careful not to commit too much support for us, now that more of the details are out there in the media, is a good indicator of how things are turning, of how the unconditional support of a few days ago is now being hedged.

Anna finally gets a confirmation from Steve that he has a court time today with Judge Cain at three o'clock. He has also made contact with a criminal lawyer in Belgium, Bartholomeus Verbeke, who is making some inquiries for us. But it is after hours in Europe and most offices are closed until tomorrow. When Steve asks about the media situation outside our house Anna tells him that they have all been very respectful and that they remain camped quietly on the street. Steve suggests we go out and offer them a statement; he'll draft something for us to say and email it over. We can refer all questions to his office, and hopefully that will be enough to get the media hounds to leave. His secretary has been monitoring the news all morning, and it doesn't look like the reporters have dug up anything *else* that we don't know.

The promised email arrives about twenty minutes later, and Anna ventures out the front door. The gaggle has grown, but Anna has experience with this, and she is not intimidated by the press of bodies on the front step nor the flashing cameras.

"If I could have your attention please," Anna says, and then reads from the prepared statement. "My name is Anna Fraser. I am the wife of Dr. Alfred Olyontombo. As you already know my husband is confined to house arrest, and this will be the last statement we make here at our home. We have engaged Steve May of Tierney, Thomas, and May as our attorney, and he will be pleased to answer any of your questions if you contact him

at his office. We appreciate your respect for our privacy and the privacy of
our neighbors."

"Mrs. Fraser, do you believe that your husband is guilty?"

"Mrs. Fraser, how much did you know of your husband's past?"

"Have you been in touch with Belgian officials yet? What did they say?"

"Has Dr. Olyontombo resigned from his clinic?"

Anna lets out a long sigh as she shuts the door behind her. This time
she lets me take her in my arms and hold her for a few minutes. I think I
need the close contact more than she does because, once I am holding her,
I don't want to let go. I imagine she must be thinking the same thing: *How
did we ever get to this?* The house is quiet and empty, the two of us are here,
but nothing is on—no lights, no television—and it's getting drab outside
with the sun hidden completely by clouds late in the afternoon. It makes
it like dusk inside the house. Leaving the lights off, we retire to the den.

Anna sits on the sofa with her feet pulled up to the side underneath
her and laughs. Not a happy laugh, or a fun laugh, but rather a resigned
laugh. "We've been through a lot, haven't we?" she says.

I'm not sure if she means the last few days, or the last few months with
the death of our daughter, or our entire relationship together, but I answer
her, "Yes, we have."

"Nothing like this though."

"No. Nothing like this."

"But we'll get through this, won't we." She might be questioning me
or telling me, there's very little expression in her voice to give me clues.

"I hope so."

Tipping her head to one side, she stares at nothing in midair and nods
slowly. "Tell me about the nuns ... and that priest," she finally says.

I tell her that there isn't much that I haven't already told her: that I
always assumed that the nuns were from France, like the priest, Savard,
who I knew for certain was. They all spoke French, and we called them by
their French names. It never dawned on me that French was also a main
language of Belgium. We talk about how much I loved the nuns, how well
school went, and how I excelled there. How much they helped me, to
escape from the animal I had become, to become human again.

"And the priest … after you … after he was dead? What did the authorities do?"

"They'd no reason to ever suspect me. You had to live through those times, Anna, to understand. Savard was a foreigner and the police made a perfunctory show of investigating, but he had been sticking his nose into politics, and as far as they were concerned, he was just another political casualty. They could barely keep up."

I divert Anna with more stories from Notre Dame de la Paix, and the distraction is good for us, keeping us both occupied until the call comes from Steve. He has just finished the hearing and is on his way over. This could be good news, or it could be bad; Anna says she can't tell from his voice. But she understands this lawyer process and knows it's better to receive the news face-to-face. I would have just begged him to tell me over the phone. It'll take him an hour to drive up to Boulder from downtown this time of day. When I complain to Anna she tells me that he wants to see us because he's our friend not just our lawyer and, she points out, he might be our only friend right now.

While we wait for Steve, Anna takes a call from her brother and gets up, leaving me alone in the den. She heads toward our bedroom seeking privacy.

"Anna," I call after her. "Let me talk to him before you hang up."

Rob needs to hear some of this from me, and I need to hear his reaction for myself. He'll have spoken to Ruth and Eldon by now, and I'd like to get a feel for the impression that they gave him. I hope they've moderated a bit since they left here this morning. With all the things that are going wrong, I don't want a split between Anna and her family. I understand if they turn against me—fair enough—but it would be a harsh cruelty to have any bad feelings amongst this tight and loving family. Rob understands Eldon and might be the force that can keep the bonds tight. When Anna returns to the den I can see that she is upset as she places down her phone.

"I wanted to speak with Rob," I say. "I owe it to him."

"He said that he didn't want to speak to you."

"What? What did he say? What did you talk about with him?"

"I told him what we know, and that we're waiting for Steve right now."

"What else? What did he have to say? How are Eldon and Ruth?"

Anna explains the conversation. It sounds like her parents are very skeptical of me; they've told Rob that I admitted to being a murderer. Neither Rob nor her parents have heard the full circumstances of my crimes, but it seems it doesn't matter—guilty on one count, guilty on all counts. Rob wants Anna to go home to Colorado Springs so that she can be with her family, and she told him that was impossible—house arrest means that someone has to be here to supervise me.

"What did he say to that?" I ask.

"He thinks I should go ... and let them lock you up."

"Rob said that?" I'm incredulous, but I mull on it for minute. In what is likely an attempt on my part to elicit some pity I mumble, "Maybe he's right."

I assume by the way Anna looks at me without saying anything, just delaying and looking at me, that she herself is thinking that maybe he's right. Maybe she should get away now before this goes any further. A month ago a reaction like this, of casting a shadow of doubt onto our relationship, would have made me weep. Even a few days ago I probably would have teared up. But after the past twenty-four hours my heart has been pounded by a sledge so many times that tears don't even form. In my mind, I am sure Anna is considering Rob's advice. So am I.

It's full darkness outside when Steve finally arrives, and we anxiously answer the door. Letting him in to our completely darkened house, I flick a switch. Anna and I see each other in full light for the first time in more than an hour. I assume that I look as pathetic as she looks emotionally drained, but Steve maintains his professionalism, not giving any indication that he has noticed.

"Would you like tea, or a drink?" Anna asks.

"Not right now," Steve replies. "Maybe later."

Steve knows his way around our house and he heads to the kitchen and opens his briefcase on the countertop.

"It went pretty much as I had feared," Steve says. "Brussels has provided more than enough for extradition. They've got a witness and fingerprint evidence. Maybe that's not enough to convict in a court, but it's enough to extradite and get a preliminary trial there. That's all they need. With our treaties, Judge Cain's hands were pretty much tied."

"So, what now?" Anna asks.

"We'll have to fight this in Belgium. I've got the contact for Bartholomeus Verbeke in Brussels. He comes highly recommended, and he's got experience at the Rwandan war crimes trials, so he should understand some of the context here. He's also supposed to have good contacts in the justice department in Belgium."

"When will things happen?"

"Very soon," Steve replies. "The DOJ wants to transfer right away to the East Coast, and then Belgium will escort you overseas with their people."

"What's 'very soon' mean?" Anna asks.

"Tomorrow night. Late in the night. That's when the regular JPATS flight goes from DIA. The US Marshals will pick up Alfred here and issue standard transfer garb. But you'll need to send civilian clothes because the transatlantic flight will be commercial, and they don't want to draw attention to the fact there's a prisoner on board."

I knew DIA was Denver International Airport, but the other acronym lost me. "What's JPATS?" I asked.

"Sorry," says Steve. "The Justice Prisoner and Alien Transportation System. That's the fed's airline for moving criminals around within the country.

"Also," Steve adds, "we've been able to do a bit of internet research on the four victims named in the indictment. The short story is that they were four nuns teaching at an old missionary school south of Kigali in 1994. It happened within a few weeks of the start of a massive genocide that killed anywhere between five hundred thousand and one million people."

I know this much already. I had surmised from the earlier television news reports that it was the good sisters from Notre Dame de la Paix who were murdered—and it was their deaths that they were trying to blame on me. I also knew about the genocide since I'd followed the news of the war crimes tribunal when I lived in Paris. Not a lot of Americans knew much about the genocide since news in the US often doesn't cover much of the rest of the world—unless Americans have a financial stake in it. I am hoping Steve can tell me something new.

Steve goes on. "Early in April of 1994 ten Belgian paratroopers, part of the international peacekeeping force in Rwanda, were butchered and mutilated. The Belgians went crazy. They began to pull all their peacekeeping forces out. The public was up in arms. Then five days later these four Belgian nuns were murdered. Apparently, it dominated the news in Belgium for a long time. Only one guy was ever convicted of the paratrooper killings, and they've never been able to convict anyone of the nuns' murders. It's still a very sensitive topic in Belgium."

"Fuck." Anna sighs. "So, we don't just have to fight in the courts over there, we have to fight public opinion as well?"

"Unfortunately," Steve says with a shrug, "that's probably true. But maybe not for a few days yet. As far as we can tell, this investigation by the prosecutors hasn't made it to the Belgian papers ... for now. We'll keep our fingers crossed."

I had never heard of the nuns' murders until just this morning. That news had never even reached me in the Nkwenda camp.

But the picture is now becoming much clearer. I played a role in the deaths of Mother Katherine and the others. I was at least partially responsible, because I left them alone. I should have stayed, protected them. These were four beautiful people, who did nothing but good for me and all the others at that school and in the local community. For the first time I begin to think that maybe punishment in Belgium will not be just some twisted justice in repayment for other crimes of my childhood, it may be rightfully due to me for the murders of the sisters, along with the other blood I shed at that school.

I leave Steve and Anna so I can sit alone in the darkened den to sort through my thoughts. The recliner is cool but comfortable, and I close my eyes to fight a debate in my own mind. On the one hand, I know logically, without any question, that I did not kill those nuns, but some illogical part of my being is equally convincing in telling me that I have culpability. Something inside me is demanding atonement, penance, justice, so that all my sins compiled as a child mercenary might somehow be erased or forgiven. I struggle to find a way to relieve my guilt. If I confess to the murders of these nuns and if they punish me for them, then perhaps that will give me the freedom my soul seeks. But I am trained as a logical thinker. I am a physician, and I know that these arguments make no sense *logically*. Logically, I shouldn't be punished for a specific crime which I did not commit, and I know where Anna's legal mind would settle on this. And, logically, it makes no sense that punishment now will make me a better a person going forward. I certainly don't need deterrence; I've worked hard for the past two decades to do everything I can to help my fellow humans and to lead a noble existence. I know all of this. So why is the illogical argument making so much sense to me?

Steve's goodbyes stir me from my reverie. He promises to get back to us tomorrow as soon as he has more news. Anna comes into the den, turns on the light, and sits.

"What else did Steve have to say?" I ask.

"Nothing."

"Well, you were talking about something. What were you talking about?"

"Nothing."

"Anna?"

"He wanted to make sure that I am considering all the eventualities."

"Meaning?"

"Meaning ... have I thought about if you are convicted there?"

"And? What other *eventualities*?"

"What we'll do if you're sentenced there," she replies.

"Did he ask you to consider that I might even be guilty? That I might be a murderer of four nuns?"

"Yes." She looks in my eyes and searches for clues of this possible guilt. "Yes. That, too."

"And what did you tell him about these possible *eventualities*?"

"I told him that you won't be found guilty."

"What did you tell him if I am *found* guilty?"

"That we'll apply to have your sentence served here in the States," she says.

"What did you tell him if I *am* guilty?"

"You're not," she replies spontaneously.

"If I am?"

She pauses to consider the question. "If you are—and you haven't told me the truth—I don't know. I don't know what I'd do." She watches me, trying to read me, and then asks, "Are you?"

"I'm thinking of pleading guilty just to get it all over with. Get what's due me."

She erupts in a sudden fit that scares me as she shouts loudly in my face, "Are you guilty? Did you kill those nuns? Are you guilty or not? Tell me the fucking truth, Alfred!"

The bluster of the arguments I had made to myself a few minutes ago vanishes amidst the intimidation I am now feeling. "Anna, of course I didn't kill them. But I didn't stay to help them, either." I try to repeat aloud the debate that I had just worked through in my mind, and it comes out sounding lame and pitiful, more so in front of a professional lawyer.

"Freddie." She has calmed down and speaks slowly, as if I am a child needing extreme clarity. "You weren't there. You didn't do it. You will not plead guilty. We will fight this. Period."

New Year's

Thursday night the marshals picked me up, just as Steve predicted. The rest of the night was spent traveling across the country as any other common prisoner would, courtesy of the JPATS airline. They delivered me to this US Immigration detention facility in Newark, New Jersey, to await pickup by the Kingdom of Belgium. Now, after two days stuck here, it is New Year's Eve, and I'm finally able to speak to Steve by phone. He tells me that Bartholomeus Verbeke, the lawyer he's arranged for me in Brussels, left him a message saying that the prosecutor's office there wants me picked up as soon as possible. He tells me that probably means Wednesday. Today is Sunday, and tomorrow will be the New Year's Day holiday, so they'll likely fly here Tuesday and take me to Belgium on Wednesday.

I lay down early for bed, contemplating my first New Year's Eve alone since before I met Anna. I've spoken to her only once in the last few days since leaving Denver. Her parents worked hard to convince her to go to their place in Colorado Springs while I am held here, in limbo. My mind starts twisting, running through scenarios of what might be happening there with her parents. Perhaps they've convinced her to stay away from me. She's very close to them, and she must be having doubts about me. Maybe they'll convince her not to come to Belgium. These negative thoughts keep me awake most of the night.

I have it in my mind that Wednesday will be the day that I leave, so I am surprised when the next day, New Year's Day, the door to my cell swings open and a guard hands me a plastic bag and instructs me to change into my own civilian clothes.

"Am I going somewhere?" I take the package from him.

"Out."

"Where?"

"No idea. They told me to get these to you and to have you put them on. Let's go," he says.

It feels good, dignified, to have my own clothes back on. I've been wearing the same prisoner attire that the marshals gave me four days ago when they picked me up at my home. I assume that they must be taking me to a hearing of some kind, and I follow my guard's instructions to walk ahead of him, back to the entrance of this facility. A new set of US Marshals await. After verifying me, I'm ordered to remove the jacket I'm wearing, and a set of handcuffs is affixed to my wrists.

"Can you tell me where you're taking me?"

"We've been instructed to get you to the airport. That's all we really know. Sorry."

This is a short ride, retracing the route of the bus that brought me out the back of the Newark airport a few days ago. We drive through the same security gate before entering the terminal building through an area marked SECURE PERSONNEL ENTRANCE. TSA staff are managing the area but there are no long lines here. My handcuffs are removed and replaced by a set of plastic ones, and I am directed into the body scan machine, instructed to hold my hands above my head, and then motioned out the other side where I am greeted by my same marshal escorts.

These two have obviously done this before because they know exactly how to find their way through the maze of corridors in the depths of the terminal. They have an electronic card which they scan outside a windowless door that allows us into a small lounge which is furnished with comfortable-looking plush chairs and a sofa. There is a table set with an assortment of drinks and snack foods. Two of the chairs are occupied by men who rise as we enter and greet my escorts. Neither of these men wears a suit jacket, and both are openly displaying holsters with pistols strapped to their torsos. The two men sound tired when they speak, making their guttural-accented English even more pronounced. No one bothers to introduce me, and I am left standing there while the four men do a verification and exchange paperwork. All satisfied that I am who I am supposed to be, they trade my plastic handcuffs for a traditional metal set, and the marshals leave me with my new escorts.

"Azikiwe Olyontombo, I am Inspector Dirk Herweyer, of the Belgian Federal Police. This is my partner, Philippe Brossard. We are escorting you to Brussels tonight. As of right now you are considered to be under the custody of the Belgian government and all laws of the Kingdom of Belgium will prevail. This includes that anything you might say to us can be used in prosecution against you. You have a right to a lawyer and one will be made available as soon as we can upon arrival …"

He continues with the full Belgian equivalent of the US Miranda warning and then hands me a sheet of paper with it all printed out in English and French. Steve had already explained the process to me, the basics of the Belgian court system and the process of prisoner transfer. Commercial flights are the most common method of moving international prisoners. It's done with discretion, and other passengers on the plane rarely even knowing that a transfer is happening. The airline personnel and the air marshals on the affected flights are the only ones aware. As an added measure of security the exact transfer flights are kept confidential, even from family and lawyers. This has left Anna with no way of knowing when I will be sent to Belgium.

"All right, with the formalities out of the way, Olyontombo, we all know what you've done," the inspector says. "We'd probably be considered heroes if we could find a reason to shoot you, so feel free to give us one.

And one is all we need. You won't be given a second chance. Unfortunately, we do have to demonstrate some discretion on a commercial flight, so be on your best behavior. The most likely reason anyone should have to suspect that you are a prisoner in transport is that I have shot you. Do you understand all this?"

I nod while trying to assess these two. The one that has done the talking, Inspector Herweyer, is quite a bit older than I am, almost retirement age, I think. The other one is quite a bit younger, not even thirty yet. I had anticipated more refinement from European police, not the surliness that this one is demonstrating. I'm not sure why I expected that.

"I'd like to make a phone call, if I may, Inspector."

"I just told you, you are now under Belgian law. Forget the American TV crap. You don't *get* a phone call," Herweyer says.

"I just wanted to call my wife and let her know what's happening."

"Not from here you don't. Have your lawyer call her when we get to Belgium."

Tentatively I ask, "May I sit?"

"There." He points to a hard straight-back chair. As I take it he flops onto one of the comfortable lounge chairs opposite me. Then, as if to deliberately rub it in, he takes out his cell phone and sets it on the table beside him.

I interpret everything so far to mean that I need to be very careful. This man obviously knows the charges I am facing, but I can't decide if he is just a jerk with a personal chip on his shoulder, or if this is an indication of something bigger, of which I'm just unaware. The younger man, Brossard, seems to have a more amenable temperament, but defers the lead to Herweyer.

Less than five minutes later, Herweyer nods to Brossard who tells me to get up and shows me how to place my arms so that they can drape my jacket over my handcuffs, keeping them out of view.

"We'd prefer if you don't draw attention to these. We'll keep the jacket here. If you've got to take a shit, do it now, because these cuffs won't come off until we land."

From the back corridors of the terminal we are led by a security guard to the boarding ramp of a Brussels Airlines 777. The plane has not yet started general boarding, but we are let on, and Brossard follows me all the way to the second to last row, where he directs me into the window seat on the right-hand side of the plane. Herweyer has a short conversation with the pilot at the front and then comes to the back taking the window seat directly behind me in the last row. Brossard sits in the middle seat right beside me.

It is a while before other passengers start boarding, beginning with some elderly people and others needing assistance, then those with kids, and finally the general public. Boarding takes a while; this is a big plane, and it's New Year's Day, but the flight appears full with the exception of the one seat to the left of Philippe Brossard and the two beside Dirk Herweyer in the row behind us.

Waiting on the tarmac for the plane to take off, my thoughts drift back to the first time I went through this airport. We were young and flush with optimism. Arriving from Paris we had a quick stopover in Newark on our way to Denver. Anna was going home, and I was on my way to meet her family for the first time. We were both about to start our studies at the University of Pittsburgh, and we were brimming with idealism. I was sure that coming to America was my opportunity to put the sins of Africa behind me, which I wanted to do so desperately. And with each passing year they sank further and further into the distance, less of a distraction, less of a burden. Our lives were charmed, each year better than the one before—until Steph got sick. Now, I've returned to this same airport that was once my gateway to freedom, leaving the accomplishments of the last sixteen years, heading toward a reckoning with the past.

Shortly after we are airborne my escort behind me leans in to let his partner know that he is going to take a nap. When I am sure by the sounds of his light snores that he is asleep, I venture to make conversation with Inspector Brossard beside me.

"I hadn't expected to be transferred so soon." I speak in French to make it easier for him and friendlier. "Just yesterday my lawyer told me that it probably wouldn't be until at least Wednesday before you came for me."

"We just got lucky," Brossard says.

"Lucky?" It's an odd choice of a word for this situation and I am curious.

"Yeah. We've known about this assignment for a while, and as soon as it came up last week we jumped on it."

"Jumped on it? Why?"

"I've always thought it'd be cool to do New Year's Eve in Times Square. The timing was perfect. That's why we're a little tired. Dirk doesn't do the late-night partying so well anymore. Says he used to be able to drink all night and then work the next day no problem. I think he's full of shit. I don't think a hard-ass like him was ever a partyer."

"Why did he want to come, then?"

"A personal feather in his cap before he retires."

"I don't understand."

"A little prestige before he goes out. You're going to be a big deal when this comes out in the news. He wants to be able to say he was the one who brought you in."

"Really …"

"Yeah, I was just a little kid when you killed those nuns, but he was on the force. He's been telling me how the whole country was sickened, first when the peacekeepers got slaughtered, and then just a week later when you killed the sisters. Dirk says that every man in Belgium who was alive when that stuff happened will want to drop the guillotine on your neck. He says there'll probably be a public call on Parliament to bring back the death sentence—just for you."

This is quite enough for me to drop the idea of conversation and I sit silently, thinking about what I've learned. He's already convicted me and is convinced that everyone else will, too. I don't know when my case will become public, but it sounds like when it does it's going to be big news. Perhaps it's better if Anna isn't there. Maybe she doesn't need to be dragged through all this if the outcome is already a fait accompli.

Some time passes in silence before I ask my escort for the time.

"That depends … New York time or Brussels time?"

"Now. Wherever we are right now."

"A little after midnight," he says.

"A little after midnight. January second, then?"

"Yes."

"My wife and I were supposed to be on a plane together today. We were going to Saint Martin. It was going to be our honeymoon trip. We never got to take one when we were married."

Herweyer laughs from the seat behind us. I hadn't realized that he was awake and listening. Without even trying to keep his voice down he says, "What kind of a bitch would marry a pathetic bastard like you? Serves you both right."

The barb stings, and I regret more than ever having brought this upon Anna. I feel like weeping, but I don't want to give these two the satisfaction, so I turn my head toward the window and wipe away the few tears that have escaped. I decide to stay silent the remainder of the flight, but an hour or so later I need to use the bathroom.

"Monsieur Brossard, I'd like to use the restroom, please."

Brossard looks back over his shoulder at Herweyer who frowns and nods to him. Brossard waits for me to exit my seat and then follows me into the galley, which is right behind us in the back of the plane. As I am shutting the tiny bathroom door a boot is thrust into it, blocking it from closing, and then it is pushed wide open. Herweyer is standing there with two airline attendants busy behind him.

"Door stays open. Security rules. I told you to go before you left."

The flight attendants are as embarrassed as I am, and they squeeze out into the aisle.

"Go ahead, macaque. Hurry up and do your business."

Upon returning to my seat I resolve not to engage this man for anything anymore. Instead, I occupy my mind thinking about the last day I shared at home with Anna, before the marshals came to collect me.

* * *

Most of the day had been spent drafting notes for the clinic, getting updates from Steve, dodging calls from acquaintances, and seesawing in my mind about what I am due for my sins. I'd kept this debate to myself since I knew Anna's position and wanted to avoid confrontation; our time left together was short and very precious at that point.

I had no idea how long I might be away so I prepared notes for my colleagues at the clinic who would have to take over my patients. Most of what they need to know is contained in the patient files, but there are a lot of things that I store in my head, little personal things, like favorite sports teams and whatnot. There are a few patients I wanted them to pay particular attention to, especially those who require ongoing care. One of these is Ricky Nunez. He'll just be starting his cancer treatments in the new year, and I'm hoping that whomever takes his case makes sure that he is actually getting to them. I'd also like them to be in touch with his mother, Pina, just to make sure that she is okay. She'll need a lot of support. Anna and I had each other when Steph was sick, but Pina is alone with an apartment full of her other four children, who she also has to look after. I also wrote out notes of encouragement that I left to be delivered to Pina and Ricky.

Steve showed up midmorning with his news from Belgium and the full complement of daily newspapers for us to read. He had spoken with Bartholomeus Verbeke in Brussels, getting familiarized with the Belgian judicial system, and a little more info on where my case was within that system. Steve explained that, not unlike the American system, all criminal felonies must go through a preliminary trial phase, roughly equivalent to a grand jury, to determine if there are sufficient grounds to proceed with a trial. Bartholomeus had finally been able to contact the public prosecutor's office, which would normally perform this role. But because of the exceptional public interest likely to be generated by this case, the prosecutor turned it over to a judicial inquiry.

Bartholomeus claimed that this is definitely to my benefit, since the investigating judge in a judicial inquiry is responsible for looking for all the facts in a case, both incriminating and nonincriminating. If left to the prosecutor alone, they would only look for the incriminating facts. The judge also has powers that a prosecutor would not have, such as dealing with detention. Bartholomeus will be applying for bail but says that it is doubtful. He'll try to get electronic monitoring if bail doesn't work.

Bartholomeus also informed us that these investigations are usually conducted without public involvement and without the public even knowing that they are going on. That's why the media there didn't know about it, or at least why they hadn't published anything. But Steve told us that it's only a matter of time, especially if the media outlets in the United States contact their counterparts in Belgium.

Our review of the day's newspapers told us that the Denver press had likely already been in contact with the Belgian media in order to get information about the murders of the nuns back in 1994. The day's stories also contained a pretty bare-bones personal history of me and a much more extensive background on the situation in Rwanda at the time.

It was from among these stories that we—Anna, Steve, and I—all learned the precise details of the murders at Notre Dame de la Paix. We were learning the facts at the same time the paper-reading public in Denver was getting them. Four Belgian nuns, Geert Grennerat, Marjon van den Bosche, Brechtie van Huejten, and Kaatje Simmons had all had their throats slit, and it appeared that at least two of them were also raped. Sisters Geraldine, Marie, and Brigit, and Mother Katherine, as I had known them, were all left stripped naked with crucifixes scratched into their flesh. The papers reported that just a few weeks prior there had been a savage murder of a French priest at the same school. At the time of the nuns' murders in 1994 the Rwandan government was in chaos. Its president and prime minister had just been assassinated, and the United Nations Peacekeeping Force that was deployed there had lost all control. Only five days before the nuns were murdered, ten Belgian peacekeepers had been killed in another horrific slaughter. Public outrage in Belgium was off the charts.

Rwanda was a former Belgian colony and Belgium still felt it had paternalistic responsibilities. Since there was no longer a government in Rwanda capable of doing any kind of investigation, Belgium immediately sent a team of its own investigators to reclaim the nuns' bodies and do whatever they could to rough-out their own examination. In searching the school the Belgian team found the murder weapon, a knife with the nuns' blood on it, in a footlocker with some other personal possessions. These were recovered and sent back to Belgium.

Now I knew the full story of the good sisters' murders.

The Denver papers also provided stories about me which they must have pieced together by talking to my friends. They contained some information from a few previous stories in the local community newspaper, the *Sun Valley Herald,* about my involvement in the downtown neighborhoods and particularly my activities at the community center next to our clinic. It wasn't a secret from my friends that I had been born in Africa and moved to France as a refugee, and then on to America to study medicine. They dug up my school records and my American Medical Association records which really said nothing, and they confirmed with the police that I had no previous record and hadn't been issued even a speeding ticket since arriving in the US. No one who would comment for the stories had any idea that I was secretly a fugitive from the law somewhere else in the world. Of course, I hadn't known this myself until a week ago.

Other stories were devoted to the conflict and genocide in Rwanda during the early nineties. These stories went into detail explaining the civil war between the minority Tutsis and the majority Hutu ethnic groups in the country. For several years the Rwandan Patriotic Front, a guerrilla Tutsi group, had been waging a civil war with the Hutu-controlled government. That prompted the United Nations to send in a peacekeeping force in October of 1993. But then, on April 6, 1994, the Rwandan president died when his airplane was shot down. The next morning the country's prime minister was murdered and the ten Belgian peacekeepers who were trying to protect her were all killed and mutilated. During the next three months, hundreds of thousands of Tutsis and moderate Hutus were indiscriminately slaughtered by the hardliner Hutus. That was when so many of us fled to the refugee camps that had been set up across the borders in neighboring countries.

I knew the story of the genocide well, having been there myself and then picking up bits and pieces while in the Nkwenda camp in Tanzania. What I didn't know at the time, I learned over the subsequent years by following the war crimes trials. In late 1994 the United Nations had established the International Criminal Tribunal for Rwanda, an international court located in Tanzania that held trials right up until the end of 2009. But it didn't finish its work and formally wrap up until December 2015.

Very few Americans had paid attention to the genocide or the war crimes trials. The Americans weren't part of the UN Peacekeeping Force and had shunned formal requests for help. What the people of Denver were reading about Rwanda in their newspapers that morning was probably more information than they received during the actual carnage in 1994. It was an eye-opener for Steve, who knew little of this history, and even gave Anna information that she hadn't picked up from me over the years.

But it seemed that none of the rest of the USA was yet getting any of this. The national news outlets had not picked up on my extradition as anything particularly newsworthy and so it wasn't being reported on the networks or in the national papers. So far it was limited to the odd minor mentions in their online sites. It gave me little comfort to know that, but Steve said the less publicity, the better.

During the afternoon, Anna approached me with a subject that was concerning her.

"Freddie, I'm worried about you."

"I'll be fine, Anna. I'll see you in a few days in Belgium. What can happen in a few days?"

"No, I'm worried about you slipping," she said.

That was part of the code we used when we referred to my bouts of depression. *Slipping* was our euphemism to avoid coming right out and calling it what it was. I had been through my funks many times over our years together, and her patience and kindness were no doubt an important part of my therapeutic recovery. We both worried, but seldom talked about the possibility that I might someday *slip* into a severe and lasting depression. It seemed this was what was on her mind.

"I'm worried that you could slip quickly, and I won't be right there to help you, Freddie."

This had already occurred to me as well, but Anna didn't need this worry on top of everything else we were dealing with. "I'll be okay, Anna. That's not going to happen."

"You don't know that."

She was right. I didn't know for sure that I could avoid falling into a depression, but somehow, I had a strong sense that it wouldn't happen. Usually my funks came on me when things were going great, not when they were going badly. When things were humming along in my life and running smoothly, I would start to have these feelings of guilt and unworthiness for being in such a good place. These were most often the precipitant of my depressions. Now I was certainly feeling a lot of guilt for having brought this situation into our lives, but it wasn't guilt stemming from things going too *well*; nothing was going well at the moment.

"I'll be fine, Anna. Honestly."

That didn't really satisfy either of us, but what else could I have said?

That last night, as the early dusk settled outside, we only turned on a few lights in the house. It was likely going to be our last night together, and even then, it was only a partial night since the marshals were scheduled to pick me up at one thirty in the morning. Our plan was for Anna to meet me in Belgium, but we didn't know exactly when we would see each other next, and we didn't know whether I was going to be incarcerated or receive bail. Everything was an unknown.

I was upstairs lying on Stephanie's bed, staring up at the ceiling, when Anna came in and lay beside me. We hadn't spent much time in there lately, not like right after Steph passed, when we'd go in every day.

"I just got off the phone with Daddy," she said.

"What did he have to say?"

"He doesn't want me to go to Belgium."

"I can't blame him, really. If I were in his shoes I'd probably feel the same way."

"Rob doesn't want me to go, either. They both say I should stay here where I can get support from them and my friends."

"What did you tell them?" I asked.

"That you need the support."

I rolled into her and kissed her on the forehead. I knew that if she abandoned me, I'd be completely alone. I could already feel the desertion that was taking place elsewhere in my life, the shunning from a distance as friends and acquaintances jumped to the easy conclusion that I must be guilty. I could feel it in the same way that one can feel the presence of another in a dark room, or the way you know someone is looking at you even when you can't see them. But I knew that even if I fought these charges, and proved them all wrong with my innocence, things would never be the same. Anna's family, my patients and colleagues—they'd all still have lingering doubts about me. We could never have the kind of tight bonds that we did only a few weeks earlier. Anna was the only one I could count on to maintain the certainty of a relationship.

What about her relationships, though? What was to happen to them? Even if I was found not guilty, the same distancing and insecurities in her relationships with friends and colleagues and family would change things for her forever. And what if I was found guilty after she stood beside me? Would they brand her guilty by association? Perhaps I should be the one to force her away now and spare her the future pain and shame.

"We need to do what's best for you, Anna," I said.

"What's that supposed to mean?"

"It means we need to think of how you will come through all of this."

"Don't start that again, Alfred, please. We've been over this more than once. Let's just be together tonight. I need to be with you. I need to feel you."

Since the time when we first met, Anna has had this uncanny ability to understand my thoughts, often more clearly than I do myself. At that moment, she must have been sensing my cerebral debate and she put a stop to it just like that.

We spent the next six hours, until the alarm on Anna's phone went off around midnight, just being with each other, not sleeping, hardly speaking, just being. We maintained touch with each other softly for the whole time, lightly stroking forearms and the backs of hands and faces, and gently wiping tears from one another when they started to flow. Neither of us even tried to use words to express our love; everything was said in the silence of intimacy.

After the alarm sounded I could feel my pulse increase and my heart beat harder in my chest. I'm sure some of it was the anxiety of being taken away by the marshals, and some of it was undoubtedly the fear of being sent to a foreign country to possibly be put in jail for the rest of my life. But what registered with me the most was being separated from Anna. We'd been apart before, one or the other of us leaving for professional conferences, sometimes for up to a week. Or her taking Stephanie and going to stay with her parents for some time in the mountains together.

Or me and her brother taking off for a weekend of hiking or mountain biking. But we'd never been separated against our wills, pulled apart when it wasn't our choice. And all of this was happening less than three months after being permanently severed from our only child.

I clamped the inside of Anna's wrist with two fingers and felt her pulse racing, just as my own was. Snuggling down, I placed the side of my head, my ear, to her sternum just above her breast and listened up close to the rapid thumping of her heart. She responded by cuddling tightly around me and stroking the side of my head, running her index finger absentmindedly along the length of my scar from my hairline, across my eyebrow, below my eye, down the side of my jaw, and back up again. Eventually we let go, kissed on the lips, and got ready for the marshals; Anna made coffee while I showered and shaved.

Belgium

Dawn isn't breaking because there is a heavy mass of gray clouds, and below those a thick fog, but the sky is lightening a bit as we taxi to the landing gate at the Brussels airport. Both Brossard beside me, and Herweyer behind me, take out their cell phones and begin a series of calls the moment the plane pulls up, but neither of them makes any motion to leave the aircraft. I watch as the last of those needing assistance are helped from the plane and then rise stiffly when I am instructed to.

In Newark we were led through the bowels of the terminal by a lone security guard. Here we are met by three heavily armed men dressed in SWAT gear, openly brandishing automatic rifles, to take us to a secure customs area. The display of force is unnerving, and I wonder if they really think it is necessary, or are they just doing it for show? I obviously have nothing to declare at customs, but apparently there is some paperwork that has to be signed. I can see that part of it includes my passport, which has somehow made its way from my surrendering it in the Denver courthouse all the way here with Herweyer.

As I am learning, all airports have a backdoor security gate, and that is where I am taken after being loaded into another van. I can see through the windshield that there is something different about this gate. There is much more activity, even at this early hour of the morning. A commotion is taking place near the gate. After passing the checkpoint and moving outside the fence, our driver slows down, deliberately I am sure. I can see a small crowd of about twenty people standing in the roadway in front of us. The crowd parts at the last minute, letting the slow-moving van pass through. Fists are waved at the window, and there are a couple of homemade signs: BUTCHER and REST IN HELL are held in the air to ensure that I notice them. Once through the small crowd, the driver speeds up, taking a ramp onto the freeway.

It's quite clear that my case has not been kept confidential. This is further borne out by the hubbub in the police station. Brossard and Herweyer are there ahead of me, and there's quite a crowd around them.

"Here's the fucking black bastard now," Herweyer says loudly in French, announcing my arrival. He basks in the celebrity among his cohorts and makes a show of ordering me through the intake process, relishing every opportunity to denigrate me. Brossard stands to the back, showing me some measure of dignity by his silence.

"I hear a lawyer is going to just be a waste of money with the case that the prosecutor has against you," Herweyer says. "Do you want to see him, or should I just tell him to go home?" He jokes loudly for all to hear. After he gets their approval with a round of laughs, he motions for me to sit down. My handcuffs are traded for a familiar-looking bracelet which is clamped around my ankle and scanned to make sure it works. Another officer escorts me away from the ruckus to a private conference room where my lawyer is waiting.

"Dr. Olyontombo, I am Bartholomeus Verbeke. I apologize for your treatment." His English is excellent, with the distinctly British accent common in Europeans.

This is the first show of respect that I have been offered in a while. He is a tall gentleman, a few inches taller than my own six foot two. His face tells me that he is probably in his early sixties, but his trim body, and the posture with which he carries it, makes him appear much younger. Balding white hair is brush-cut short, and astute gray eyes inspire confidence and ease.

"Mr. Verbeke, a pleasure to meet you," I say. "No need for you to apologize, sir."

"Doctor, how would you like me to address you? The official paperwork here says Azikiwe."

"That's a name I have not used in a long time. My name is Alfred now, sir."

"Not sir. Bart. Please call me Bart. I have a car waiting for us outside. We should get out of here. I'm sure you're tired. I'll fill you in on the way."

I *am* tired, very tired. It's well after midnight New York time. We continue our conversation in the back of the car he has arranged for us.

"I've negotiated with the investigating magistrate to have you released into my custody, subject to the electronic monitoring. It was a generous gesture on his part, but despite the seriousness of the charges, you come with an impeccable reputation. However, I should warn you, if this makes it to the stage of a full trial you'll have to expect to be held in jail.

"I've arranged a small apartment for you and your wife. We'll take you there now."

The mention of Anna almost chokes me up.

"I haven't been able to speak with her for a few days."

"So she told me," he says.

"When did you last speak with her?" I ask.

"A few hours ago. While you were in the air. She's been trying to reach you."

I'm relieved to hear that she tried. I was more than a little worried, and still am, that Anna might have succumbed to the wishes of her father and brother.

"Where is she? And what did she say?" I ask, not completely sure I want to hear the answers.

"She didn't know that you were being transferred here already. None of us knew that they would be ready to bring you over so soon. She says she'll be here tomorrow. She'll bring your things with her."

I close my eyes to savor this news. It's a relief and the best thing I have heard in over a week.

"Nothing is going to happen here in the next few days," Bart says. "So why don't you get settled in with your wife and rest, adjust to the time difference. I'll come and see you on Wednesday. I should know more by then and be able to give you a full update."

"Bart, when I left the airport this morning there were protesters. Were they there because of me?"

"Likely, yes."

"How would they have known I was going to be there? You said that you didn't even know when I was arriving."

"Alfred, your case has been going on for more than a year ..."

"A year? And nobody told me?"

"The investigation has been taking place for a year. It's like any investigation. The authorities don't want to tip their hand until necessary. It would have been started by a prosecutor based on some level of information, and then, because of the international connections and the likely public interest, it was turned over to a judge for a full judicial inquiry. It's the equivalent of your grand jury process."

"And those protesters ...?"

"There's a lot of sensitivity amongst the public to what they are accusing you of. It's impossible with all the investigators and police that are involved in this to keep it quiet. Someone's obviously leaking. Probably family members of the victims. Perhaps they know this was going on and will have a lot of sympathizers among the police and elsewhere. We'll talk about it more in a few days."

Our car pulls up to a nondescript four-story building along a street lined with similar buildings.

"This isn't fancy, but that serves a few purposes." Bart nods toward the building. "First, it's not too expensive. We have no idea how long you'll be here, and I didn't want to break your budget. But more important, it's less likely that it'll be found out as your residence if it's one of the common places. When they do find out you're here, as they eventually will, we're going to have a lot of public sentiment against us.

No sense antagonizing them further by having you holed up in the Ritz-Carlton."

The inside is furnished adequately, and this is really not a concern of mine anyhow. It's certainly far nicer than the detention-center room in Newark.

"Here are my numbers." Bart hands me a typed-out page. "I've included some other information that you might need. I've had some food brought in, but you might like to go to the market." He hands me some money. "Here are some euros to get you by until your wife arrives."

I lift my leg a bit and point down to my ankle.

"We'll see if we can get that off soon. In the meantime, you're still pretty free to go where you like. You just can't leave the country."

The first thing I do after Bartholomeus leaves is try the phone, finally reaching Anna, waking her a little after midnight Denver time.

"Are you okay? Where are you?" she asks without even saying hello.

"I'm fine. But I was worried about you."

"I'll be on the flight tonight."

I've only been away from her for five days now, but it seems like much longer. In fact, my life before all of this blew up seems like it was ages ago. I wonder if incarcerated time always passes so slowly. Attempting to organize these thoughts, I count on my fingers from the day the Denver police showed up in my office until now. Not even two weeks, but so much has happened. It all seems impossible, surreal. Two weeks ago I had not the slightest inkling that my life would ever take a turn like this.

I badly want to make my way to the airport and see Anna as soon as she gets off the plane, but with the monitor I'm wearing I'd just cause a commotion with the authorities. Instead, I wait in the isolation of my apartment for Bart's car to arrive with her. The desperation and loneliness that had built up in me since we parted only a few days ago is overwhelming, and I find myself fidgeting and shaking, peeking out the curtains every few minutes. When she finally steps through the doorway, dispelling my lingering thoughts that perhaps she would abandon me, I wrap myself around her not wanting to ever let her go. Anna truly is the center of my universe.

As he promised, Bartholomeus arrives the next day at our little apartment, but he doesn't have much news for us. He tells us that he applied to have my ankle monitor removed, but the request was declined by the presiding magistrate, ruling that it did not constitute unreasonable confinement especially since my case met both tests of Belgian law for such monitoring: the probable indication of guilt of a serious crime and the special circumstances of the case.

"What are these special circumstances?" Anna asks.

"Mrs. Fraser—"

"Call me Anna, please."

"Anna," Bart continues, "it's impossible to underestimate the national sentiment that is likely to surface when this becomes public. There are heavy political implications here in Belgium that could be related to your husband's trial."

"Political implications? How can politics be involved in this?" Anna asks.

"Perhaps I should explain some of the history to put this in context for you." Bart motions toward the chairs, and we all take a seat. "Belgium has long prided itself on its neutrality. We held off picking sides during the Second World War until we were overrun by Germany. We've always considered ourselves one of the world's great peacekeeping nations."

"Alfred has told me about the Belgian peacekeepers that were murdered in Rwanda," Anna says. She is curious. She's a lawyer and wants as much information as possible.

"Yes, April 7, 1994. The date is etched in Belgian history. Extremely brutal murders," Bart continues. "And our government was frustrated at the lack of UN support. The country was outraged. The government ordered a withdrawal of the remaining peacekeepers, but before they even got out of the country the four Belgian nuns at Notre Dame de la Paix were murdered. It was in an equally savage manner and resulted in the sisters becoming a lightning rod of national indignation. They became known as *Le Quatre Soeurs de la Paix*, 'the Four Sisters of Peace.'"

"And no one was ever charged with those murders?" Anna asks.

"Not the nuns' murders," Bart says. "But one man, a former Rwandan

Army major, was convicted here in Belgium in 2007 of the ten peacekeeper murders."

I was confused by this and stopped Bart. "I thought the trials were in Tanzania? I know that the United Nations set up the war crimes tribunal there. Why a conviction here?"

"You're right, Alfred. When those trials in Tanzania didn't convict anyone for our peacekeepers' murders, Belgium sought extradition of this one known participant. In fact, that case went all the way to our Council of State, your Supreme Court equivalent, to establish that we had the right to convict for crimes against our citizens on foreign soil. That's the basis for being able to extradite you."

Anna has been listening intently. "So, Bart, no one has ever been convicted for the deaths of the nuns?"

"That's right, Anna. Only one conviction for the ten peacekeepers, and none for the Four Sisters of Peace. It's a national sore point that has festered in this country for more than twenty years." Bart sits up straighter in his chair and takes a deep breath. "So, you can see how once it gets around that the prosecutors have a suspect, there will probably be a tide of public revenge stirred up."

He pauses, giving us time to let this sink in.

"Bart." Anna picks up the conversation again. "You said that Alfred's case has political implications. How is that?"

Bart fills us in on the current state of political affairs in the country: the ruling political party in Belgium is currently clinging to power in a minority government situation in the Parliament. The prime minister and his cabinet know that a public trial at this time could pull the country together in a common cause that would go a long way toward getting them reelected.

"It's only a matter of time until this explodes in the press," Bart says. "It'll be impossible to stop that happening, and it's going to make it a real uphill battle for us."

Anna nods, thinking for a moment, and then asks about next steps. I just listen, taking it all in.

"We'll have a discovery hearing next week with the judge," he says.

"That's when we'll get to see all the evidence they have gathered so far. Until then there's not much we can do."

Bart picks up his briefcase and stands. "We'll reassess right after that and begin to plan for a defense," he says, as we show him to the door.

The elation I was feeling from having Anna back at my side for the past twenty-four hours begins to quickly evaporate. We try to divert our attention until next week's hearing by getting out and seeing Brussels, acting like tourists. It's not lost on us that these are the exact days we were supposed to be spending together in Saint Martin, on our once-again-delayed honeymoon.

"Well, Alfred, we do have something of Saint Martin here in Brussels," Anna says.

"Not the weather, that's for sure." The sun has not come out for even a minute in the week since we arrived in Belgium. It's been cloudy and rainy and foggy the entire time, and even though the temperature is a little above freezing, the constant dampness makes it feel much colder. There's a penetrating achiness that stiffens my joints and makes me physically hurt all over.

"No, it's not Saint Martin's weather, that's for sure," she says. "I was thinking of the combination of Dutch and French."

Anna, always the optimist, forever looking to the bright side. That was one of the things we were looking forward to in selecting Saint Martin, the variety of two languages. And we have those same languages right here in Belgium. The country is pretty evenly split between Dutch and French speakers, with most people in the greater Brussels area fully fluent in both, even if French is more commonly heard. German is a third official language of the country, but we don't encounter much of it. Almost everyone in Brussels, especially anyone under forty, also speaks English with fluency, but Anna and I speak French, enjoying the opportunity to converse in the language that we've hardly used since leaving Paris.

We impel ourselves to be out and about during the day, sightseeing to occupy our minds and walking to make sure that we are getting some exercise. The evenings are spent inside our little apartment where I pass hour after hour on my laptop voraciously soaking up any information

I can find on the Belgian involvement in my birth country of Rwanda. I also take in as much news as I can about the current state of affairs in Belgium, reading several news sites and sources thoroughly.

It's while doing my nightly news search on the eve of my first hearing in front of the judicial inquiry that I come across a small article on the Reuters European service, *Media Seek Admittance to Four Sisters' Inquiry.* This is the first real proof I have seen that the media do in fact know something of what is going on with my case here in Belgium and that they do have a solid interest in it. The article states that several media outlets have banded together to petition the judicial inquiry to allow them access to the hearings. Under normal circumstances this would not be done, but it is not unheard of, especially in cases of significant national concern. The article goes on to give a brief background, stating, *Sources have confirmed that Azikiwe Olyontombo, an American physician and former Rwandan national, has been extradited recently from the USA to Belgium where he is facing charges in the murders of the Four Sisters of Peace.*

"Bart warned us it would come," Anna says when I show her the story.

"I'd just hoped it wouldn't come for a while longer," I say.

Sure enough, it arrives the next morning. After being delivered by the car Bart sent for us, he greets us anxiously at the courthouse. "I'm afraid the media is onto this already. I don't think that it is worth any effort for us to oppose their request to be present in the courtroom. It's most likely that they'll be successful anyhow. We could try, but we're probably just delaying the inevitable and maybe even hurting our position by looking more guilty in the eyes of the public."

I look to Anna for her guidance. "I can't disagree with you, Bart," she says. "Let's just get on with it."

Our hearing begins in a small room with Bart, Anna, and me, as well as several court officials, the presiding magistrate, Dieudonné Gelineau, and a single lawyer representing the media outlets. After giving leave to the media lawyer to present his argument first, Judge Gelineau promptly grants the request without even consulting either me or my lawyer and swiftly adjourns the proceedings for thirty minutes to allow time to find a larger room.

Once summoned to the new room we enter to find it packed with journalists. It's too full, and the judge promises that a larger room will be found for the next time. Neither Anna nor I, in spite of Bart having tried to prep us for the high level of interest that would be coming in the case, could ever have imagined this much attention. Even Bart admits that he is shocked at the numbers that have shown up for the first day of the inquiry.

The formal proceedings begin with me being offered the choice of which official language I would like the hearing to be conducted in. They also offer me a translator. Bart has already explained to me that during a judicial inquiry the judge will be addressing me directly, unlike the custom in the United States where lawyers do all the speaking for their clients. Bart's role is strictly to advise and object on legal procedure only. I tell the judge that French will be fine and that I am fluent in it.

The whole proceeding seems rather informal. The court attendants present the framework of evidence that they have compiled in complete detail, submitting documentation and identifying it with numbers as copies are physically piled first on the table and then on the floor when space runs out. Great detail is presented about the four nuns, Sister Marie, Sister Geraldine, Sister Brigit, and Mother Katherine, and their backgrounds and work at Notre Dame de la Paix mission school. When their smiling photos are held up I instantly recognize them, and then when the crime scene photos of their bloodied and mutilated bodies are shown I have to turn away. I can't bear to see them looking like this, and many more memories flood back into my mind of other similar atrocities that I have witnessed. I hang my head low, looking away from the photos. Both Anna and Bart lean into me at the same time.

"Alfred," Bart whispers, "sit up. Your body language is incriminating."

I try to do as he instructs, but I can't look at the photos and I remain turned away until they move on to the next evidence.

"Several items were recovered by the investigative team which the government sent to the site," one of the officials says. "Included are these contents of a footlocker in the dorm room belonging to, according to school records, Azikiwe Olyontombo."

One at a time, from a box in front of him, he begins to lift out the few possessions I owned and left behind at the school when I fled. I had fully intended to go back to the school within a few months and retrieve my belongings, but I never made it. I ended up staying at the Nkwenda refugee camp for four years, long forgetting those few possessions at Notre Dame de la Paix.

Each item is contained in a sealed clear plastic bag: a few clothes, a few toiletries, several notebooks with my name on them, and two textbooks with my name on the paper covers I made for them. I gasp, along with the rest of the courtroom, as the last item is ceremonially withdrawn from the box and reverently displayed for everyone to see.

The court attendant pauses, as if for dramatic effect, before continuing a little more loudly and clearly than he was previously speaking. "The inscription on the handle here is marked *Azi O* and the fingerprints lifted from the handle back in 1994 match those that the Rwandan army had on file for Azikiwe Olyontombo. The army maintained copies of his prints from the time they first arrested him and placed him in the school in 1990. These same prints have recently been matched to the man living in Denver, Colorado, under the alias of Alfred Olyontombo." There is another audible gasp in the courtroom. "In addition," the court attendant says, "the blood on the knife blade has been identified by DNA as matching the blood of all four victims." Murmured conversation fills the room.

I'm perplexed at seeing my old knife there, Kakengo's ivory-handled knife, the one I used to kill him and which Idi had given me as a reward. I can see from here the inscription of my name that I had carved out in the handle over several nights by the campfire. It is the same knife that I also used to kill the priest, Savard. But how did it get in my locker?

The court attendant lingers with the knife in the bag, making sure that everyone, Judge Gelineau, us, and especially the news reporters, all have adequate time to contemplate the condemning evidence he holds.

Next, he lifts a small stack of ledger-like books. "These are the log books recovered from the administration files of Notre Dame de la Paix. They show that Azikiwe Olyontombo was a student at the school from early in 1990 until the murders on April 12, 1994. Birth dates shown in the records indicate he was sixteen years of age at the time." These, he places alongside all the other evidence. "And this," he says, picking up an old file folder, "is a report from the Rwandan army giving details of how Azikiwe Olyontombo was arrested after a shootout between the army and a rebel group in northern Rwanda in early 1990. This rebel group was responsible for the murders and rapes of many villagers in the northern mountains of Rwanda. And it can be seen from these reports that at the time of his arrest he bragged to the soldiers of his role in those murders."

I can't help it, I bury my face in my hands, regretting those moments which I can clearly recall. The pit of my stomach feels hollow and I think that I might throw up. I did indeed brag when they captured me, and I was party to many murders. I may not be guilty of killing the four sisters, but I am certainly guilty of the deaths of others.

I'm so lost in my regrets that I don't even hear that Judge Gelineau has called a ninety-minute recess for lunch. And I don't feel Anna's arm wrapped across my shoulders until Bart puts a hand on the back of my head and says gently, "Alfred, let's go." My legs are unsteady as I stand, and I look around noticing, for the first time, that the courtroom is completely empty. Anna and Bart each take an arm and escort me to a small room down the hall.

Coffee and sandwiches are laid out, but I am not the least bit hungry. I find a chair and sit quietly. Anna, who was the consummate professional in the courtroom, sits beside me and begins to cry.

Leaning in, I pathetically attempt to console her. "I'm so sorry, Anna. So sorry."

Bart squats down directly in front of Anna and takes her firmly by the shoulders. "Anna, nothing is proven yet. We have to review everything. We'll put together a defense. You know how this works."

Anna looks him in the eye. "I know, I know. I just had to get this out." Wiping away the tears, she sits up straight and takes a few deep breaths.

"No." I clench my jaw, shake my head, and look back and forth from Anna to Bart. "No, I will confess."

"I'm not going to ask you if you did it or not, but I have to advise you against a confession, Alfred," Bart says sternly.

"No. I'm not going to put Anna through any more of this. I might not be guilty of these murders, but you heard that I have already confessed to other murders—even bragged about them. Every reporter in that courtroom thinks I'm guilty. The judge thinks I'm guilty. You probably think I'm guilty, too. No. I deserve punishment. Anna doesn't deserve any more of this."

"Stop it!" she screams. "Stop it! Stop it! Stop it!"

I stop talking and just shake my head side to side.

Bart steps in. "We all need a few minutes. Let's not decide anything yet. Let's see what happens this afternoon. We'll sleep on it and talk about it again tomorrow."

We all try to compose ourselves quietly and say very little before returning to the packed courtroom for the afternoon session. A video monitor has been set up at the front of the room, and a technician is fiddling with the equipment as we enter. I can feel the penetrating stare of every eye in the room.

"Is this ready to go?" Judge Gelineau asks.

"Yes, Your Honor," one of the court attendants answers. "We have a videotaped statement from a witness to the murders. This witness claims to have been present and tried to stop Mr. Olyontombo from committing the murders but was unsuccessful."

"And how did you come upon this witness?" the judge asks.

"The information was volunteered last year. He came to us."

It is explained that the witness was originally convicted by the ICTR, the International Criminal Tribunal for Rwanda, of war crimes against humanity committed during the Rwandan genocide. Although he was not a Rwandan, he had apparently led a notorious mercenary band hired by officials within the Hutu government to eradicate several villages sympathetic to the Tutsi rebel movement. He was convicted in 2009 and sentenced in Tanzania to natural life imprisonment. Then late in 2015, just as the ICTR was wrapping up and closing down, he came forward offering information about the Four Sisters of Peace murders in exchange for commutation of his sentence to twenty years. Naturally, the Belgian government was anxious to get the information and, as a major contributor to the criminal tribunals in Tanzania, it arranged the deal with the ICTR.

Judge Gelineau is listening very carefully, as indeed we all are, to this background information. "And how do we know that this witness is telling the truth?" he asks. "How can we be sure that it is not just a ruse to shorten his sentence?"

"Your Honor," the attendant replies, "the witness was able to provide specific details of the murder and crime scene which were never made public by the investigators."

"Such as …"

"Such as the fact, Your Honor, that the murder weapon was found in the footlocker belonging to Azikiwe Olyontombo and that it contained the inscription *Azi O* carved into the handle. Our witness was then able to give us the alias 'Alfred,' which Azikiwe Olyontombo is now living under, and the information that he left Tanzania for France in 1998. It became easy for us to trace a Rwandan refugee in France who was living under the assumed name of Alfred Olyontombo. Mr. Olyontombo then left for the US in 2001, where he eventually applied for and received American citizenship. He has been living up until now in Denver, Colorado. New fingerprinting confirms that his prints are the ones found on the knife at the murder scene."

"Very well," says the judge. "Play the tape, please."

The attendant points a remote control toward the screen in front of us, bringing it to life with a mug-shot image. But before he can speak any words I am smacked by the photo staring out at us, and I jerk involuntarily in my seat. Anna and Bart both reach out from either side of me to lay a calming hand on my arm.

"The man pictured here, You Honor, is our witness who has come forward in Tanzania. His name is Idi Mbuyamba."

The next few sentences don't even register with me. I am too struck with the image of Idi in front of me. It is unmistakably the nemesis of my childhood, pictured now almost twenty years older than when I had last seen him as I left the Nkwenda camp.

The screen changes to a prerecorded session with an interviewer asking precise questions of Idi who answers in confident and clear tones. When the camera is directly in front of Idi, he looks straight into it and right out through the screen as if he is speaking to me directly, personally. He probably was. He probably knew when they filmed it that he would be able to reach out to me one more time, ominously bringing back to my mind the last time I saw him. We were leaving the Nkwenda refugee camp, and I turned to look through the back window of the van. Then, as now, as if to emphasize his videotaped message to me, he raises his right arm to where the camera can clearly see it, displaying his severed stump.

That son of a bitch. He ruined my childhood, haunted the rest of my life, and now, twenty years later and thousands of miles away, he still seeks to ruin everything that I have left.

I'm sure that everyone in the room must have witnessed my spontaneous reaction to seeing Idi on the screen. It wasn't subtle, but now I will myself to find composure and sit up straight, focusing on the video screen along with everyone else. I am able to listen carefully to every word Idi says. They are deliberately spoken in Swahili and accurately translated by an interpreter for the camera. Idi tells how I asked him to help in the murders, but that he refused and tried to reason with me. He claims that he told me not to kill the foreigners because it would bring too much interest from the authorities and goes on to explain how he watched as I took the bloodied knife and stashed it in my footlocker.

I thought at the time that I was being clever when I killed Savard and left my knife with Idi, hoping he would take the blame for it. It bothered me not at all that my crime might be falsely attributed to him; it seemed like small compensation for his having totally ruined my childhood and perhaps my future as well. But I hadn't counted on *his* cunning. He turned the tables back on me by murdering the nuns and ensuring that the knife pointed right to me for those killings. Shaking my head, I mumble under my breath, *Fuck, fuck, fuck.*

After fifteen more minutes of condemning interrogation the video ends. The reporters behind me shuffle out of the room. They have more than enough for their stories and don't hang around to hear the last of the discovery process, preferring to get the salacious information filed with their editors as quickly as possible.

Upon completion of the presentation of the evidence against me, Judge Gelineau begins to address me, "Mr. Olyontombo—"

"*Doctor* Olyontombo," I clearly and firmly interrupt him as I rise from my seat to stand tall.

"Pardon me?" Judge Gelineau asks, obviously perturbed at my interjection.

"I said '*Doctor* Olyontombo.' I have a professional designation, Your Honor, and I would respectfully request that I be addressed by it as a courtesy of this inquiry."

Bart and Anna look up at me from their seats. Both are clearly taken aback at my sudden affirmative and challenging disposition. I stand tall between them, feeling empowered by my newfound defiance as I wait for the judge's response. He too is surprised at my changed demeanor and takes a moment to assess me before finally replying.

"Certainly … *Doctor* Olyontombo. My apologies," he says. "Dr. Olyontombo, the only interest of this inquiry is to ascertain the truth. Enough so to either freely discharge you or to formally send you to trial on the charges of which you are accused. You have seen all the evidence against you, and you have the right to both refute it and to bring your own supporting evidence before the inquiry. Do you wish to do so?"

I look down at Bart, and he gives me a small nod. Anna too is nodding her head, emphatically. But I don't need to see this from either of them. I straighten myself even taller, pulling my shoulders back and lifting my chin slightly higher. "Yes, Your Honor, I do. I concede nothing to this man and his false testimony. But I will need some time."

"Absolutely. You can have Mr. Verbeke contact my office to make arrangements."

Back in our little conference room, the stale sandwiches and now-cold coffee are still on the table. I grab one sandwich in each hand and eat heartily as I sit down. Seeing Idi's face on that video screen has given me a new vigor—not more confidence in my ability to challenge the case against me, but a new resolve to not go down without remonstrating. I don't want to give that man another victory over me without a fight.

"Alfred, I'm glad you've changed your mind," Bart says. "We'll get started tomorrow on a defense."

"No," I say.

Anna springs from her chair. "Freddie, we have to. You can't just give in to this. We have to find a defense here."

"No. We won't wait until tomorrow," I say. "We should start right now. I'm not guilty of those murders, and I don't want to waste a minute letting anyone think that I am."

Anna and Bart look at each other in surprise.

"Very well, then," says Bart, pulling a chair to the table.

Moving around behind my chair, Anna gives me a small hug and then plants her hands firmly on my shoulders. Bart plops a briefcase on the table, takes out a notepad and pen, tapping the end of it like a metronome on the paper.

"Okay," he says, "there are two critical elements in the evidence that we will have to overcome—the fingerprints on the knife and the testimony of Mr. Mbuyamba. Was it your knife?"

"Yes."

"Okay, what about Mbuyamba. Do you know him?"

"Yes, I know him well."

"Would he have any reason to lie about you killing the nuns?"

"He has very good reasons to lie about that. Several of them."

Bart looks at me and then up at Anna who is still standing behind me. He thinks for a moment about the answer I have just given him. "Another problem is that your passport shows the name 'Alfred,' which the state is claiming is an alias. That might seem to some like an indication of guilt."

I'm nodding my head as he is saying this, going over the events of the past in my mind.

"Thoughts?" he asks.

"Lots of thoughts. I'm just not sure what to say to these things."

We sit silently for a moment while Anna walks around to the other side of the table and begins pacing. "Freddie, you told me your story of Africa—the time you spent in Zaire and Rwanda—but there's more, isn't there?"

She stops talking, waiting for me to answer, and I nod my head.

"Yes, Anna. There's more."

I had told Anna the story of my childhood, the part that continued to haunt me with guilt. I had told her everything right up to the last person I killed, Father Michel Savard. I had turned my life around after that and didn't think that anything from that point on could possibly be the source of the extradition proceedings against me. Anna already knew much of the rest of my story of my time in the Nkwenda camp in Tanzania. I certainly hadn't killed anyone during that time period. But the ensuing events, especially Idi's involvement, make me now agree with Anna that the rest of my story must somehow be relevant, so I pick it up where I had finished before, omitting no details.

Nkwenda

My childhood ended February 20, 1994, the moment I killed that bastard, the priest, by slicing open his belly. I did it in cold blood, planning it ahead of time. It might have been calculated and committed in a sense of rage over the suicide of Little Gabe, and as a result of Savard's pedophilic abuse at the school. Nonetheless, it was my conscious decision. Up until that time I had the excuse of coercion and childhood innocence for all my crimes, but not that one. From that moment on I was no longer a child.

After leaving Savard to die with his pants down and his entrails spilling out on the floor around him, I snuck back into the dorm and took off my clothes, wiped the blood from the blade of the knife, wrapped it in a plastic bag, and showered the blood off me. A long hour passed as I waited until Sister Brigit came knocking for me.

"There's a man to see you, Azi," she said.

I calmed my breath, relieved that another cog had fallen into place for my plan. Major Ntagura had gotten my message to Idi, and he had come for me as I was pretty sure he would. "Thank you, Sister. Can I see him in the cafeteria?"

"Of course," she replied, and I followed her out.

"Sister Brigit, I'd like you to meet Idi Mbuyamba." I lingered on his name, making sure that she heard it clearly. "We'll only be a few minutes."

With that she left us, and Idi smiled. "So, you've finally decided to be a man, Azi. Good. We can use you."

"I'll be around in a few days, a week or two at the most," I said, handing him my knife wrapped in the bag. "Take my knife and hold it for me until I get there. You remember this knife, Idi? You gave it to me after I ... after Kakengo died."

"I remember it well, Azi." He slipped the package under his coat. "We'll be glad to have you." He hugged me like a comrade.

"Don't lose the knife," I said. "You know how much it means to me."

"Don't worry, Azi. We have plenty of weapons for you, brand-new ones."

"Give me a few days, and I'll get back to Major Ntagura," I said. Then I showed him out of the compound.

I went straight to the nuns' dorm and knocked on their door, finding all four of them inside.

"Sisters," I said, "if this man that was here tonight, Idi Mbuyamba, comes looking for me again please do not show him in. He is a very evil person, and we'd all be better off without him around. I know that he is a murderer and is running with the militias now. He wanted me to join them, but I've told him to stay away."

The next morning, when the housekeeper found Savard, the police were summoned. We were all interviewed, and the compound was thoroughly searched, nothing of any value to the case turning up. But the police in those days in Kigali barely had time to make an appearance at all the murder sites in the city. The country was on the verge of civil war and murders were steady. The police made a little more of an effort in this case because of the nuns and the foreign connections of the school, but they were not equipped for forensic investigations. Once the sisters and I informed the police that Idi Mbuyamba had shown up the night before, the case was pretty much closed. Idi was well-known to the authorities, and they were happy to have the case solved quickly. If they ever caught up with him, as I hoped they soon might, the knife, which I had given him, would surely add to his culpability.

During the two weeks after I dispatched Savard to his god, the lid blew off the pressure cooker that was Rwanda. The rampant murders turned into overt slaughters; one of the worst genocides in history was underway. The good sisters at Notre Dame de la Paix sent me away to find refuge in one of the several camps that the United Nations had established in the surrounding countries, and I left in the wee hours of the morning traveling east and north, making my way to Nkwenda in Tanzania.

I arrived in the camp, like everyone else, on the verge of starvation. I carried on my back the bags of an old woman who had fallen by the roadside less than a mile from our destination, and I had the woman herself slung over my shoulder. I set her down as gently as I could in front of the large white tent with the bold letters *UN* emblazoned on the roof. She slumped lifeless into a heap of skin and bones, and I tried to stretch her out to give her some measure of dignity.

"Don't leave her there. Take her to the morgue," said a pompous local guard. He pointed to the far side of the camp, downwind from the tented village, to where a dense column of smoke rose.

"What about food?" I asked. "I need some food. Please."

"You won't get food here without registering first." And he pointed to a long line of desperate-looking refugees snaking out from another white tent farther down the dirt road that functioned as the main street for the camp. I was hungry, having last eaten two days earlier, and completely exhausted after having carried the old woman and her possessions for the last hour. I started to leave, walking in the direction of the line he pointed toward.

"Don't leave her here," he called after me. "You'll get nothing until she's looked after."

Turning back around, I hefted her over my shoulder again and trudged toward the morgue. There just wasn't enough strength in me to bother with picking up her bags, and I left them. I hadn't taken but a few steps away when the guard pounced on the belongings, scavenging for whatever he could use or sell or trade.

The morgue gave me my first taste of what I was soon to learn is what refugees spend most of their time doing in such camps—standing in lines. Everything is a line, and if bureaucrats the world over are adept at inefficiencies resulting in lineups, the inefficiency of the United Nations' personnel and the lines that they generate set the gold standard. To be fair, there are good reasons for the lines in the camp. Many of the people employed by the United Nations are locals, and they have no training or skills for the jobs they take on. The international personnel did their best under the circumstances, and the lineups were no doubt unavoidable. The UN is also almost always operating on a shoestring budget and simply doesn't have the money to either employ enough people or aid them with the technology and materials they need to make them more efficient. But we all became immune to the lines, accepting them as a part of life. There wasn't really a whole lot else to do, anyhow. One could sit in the dirt of the streets and wait for the months and years to pass, or one could get in line and wait. So, we got in lines—lines for food, for water, for medicine, for tents, for official papers, for permissions, and for the morgue.

There were a good twenty or so living bodies ahead of me in line. The living bodies shuffled along the dead ones, rolling them in carts and wheelbarrows or carrying them in blankets supported by two or more living bodies. My dead body was too heavy for me to hold any longer, so I let her down into the dirt. I wanted to show her as much respect as I could, but physically I couldn't do it anymore, and I ended up just dragging her along until I got to the front.

While waiting in line at the morgue I learned two other important functions of lineups in the camp: they were sources of information—some of it possibly correct; and they were sources of gossip—most of it always incorrect.

The information I gathered while waiting in that line was that the camp was currently home to nearly twenty thousand individuals, all fleeing the bloodshed in Rwanda. Hundreds of others, like me, were arriving each day, and the United Nations was being overwhelmed with the need. They'd originally built the camp for five thousand, and tents and food could not be shipped in fast enough to support those already there, let alone the newcomers that showed up each day. Proper sanitation and medical care were almost nonexistent, and starvation was the norm, hence the continuous lines at the morgue. The dead arrived at the morgue by the dozens every day, and officials had to make some arbitrary rules to accommodate them. Last rites and funeral services were to be conducted by families within one hour of the death, and the bodies had to then be delivered to the morgue immediately, day or night, where they were incinerated. Only the Islamists would avoid cremation by being trucked to mass graves ten miles away. This was the only way to keep the bodies from putrefying and further contributing to the spreading diseases.

Finally relieved of the old woman, I trudged to the second line that the guard pointed out. It had grown even longer than what it was just a few hours earlier. We squatted and sat on our behinds, shuffling along in the mud as the line ever so slowly moved forward. In this line I was treated to some more information while making chatter with a few others around me.

"Where are you from?" one of them asked.

"Kigali," I replied.

"Kigali?" he asked. "Is it true what they say is happening there?"

"If you mean that things are out of control and the war has now reached the city, yes, it's true," I said.

"What's your name, son?" another of the older men asked me.

"Azikiwe … Azikiwe Olyontombo," I said.

"Truthfully?"

A flush of panic set over me. I wasn't sure what he meant. Surely they weren't looking for me for Savard's murder. They couldn't have known it was me. The police were content with having Idi to blame for that.

"What does my name matter?" I asked.

He drew a little closer to me and lowered his voice to a whisper. "Many of those here are not who they say they are, and it's bound to get worse. Trust me. I've been through this in the camps in Uganda once already. You'd be wise not to be so free about bandying your name around like that. Guard what little bit of privacy you have here."

"Thank you," I said, sitting in silence for the next couple of hours as the line slowly progressed.

When my turn finally arrived to enter the open-air tent I rose from my haunches and approached the desk. The woman seated there asked me in the finest bureaucratic banality, "Name?"

"Alfred. Alfred's my name."

"Alfred *who*? Have you got your papers?"

"Alfred Olyontombo," I answered. "And all I have is my baptismal certificate." I showed it to her and she copied my name from it, Alfred Olyontombo.

The intake interview and registration yielded me a laminated UN card with my name and number. "Don't lose this," the woman said. "You'll need it for everything in the camp: food, water, supplies. You're required to produce it whenever you're asked by anyone with a UN identity badge inside the camp. You're not to leave the camp without a movement pass. You are now a Rwandan under the protection of the United Nations, but only so long as you remain within the bounds of the camp. If you leave the camp, you will be considered an illegal immigrant in Tanzania and subject to immediate arrest. Next."

While waiting in the line I had considered what the older man advised me. The more I thought about it, the more I liked the idea. If, for some reason, they were ever to come looking for me for Savard's murder, I could hide behind my new name. But even more intriguing was the opportunity to put the horrors of my past life behind me. For four years at Notre Dame de la Paix, I'd wanted to bury that past and disassociate myself from the person of my childhood. I hated Azikiwe. I became Alfred on that day, and I never used the name of Azikiwe again. In an ironic twist of fate, Savard's christening had given me my new identity.

Shortly after my arrival in the camp I waited like everyone else, in another line, for my turn to see a doctor. Some people were so desperate, and doctors were in such short supply, that they waited through the whole night, forming a line outside yet another dirty white tent with large *UN* letters stenciled on the roof. It wasn't uncommon for the line to stretch to several dozen, sometimes more than a hundred people at a time. Those of us who could sat on our heels to avoid having to sit directly in the mud, mud that was mixed with the human excrement that had nowhere to go but to pile up throughout the camp. I avoided, for as long as I could, getting into the medical line, but puss had been oozing around my right eyeball for more than a week. In the last few days it had swollen my eye and sealed it shut. I had seen many people lose eyes to infection and violence, and I desperately didn't want to lose mine. I took a place in line next to all other manner of disease, infection, and wound.

Children in the line wailed, adults moaned and bickered with each other, but most people were simply resigned to sullen despondency, clinging to desperate hope that the foreign doctors might be able to salve their misery. This despondency was pervasive in the camp. The mass of migrants had become resigned to the fact that they had no homes to go back to, many in their families had been killed in the recent purges, and now starvation or illness was probably going to take the rest of them—of us.

As my place in the line finally neared the open-walled tent that served as clinic, emergency room, and surgery center, all in one, a mother came running, wailing up the mud street carrying a child with the head of a three-year-old and the body of a baby. She attempted to run straight into the tent, but several of those at the front of the line ahead of me grabbed her and barred her. Some shouted at her in Kinyarwanda, some in French, others in Swahili and another dialect. She shouted back in another tongue that none of them understood. The kerfuffle brought a white man outside the tent. He wore only shorts and American-style sneakers and a stethoscope. He asked in French what was going on, and one of those in line explained that the lady had not waited her turn like the rest. She was thrusting her child toward him. When he asked her the problem she blabbered through her tears but no one understood her. I stepped forward and said that she was saying her son had been bitten by a snake while they gathered sticks for firewood. The child's arm was swollen, and he had begun to convulse.

By now the crowd at the front of the tent had grown curious, and several were shouting to know what was happening. I raised my voice and repeated the explanation in the four languages that I heard being spoken.

The doctor took the child in his arms, ordering me to come with them. There was no antivenin in the medical supplies. There was barely enough outdated antibiotics sent by aid organizations in Europe and America. But the doctor was able to offer tangible empathy to the soon-to-grieve mother. I translated his instructions for care of the boy, and the mother left quietly with the child held to her bare breast.

"Come sit here. Let me look at that eye." He had moved me ahead of the line waiting outside. And while he swabbed the crusted puss to loosen it, he asked me in French, "What language was she speaking?"

"Not really a language, sir, a dialect from the mountains in the west," I replied.

"Are you from there as well?"

"I've been there, sir."

"But you speak her dialect?" he asked.

"Yes, sir, I speak several of the mountain dialects. They come to me easily."

"And your French, it's not the Rwandan slang. Where did you learn it?"

"No, sir. I was schooled by the white sisters in Kigali."

He had pried my eyelid open and had to keep swabbing it to clean it, since there wasn't enough fresh water to waste on flushing it properly. He continued to talk as he worked. "What grade have you finished?"

"Third secondary level, sir. Almost."

"Secondary? And how old are you, son?"

"Seventeen," I said, without hesitating to bother with accuracy, further perpetuating the lie I had almost come to believe myself.

"Would you like a job when we get this eye fixed up? Actually, a volunteer position, but I'd see if you could eat in the Admin tent."

That was my first encounter with Vincent Bergeron, the French doctor. I took him up on his offer and gladly traded my idle boredom in the camp for his offer to eat rations with the UN personnel in the Admin tent. The associated benefits ended up going far beyond what I could have ever imagined. Aside from simply having something to do and a purpose inside the camp, I was treated to the companionship of one of the world's finest, most compassionate citizens, *and* I was introduced to the opportunity to make amends for some of the suffering and carnage I had perpetrated.

I started the next day, spending much of the next four years as Vincent's shadow, initially acting as an interpreter for him. The camp was a mixture of people from all over Rwanda. Most of them spoke French, but many could only speak Kinyarwanda, and Dr. Bergeron had no knowledge of this language. Others in the camp could speak only Swahili, another language not mastered by the doctor, and still others, like the woman with the snake-bitten child, only spoke the dialects of the villages. I was fluent in the three main languages and passable in many of the dialects, and I quickly proved my worth to the doctor. The United Nations' staff was a conglomeration of personnel from all over the world, and the common language spoken among them was English. I'd had very little exposure to English prior to this and enjoyed the opportunity to work on another language. There was no shortage of those with whom to practice since virtually all the locals who were employed by the UN were Tanzanians and English was their common language. Vincent could speak very good English and became an excellent tutor, refining what I could pick up from others and practicing with me.

In tagging along with Vincent as his interpreter, I kept myself busy and useful in as many other ways as I could find, assisting him in anything that he would entrust to me. He showed me how to clean and sterilize, within our limited abilities, but stressing the importance of doing everything as best as we possibly could. Lacking, as we were, many of the essentials, it became even more important to reuse instruments and materials whenever possible. Eventually we got comfortable enough that I would act in place of a nurse for him when there were none available. I took a keen interest in all these activities, and Vincent could see that I was a quick understudy. After about six months he came to me with a question.

"You're enjoying this, Alfred? I don't mean the camp. I mean working around the medical staff."

"I do, Vincent. I like it a lot."

"Have you thought about your future? I mean, after you get out of the camp?"

Of course I'd thought about it. I'd thought about it a lot, but in reality there weren't a lot of choices to consider. Even if the war hadn't been going on in Rwanda, there were very few options for all but the richest to do anything except some sort of menial labor.

"What about continuing your school? Maybe going on to university?" he asked.

"I've had it in my mind, Vincent. The sisters told me that there are opportunities for scholarships. But I don't know, with the war and everything."

"The camp's been open for almost a year now, and the administration is finally getting around to opening a school. They can't possibly take everyone, but I might be able to get you in."

"Vincent, I'd like to go to school, but I don't want to stop working with you."

"I figured that," he said. "I think you might be able to do both."

The school opened using a combination of teachers from Tanzania, paid by the UN, and volunteers from among the refugees themselves. While many of us refugees came to the camp with no skills, there were also many arrivals with considerable skills, and they volunteered their services in many ways. Some of them acted as nurses, and even a few doctors stepped forward. Others picked up their trades as shoemakers or tailors or barbers. The teachers who came forward were among some of the brightest in the camp and did an admirable job with their limited resources. I was able to convince one of the Tanzanian teachers to start an English class, in which I could devote a full hour a few days per week to practicing my new language. Vincent arranged for me to attend classes the day the school started, and by going daily, from eight each morning to noon, I was able to more than gain my secondary school equivalency. The moment I finished at noon, I shot over to the clinic to start work with Vincent.

Vincent became a role model for me, the one person in my life that I most wanted to emulate. The gentleness and heartfelt empathy with which he cared for each patient astounded me. No matter how tired he was or how hopeless the situation he was treating, he gave his all toward making each patient feel special and gave them all a measure of hope. For me, he gave me hope for mankind. If he could be like this then surely I could, too. And if we did it, maybe some others would join in, and little by little we could make a difference for the camp, for others, for the greater world.

Vincent wasn't just a good person, he was a skilled and meticulous doctor. These too became traits I sought to emulate when I made the decision to try to move into medicine as a career. Vincent explained things to me with endless patience, impressing upon me the basics of caring for the infirm. One of the things that I noticed Vincent doing far more than any of the other doctors was taking notes. In fact, when he was too busy to make the notes himself, he would sometimes dictate to me as he worked, and I would scribble his words down exactly as he spoke them in his logs.

"A good doctor can never take too many notes," he once advised. "You'll see hundreds of patients. You have to have good notes about them."

Vincent actually saw *thousands* of patients, and he made scrupulous notes about every encounter and every treatment. And even months later, when I had completely forgotten one individual or another, a patient would show up and Vincent had a recollection of them.

"Just by taking the notes, your memory is stimulated," he said. "And then when you need to refer back, if you have a good classification system, you can easily recall previous encounters with the patient. Sometimes this will make a big difference in how you approach their treatments. And don't forget the personal notes. Your personal notes can heal the patient. Treatment notes will help you treat the patient; personal notes will help you heal the patient." He emphasized this over and over. It was what set him apart from, and above, other doctors. Vincent took notes about things which, at first, I thought were insignificant—things like a little boy's favorite toy or how a woman's aging mother was doing. He insisted that these were the things that healed patients. When he would look to his notes after months and sometimes even years and pick out these little details, he was able to instill a confidence in the patient. "Healing," he said, "is about confidence, positive outlook, and willpower. Treatment is of no value if you can't heal someone, for that you have to make them trust you, believe in you, give them confidence."

At the end of each day, unfailingly, usually while I tidied up and prepared for the overnight shift of nurses, Vincent would make entries into his daily log. This was his personal diary. Of course, it was always in his own handwriting, and he would never dictate these notes to me. And even though I never saw the contents, he told me that he would summarize his day, the highlights, the problems, and his personal feelings about things.

By the time I had been in the camp at Nkwenda for a couple of years, I was well entrenched in my studies at the school and my apprenticeship in the clinic. The camp itself had grown exponentially and now approached nearly fifty thousand. The UN struggled mightily to keep up, but it was impossible. The squalor and disease and destitution multiplied. We were inundated with more and more patients in the clinic, able to do less and less for them.

Following Vincent's example, I chatted with the patients and used humor to comfort them and turn their minds away from their ailments. One day while stitching up one of the patients I asked him how long he had been in the camp.

"Only last week, Doctor," he answered. Many of them called me "doctor" and Vincent suggested that it was better not to confuse them by explaining that I wasn't.

"Where have you come from?" I asked, trying to keep him occupied while I sutured him without any anesthetic. "Any hope on the outside?"

"I've come from Kigali," he answered. "And no, there's not much positive news to give you. If there were, I probably wouldn't have come here."

"True enough, true enough. Where in Kigali?"

"The south of the city."

"That's where I'm from," I said. "You wouldn't happen to know of any news from the school run by the white sisters there, Notre Dame de la Paix?"

"Oh, Doctor. The depravity of some men knows no lows. They closed the school more than a year ago."

I just nodded my head. I had expected as much. The sisters had said if things got too bad they would be forced to go home. It was sad news for me. I had spent four good years there turning around my life, largely thanks to the generous nuns. I had pretty much given up hope of ever being able to return there, and with this news it was finalized.

Not even a week later, Vincent came to me in the clinic and said there was a man asking for me. "He claims he knows you, says he has news of your old school."

Thinking it must be the man I had stitched up last week I walked out to the front looking for him.

"Right here, Azi. Right here," a whisper came from behind.

I knew the voice instantly and grew cold at the sound. Turning to face him, just inches away from me, I could smell the stench of his breath and felt it blowing hot in my face. He surprised me when he lit up with a big smile.

"Azi, they told me I could find you here."

I cut him off. "Alfred," I said. "I am Alfred here, Idi."

"Alfred. Of course. I understand. And I'm not Idi. I'm Erasto."

I smirked when he said this because I knew the name. It was a common one across the eastern parts of the country and it meant "man of peace."

"What are you doing here?" I asked.

"The same as you," he said. "Laying low. Waiting for the shit to clear so we can go home. I see you've done well … playing doctor. You're just the man I need, Azi. Oh … I'm sorry … Alfred."

"I've changed." I shook my head. "You don't want me anymore."

"Oh, yes. I do. I have a job for you. I want you to get me some drugs out of the hospital. Anything you can get your hands on. I can sell it all here in the camp."

"I'm not doing that," I shot back at him quickly. "Now, get the fuck out of here."

"Azi, you owe me," he whispered.

"I don't owe you anything."

"Yes, you do, Azi. How could you forget that I took the blame for you killing Father Savard?" He grinned sarcastically at me. "Did you think I wouldn't figure out your little plan when you gave me that knife and never came back? It didn't me take long, especially when Major Ntagura told me that they were looking for me for a murder I had nothing to do with. Damn-fucking-right, you owe me."

He gripped me firmly by the arm and pulled me in close as if to emphasize his words. "Azi, there's a good business here for me—for both of us. See what you can find for us. I'll be back in a few days."

I didn't know how long Idi had been in the camp. With so many thousands now living here it was easy to get lost in the masses. And it was well known that's exactly what a lot of people were doing. By this time, more than half a million Tutsis and moderate Hutus had been slaughtered in my homeland. It takes a lot of people to carry out that many murders, especially when most of the killings are committed in close contact and not with the use of long-range bombs and artillery. In fact, nearly all of the murders were committed by mobs using clubs and machetes, literally beating and hacking their helpless victims to death. And this was precisely Idi's specialty, killing up close and personal to witness the terror in the eyes of his victims. Thousands of killing-squad members, like Idi, had fled the country after the holocaust, taking asylum and hiding out in the UN refugee camps that were meant for the truly displaced. Once they arrived in the camps they organized themselves into gangs, creating an underworld that continued their terror and illegal activities right under the noses of the United Nations officials.

Like all other societies, ours at the Nkwenda camp had its own underground economy fueled by drugs and other illicit operations. The security force we had in the camp wasn't even adequate to perform normal policing operations, let alone try to suppress the gangs controlled by war criminals like Idi.

I spent the next several days anxious about my predicament. There was no way that I wanted to help Idi with his crooked business, but neither did I want to be turned over to the authorities for the things I had done in my past. I was still considering the situation in my mind when Idi caught me by surprise on my way to the school one morning. He was flanked by two of his lackeys. One of them, a boy only a little older than I was when I ran under his influence, carried a machete which dangled by his leg.

"Azi, what have you come up with for me?"

"I can't, Idi," I said. "Everything is kept locked and inventoried. Only the doctors are allowed to sign out any medicine."

"Bullshit. You're a smart boy. You can figure something out."

"Even if I could, I wouldn't." I had decided to take a stand.

"Oh yes you will, Azi. You fucking well better." He reached out, and the boy at his side handed him the machete. Idi slapped the blade in the palm of his hand. "I'll meet you here tomorrow at this time, and I want you to have something for me."

"Fuck you, Idi." I surprised myself at my audacity, and the boldness infuriated him.

"You fucking ungrateful wretch," he said. "After all I have done for you over the years."

"After all you've done for me?" I began shouting, incredulous at his claim. "You killed my family, stole my childhood, ruined my future." A crowd was gathering at the sound of the argument, and I raised my clenched fists barely able to control myself.

Idi must have thought I was about to hit him and countered by raising the machete over his shoulder and swiping down at me. Reacting instinctively, I raised my left arm to block the slash but was only partially successful and I felt the steel blade strike my face. For a split second it was the force of the blow that I noticed, and I didn't think of the slicing damage until a thick syrup of blood completely blinded my right eye. Blood quickly began to cloud the vision of my left eye as well, and I knew I had to do something before I lost all my sight. I could see Idi raising the machete for a second strike, and I lunged into him reaching for his arm that held the blade. We struggled for several seconds for control of the large knife, but I was now thoroughly blinded by the blood that covered both my eyes. It ran down in streams, soaking my entire chest. Suddenly feeling, but not seeing, the handle of the machete in my own right hand I stepped back and swung it wildly at the air attempting to keep distance between Idi and myself. On my third blinded swing of the blade I felt it ever so slightly meet some resistance, like slicing through a green bamboo shoot. A moment later Idi let out an agonized scream, and the commotion in the crowd around us stopped. All else went silent.

I could feel the blood running from my face in such a steady stream that it now soaked my entire shirt and was wetting the front of my pants as well. Unable to see anything, I crouched in a defensive position, holding the blade out, ready to swing it at anything that threatened me.

Idi began shrieking over and over, "My hand … my hand!"

"You've cut off his fucking hand!" Idi's boy screeched.

I tried to gather my wits but was beginning to panic at my own loss of blood.

"Is it completely severed?" I asked, still ready to swipe.

"Yes, yes!" the boy wailed. "It's lying in the dirt."

I knew I needed to stay focused, remain controlled. "Somebody tie off his arm. Quickly. Take us to the clinic and bring the hand with us."

Someone gave me a rag to cover my own wounds, and I pressed it against my face and did my best to stop the flow of blood. The small crowd guided us through the dirt streets of the tent village, hurrying us to the clinic. Upon entering I heard Vincent's voice calmly taking command of the situation. "Bring them here. Sit this one here. Lay the one with the face wounds on the gurney. Nurse, stop the bleeding. I need a proper tourniquet on this arm, quickly. Someone tell me what happened."

A voice spoke up, "That one first struck this one, and then he took the machete from him and cut off the other one's hand."

"Where's the hand?" I heard Vincent ask.

"Here, Doctor."

I heard Idi ask in a shocked voice, "Can you put it back on, Doctor?"

"No," Vincent answered. "But you're lucky, the sever was clean and you'll be able to keep the arm. I'll sew it as soon as they get it disinfected and get the blood clamped off properly."

Someone was pressing firmly on the wound on my face, while someone else tried to mop blood. I could feel the sticky wet of it covering my face and, now that I was lying down, it was running back over my head as well, soaking the pillow underneath me.

"Is he still conscious?" I heard Vincent's voice close over my face. "Can you hear me, son?"

I realized that I must be so covered in blood that Vincent didn't even recognize me.

"It's me, Vincent, Alfred."

For the first time since I had known him I heard a fleeting flash of panic in his voice. "Oh my god, Alfred. What's happened?" And then, in a brief moment of unprofessionalism, I could feel his two hands gently take the sides of my head, and his lips touched down on my bloody wet forehead and kissed me. "You'll be all right, Alfred. You'll be all right," he whispered to me.

After that it was total professionalism. Vincent worked back and forth between Idi and me with the aid of two assistants. He sawed another section of bone away from Idi's wrist leaving enough flesh to draw the skin around and make a proper stump out of it, and painstakingly sutured twenty-two stitches into the cut above my eye socket and twenty-two into the one below which ran down to the side of my jaw. In the eyes of the good doctor we were equal patients needing comfort and healing, and he did all he could to help the two of us. His skills proved ample as we both mended fine, except for the permanent reminders we were each left with. Idi's stump was much more of a disability than my scar, nonetheless the reminders would be with each of us for the rest of our lives.

In explaining the incident later to Vincent I practiced my lying by omission and only told him the part of the story where Idi had demanded that I steal drugs from the hospital. I didn't want Vincent to know of my horrid past with Idi, and I continued to try to forget it by never mentioning it to anyone, not even Vincent.

Around the time of my disfiguring encounter with Idi, the camp peaked in size. Many had arrived only to find that the UN was so overextended that they might have been better off where they had come from. And, with all the war criminals who were flocking to the camps, many new arrivals were feeling that perhaps they would have been safer back in their home communities. Eventually word filtered in to us that a new provisional government was slowly regaining control inside Rwanda. The few trickling out of the camp gradually increased to a steady flow, and the population finally began to decrease to a manageable number. In October of 1997, Vincent brought news from the head of the UN mission at Nkwenda.

"Alfred, we've just heard that they'll be decommissioning the camp. Closing it."

"When?" I asked. "How soon?"

"Next year," he answered. "It'll take them at least six to twelve months to completely close it up."

"What'll you do, Vincent?"

He laughed. "The question is not what I'll do, it's what you're going to do. I'll go back home to France and get reacquainted with the bureaucracy at my hospital in Paris, for a while anyhow. But you have some choices to make, Alfred."

I hated thinking about this. I had dreaded it and avoided it for a long time. I knew that the camp was not permanent, and God knows that I wanted to get away from the place as much as anyone. But I had no place to go, no home to go back to.

"Have you thought about leaving Africa, Alfred? For a while at least, maybe not forever." He paused to assess my reaction before continuing. "Why don't you come to France? You can go to university there, perhaps medical school. I can't think of anyone better equipped to go into medicine than you."

I was flattered by his comments but was much too practical to take them seriously. "You know that would be impossible, Vincent."

"Not if you really wanted to, Alfred. There are ways. France has a very open and generous refugee program. Nothing's for sure, but you could apply. I'd like to act as your sponsor, if you'd allow me."

I was overwhelmed with Vincent's proposal and wanted to respond, but I was afraid that if I spoke I would begin to cry. It took all my control to just nod without letting tears form.

Vincent and I had become close, very close, over the past three years. He'd long ago begun to treat me as more than just a translator or a medical assistant. We were close friends, each other's only family in this lonely despondent place. I was the apprentice, he was the mentor; I the fatherless son, he the epitome of benevolence. I suppose in some ways we filled a void in each other's lives, but at the time I only recognized the huge part he played in mine. It wasn't until years later, when I thought back and reflected on our relationship, that I linked it to something I had once heard Vincent say to a news reporter.

A camera crew from France had trundled into the camp about a year earlier. They were doing a story on the French organization, Médecins Sans Frontières, and had somehow found their way to Nkwenda. I watched them interview him.

"Dr. Bergeron, what would make a successful physician from the West want to come to such a forsaken place as this and work under such deplorable conditions?"

"There are plenty of good reasons," Vincent answered. "Look at this poverty and suffering. Where else could I possibly help so much? Where else could I be so needed?"

It took us a full year to get the necessary approvals from France for me to accompany Vincent home as a refugee. The Rwandan government did nothing to help speed the process by taking nearly eight months to issue me a passport. It probably would have gone faster if they could have located a birth certificate for me. When we initially wrote away to the Office of Civil Registration in search of one, I had to come clean to Vincent and tell him my real age. He was surprised that instead of being twenty, as I had led him to believe, I was only nineteen. The office was unable to locate any reference to my birth. To be fair to them, the records might have been lost during the war or, as often happened in those days in the rural parts of the country, there might never have been anything filed in the first place. Using my baptismal certificate we were able to establish citizenship and then finally obtain a passport.

While this process went on Vincent helped me to begin the refugee application process for France, acting as my guarantor and sponsor. As soon as we received my Rwandan passport things went more smoothly with the French authorities. Nkwenda camp had almost emptied out and we were among the last handful of volunteers and United Nations personnel still there when news came in the fall of 1998 that my final paperwork had arrived from France and was waiting for us in Dodoma. It was a bittersweet departure that we made from the camp at Nkwenda. Bitter in that it closed a chapter in my life in which I had matured into a man, and sweet in that I was beginning a new one with boundless optimism for my future in Europe. The moment, however, was indelibly blemished by the sight of Idi ominously waving goodbye with his stumped arm.

Brussels

By the time I finish relating to Bart and Anna the rest of the story about my time spent in Tanzania at the Nkwenda refugee camp, and then giving Bart the short version of my earlier childhood spent with Idi, we are exhausted. It had already been a draining day, beginning with the presentation of evidence through the morning, then the playing of Idi's video testimony after lunch, and now my own tale being laid out in the open.

"This is good," says Bart. "Definitely a lot more for us to work with than I thought we had a few hours ago. Give me some time to think about this, and we can start fresh tomorrow."

As the three of us pack our things and prepare to leave the courthouse Anna is in significantly improved spirits, not so much because of anything that I just told them but rather because I have new fight in me. She is glad that I am refusing to just give in to my old feelings of guilt, that I am ready to go the distance to prove my innocence in the murders of the four sisters. I, myself, feel as if I have shaken off another layer of the load that has been burdening me for so many years, and the three of us walk with purpose down the empty after-hours halls of the courthouse.

Even the throng of reporters and media people that have waited for hours to assail us at the front door doesn't daunt us. The cameras that were absent in the courtroom begin flashing, and videographers jockey for position to get the best angles. Bodies and microphones crowd us, and questions are flying in several languages, each reporter trying to outshout the other.

Bart takes command of the situation by opening his hand and raising it in the air, quieting things quickly.

"I have one short statement to make on behalf of Dr. Olyontombo," he says. "First, he strenuously denies the charges against him. He was not present at the murders of the Four Sisters of Peace and was not even in Rwanda at the time of the offenses. Further, Dr. Olyontombo was not even of accusable adult age at the time of these murders. We intend to prove all of this and look forward to his full exoneration before this inquiry."

For the first time in weeks I go to bed with a sense of hope. I feel positive and energized. Seeing Idi glaring at me through the camera lens has inspired a determination to put my childhood transgressions behind me once and for all. Even the crowd of media that sets up camp outside our apartment can't bother me, and I don't let the stories that flood the internet in Belgium get to me. Predictably, they report how the case against me is ironclad and how justice will finally be served for the deaths of the Four Sisters of Peace. However, my optimism is so solidly based in my antipathy toward Idi Mbuyamba that I blindly ignore this practical consideration and fall asleep in good spirits.

Unfortunately, the night's sleep is sobering, and I awake the following day with reality facing me head-on. I have to leave all the blinds shut to avoid the peering telephoto lenses that are set up on the sides of the street. Police have erected barricades on our little neighborhood lane, allowing no through traffic. They have helped to set up a media zone with a half-dozen broadcast vehicles jacked up on stabilizers. There are many more reporters gathered outside than were at the courthouse yesterday, and it's not yet even seven o'clock in the morning. The police themselves have a command-post vehicle parked a little farther down the street. I take to my laptop for the news websites that I have been monitoring, and every single one of them has the inquiry as the lead story in prominent bold headlines. By now, they all have photos of me. Some were shot yesterday outside the courthouse, some were probably obtained from the Denver media, of me on the steps of my home in Boulder. There are also some court sketches of me from yesterday with my head hanging low. The courtroom artists have depicted me with a look of shame and guilt, and they emphasize my facial scar as if it is some sort of confirmation of demonhood. The stories take all sorts of angles: some are rereporting the whole tale of the murder from 1994; some report the new facts presented yesterday; some are telling the stories of the war crimes trials, including new updates about Idi; and some have new angles on the Rwandan civil war and genocide. There is no shortage of experts to provide commentary: war experts, legal experts, experts to explain the court process I am facing, experts analyzing my body and facial language from the inquiry, forensic experts, and experts on what my likely sentencing will be.

Overnight, the newsrooms have all had time to get their editorial departments working, and they have come up with lots to pontificate about. Praise is offered to the national police for finally, after so many years, being able to crack this case that was such a scathing wound to the entire Belgian state, conveniently forgetting that the police didn't actually have anything to do with solving it; Idi apparently came forward on his own. Other editorials outright condemn me without even the benefit of a court hearing, relying totally on the evidence presented yesterday, and some are making suggestions that a life sentence will hardly be adequate justice. The columnists are in their full glory, appealing to nationalism and prejudice and fear.

The internet news has further diluted my exuberance from yesterday. By nine thirty sizable crowds have formed at each end of the street, just outside the police barricades, and their negativity seeps into the apartment with Bart's arrival. It seems that even he had underestimated the interest and animosity of the rest of his countrymen.

"Not a damned one willing to give justice a chance to play out." Bart shakes his head with a look of mild disgust. But he quickly catches himself and tries to deflect from his gloomy greeting by adding, "We better get started if we're going to prove them wrong."

I'm not sure how he intends to prove them wrong. Anna has already talked about this with me this morning, and she has pleaded with me to stay positive and just go along with whatever my lawyer suggests. She has seen many cases that looked doomed at the outset but, with preparation and attention to detail, were able to turn favorably.

"Remember," she said, "we don't have to convince the public or the media. There's only one single person that we have to convince, and that's the judge."

"And he's not influenced by the papers and the crowds?" I asked.

She didn't have an answer to that, so responded instead by giving me a glare of admonishment.

Bart has brought with him a secretary, and she sets up in the living room with her computer. When she's ready Bart begins what I assume is a standard method used by lawyers for initiating the prep work for a case. He starts with my past, and I spend several hours telling him of my childhood, the same story that I had recently unburdened myself of in the Denver police station when I shared it with Anna. Bart listens carefully but is much more interrogative than Anna was, stopping me many times to ask questions and probing for details that I sometimes have to think hard about to recall. He makes me recount every possible thing I can about Idi Mbuyamba, right from my first encounter, when he took me after Kakengo had killed Uncle Dzigbote and Auntie Nyaka. He wants every small detail about the killing of the priest, Savard, and exactly when and how I turned the knife over to Idi. Bart tells me that it is going to be tricky convincing the judge that I gave the knife to Idi before the nuns were murdered without implicating myself in the priest's killing. We then pay special attention to the incident where I had taken Idi's own machete and left him without a right hand. He makes me recall the names of any witnesses who were there at the time. These, I tell him, may not even be possible to find. "We'll see," he says and continues with his methodical interrogation.

Shortly after three o'clock Anna's phone rings, and Bart suggests that it is a good time to quit for the day. We have only stopped once for a short snack at noon and we are getting exhausted. About ten minutes after taking the call in the other room, Anna rejoins us.

"That was Steve," she says. "He said the story has been picked back up in the Denver media. It's on the front pages again after yesterday."

I'd been watching the Denver papers. Since the day I was extradited the story had dropped out of the headlines, with other, more current items filling the void. But it seems that interest has been renewed with the revelations from the inquiry yesterday.

"Is there anything we can do about this?" Anna points to the crowd outside as Bart and his secretary prepare to leave.

"We'll just have to hope that it doesn't get any worse and be thankful that the police are keeping it organized," says Bart. "Unfortunately, there's going to be a high level of interest throughout the case, but the media will have to move on to other stories soon. We'll send food in so that you don't have to go outside for a few days. It's still a lot better than jail."

That is true. I have Anna here with me and access to my computer, both important things that I wouldn't have in jail. I can see I'm not going to be able to get much exercise for the next few days; we won't be doing the walking that we had worked into our routine when we first arrived, but we can live with this inconvenience.

"Let me know if there's anything you need, and I can have it sent in," Bart says before leaving for the day.

By dusk not only have the Denver papers picked up on the story, but the national media in the US is reporting on it for the first time. Once one news service headlines a story, the rest follow like sheep. Only none of them have done any of their own reporting, they are all just regurgitating everything that the Belgian media has said. I can tell by the slant of the articles that the great bastion of freedom and fairness, America, has no interest in waiting for judgment. The sensationalism of the story outweighs that, and they are gobbling it up, having already followed the Belgian media's lead and proclaiming guilt. Normally the American press shows concern when an American citizen is put on trial in a foreign country, but I'm perceived as a second-rate citizen. I'm a black man who comes from a backward African country and who only *became* an American citizen, a transplanted refugee, no less. It's the salaciousness of a professional medical doctor violently raping and mutilating four nuns that attracts them. That's the story the press wants, not the truth.

Before yesterday it wouldn't have bothered me what the press thought. I was prepared to take my lumps and let them condemn me. But after seeing Idi practically gloating at me in his video testimony, I am determined not to let him have any more satisfaction. It irks me that the press has jumped to presumptive conclusions.

It's not long before Anna's father calls to say that he has seen the morning news in Colorado and begs Anna to come back home. She leaves me to take the call alone in the bedroom and returns about ten minutes later visibly upset.

"What did Eldon have to say?" I ask her.

"I'm too ashamed to repeat it."

I just shake my head knowingly to her, not wanting to hear it any more than she wants to say it.

"Then he tried to make it sound like Mom thinks the same way," she says.

"She might. Did you get to speak to her?" I ask.

"He put her on."

"And what did she say?"

"I don't think she really feels as strongly as Dad does. But you know how she pretty much goes along with anything he says. She did say that she loves us both. Daddy couldn't bring himself to say that."

"Anna, I never wanted to come between you and your parents. What would you say about going ahead home? I can stay here with Bart. I promise you I'll fight this. And Bart seems more than competent. I'm not going to give in now."

She doesn't even take a moment to think about it. "Not a chance. I'm not leaving you."

"It won't be leaving me. It'll be saving your relationship with your parents. You have to think of that, regardless of the outcome here. Eventually you'll have to go back there, one way or the other. And it might be easier on them, and you, if you go now."

"Even if you don't need me, Freddie, I need you. After what we've been through with Stephanie, this pales. I'm not leaving you, Freddie—ever—and that's it. It's settled, so don't bring it up again ... please."

Pulling her close, I kiss the top of her forehead. I savor the feel of her body close to mine. I've always thought that we were an impeccable fit together. The curves of her slender frame just seem to fit perfectly against my larger body. Standing here like this, or slouched together on the couch watching a movie, or in bed sleeping spooned on our sides, or making love with her in any of many ways—everything just seems to fit. It's like a lock and key, created perfectly for one another, and no other.

On the second day after the hearing most of the media crews clear out from in front of our apartment. A few stick around, probably waiting for the last of the demonstrators to also leave, but the media now knows that nothing more will happen until after the next inquiry appearance. Bart can't arrange that date until we decide on a plan of action. He tells us that, like the press, the demonstrators will also likely thin out in a few days, but it's possible a few will continue to hang around on the streets. He suggests that we be patient with them since those who are the most persistent are quite likely family members of the murdered nuns.

We sit down to get started with today's session. "I've been thinking overnight about what our next steps should be," Bart says. "First, the knife. You said that you gave it to Idi Mbuyamba. It's a long shot, but we need to get the original reports and see if there were any other fingerprints on the knife besides yours. If we get lucky, his might be there. If there's nothing in the report we'll ask for another fingerprint analysis. If the blood is still there, there may still be prints on it that were missed.

"Second, somehow we've got to get proof of your real age. We'll send someone in Rwanda to search birth records there. Your baptismal certificate was used as a basis for your first passport to get you out of Rwanda and into France, but if we can find an original birth certificate it may be able to corroborate your real age and prove that you were only fifteen at the time of the murders. If you really hadn't reached the age of sixteen, Belgium can't try you for crimes committed as a youth.

"Third, we've got to try to get some proof that you were not in Rwanda on the date of the murder. I'm going to have someone contact the United Nations and see if they have kept any records from the Nkwenda camp.

"And last, we need witnesses, anyone who can vouch for any of your story. If we come up empty with the birth info and the UN records, they might be all we have. What about the French doctor … Bergeron? Do you have any way to contact him?"

I had stayed in touch with Vincent over the years. Initially, while in med school, we'd corresponded a lot, but gradually over the years our emails became less and less frequent. We saw each other only once after I left France: he made a special trip to Pittsburgh for my graduation. He and Anna had conspired to surprise me, and it gave me a whole new level of pride in my accomplishment to have him there to share the moment with me. Vincent had never stopped spending most of his time away with Médecins Sans Frontières, returning only periodically to France. Several times I had promised him that I would do a stint with the organization, but the timing just never seemed right. First I was doing my residency, and then Stephanie was born, and then I was trying to get my practice going—something just always seemed to get in the way. The last few years we had only made a point of touching base with emails at Christmas. I had sent him a note this past November to tell him of Stephanie's passing and heard back from him in early December. It took him a while to respond since he is currently working in sub-Saharan Chad, where Islamic extremists are waging a guerrilla war, and he is often away from internet connectivity.

In response to Bart's question I answer, "I can reach him, maybe. Though not immediately. But I should be able to get an email through."

"Do you think we could get him to come here?" Bart asks.

"I can see what he says. He's working in Africa right now."

"Of course we'll get him to come," Anna jumps in. "We have to. His testimony could be all that we have. He'll come. I know he will."

Bart leaves us with the proposal that he schedule our next inquiry time with Judge Gelineau for one month from now. Anything that we have come up with during this month we can present to him, and if we need more time we'll ask for it. We're all in agreement that the sooner we can deal with things the better.

I draft and send off several emails this afternoon. I am especially saddened to have to send the one to Vincent. I feel ashamed at the position I am in and had hoped that somehow, he wouldn't have to find out. I feel like a child who has done something which they know will bring disappointment to their parents. I explain in quite a bit of detail my predicament, how I arrived at this point, and how I am hoping that he could come back to offer his testimony on my behalf. Several times throughout the email I apologize for having to inconvenience him and take him away from his work in the remote communities of Africa.

I also send a follow-up email to my clinic in Denver. I had sent them one a week or so earlier, asking for them to forward me an email contact for Ricky and Pina Nunez. I am concerned for them both and want to hear how Ricky is making out with his cancer treatments. I learned early on in practice that this extra bit of interest and involvement in my patients' well-being inspires a lot of confidence and positivity in their attitudes, which translates into better outcomes. All my other patients know that I'll be away on vacation until February, so there is no need to connect with any of them. I ask Rosa if she could please get me the email address I need for Ricky.

I don't really expect a quick answer from Vincent, but I get a prompt one back from my clinic. It isn't Rosa who answers, but instead, Mark. His note is quite straightforward: *Alfred, All of us here at the clinic wish you all the best. Brie, Luis, and I have decided that under the circumstances it is probably not appropriate for you to be contacting any of the clinic's patients. Thank you.* And that was it. It doesn't take much for me to read between the lines, or rather, the lack of lines, and understand that they are trying to distance themselves from me. It saddens me a lot to think about this. These, of all people, ought to know my personal integrity; their response speaks to me like a megaphone.

A couple days pass, and no one is showing up out front to protest, and so the media is also completely absent. This allows Anna and me to get out and start walking again. We've been cooped up inside for too long. We're both used to a lot of exercise, and when I don't get it nothing feels right in my body. I am stiff and yearning for some fresh air, and even the cloudy, damp weather of Brussels beats being indoors for a whole week.

But as the days go by the fresh air and exercise aren't enough to counteract the disappointing news that flows in. Even Anna, ever the optimist, has turned a bit sour at the news that Bart received back from the United Nations. Hard-copy logs from Nkwenda that would have shown the dates of refugee entry into the camp had long ago been destroyed. There are some computerized records that have been maintained, and they show that Alfred Olyontombo was indeed at the camp for a period of several years, but there was nothing to confirm the date of his arrival. That one piece of information would have solidified my alibi, and we placed a lot of hope in it. On top of this, new forensic fingerprint tests, which Bart had ordered on the knife, come back empty with not a trace of anyone else's prints other than mine. The very day after Bart breaks this news to us he calls to say that his researchers in Rwanda and the Democratic Republic of Congo have all reported back that there are no birth records to be found for Azikiwe Olyontombo in either country.

Then finally, nearly two weeks after having sent my email to Vincent, I get a reply. I must admit, I had begun to wonder if he too wanted to avoid me. I am glad to see that he was away doing his circuit among isolated villages, and his delayed response was only due to his lack of access to a computer. Unlike everyone else who seemed to be abandoning me to a presumptive guilt, Vincent gives me a boost by saying that he'll be in Belgium within a week. It's the soonest he can make arrangements, but not to worry, he will do everything he can to help me. This shot of good news is welcome, not only to my spirits but Anna's as well. Amidst all the recent negative news, just the fact that Vincent is coming is an elixir to both of us. And we desperately cling to shreds of hope that he can be of some help in clearing me.

Anna and I greet Vincent at the airport like the long-missed family member that he is. The anticipation of his arrival is a very emotional stew for me: a mix of guilt at not having made more effort to see him over the years, joy to finally see him now, thanks that he is coming to help, sadness that our reunion is under these circumstances, and shame that I have let him down. On my way to the airport I resolved not to let these sentiments overwhelm me.

Pulling his worn and dirty suitcase through the customs arrivals doors, my first impression is of how serene and contented he looks amidst the bustle of the travelers around him, always a calm and reassuring presence wherever he is. There is not the slightest evidence one might expect from the deprivations and hardships of his choosing to practice medicine among the poorest of the world. On the contrary, he is spry and possesses an aura of exuberance. I still pictured him from the last time I saw him, more than a decade ago, and am not prepared for the effects of natural aging that I should have expected. The receded brush-cut, his stubbly beard, the hair on his arms are all totally white now. But the deep crinkles at the outer edges of his eyes just serve to highlight the radiance of his tranquil blue irises, more so when he spots us and lights up with the same joy that we are feeling.

The three of us meet in a hug, each pulling the other two tight together. My determination to control my emotions is abandoned in the moment, and I let the tears run freely down my face. We stay locked together in this little display of solidarity for several moments before stepping back to look closely at each other. Vincent, eternally compassionate, and with great tenderness wipes the tears from my face with his bare hands, as a father would his small child, and then he wipes his own. After composing ourselves we hug again, upright and with strength, patting each other on the back. Anna waits her turn to receive Vincent's kiss and sincere affections.

We avoid discussing my situation until we are back at the apartment and are caught up on all that Vincent has been doing for the past few years. But it could be evaded for only so long before Vincent asks about it. I tell him of the suddenness with which things had developed, how I had been arrested in my office and extradited within ten days. We explain in detail the process that is unfolding here in Belgium and the desperation of the situation.

"So, you think that Idi is pointing the blame at you as revenge for taking off his hand?" Vincent asks.

"That … and more." Vincent knew nothing of the death of the priest, and I go on to tell him the previous chapter of my life, my youth he still knows nothing about. Vincent listens to my story with his usual serene compassion.

"So, you see," I say, "he knows I set him up to take the blame for Father Savard's death. Another good reason to hate me. And then just the fact that I turned away from him, that I wouldn't fight with his mercenary band in Rwanda, and then openly opposed him at Nkwenda. Each of these alone is reason enough for him to lie about me murdering the nuns, especially if it lessens his own sentence."

"Wow." Vincent shakes his head. "How can I help you?"

"Ideas, if you have any," Anna says. "But at the very least we'd like you to stand as a character witness and tell them what you knew of Freddie in the Nkwenda camp. Maybe what you knew of Idi."

"Of course, I'll certainly do that."

"We have another angle we are trying to work from," Anna says. "The school records and the army records both say that Freddie was sixteen at the time of the nuns' deaths, but he says that he was actually fifteen. You helped him obtain that first passport in Rwanda in order to get him his refugee papers for France."

"I remember that," Vincent says. "He told me in the camp that he was sixteen when I first met him, but when we went to apply for a birth certificate he admitted to me that he was actually a year younger than what was printed on his baptismal certificate, and a year younger than what he had led me to believe. It didn't make any difference to me at the time. Unfortunately, we got nowhere trying to locate his birth certificate. It seemed that either there never was one, or in the confusion of civil war the records were destroyed or lost. We ended up having no option but to obtain the passport with the use of the baptismal certificate. It was the only ID available. Besides, he had been calling himself Alfred for nearly four years and wanted to continue. He said Azikiwe was a person he wanted to completely forget. Now I understand why."

"If we could get you to speak about that it might help to prove his real age. That could be critical because we need to establish Alfred's accurate age when the sisters were murdered."

Vincent takes a few minutes to go over all that we have been telling him before coming up with some thoughts of his own. "I need to go home to Paris for a few days. There are some things there that I need to get."

* * *

With the judicial inquiry scheduled to resume at the end of the week, and Vincent back in Paris to attend to his affairs there, Bart has been prepping me for how we should proceed in our presentation to Judge Gelineau. Even though Bart will be there with me, representation by a lawyer is not allowed during judicial inquiries in Belgium. I will have to make the case to the judge myself. Bart will have the right to intervene on my behalf in very limited circumstances, mostly only to question points of law.

One small story in the newspaper stating that the inquiry will recommence in a few days reenergizes a flurry of activity in the media and reawakens the protesters. Making things even worse this time, the politicians stir the embers and inflame public outrage when they adopt my case as their cause of the week. One of the small right-wing opposition parties in Parliament has called on the government to bring back the death penalty *so that proper judgment can be brought upon the Rwandan murderer who took the lives of good, innocent Belgian citizens, the Four Sisters of Peace.* There is a sizable portion of the population that is in favor of this, and an online petition receives nearly half a million signatures in the first day alone. Under pressure, and in response, the governing party stands in Parliament to announce that the justice department is pursuing the case with full vigor and that the strictest enforcement of penalties will be brought to bear on the guilty offender.

The debate now taking place in the media is not whether or not I am guilty—it seems that they have already established that—it is whether a sentence of natural life in prison is severe enough. So now, we don't just have demonstrators on the street proclaiming my guilt; there are two sides lined up to debate the broader issue of capital punishment. For the few days before the inquiry is to start up again, we are once more confined to the apartment. The crowds outside are several times their previous size, and the media is out in even larger numbers, having even more angles to promote now.

And, as if to muddle things even more, there is another group that has curiously jumped on the bandwagon to have me summarily convicted.

There is a large population of African expatriates living in Brussels and, ever since the judicial inquiry began, there has been a growing backlash against them. It seems that hard-line, white-nationalist extremists have been stoking hatred against the entire black community in the city, lumping all Africans with me and blaming them for the murders of the Four Sisters of Peace. In order to protect their delicate standing within the greater community, the Africans have come out against me, condemning me and isolating themselves from me. And to further prove their point, they organize their own groups to demonstrate against me out in the streets.

With all these disparate groups using my case to push their own agendas, the media is having a field day. Commentators and prognosticators are making the most of their time in the limelight.

The morning of the inquiry we are greeted at the courthouse by even more reporters and cameras than before. And thousands of protesters, each with their own pet cause, are trying to outshout the others and jockey for spots in front of the television cameras. There are political protesters, urging their respective parties toward firm stands; death penalty advocates shouting for it to be reinstated; abolitionists arguing against them; anti-immigrant protesters claiming that all foreigners are causing harm to Belgium; coalitions of African organizations claiming righteousness and disavowing me; Belgian nationalists affirming the greatness of their country; and somewhere lost in the throngs are the families of the Four Sisters of Peace, simply looking for justice or revenge or just closure.

Judge Gelineau has anticipated the level of interest, and we use the largest room in the building to accommodate the media. With Vincent and Anna flanking me on one side and Bart Verbeke on the other, the judge reminds all of us that this is not a trial, but rather, a hearing strictly to determine whether there is a prima facie case with which to proceed to a trial.

"Dr. Olyontombo," he says. "More than a month ago, you were provided with the evidence of the state against you. As is your right, this is your opportunity to either refute with proof, or explain with cause, that evidence. You also have the right to say nothing and are not expected to answer anything that may further incriminate you. Do you wish to proceed?"

We have very little solid evidence with which to proceed, the entirety of my case will rest with what Vincent is able to convince the judge of.

"Yes, Your Honor," I say. "I would like the opportunity to show you how I was not the one who committed the crimes of which I am accused. I have with me Dr. Vincent Bergeron who would like to address you."

"Dr. Bergeron, you are familiar with the evidence that was presented?"

"I am," Vincent replies.

"What can you tell us?" the judge asks.

"Your Honor, I have known Dr. Olyontombo for twenty-three years. From the time I met him in 1994 I have always found him to be of the highest moral character and standing. He is outstanding in his profession and—"

"Dr. Bergeron," Judge Gelineau interrupts. "Dr. Olyontombo's character and competency as a doctor are not in question here, and frankly they have no bearing on the evidence that is presented against him. It is not this inquiry's duty to judge Dr. Olyontombo, only to judge the evidence. Do you have anything of relevance to the factual evidence?"

"I do, Your Honor," Vincent replies. "As I said, I have known Dr. Olyontombo for twenty-three years, from even before the date on which the murders of the four sisters occurred. And I have proof here that he was not in Kigali at the time of those murders, but rather was in the Nkwenda refugee camp in Tanzania."

The judge interrupts Vincent again. "Dr. Bergeron, if you were familiar with the evidence you would know that we have investigated Dr. Olyontombo's tenure at the camp and found no conclusive proof of the day that he arrived there."

"Your Honor, I have with me my own personal notes from those days in the camp. I would like to present you with my handwritten diaries, in which I make mention of my first meeting with Dr. Olyontombo on April third, 1994. I had treated him for an eye infection. My notes also show meeting him nearly every day after that, including on April twelfth, the date of the murders."

"May I see your diary, please?" The judge reaches for the notebooks.

When Vincent returned from Paris a few days ago and proudly

produced these old diaries, I thanked the gods for all the times he had insisted on my patience at the end of the day while he carefully made his notes. These old journals had been kept by Vincent all these years in his home in Paris. He cherished them and maintained a full complement dating all the way back to his first placement with Médecins Sans Frontiers more than thirty years earlier.

"I have marked the pages." Vincent hands over the first book. "In this one," he says, as he holds up a second notebook, "I have flagged the pages of the dates when I treated Dr. Olyontombo for the wound which you now see scarring his face, as well as treating his accuser, Idi Mbuyamba, when his hand was severed. The two men had previous disputes, and when Dr. Olyontombo was attacked, he was forced to defend himself. I can personally attest to the fact that this is one very good reason why Mr. Mbuyamba would falsely accuse Dr. Olyontombo."

The audience of reporters behind us is shuffling and talking, tapping out messages on their cells. I watch Judge Gelineau very carefully as he thumbs through Vincent's notebooks, taking plenty of time to read the pages that Vincent has flagged with Post-it tabs. The judge's face gives nothing away, but he does take a second look through the notebooks. A full five minutes pass while no one speaks.

Finally Judge Gelineau looks to Vincent. "Are you prepared to submit these for forensic analysis, Dr. Bergeron?"

"Of course."

"And current handwriting samples?"

"Most certainly," Vincent replies.

This was the most conclusive evidence we could provide. As expected, the search in Rwanda for my birth certificate came up empty. I try to explain that the age shown on my baptismal certificate, which I had used to secure my original Rwandan passport, was based on a lie that I now regret. I realize that the explanation I give of how my age was recorded in the army and school records and on the baptismal certificate is only my account, and I have nothing to back it up. But I am desperate and need to raise every shred of possible evidence.

After we finish in court, the four of us—Vincent, Bart, Anna, and I—

hash out the happenings of the day over takeout dinner in our apartment. We all agree that Vincent's diaries will be very compelling in establishing my innocence and undermining Idi's already shaky credibility. But none of us are confident that they will be enough to overcome the evidence which points to my guilt. There was nothing that I could say to address the fact that the nuns' blood was found on my knife. I could not tell the judge how I had given the knife to Idi in the hope that it would incriminate him for the murder of Savard, the priest. That would only have implicated me in that death—and I certainly didn't need any more trouble with the law than I was already facing. It's going to be up to how Judge Gelineau weighs it all out in his own mind.

The judge has set a date for one month hence to deliver his finding. Like the last time, it takes a few days for the last of the protesters to get tired and leave, and the same amount of time for the media to lose interest and move on to other, more topical stories. They'll wait until a few days before the next inquiry date, at which time they'll resurrect everything again. In the meantime we have nothing to do but wait. This time though, we have a bit of hope in the backs of our minds, hope we didn't have a month ago. Vincent's diaries have been a godsend, and his time spent with us has given us back some of our missing faith in mankind. Vincent's calm and consoling words, his controlled and positive attitude, and most of all, his simple acceptance of life and his contentment with it are inspiring to both Anna and me. Bart has only been around him for a few days yet is compelled to comment on how he has never met anyone quite so selflessly devoted to the good of others as Vincent.

Unfortunately for us, that selfless devotion is beckoning him back to his work in Africa, and he can't sit around here for a whole month waiting on Judge Gelineau's decision. He indulges us with one more week, during which the three of us become tourists, seeing the things that Anna and I had already seen, but this time, seeing them with a joy we missed the first time around. Evenings are spent quietly in the apartment, just being together and absorbing the gentle and easy comportment of our friend.

The week is followed by a sad farewell at the airport with several promises being made. Vincent promises to be back if we need him for anything at all, none of us outright mentioning the possibility of needing to go through a full-blown trial. And Anna and I both make promises, not hollow promises, but sincere ones, to visit Vincent in Africa soon after this is past us. We are determined to take time away from our respective practices and go to volunteer at Vincent's side for at least a few weeks. We no longer have the care of Stephanie to hold us back, and this whole experience has completely refocused our perspective on what we want to do with our futures. We can now better understand the fragility of status and relationships and see the folly in accumulation and ownership. We are both committed to helping repay Vincent some small amount of the debt we owe him. When we try to mention it to him in these terms, he replies that there is no debt, but rather that all our deeds are simply entries in the eternal ledger.

The next three weeks waiting for Judge Gelineau to come out with his ruling are tempered by the week that we spent with Vincent. The media and the protest groups and the general public build up their steam as the last few days go by. Columnists, experts, and armchair quarterbacks spend countless hours debating the likely ruling, many of them switching their opinions from one day to the next. The only thing that seems consistent, and certain, is that no one will be happy if I am exonerated. The entire country, now that the wound has been reopened, wants me to pay for the murders of the Four Sisters of Peace. It doesn't matter that I may not be guilty. All that matters is satisfying the national yearning to finally put this sore point of Belgian history to bed. If that doesn't happen by finding me guilty, the wound will simply continue to fester.

In spite of all this attention and the outright hatred toward me, our time with Vincent has taught us to find contentment and a measure of peace, and although the three weeks pass slowly, they are more bearable than they otherwise would have been. Anna and I spend almost every moment together. Our relationship has a new peacefulness to it that we never even knew we were missing. The beauty and the strength of this woman never cease to amaze me. Before he left, I had the opportunity to talk with Vincent about my long-harbored feelings of not being worthy of Anna. He pointed out to me the things he knows that she sees and loves in me. His arguments are partially convincing. Nonetheless, I continue to hold her in awe, and I marvel at her as a goddess. Anna and I try not to speak of the possibility of an unfavorable decision, and instead make plans for what we will do when we get back to Denver and how we can repair the relationships with her family. We both intend to be totally forgiving of all those whom have distanced themselves from us. We understand how things must have looked to them and just want them back in our lives.

Oddsmakers have been taking bets on the outcome of the inquiry as if it were a football championship, and since most people bet with their hearts and hopes and not any sense of objective logic, most of the bets are against me. A few days before the ruling is scheduled to come down, the Belgian Parliament bends to relentless pressure from the media and the public and agrees to make an exception and allow cameras into the inquiry room for Judge Gelineau's decision.

On the morning we finally arrive at the courthouse, we are greeted by the usual groups of protesters and an even larger representation by the media. Reuters, AP, and all the major international wire services are here, and I even notice that CNN and Fox have a visible presence. I have been following their coverage on their websites. CNN has been reporting the details of my case, albeit strongly highlighting the salacious portions; Fox worried less about accuracy, instead using me as an example of the need to change immigration policy.

In the inquiry room, Anna and Bart sit on either side of me again. I am conscious of my heart racing, and I will it to slow down, unsuccessfully. Anna senses the vibration of my speeding pulse and the clamminess of my large black hand held in her tiny white one, and she squeezes firmly. I am oblivious to the constant flashes and clacks of cameras. My body tenses up as the judge takes his seat and starts to speak. As before, he begins by reminding us all that this is not a trial, but rather an inquiry to determine if I should stand trial. There will not be a finding of guilt or innocence.

After an exhausting repetition of all the evidence he has considered and an explanation of the applicable laws of the Kingdom of Belgium, with perspiration beading on my face and soaking my back against the chair, I close my eyes tightly and hear his every word clearly articulated in the auditorium of my head.

"The evidence presented of the forensically validated entries in the diaries of Dr. Vincent Bergeron establishes that on the balance of likelihood Azikiwe Olyontombo could not have been present in Kigali at the time of the deaths of the four nuns, and further it calls into question the testimony of the witness, Idi Mbuyamba. Legitimate doubt is raised about the truth of the state's primary witness. Considering the aggregate of the evidence presented, it is this inquiry's opinion that it is unlikely that a finding of guilt beyond reasonable doubt could be established at a trial in a court of law. In view of this, it is the opinion of this inquiry that there is not sufficient evidence to proceed with a trial of Azikiwe Olyontombo. Dr. Olyontombo, you are free to go home."

I must have been holding my breath because I feel the wind rushing out of me, and I'm unable to stop an instantaneous flood of tears. I cry uncontrollably, in gasping pants. The courtroom erupts in commotion, and several photographers take advantage of the confusion to scramble around in front of us where they shouldn't be and snap photos. A gavel is banging, and I sob through it all, finally gaining a measure of composure with several large breaths. Anna is clutching me and crying and laughing at the same time. After a few moments of watching her and savoring her extreme emotion I extricate myself from her grip and rise to stand. The entire room quickly comes to a hush.

"Your Honor," I say, "I want to thank you for your honest and fair decision."

No sooner do I get the words out of my mouth than a loud shout comes from the seating behind me, "You guilty fucking bastard … you deserve to die!"

Judge Gelineau bangs his gavel, but the courtroom explodes in tumult a second time. Two security officers rush toward us and take Anna, Bart, and me by the arms, leading us out through the entrance the judge used. We convene in the judge's chamber where I am able to shake his hand and properly thank him. It can't have been an easy decision for him, not with the public and the politicians all pressuring him to send me to jail for life. On his advice, we decide that I should not go out to face the press, or more specifically, the public. Bart will act as envoy and speak on my behalf. This will probably be best for the next few days, until tempers cool and things calm down. The judge arranges for us to be taken out through the prisoner docks and escorted home in an unmarked police car. I would have preferred to hold my head high and walk right out the front door, but I know that this would not be safe. Before leaving the judge's chambers I lift up my leg and rest my foot flat on the seat of a chair. My pant leg slips up, exposing the monitor still fastened to my ankle, and I patiently wait for it to be removed.

Before we're even out of the courthouse Anna is busy with her phone, sending an email to Vincent. We're not sure where he might be or how long it might take before he accesses a computer to read it, but we definitely owe it to him to be the first one that we notify. Within seconds of sending it off Anna's phone rings.

"Vincent," she cries joyously. "Just a minute, let me put you on speaker."

"Congratulations, Alfred." Vincent sounds just as happy as we are feeling. "Justice is properly done."

"We can't thank you enough, Vincent. It wouldn't have happened without you."

"I'm going to hold you two to your promise." He chuckles. "A visit here in Africa, soon."

"Count on it, my friend. We'll be there," I say.

A second call comes in right after we say goodbye to Vincent. "It's Steve," Anna says. "Steve, you're on speaker with us both. We just got the decision."

"I know. Congratulations. CNN just reported it. Fantastic news. What're your plans? Are you coming right home?"

"We've some things to wrap up here, but we'll be back in a few days," Anna says. "Steve," she pauses, "thank you. You're a rock."

"We'll celebrate when you get home."

Finishing that call, Anna begins tapping in another number. "I've got to call Daddy."

I agree. "Yes, call him right now."

We climb into the waiting police car as the call goes through.

"Daddy, we're coming home." Anna starts to cry as the words come out. "Yes. We did it. It's all over." But Anna is crying too much to talk anymore and hands me the phone.

"Eldon, it's Alfred. Anna's a little excited here."

"You won, Alfred?" he asks.

"I didn't win anything, sir. There was nothing to win. Just something to prove."

"Congratulations, Alfred. Well done. When will you two be coming home?"

"In a few days," I reply. "We'll let you know. Please give my love to Ruth."

It does hurt a little bit that Eldon doesn't offer any apology, doesn't say he's sorry for having assumed I was guilty. But Anna and I have already talked about this. We don't expect it from anyone when we go back. We know that everyone—our friends, the partners in my practice, our relatives—will all be happy for us, but no one will ever want to admit that they had given up on me. This call with Eldon is just my first direct experience with it, and it stings. But I'll get used to it; we've agreed to take the high road and not begrudge anyone.

Back in the apartment, while we wait for Bart to arrive, we start firming our plans to return home. We had been careful about making solid commitments, but now we can get on with it.

"Anna, we missed our honeymoon trip to Saint Martin, and it's already the middle of March. Do you think we should go to Le Mont-Dore for our anniversary?"

Le Mont-Dore was the little mountain ski village that Anna and I had traveled to when we first started dating. It was where she lured me in and then trapped me, as we jokingly told our friends. It has special meaning for us because it's where we first made love and spent a whole enchanted weekend in bed. We've been celebrating it over the years as one of our anniversaries and always said we'd go back someday, but never had the opportunity.

Anna is sipping wine as I make the suggestion.

"We could either rent a car or take the train. It's only about eight hours away," I say, while she thinks.

"We've told Mom and Dad that we'd be coming right home," she finally says.

"Do we really owe them anything right now? A few more days won't matter."

"Then why don't we just go to Saint Martin?" she asks.

"We don't have anything with us for a beach vacation."

"They have nude beaches there; we don't need anything."

I'm not sure if she's serious or joking, until she can't help but smile and starts to laugh.

That night the media has a field day with Judge Gelineau's decision. It has been soundly lambasted in Parliament, and the public is solidly unified in condemning it. Despite the professional opinions of several forensic handwriting experts that Vincent's diaries are genuine and could only have been written during the relevant dates back in 1994, no one wants to believe it. It leaves the murders of the Four Sisters of Peace unsolved, and everyone would have preferred to have put it all to bed by locking me up. We try to avoid the fracas over the next couple of days while we tidy up things here and finalize our plans for our trip to the Caribbean, but it is impossible to escape. The crowds are still assembling each morning outside our apartment to protest, and the media is hounding us to do interviews.

Bart strongly advises against any media contact for a few months, until things quiet down. "In fact," he says, "put your phones away, don't even look at your computers. You both deserve a break. Just get on that plane in the morning and forget everything for a few weeks. Start right now."

"Hear, hear." I raise my glass in a toast.

We are having one final drink together before leaving Brussels. Bart has provided sure guidance thus far, and I take this advice to heart, ceremoniously shutting down my cell.

We couldn't be much happier as we carry our bags out the front door and load them into the car that Bart has arranged to take us to the airport. This whole messy chapter in our lives is at last over, and we can finally move forward. We'll fly from Brussels to Paris and then direct to Saint Martin, where we'll totally escape everything. With the jinx of my childhood sins hopefully put to rest forever, Anna and I are both floating as we climb into the car. She slips into the back seat and slides across behind the driver, and I climb in beside her. The car pulls away, directed through the crowds on our cordoned-off street by the policemen who have been stationed there. Spring is close in Brussels, and there is a hint of it, a crisp freshness blowing in the air. The sun has been in and out, playing peekaboo from behind the billowing gray clouds all morning, but right now it's radiant, contributing to our giddiness.

Two blocks away I twist around toward Anna to look behind us through the back window of the car, taking one final look at my Brussels prison. Glad to be leaving it behind I turn back, leaning over to kiss Anna's smiling face beside me. I pay no attention to the car that has slowly gained on us in the lane directly to our left until I am just about to kiss Anna's cheek and vaguely notice two black men, one in the front passenger seat and another in the back, looking at us. In one swift synchronized moment both men raise stubby automatic assault rifles to their open windows and blast in a single continuous barrage, emptying their magazines into the side of our car in a matter of seconds before speeding off.

The whole incident happens so fast that by the time my brain processes what is going on it's over. Anna screams while we're thrown violently forward into the back of the front seat, our car slamming to a dead halt, ramming into the bumper of the bus stopped ahead of us. The horn blares loudly. An airbag is pinning our driver to his seat, and Anna slumps sideways into me. I reach around her needing to comfort her and instantly recognize the sticky wetness on my hands.

"Oh God, no!" I scream. "No … no … no! Anna? Anna?"

I turn her slightly to see her wounds. The left side of her head and neck have several small punctures, each is bleeding a trickle. I keep talking to her, "Anna … Anna … can you hear me, Anna? Come on, Anna … speak to me."

I am desperately willing her to life when she opens her eyes and looks at me with a soft smile. In the depths of her gorgeous blue eyes I can see her life evaporating right before me. Her breath is in short quick gulps, and with the last of it she asks, "Freddie … Freddie … are you okay?"

I wait, wanting another breath to come from her, imploring one with sheer willpower, but there is none, and her eyes go milky and sink.

I don't notice that the doors of the car have been flung open and a crowd has gathered around. Someone is reaching in with a hand on my shoulder. "Sir … sir … are you okay?"

Anna's last words play over and over in my mind. "Are you okay? Freddie, Freddie, are you okay?" Even as she lay dying in my arms, Anna was concerned for me. Her thoughts were for my well-being, not for herself. Mortally wounded, she was still worried about me. What a curse I am. My angel taken, because of me. Will there never be an end to the death around me?

Denver

The great open fields of Kansas lie below me, and I scan them absentmindedly, watching one approach and then pass beneath out of view, sighting another one and following it until it too disappears beneath the wing. The last several months of my life have been a hellish nightmare, but there are no possible words to describe the past few days. The shock and total loss leave me empty of a soul, with no will to continue. I will bury Anna as she deserves, in the small family plot next to our treasured little Stephanie on the farm her father owns, with the peaks of the Rocky Mountains forever looking down on them both.

Steve said he'll meet me at the airport. He was her friend and partner at work, our friend, and the only one who stood with us through this whole ordeal, the only one who now remains and seems willing to talk to me. He called me immediately after the shooting saying that it had been reported almost instantly on the cable news in America. I've tried repeatedly, but her father won't return my calls. I've tried her brother with the same results.

In the couple of days directly after Judge Gelineau made his decision, the media in Belgium was relentless, milking the story as much as they could, egging on the public and the politicians. Despite the ruling, I was vilified, guilty, and being allowed to literally get away with murder. The American press was slightly kinder, but the damage to my reputation was done. Anna and I had planned to work around it, just enjoy our trip to Saint Martin, and then deal with things.

I remember little of the actual events in the immediate moments after the attack—lots of people, police, ambulances—but I very clearly and distinctly remember shouting at the emergency workers to let me lift her from the car. I took her in my arms for one last time and hugged her tight to me, oblivious to the blood that spattered us both. She was smiling as she slept there in my arms, like she always did, so peacefully smiling in her sleep, this time forever.

The police made me lay her on the gurney and then pried my fingers from her one at a time. They took me to a safe house while they tried to figure out who might have done this. We all knew it could have been any one of the many groups that despised me. It could have been a couple of lone crackpots, but I am certain in an instinctive way that it was the long tentacles of Idi. Of course, there is no way to prove that, and the police have almost no concrete leads to go on. But I feel in my marrow that Idi was settling his account, as he had once vowed he would.

The police kept me in protective custody for ten days, not even allowing me to see Anna's body until it could be released to take back home. I was alone with little to do except regret, and I regretted a lot. I regretted the path I chose when I was so much younger, regretted not letting the crocodiles take me rather than submitting to Idi. I regretted not killing him during any of the many chances I had to do so. I regretted having killed so many innocent people while under Idi's spell. I regretted killing Father Savard. And then I especially regretted trying to pin the blame on Idi, knowing that if I hadn't made that mistake the four good sisters and Anna would all still be alive. None of this would have ever happened if I had chosen differently at any one of those times. I regretted letting Anna get too close, I regretted not having pleaded guilty so there wouldn't have even been an inquiry, I regretted letting her sit on that side of the car, I regretted my whole pathetic life.

I tried desperately to reach Vincent. He needed to know what had happened, and I needed to hear his voice and consolation. But he was away on the circuit of his village routes, and now I am almost back home and about to bury Anna and he doesn't even know she's dead yet.

When I exit the customs area Steve is waiting for me, as he said he would. He greets me solemnly. "I'm so sorry, Alfred ... so very sorry."

"Thanks, Steve. You were a good friend to her. You've been good to both of us. Thank you."

The funeral is four days later, and Eldon and Ruth have sent word through Steve that they don't want me at the wake. I understand. Virtually everyone blames me and my troubles for Anna's death, and there will be very few people there who would care to see me, anyhow. But I have Steve ask them to please let me attend the funeral. Please.

Steve and his wife drive me down to Colorado Springs for the funeral in the same church that Anna attended as a child. I sit with them and the others from the law firm, away from Anna's family, as they requested. She was my wife, so I could have laid out all the rules. I could have had the service in the manner of my choosing, but out of deference to them I let them do as they pleased. It is a tragic loss for them as well, and they certainly weren't contributors to Anna's death like I was. The only thing I wanted was for her to be buried alongside our little angel, and of course Eldon and Ruth wanted the same, so I made no comment about any of it.

At the grave site I stand at the back of the congregation and cry what few tears I have left. It takes all my will to hold back, biding my time to spend a few private moments with the two loves of my life after everyone else leaves. As the ceremony finishes and the gathered turn to leave, the family walks in my direction and Anna's mother steps toward me. "I'm sorry, Alfred. She loved you, and I know that you loved her."

Ruth moves forward and hugs me, reaching up to kiss me on my wet cheek.

"Thank you, Mom," I reply. "I'm sorry, too."

My father-in-law steps in beside his wife. "You son of a bitch," Eldon says. And that's all he says before taking his wife firmly by the arm and turning his back on me.

The next few days I spend alone in the house, going through Anna's things. Touching everything, smelling everything, remembering everything, trying to save whatever small pieces of Anna are left. Anna and I, together, went through this very same exercise with Stephanie's things just five months ago. We had each other for comfort and commiseration; this time I do it alone.

I don't have a practice to go back to. The first day, while I waited in protective custody for the authorities to prepare and release Anna's body to me in Brussels, I received an email from my partners in the practice. It had been date stamped and sent late the night before Anna was killed. I'm sure that the way things happened that next day they must have regretted the unfortunate timing. I didn't regret not having opened it sooner since it would have just dampened our excitement of leaving Brussels. Basically, the email informed me that they had voted to buy out my share of the practice; the publicity surrounding my circumstances was taking its toll on business and they could no longer afford my negative impact.

On the fifth day after the funeral, after spending the previous few days alone, I get in my car and drive over to the neighborhood sporting goods store. I pick up a couple of brand-new basketballs, a football, and five Broncos jerseys. Making the half-hour drive downtown into Denver, I park out front of Pina Nunez's apartment. I've thought on and off over the last months about Pina and Ricky's battle with cancer, how they must be struggling. I have no idea how the treatments are going, and I am anxious to follow up with him, even though he is no longer my patient. With the box of goods I have just purchased I walk in through the open front door of the building and up to their apartment. Standing before the door, I hear the sounds of a family inside. One of the boys is shouting at another, someone's wrestling or rolling on the floor, the TV is going, and pots are clanging in the kitchen.

In response to my knock Pina shouts from inside the apartment, "Yeah? Who's there? Marcus, answer the door, would ya."

When Marcus doesn't answer, I give another knock and Pina opens it instantly. "Dr. Olyontombo?" She's surprised to see me. "What's all that shit been going on with you? I don't think you should be around here."

And she shuts the door, clicking the lock from the other side.

Pina Nunez's rejection sears. It's the final punctuation of what is left of my life. Within five short months I have lost my daughter, my practice, my family, my friends, and Anna—the love and rock of my life. All of it because of Idi Mbuyamba. That monster stole my childhood, caused me decades of guilt, and now has taken everything else that ever mattered to me. The vision of him smirking from the video screen, gloating, plays over and over in my mind as I sit alone in my den, dusk darkening the silent house. I let the doorbell ring until I think that whoever it is has finally left, and then it rings one more time. Weary from life I plod to the front door.

"My god, Alfred, I'm so sorry." Looking several years older than when I last saw him just six weeks ago, Vincent sets his bags at his feet and steps in to hug me. The sorrow I read on his face is a message straight from his heart. We stand together in the open doorway embracing tightly, sobbing on each other's shoulders.

The next two days we spend with each other, much of it in silence, just being together, before Vincent finally broaches things. "Alfred, what will you do now?"

I shake my head while staring at the floor. "I don't know. I have no idea, Vincent. He's stolen everything I had. Everything that means anything."

"He's not the only Idi, you know? And you're not the only Alfred."

"What are you trying to tell me, Vincent?"

"Africa is full of Idi Mbuyambas. And they keep on ruining the lives of thousands. Hundreds of thousands … of Alfreds."

I nod my head in understanding.

"Come home with me, Alfred. Come back to Africa. Come help me stop it."

The Beginning of the End

My body feels good—limber, loose, and agile, like I haven't felt since my youth. I have no more time for the silliness of gyms and spin bikes. Miles of walking, climbing rough terrain, carrying, lifting, bending, moving continually has adapted my muscles. They've returned to the long sinewy form of my younger years. They're no longer swollen and twisted with knots, always stressing joints filled with inflammation. I can rise in the mornings with ease, ready for the movement of another full day of work.

I am taking in far fewer calories, but I maximize them all, sucking every last vitamin and mineral into my bloodstream and delivering them efficiently to my bones, muscles, organs, brain. I can retain and process information and retrieve memories quickly again. My brain no longer tricks me by spinning in loops of regret and negativity.

The continual fresh air provides my body with a clean source of oxygen that pulses through my veins cleansing every cell, fueling positivity. It's a catalyst during the day and a sedative at night. I sleep the sound, restful sleeps that Anna once did, and I'd like to think that perhaps there is a smile on my face, like she always had when she slept.

I miss her immensely and think of her constantly, fondly remembering the life we shared, the child we shared, the closeness, the bond that I'll never have with anyone else again. I have come to understand there can never be absolution for me for whatever part I played in her death. I will never be able to make reparations for all the other deaths I have caused. And if my karma was in any way responsible for shortening the life of little Stephanie I will never make satisfactory amends. I accept these things that I can never change, and I'm prepared to assent to my dues. I heard the whispers when I left Denver, that I was running away, hiding. And perhaps there is some truth in that. But I don't believe that's what's motivating me. I'm moving forward, determined to do what I can to make the lives of others better, not in the hope of achieving some measure of eternal salvation, but simply because it is the right thing to do. I, Azikiwe, concede nothing to the evil in this world.

The equipment that I was able to purchase with the sale of my share of the practice in Denver has been invaluable. We've set up a mobile surgical unit and are able to treat patients who would certainly have died otherwise. Two of us working together can accomplish several times what each person can do alone. We feed off each other, sustain one another, and complement the skills of the other.

I have taken to learning Arabic, since it's the most widely spoken of languages here, and I'm enjoying the challenge. After working at it for a little more than a year now, I can converse pretty well in it; well enough that Vincent has asked me to deal with the television reporter who has just arrived from Cairo. She's doing a story for Al Jazeera on the carnage caused by the militant Islamic rebels. She and her cameraman have been observing me work all day, repairing the damage to the bodies of blameless victims and treating the ailments common to the undernourished living in the unsanitary conditions of much of this part of rural Africa.

A boy of eleven or twelve is carried in amidst a commotion of bickering. His right arm has been blown apart by a malfunction of his automatic gun. His escorts are arguing whether he should be brought for treatment or left untended. He's still wearing the bandoliers of the militia rebels, identifying him as the enemy. I quickly dispatch those who brought him in and set to work doing what I can to save his life, and some of the arm, first securing a tourniquet to staunch the blood. The boy is in shock and crying, asking for his mother. I take him in my arms and hold him tight to my chest, gently patting the back of his head, softly kissing his forehead and whispering to him that he'll be all right. After doing what I can for the youngster, the Al Jazeera reporter asks if we could now do the interview.

She begins by speaking in Arabic directly into the camera. "I am with Azikiwe Olyontombo, a physician from the United States of America, who has been working in this remote area of Chad for the past sixteen months. Dr. Olyontombo, we've just watched you work on saving the life of an enemy combatant. Why?"

I'm a little offended at the question, but know it needs answering. "A twelve-year-old boy can never be the enemy. I am a doctor. My only enemy is suffering."

"Of course." She shrinks, as if sorry for having asked, before continuing. "Doctor, what makes a successful practitioner leave the security and comforts of Europe or America to come to work in a situation like this?"

Another question that, at first, I consider to be frivolous. I catch myself as I'm just about to roll my eyes, realizing that what is so obvious to me isn't to many others. "Just look around us. Look at the poverty, the suffering. We can make a difference. Shouldn't we all do our little part?"

"Yes, Doctor. But there must be more to it than that. What is it that *really* draws you here, so far from your home, your family?"

For a fleeting moment I wonder if this woman knows something personal about me. I take time to consider her question and then answer, "This is my home."

She is surprised and a bit confused. "You're an American, though?"

"I am American. But I was African first."

"You mean ... you are an African American?"

"I was born in Africa."

"Really? And have you actually experienced this?" She sweeps her arm at the generality of those around us. "From the other side, so to speak?"

"I have. Yes, I have." I stare off absently, but quickly reel myself back in before she can ask another question. "I know firsthand what these people are going through."

"How unusual." It's clear she is intrigued. "Can you tell us about your personal experiences here in Africa, before becoming a doctor … before going to America?"

"Not so unusual … unfortunately."

"But it is unusual to come back to it. Why do you?"

I think about some of my deepest reasons: escape, the need to be needed, my attempt to reconcile—to even—the eternal ledger of fate. But I can see no use in beginning that discussion, so I answer with honesty, "Every little kindness helps."

THE END

Acknowledgments

This book began as a solitary process—a hermit finding pleasure in creation. It culminated as the product of the collaboration of a cast of professionals. And in between the beginning and the end was the invaluable support of family and friends.

First among these is my wife, Rosanne. She is my granite and my mist, the one that dabs my tears of sadness and spawns my tears of joy. She is the one that tolerated the hermit at whatever hour inspiration struck. Thank you, Rosanne.

My brother-in-law, John Lindsay, was my first reader and the only reason anyone else ever got to see the story. It was his encouragement and enthusiasm that gave light to the project. Judith Sellick, among the earliest of readers, has been a friend whose wisdom and opinion always matters. My sisters, Marilyn and Margo, have forever cheered me on, and as early readers their praise was motivation to persist. My four children and their spouses, endless wells of ardor, are my incentive to always try to leave things a little better than I found them. Thank you, all.

There would be no book were it not for my agent, Laney Katz Becker, at Massie and McQuilkin. She is the one that rescued me from the slush pile, took a chance when no one else did, and placed the book in the capable hands of Blackstone Publishing. She went well beyond the call of duty, also becoming my first editor and my mentor. Thank you, Laney.

The entire team at Blackstone Publishing has been phenomenal: acquisitions, editors, designers, publicists, and all the others that work behind the scenes. To all of you, thank you.

Even before any of this, there was a germ of inspiration provided by my dear friend Dr. Dieudonné Detchou, LLD. Dieudonné embodies the dream of fairness and justice in Africa, and he has made it his mission to work toward that end in his homeland. I would be honored if I was able to say that this story contributed to raising awareness of the troubles that he works to solve. I am indebted to Dieudonné for the seed he planted and the example he is. Thank you, Junior.

Author's Notes

Truth, by Omission is a creation of my imagination; however, it does contain numerous historical events revolving around the Rwandan genocide of 1994. I would like to identify here those facts so that history may be credited where it should.

The insurgencies and guerrilla groups which are mentioned in the book, including the Rwandan Patriotic Front and the National Resistance Army, were rebel organizations that played key roles in the lead-up to the genocide. The deaths of the Rwandan president and prime minister on April 6 and 7 in 1994 actually happened as described in this story and are seen as the ignition sparks of the genocide. Sadly, the capture and mutilation of ten Belgian paratroopers, as told here, was also a factual event. And, as described in this story, it set off a fury in Belgium which resulted in the recall of all of Belgium's peacekeeping troops from Rwanda.

Only one person was ever convicted of these crimes and it has remained a national sore spot in Belgium ever since.

All names used in this story are fabrications with the exception of Bernard Ntuyahaga, the former Rwandan army major, who really was extradited to Belgium in 2004 and convicted in a Belgian court in 2007 of the peacekeeping murders. This fact is used in the story as justification for Alfred being extradited from the United States for the murders of Belgian citizens.

Coltan (columbite–tantalite) is a real "blood" mineral that was mined, including with the use of slave labor, and sold through the Rwandan army as described in this story. It continues to be a valuable commodity in the manufacture of electronics but has since been discovered in several other places outside of the Congo and Rwanda, which were its main sources for many years.

The "Four Sisters of Peace" are a total fabrication for the purposes of this story. However, the horrors of the public display of severed heads, the stuffing of genitals in the mouths of victims, and the slicing of Achilles tendons are violent practices still employed in parts of Africa.

The UN refugee camp at Nkwenda, which is an important part of the story. is also a fabrication. Nkwenda is a real village in Tanzania and the UN did establish several refugee camps for fleeing Rwandans, but not at Nkwenda. However, the Rwandan war crimes tribunals which are referred to in the book actually did take place in Tanzania and in the time periods that are stated.

Unfortunately, child and forced slavery remain as serious problems in contemporary Africa, as does the use of children as soldiers. It is estimated that there are 120,000 child soldiers on the continent and further 100,000 children are brought into slavery each year. These children are all too real. As are the millions upon millions of displaced refugees and millions more that live in poverty.

This novel is an imaginative creation meant to entertain. If it does that, I am happy. If it should raise any awareness of other important issues facing Africans, I am doubly pleased.